SOUL SCEPTER

TIME MARAUDERS

ERIC WESTERGARD

CROFTON

Soul Scepter: Time Marauders is a work of fiction. Any references to historical events, real people, or real places are used fictitiously. Other names, characters, places and events are products of the author's imagination, and any resemblance to actual events, places, or persons (living or deceased) is entirely coincidental.

Publisher's Cataloging-in-Publication data.

Names: Westergard, Eric, author.

Title: Soul scepter : time marauders / Eric Westergard.

Series: Soul Scepter

Description: Phoenix, AZ: Crofton Publishing, 2023. | Summary: Sixteen-year-old Will Donovan must find reasons not to give up on himself and people in need while trying to survive time traveling to medieval England.

Identifiers: LCCN: 2023905456 | ISBN: 979-8-9879363-1-3 (hardcover) | 979-8-9879363-2-0 (paperback) | 979-8-9879363-0-6 (eBook)

Subjects: LCSH Time travel--Fiction. | Great Britain--History--Medieval period, 1066-1485--Fiction. | Science fiction. | Adventure fiction. | Historical fiction. | BISAC YOUNG ADULT FICTION / Science Fiction / Time Travel | YOUNG ADULT FICTION / Fantasy / Historical YOUNG ADULT FICTION / Historical / Medieval | YOUNG ADULT FICTION / Action & Adventure / General

Classification: LCC PS3623.E78 S68 2023 | DDC 813.6--dc23

Book Cover Art by Purwanto Afdan

1 3 5 7 9 10 8 6 4 2

First edition 2023

Dedicated to those craving more from life.

1

———

Will Donovan panted as he took in the approaching menace on the other side of the volcanic crater. The black pit he and the other boys stood in was the size of a football field, strewn with sagebrush and beige Idaho soil.

Hours ago, Will had seen the jagged walls surrounding them as epic, but now the rock faces seemed to be caging him in. He tore off the paintball mask over his dark sweat-tinged hair and sized up the four angry guys marching toward him.

The game was over; it was only meant to be a game. But now it seemed like a real fight might be coming. The largest of the pack, Tanner, walked several strides ahead of his rabble. His eyes blazed on his heat-reddened face.

Will turned to one of his teammates, his only friend present. "What's got him so butthurt? He didn't even get shot."

Danny's desert camouflage mask was pulled up and perched atop his ruffled blond hair. He and Will were sixteen, but the others were a year older. The usual playfulness was gone from Danny's face, and his eyes hinted distress. "I think you were being too smart for your own good again."

The pack closed the distance. Will rested his gun on a volcanic boulder and held out his hand for a fist bump. "Hey, guys. Good game."

"Really, terrorist boy?" Tanner let his gun hang on the sling over his shoulder and drove both fists at Will's chest like battering rams.

Will deflected one of the blows with his extended hand and took the other in the chest, sending him back several steps. The words hurt more than the slug. "What's your problem?"

"I don't like playing with cheaters," Tanner spat.

A familiar pain drifted to the surface, and Will hoped he could steer the conversation toward the game instead of Tanner's initial insult. "I didn't cheat. You were the one who wanted to play with *safety* kills so you wouldn't be shot at close range."

Tanner nodded to his friends. "I did that for them—because I saw *you* show up. I'm okay with someone calling out a player rather than shooting them from inches away. But you didn't have any ammo left, so you shouldn't be able to do safety kills."

Will kept a practiced, calm expression. "I've never heard of that as a rule. I can play by whatever rules you want. You just have to make them up beforehand."

"Rules to compensate for playing with someone like your dad?" Tanner said.

"Whoa, back off!" Danny demanded. "If he has the guts to rush your position with no ammo and doesn't get shot—you deserve to lose."

"Shut it!" said a guy on Tanner's team. Of the eight boys present, Will and Danny were the outsiders, and this was their first time competing with the others. Even their two teammates shifted to stand with the others in Tanner's crew.

Danny had told Will earlier that day that there was a group

of six looking for two more, and Will was eager enough to play that he hadn't asked for everyone's name. He recognized most of the older boys from school but didn't know them well.

In contrast, Will was weary of everyone seeming to know who he was. He couldn't count the number of times he'd overheard people whisper, "That's Michael Donovan's son." The only name from this group that would have meant something to him was Tanner's. Will had disliked him from a distance because of some cruel things he'd overheard Tanner say at school about a stray dog. He sorely regretted having anything to do with this guy or his friends.

Tanner's eyes narrowed. "You're just as sick as your dad. You come here with your ratty clothes and crap gear, and then do a suicide run on our position."

Will's eyes flitted down to his gray shirt and jeans. Besides Danny, who was decked head-to-toe in army camouflage, the rest wore flashy, brightly colored speedball jerseys.

He glared back at Tanner. "The main difference between the clothes you and I are wearing is that yours have been covered in paint all morning."

Tanner glanced at the others as Danny laughed. Was this show of aggression just because Will had made him look bad in front of his friends?

"At least I'm not the spawn of a mass terrorist," Tanner growled.

Will fought to keep a glass face, but the words burned so hot inside of him that it felt like his facade would melt. "You know I had nothing to do with that. I was just a baby."

"But the apple doesn't fall far from the tree. Your dad blew up hundreds of good people—including lots of government agents. And then there's your mom."

One of the other boys snorted a laugh. Every particle of Will's lean muscles tensed.

"I saw her at school once," Tanner continued. "Biggest crippled, drooling freak on wheels I've ever seen."

Will winced inside as he thought of getting a prescription bottle for his mom that morning before hugging her and rushing out the door. "My mom doesn't drool. What is wrong with you? So what if she needs a wheelchair? There's no reason for you to be so caustic."

Tanner stepped closer. "Me? Your existence is caustic."

Danny rushed forward, but several other boys held him back.

Will's hands curled into fists at his sides. He thought of the vulnerable places he could pummel Tanner—places that might bring him down with a single blow. *But there's no winning if I act like what he accuses me of being.* Then he felt a familiar pang—he hated feeling like he wasn't allowed to physically stand up for himself.

Tanner handed off his paintball gun to a lackey and shoved Will again. Will deflected the advance and stepped to the side. He had a clear shot at Tanner's head but ground his teeth. "This doesn't benefit anyone. Just stop."

"What? Are you a coward?" Tanner said.

"Take him out!" Danny yelled as the other boys kept a tight grip on him.

Every ounce of Will wanted to heed his friend's advice, but he forced himself to sound calm. "We don't need to fight each other. Look, if I did something to offend you, I'm sorry. Why don't we all just get back to playing or call it a day?"

Tanner held up both palms. "Hey, all right, I'll stop." Then he lunged forward and pushed Will over into some coarse sagebrush.

The branches dug at Will's back as he scrambled to get up, only to see the bottom of Tanner's boot striking him in the face.

He fell backward again, through the bush and onto lava

rock. He began to rise but was stopped once more by a kick in the gut.

Will rolled away, holding a hand to his side as he rose to his knees. Danny was yelling and trying to throw fists at Tanner's friends, who were still blocking him from intervening.

As he rose to face Tanner, Will sent a death glare. "Terrorist? You're the one who's taking cheap shots and kicking me while I'm down."

"Because you're an animal that should be put down—just like your crippled mama."

Will's inhibition disintegrated. He seethed as he tackled Tanner to the ground. The other boys dragged Will off before he could land any blows, and someone struck him in the face.

Will pushed away. Tanner was back on his feet, but Danny broke free and stood ready with Will.

A hint of embarrassment flashed across Tanner's face, but the expression soon vanished, replaced with a tightened jaw and curled lips.

Will stood ready for an attack, but Tanner stayed back, his eyes like daggers. "Someone *does* need to put you down before more innocent people die."

The icy change in tone surprised Will. The words hung in the hot, dry air. Will's fists were up, and his eyes darted to each of the boys, searching for any sudden movements. He took a deep breath, keeping his voice even. "I think the heat is getting to you, Tanner. You're not making any sense."

Danny's lip was bleeding, and he stood in a martial arts stance next to Will.

"Well, look at this," Tanner said, stepping toward them. "Soldier wannabe and the terrorist boy. Why don't we do one last shootout?"

"No way," Danny said. "We aren't doing anything else with you."

"I'm surprised you haven't gotten tired of losing by now," Will said, holding his chin up, trying to ignore the pain throughout his body.

"We won't lose this one," Tanner said in a fierce tone.

"What are you talking about? We're not playing anymore," Danny said.

Tanner's eyes darkened. "You will . . . or we'll leave you out here in the desert."

Will's mind raced as he scanned the angry faces looking back at him. He kept his fists ready—he wouldn't let anyone take any more cheap shots.

"If those are Tanner's terms, then you're not riding in my truck either," said the only other driver.

"I don't want to be on their team again," Kenneth said.

"Same teams," Tanner ordered. "Simpler scenario—elimination."

"Simple would be good for you," Will retorted, feeling resentment win out over fear.

Danny put a hand up between them. "No, we—"

Will grabbed him by the shirt and began to back away. "It'll be fine."

Danny shoved Will's hand away. "No, it won't!"

The other six boys walked away and conversed while glancing over their shoulders.

"Hey, team!" Danny called. "Aren't we going to make our own plan?"

Kenneth ignored them, and Zeke smirked. "Yeah, in a moment."

"They don't want to have an actual match," Danny said as they watched the group. "They're just going to empty their guns onto us."

Will was so worked up he was quivering. A storm of conflicting emotions whirled inside him, fighting over what he should do. His mom would want him to run away, but he was so sick of retreating, apologizing, and caving.

"What's going on with you?" Danny said. "They're jerks, but this is no longer any type of competition."

"It is, and I have to beat them," Will said, resolved.

"There's no beating them. If you wanted a fair fight with Tanner, you had your chance. I would have just torn into him if he had been saying things like that about my family. It wouldn't have mattered that he's huge."

"That's great for *you*. I can't do that."

"What are you talking about? There's nothing wrong with y—"

"Isn't there?" Will cut in. "You remember what happened in second grade, when I was getting made fun of for being the kid of a terrorist, and I got in a . . . scuffle? No one got hurt."

"Oh yeah, and then it made national news. Because they said you, uh . . ."

"That I displayed 'violent genetic predispositions,' and there was even online chatter that someone should kill me for public safety. My family received death threats!" Will thought back to how his mom had begged him to promise never to fight again. He swallowed hard and nodded in the direction of the other guys. "Look."

"Yeah, that sucks," Danny said as he turned. "Hey! You know that's not safe!" he shouted as he saw the others turning up the velocity on their guns.

They ignored him and continued to adjust their weapons, firing test shots into the black crater walls. Two of Tanner's teammates looked nervous, as if they weren't fully on board with what was happening. Tanner barked at them to hurry up, and they dutifully began twisting Allen wrenches into the side of their guns.

"Someone could get killed!" Danny shouted. "You shouldn't max out the velocity, especially on a high-end gun!"

"I'm not worried about it," Will said.

"Agh! Will, getting shot at close range with the velocity illegally turned up—that's the hospital, at least. But depending where they hit you . . . This isn't a game anymore. So what if we get abandoned in the desert? We aren't that far from the highway. This isn't worth it. It's not worth dying over."

For Danny's sake, he didn't say it, but he ached inside: *It's living that's giving me problems.*

"I know what I'm capable of," Will said, his voice steady, his nerves still on edge.

Danny froze. "You—you're going to go—all *Will Donovan* on them?"

Will nodded, not taking his eyes off Tanner.

"Well, do you have a plan?"

"You should go," Will said sternly.

"You know I'm not going to leave you alone with these guys!" Danny let out a sharp exhale. "What are you going to do?"

"I'm going to go along with this farce. Take on Tanner on his own terms."

The group walked back toward them. "You ready?" Tanner growled.

"No," Will said, trying to hide the resentment in his voice. "I haven't had a chance to touch base with my teammates."

"We're good," Zeke said as he walked past Will and Danny. "This is a simple scenario. Nothing to talk about."

"All right, let's split up," Tanner said. "See you soon."

The two groups of four moved to opposite ends of what they called Hell's Arena.

"So, where are you two going after we start?" Will asked.

"We'll split to the sides," Zeke said. "Why don't you and Danny stay inside the fort?"

"That works," Will said, sounding committed. "You can keep them back for us."

He pulled Danny aside. "Grab your gear. We might not be able to come back for it. Go to the back corner of the crater, and I'll go to the trench. That way, we'll both have an angle on anyone between us."

"Dude," Danny said. "If they don't stop shooting after you're out, just run." He swallowed and gestured a "hang loose" sign with the thumb and pinky extended. Will hesitated but returned the gesture. It was a custom they shared, but now it felt painfully out of place.

They joined up at the plywood fort, which was shaped like a military pillbox.

Kenneth scoffed. "Why are you carrying your packs into the game?"

"Oh, I brought extra ammo. You know, in case you run out and we need to share," Will said, trying to sound friendly.

He pulled his mask on. Now that he wasn't trying to force a brave face, he felt a wave of fear thrashing him in the gut. Will tried not to let his hands shake, and his fingers felt slick with sweat against the smooth metal surface of the gun. He couldn't remember ever being this scared.

The other boys pulled their masks down. "You ready?" Tanner shouted from across the crater, near their side's fort.

"I'd hate for there to be an accident," Kenneth muttered.

Zeke shot him a look and a clenched fist. Then he glanced at Will and relaxed his arm.

Will knew they would try to brutalize him, but the full realization of what was happening hit him like a boulder spat from a volcano. *An accident,* he thought. *If Tanner "puts me down" in a game, it won't be murder—there will be witnesses agreeing it was just an accident.*

He remembered overhearing Tanner at school going into detail about killing a stray dog. *I'm just another animal for him to slaughter. But what about Danny? What are they going to do to him?*

"Ready!" Zeke shouted back to Tanner.

The boys on the other side of the crater whooped, and Tanner bellowed, "All right! Three, two . . ."

"Danny! Go!" Will yelled, and he and Danny turned and sprinted in opposite directions.

"Hey! You can't move yet!" Kenneth demanded.

"Get 'em!" Tanner yelled, and his team surged up the field.

Zeke and Kenneth opened fire on Danny and Will. Danny's massive duffle bag slowed him down but also protected his head and back as multiple paintballs hammered into it.

Will ran, staying low to the ground, teeth clenched, heart racing. He wove back and forth as shots pelted the sagebrush and rocks around him.

Just before he reached the trench, his sneakers slid on loose black pebbles, and for a moment he was airborne, desperately falling face-first. His body landed with a hard thud, and the plastic hopper holding his paintballs rattled across the lava rock as it spilled out its precious contents.

Will rolled into the trench as projectiles whizzed overhead, but his hopper and rolling ammo stayed behind.

"No!" Danny screamed.

"He's dead!" Tanner yelled as he and the others rushed forward like jackals moving in for the kill.

Danny fired at the group. "Stop!" he yelled. "Stop!" He hit several of them, but they kept going.

"Light him up!" Tanner ordered.

The predators eagerly shot at the rim of the trench as they

ran. Zeke was the first to reach the edge, where he thrust his gun down like a bayonet.

As soon as he did, his head jerked backward. The goggles of his mask were obscured with orange paint.

Will was fifteen feet down the trench from where he'd fallen in, with another hopper attached to his gun, quickly unloading paintballs into the faces of those standing unprotected at the edge.

Zeke and Tanner brought up their guns and fired blindly in Will's direction despite their muddled vision.

Will shot both of them in the groin, and they let out shrill yelps and lurched forward. Zeke dropped his gun, almost falling into the trench.

"Point your guns in the air, and get off the field. Now! Or I'll keep shooting!" Will ordered as he continued to blast paint at their masks.

Everyone but Tanner complied. He knelt in pain, wiping at his mask in desperation while trying to aim. Will shot him in the armpit, then again in the groin.

"Stop, stop," Tanner whimpered as he crumpled forward, bracing his gun over his head.

Will climbed out of the trench and stood over Tanner for a moment. Will's lip trembled behind his mask. He felt the urge to continue attacking, to let out the frustration built up over a lifetime's worth of bullying on the feeble ball cowering before him.

A sick feeling sank to the bottom of Will's gut, and he ran toward Danny.

"Let's get out of here!" Will panted.

"Yeah, I don't think we're getting a ride." Danny ran back toward the group of boys gathering around Tanner, who was still lying in a heap on the desert floor.

"What are you doing?" Will hissed after him.

Danny got within range and fired a paintball that connected with Kenneth's left butt cheek.

Kenneth leaped off the ground, grabbing his flank. A chorus of insults and paintballs fired back at Danny as he ran away.

"Got him!" Danny shouted as he returned.

"What was that all about?"

He thumped Will on the back. "If I'm going to get ditched out in the desert, I might as well deserve it. Let's go."

They climbed through a crevasse in the crater wall and ran for several minutes until they were sure the other boys weren't chasing them. Then they hid behind a large wall of lava rock and collapsed to the ground.

"My heart is pounding," Will breathed. "That was insane."

"Mine's about to stop after running with the duffel bag," Danny panted. "It probably did stop when I saw you fall. I thought they were going to—to get you. I'm so glad you were able to get another hopper on and loaded so fast."

"What?" Will said, pausing between breaths. "You think I'd let the hopper fall off my gun?"

"Yeah, everyone saw it."

"You saw my *spare* hopper spill across the ground—I wedged it between my back and my backpack and tightened the shoulder straps so it wouldn't fall out as I ran. I pulled it out right before my *stunt* fall."

Danny's jaw dropped. "That was your plan? Why didn't you tell me you were going to do that?"

"Because you would've tried to talk me out of it," Will said, trying to suppress a mischievous grin.

"Yeah, but that was really crazy. They could have killed you!"

Will muttered, "Most people would probably be glad."

"What? You know that isn't true. Even if you have some kind

of death wish, I don't, and they could have done the same to me too."

Will's expression fell. "I'm sorry . . . I let you get dragged into it, but I told you to leave."

Danny shook his head. "It's like it's not human—that you can pull off stuff like that. Maybe if you just tried not to stand out as much—"

Will flinched, and Danny stopped. Was his best friend telling him not to be himself or that he didn't already stand out without trying?

"That came out wrong," Danny said. "I just don't like the way some people treat you."

Will waved his hand dismissively. "Don't worry about it. I just needed to get back at those guys and—" His face blanched, and he brought both hands to his head as he stood in horror. "No, no, no!"

"What is it?"

"I think . . . I really hurt Tanner." Will's face paled.

"He deserved it," Danny huffed.

"That's not it. I think they'll post about this on social media."

"They won't post how they lost."

Will shook his head and bit his lip.

"Oh, they'll post that *you* hurt them," Danny said.

Painful emotions welled up inside from making headlines as a seven-year-old. "Even though this was just supposed to be a game, a game that I never should have started playing—they'll have photos of their welts to prove it."

"Hopefully, they don't take pictures of *all* of their welts."

"Right—but you know the media will twist the headlines to make it sound worse than it was. They'll write something like 'Son of Terrorist Shoots Six Children, Leaves Them in the Desert.'"

"They're leaving *us*!"

"Yeah, but they'll make it sound as bad as they can."

"I don't know. I think 'Guys Shot in the Balls Share Woeful Regrets' is pretty good clickbait."

Will smiled. "The world won't go that easy on me."

Danny laughed. "Dude, chill out. What's done is done, and there's nothing you can do about it."

"I know. I'm painfully aware that I can't change the past." His thoughts went to the many lasting effects of the hotel bombing in Washington, DC. When his mom had received the news, she was so distraught she wrecked the car, resulting in her physical struggles. In the accident, Will's car seat was thrown through a window and into a river.

A news commentator had said Will was the only one who should have died that night.

Will squeezed his eyes shut for a moment, dreading going back into town to a life of people telling him who he was and how he should let himself be walked over. He thought about his uncle, who worked at a laboratory deeper into the desert, but he hadn't seen the man in months. "I just wish I could go to a place where no one has heard of me."

2

———

Fifteen miles deeper into the endless sweep of sagebrush and lava-rock-scarred earth resided a heavily guarded government facility. The Idaho National Laboratory was the home of fifty-two nuclear reactors and a newly constructed classified research building that had sparked public interest. The structure's purpose, however, remained an enigma to outsiders.

Within its walls stood Will's uncle, Dr. Chase Donovan.

He waited behind the entrance to a small auditorium stage with the facility director. The older man firmly gripped him by the shoulders, his thick white eyebrows furrowed. "What they think of your demonstration could determine the fate of our country. Don't screw this up."

Chase's steady, roguish expression didn't change. "Of course not."

"Keep it simple. Just remember, that's the president of the United States in there. He and his officials could shut this whole place down on a whim. Forget about any theatrics. You're a scientist, not a rock star."

"It sounds like you think I'm becoming more grounded. Last week, you accused me of playing God."

"Chase!" Dr. Tooley implored. "You're already on thin ice with them for refusing to put your nephew in protective custody. The kid has a right to know about your family's unhuman abilities."

"That's between my family and me," Chase said, trying to hide the annoyance in his voice.

"Just don't embarrass us. And don't get our funding cut!"

Chase pulled away impatiently. "You mean the extra funding we get because of me? Trust me. I've got this."

As he waited to be introduced before taking the stage, he thought over his reasons for not involving his nephew as a test subject. Up until this morning, it had been the right thing to do. Chase checked his phone for seemingly the hundredth time that day to see if anyone had been able to get ahold of Will.

A lot of people are going to loathe me. However, that didn't matter as much as protecting those he cared about.

The auditorium could seat over a hundred, but today, there were only thirty-two—a mix of government officials and other scientists seated right up front.

Chase took the stage wearing a collared shirt with the top two buttons undone. On many men, it would have looked unprofessional given the setting, but it worked for him—like his one-day overgrowth of even, light brown stubble. His gray-green eyes scanned the audience like a hunter surveying a herd.

"Mr. President and distinguished guests, prepare for an astounding update on Project Black Hammer." He projected his voice, declining to use a microphone. "But first, we need to rectify a problem."

Dr. Tooley shifted uneasily in his chair.

Chase stretched out his arm and let three tiny black objects fall from his hand. One by one, they clattered on the stage. "I found these this morning as I was prepping the laboratory for the demonstration. Look familiar to anyone?"

"What are they?" President Torres asked from the front row.

"Spy cameras," Chase said with an edge to his voice. "With broadcast capabilities. Only a few people have ever been in the lab room where Black Hammer research has been done, and I've arranged for all of them to be present."

"What the—" Air Force General Harris said, almost to himself, as people looked around at each other.

"Why didn't you tell me about this?" Dr. Tooley demanded.

"Oh, I didn't want to spoil anything," Chase said. "Besides, who doesn't want to rule out traitors?"

"Is *this* room even secure?" Agent Jennifer Carlsberg asked.

"It's been swept with equipment that would detect any other devices," Chase said.

"Dr. Donovan," President Torres said, clearly trying to stay calm, "is your nephew safe? People with malicious intentions who wanted to use Black Hammer could easily get to him."

"The first thing I did when I found the cameras was to reach out to his mom and grandparents."

"And? Where is he?" General Harris asked.

Chase was stone-faced. "I can't respond to that yet in present company."

"Dr. Donovan," President Torres said, "I'm deeply concerned about this breach in security. Besides you, has the artifact responded to anyone else?"

"Not yet."

"But you still think it's responding to you because of your peculiar genetics—and that your nephew should be able to activate it as well?"

"Yes, sir."

"This is a national security risk. An intel leak was the

primary reason I wanted to make sure your nephew is secure," the president said.

"Oh, like me?" Chase said. "I haven't been allowed to leave the facility in six months. You have no idea what Will has gone through growing up. He doesn't need to be caged for the rest of his life."

"I can see how this is frustrating," Agent Madoc Morgan said. "We'll figure out who did this and work things out for you and your nephew."

"Oh, I'm absolutely certain." Chase tapped on a remote. An image appeared on the large projector screen behind him. "This is an aerial view of the closest National Guard armory at six this morning."

The image changed.

"This is the armory thirty minutes ago. Looks the same, doesn't it? So where did all of the National Guard vehicles come from that rolled into our facility two hours ago?"

Members of the audience exchanged glances. General Harris said, "The vehicles are probably just from a different armory."

"No, none of the vehicles are owned by the Department of Defense. A global aerial database I've generated over time indicates that the vehicles came from this location."

The image on the screen changed to show a military compound in the desert. Chase continued, "This is a compound in northern Nevada owned by militant fundamentalists with ties to an organized crime network called the Imperial *Dreizack*—dreizack being German for 'trident.' Now, I'm very interested in why they were given permission by someone aboard Air Force One to masquerade into our facility."

"Who made the phone call to the Guard unit?" demanded the president.

Everyone denied making the call, and the chief of staff

stood up with his phone in hand. "I'm calling Secret Service outside."

"Wait," Chase said. "There's one more thing we need to target before you do that."

"Why didn't you report this information as soon as you were aware of it?" General Harris demanded.

"Because I'm a scientist, and I want answers. Because I'm a hunter, and I didn't want to scare away my prey. And because whoever did this put my family at risk. I want them in hand-cuffs. So—last question—why does one of you need to sneak a widely illegal knife past metal detectors?"

The image on the screen changed to show a cropped medical image of a leg exhibiting bones, soft tissue, and a folded ceramic butterfly knife secured to the calf.

"A lot of you understandably carry guns, but this doesn't seem very . . . *government issue*," Chase said.

"Just tell us who it is," President Torres said.

"Of course, sir. I'll not only tell you; I'll show you."

The screen changed to a live video feed of the audience.

"Chase, what are you doing?" Dr. Tooley asked.

"When I told you about the cameras and the illegal knife, all of you initially looked concerned, then upset—all except for one of you. The individual I suspected briefly looked horrified, then immediately forced a calm expression—on both occasions. That person also happens to have the knife."

"It isn't your place to meddle with security measures!" General Harris said, his face reddening. "If those soldiers outside aren't ours, we should have been alerted immediately."

"Normally, I would absolutely agree," Chase said. "But you have a mole in your inner circle that you've been too incompetent to deal with, and it only took me a few minutes to figure out who it was. This person needed to be stopped before giving any more orders to the heavily armed criminal organization on my doorstep."

"Look, Dr. Donovan," Agent Madoc Morgan said with a strong, confident voice, "we all respect you here, and you don't have anything to prove. I'm a CIA agent, and I was in the Marines, so yeah, I carry weapons. The knife is mine, but this whole ordeal you've fabricated regarding 'facial expressions' is just a witch hunt. I've been a big advocate of your work for a long time. I can't believe you would jump to something so preposterous."

"Madoc, I'm surprised you would be a part of something so preposterous," Chase retorted as he played back the agent's brief reactions on the projection screen. "Apart from the scientists who work here, you're also one of the few people who has been inside the main laboratory."

Agent Morgan scoffed and gestured at the screen. "So I don't like the idea of being infiltrated by radical fundamentalists." He raised his voice and pointed at Chase. "If anyone should be under scrutiny—"

President Torres cut him off. "Agent Morgan, you were highly in favor of bringing in additional security."

Morgan threw up his hands. "Who wasn't in favor of it?"

"No Secret Service agents are answering!" the chief of staff said.

"Morgan, surrender your firearm, and your phone too," General Harris growled. "And that knife."

"You've gotta be kidding me!"

"I'm not kidding," the general seethed. "And Mr. President, we should get you out of here until we have a better idea of what's going on."

"Agent Davis!" The chief of staff shouted for one of the lead Secret Service agents, who was outside the door. "Agent Davis!" He hurried toward the auditorium doors and then froze.

Gunfire sounded from the hallway.

Horror fell over the faces of those in the room as they heard cries of pain and what sounded like bodies hitting the floor.

General Harris motioned for everyone to get on the ground. Several people pointed handguns through the gaps in the auditorium chairs toward the two sets of doors at the top of the room's sloped aisles. Agent Jennifer Carlsberg climbed over a row of seats to help defend the president.

General Harris hissed, "Morgan, put your gun on the ground and slide it over to me."

Agent Morgan was crouched behind a row of seats but hadn't drawn his gun. A smile slowly climbed from his prominent chin to his high cheekbones. He drew his gun and tossed it to General Harris.

Harris reached out and caught it with an angry grunt.

Morgan shrugged. "You'll need it more than I will."

Several people gave Morgan shocked glances. Carlsberg waved for everyone to stay quiet and sent Morgan a death glare.

Chase crouched behind the podium on the stage. He watched President Torres lying in the front row, tapping General Harris on the shoulder. The president pointed to Morgan's gun. "Give me a gun," he whispered. Harris shook his head and motioned for Torres to stay on the ground.

All of Chase's bravado washed away in a tsunami of concerns. He was furious at Morgan and his cohorts but also engulfed with guilt for all the people he had put in danger. He was terrified for them and wished he could help. Chase looked around for a weapon, but all he had was a pen, a laser pointer, and his phone.

The hallway fell silent.

Then the building's lights shut off, and several people gasped. Even the lights in the hallway extinguished. The only glow in the auditorium emanated from the green exit signs above the dark doors. Everyone in the room stared at the ominous black spaces below. The hazy green signs seemed to taunt them. *Exit,* safety this way.

A deafening boom rang out as both doors exploded inward.

The officials with the president fired into the spaces below the exit signs, sending a thundering echo throughout the room. However, no one was in the doorways.

Several dark objects were thrown from around the door-frames, clinking as they rolled down the inclined auditorium.

"Grenades!" General Harris shouted.

Chase plugged his ears and squeezed his eyes shut just before the ear-splitting explosions and bright flares of light. The stun grenades created minimal shrapnel but temporarily blinded and deafened those nearby, distorting their sense of balance and impeding their ability to move.

Chase glanced around the podium. The lights from the exit signs were barely enough for him to see silhouettes of men in tactical military apparel rushing into the room with assault rifles and night-vision goggles mounted to their helmets.

The agents on the auditorium floor returned fire and hit several intruders but were cut down by the opposition's superior firepower and visibility. The hostiles ran down both aisles, their guns spitting between the rows of seats wherever they met resistance.

Four of the intruders ran onto the stage and cornered Chase behind the podium. He stood and backed away.

"Put your hands on your head! You're coming with us!" one of the men yelled.

"Okay, okay, hands on head," Chase said as he complied, facing the man in tactical gear closest to him. His hands weren't empty, though—he pressed the button on the laser pointer.

The red beam flashed into the night-vision goggles. The light's intensity, magnified by the lens, made the man's head jerk back. Chase grabbed the barrel of his gun and spun it to the side. In one motion, he smashed his elbow into the man's face and swung his body around, using it as a shield. Then he fired the weapon at the other three Dreizack soldiers, dropping them to the ground. Chase knocked the man he was holding unconscious with the butt of the rifle and took refuge behind the podium.

He fired high above the heads of those in the room, causing the remaining assailants to take cover. The flash from the weapon's muzzle shed light on the front of the auditorium, where Chase desperately hoped to see some of his colleagues unharmed.

The magazine ran out of bullets. For a split second, Chase was tempted to make a mad dash for the exit. However, he felt sick about abandoning those in the room.

Then he saw movement.

Chase threw the rifle toward the back of the auditorium, hoping the clatter of the gun might buy him another second and that the Dreizack had orders to take him alive. He scooped another assault rifle off the ground, fired several shots, and leaped from the stage into the blackness.

"Dr. Donovan, surrender!" a man yelled from the other side of the room.

Chase rushed to President Torres, who was pressed to the ground, his hands desperately searching across the floor, stopping as he grasped a handgun.

"Get up," Chase whispered, tugging on the president's shoulder.

Torres's head whipped around. "You?"

"You have to trust me. I'm going to try to get you out of here."

Both of them stayed in a crouched position as they clambered to a side exit. Chase stayed between Torres and the killers, firing several rounds behind him. The hostiles shouted and fired back, but their shots flew high overhead.

Torres fired once behind him before Chase pushed him into the hallway. They both recoiled at the sight of the dead Secret Service agents on the ground.

"We have to keep going!" Chase said. "Follow me!"

The president took a deep breath and nodded. "All right." He had been an amateur boxer decades ago and had a reputation for trying to stay fit. Sweat dripped from his black hair, no longer in a neat business part, and down his taut jaw muscles.

The two men ran down several hallways before ducking into one of many labs.

"Hurry, climb on the table. We're going up into the air ducts," Chase said as he got on the lab table and started removing the cover on the ventilation chamber.

Before following, Torres flipped the safety on the handgun, then slipped it behind his back and under his belt.

Chase raised an eyebrow. "That looked natural."

"I grew up in a rough neighborhood. What's your excuse? You seem to be uncannily comfortable with these bigger guns."

"The thing is that I never really grew up—I just found bigger and better toys."

"That's concerning on many levels right now."

"Yeah, I know." Chase laced his fingers together for the president to step onto so he could boost him up into the chamber. "It's part of the reason you guys locked me up in the middle of the desert."

Torres followed Chase as they crawled through the air ducts, trying not to make any noise. They froze in place as an eerie voice sounded over the building's loudspeakers.

"Chase, I know you can hear me. You don't need to run anymore. We have no intention of killing you." It was Morgan.

"You know we can do great things together. We could have

spoken under more relaxed circumstances if you hadn't blown my cover. Your friends have died because of your foolishness. Don't let the blood of more people stain your hands. There is no way for you to exit the building. We don't need President Torres. If you want us to let him live, surrender yourself."

Chase shook his head and whispered back at the president, "I'm not going to."

Torres's face was illuminated by narrow slits of light. He swallowed and gave a nod.

Morgan's voice sounded again. *"I would prefer to work with you, Chase—it would make things so much easier. But you know I don't need you. We can use your nephew."* There was a pause. *"I'm sure Will would be much more pliable than you are proving to be. Don't be irrational."*

Chase clenched his teeth in anger and pressed onward.

Their progress through the ducts was slow as they tried not to make any noise, and soon the voice echoed again. *"Chaaaase, I'm beginning to lose my patience. You have one minute to turn yourself in before my order to capture you alive expires. I will use your nephew instead. There are only so many places you could have gone. If you're in the building's ventilation chambers, it won't be difficult to flush you out. Let go of your ego. You have fifty seconds."*

They continued to crawl long past the end of the one-minute ultimatum until they reached a duct that exited into what looked like a large personal garage.

"Where are we?" Torres whispered.

"It's part of my place. I've made so much money for you guys that a pittance of it was allowed to go toward living quarters for me and a workshop for personal projects."

Chase dropped down, ran out a workshop door to his living quarters, and returned with a black metallic carrying case.

"Is that it?" Torres asked.

Chase nodded. "Black Hammer is inside. I moved it from

the main vault after discovering the security breach." Chase pulled a white sheet from a car in the center of the workshop, revealing a highly customized metallic red coupe with black-and-white racing decals down the sides. The wheels had thick all-terrain tread, and the body exuded an essence of brute strength and aerodynamics.

"I've made a lot of customizations to her. She's bulletproof and has a lot of driving versatility. I started integrating a weapons system, though that part isn't finished."

"You built yourself a Bond car," Torres quipped.

Chase suppressed a grin. "I like mine better, though—when it's done." He ran to a corner of the garage and picked up a rocket launcher and several rockets. "You'd be surprised by what I can get ahold of if I say it's for research and development. Now, I really wish I had integrated these. A lot of the weapons can only be used manually."

Torres continued to take in the car. "Let me drive, then. You can manage the weapons."

Chase loaded the rockets and launcher behind the front seats. "No way. You aren't driving my car."

"I can drive well, but I've never used one of those," Torres said, pointing at the rocket launcher.

"When was the last time you actually drove a car? You get chauffeured everywhere you go."

Torres's face reddened. "When was the last time you fired a rocket launcher while driving?"

Chase huffed and slapped a single key into the president's outstretched hand. "Fine. Don't get us killed."

A smile tugged at the corners of Torres's mouth. "That's the general idea."

As soon as the armor-plated garage door rose high enough for the car to clear, Torres slammed on the accelerator, and the car sped out onto the pavement. Two militants outside dove for cover.

The drab concrete plaza outside was surrounded by desert-brown research buildings. Men in camouflage opened fire on the vehicle. Chase shouted directions to Torres while punching commands into the console screen.

Bullets hammered the side of the car.

"Activate machine guns," Chase ordered. The display screen on the console showed a video feed with crosshairs. He redirected the crosshairs to aim at hostile targets as the car's artillery roared.

Three intruders were hit as more armed men poured out onto the plaza. Bodies of Secret Service personnel and INL security staff lay in front of the research facility. More bullets thundered against the car's windows, cracking the glass and obscuring visibility. Torres weaved the car as he raced toward the main road.

Bullets trailed behind them. A lone Secret Service agent lay flat on a rooftop, firing back at the Dreizack soldiers behind the sports car.

"That's Agent Hayes!" Torres said. "We're taking him with us! I've seen too many good people die today."

"Me too. But they're after you, me, and Black Hammer. He's much safer up there."

Torres skidded to a halt alongside the building, and another bullet ricocheted off the side of the car.

The president opened the sunroof and beckoned with his arm. "Hayes! Get down here!"

The agent shook his head, waving aggressively for them to move on. "I'll cover you! Keep going!"

Torres clenched his teeth and dug his fingers into the steering wheel before finally crushing the gas pedal to the floor. "I hate leaving my people behind!"

They sped around a corner, now facing the stretch of road between them and the closed security gate. A large military truck and about a dozen men blocked the gate from the inside.

"Where to now?" Torres demanded.

"That checkpoint is our only option. Anywhere else will take too long."

"But there—"

"Just trust me. Floor it!"

Torres sped forward. Chase hoisted the rocket launcher out of the sunroof and anxiously steadied the large weapon on his shoulder. It spat a trail of smoke, and the rocket connected with the truck, which exploded into a massive ball of fire. The men nearby scrambled to escape the flames.

Chase settled back into the car. "Keep driving!"

They drove around the burning wreckage and crashed through the security gate.

"Yes!" Torres yelled as they sped away with nothing but open road ahead of them.

"Outstanding driving!" Chase said and held his hand out for a high five.

The president glanced at the outstretched palm, hesitating before giving it a hard slap. Then he exhaled. "It's been years since I've felt that—in danger."

"We're not out of it yet. Get onto the highway."

"We should encounter our own incoming troops," the president said as they continued to speed down the desolate stretch of road.

"I hope so, but I don't know what else this well-networked group was able to pull," Chase said. Hopefully someone could protect Will until this mess was sorted out.

Torres let out a deep breath. "Anyway, thank you for saving my life."

Chase frowned. "Yeah, sure—I wish it was more than just me and you."

"Me too."

For a long moment, there was only the sound of tires tearing down the dusty road.

"But," Torres said, "you didn't have to help me. Why did you do it?"

Chase winced and looked out the side window. "How could I not? After what I did led to all of those people dying. Also, you've expressed more concern for me and my nephew's well-being than just about anyone else."

"I have family too," Torres said. Then he glanced in the rearview mirror and gasped. "No!"

"What?" Chase said, turning to see a black military helicopter with a gunman perched on its side rise from the INL and begin moving in their direction.

3

———

The sun beat down on Will and Danny as they stood at the edge of the lonely two-lane highway. They watched the waves of heat radiating from the asphalt as they waited for Danny's twin sister and her friends to pick them up.

Will still felt shaken from the confrontation. Glancing once more for the Barrington family Suburban, he wished it could take him to a place where his troubles didn't exist—instead of seemingly right back to them.

A low rumble sounded in the distance behind them, in the direction of the INL.

"What do you think that was?" Danny asked.

"One of the nuclear reactors blowing up? I guess we'll know if we start turning green."

"Nah. Those things are totally safe. Does your uncle still work out there?"

"Yeah, he practically lives out there. We haven't seen him in months. He's always working on something big, but he can hardly ever tell us anything." Will sighed and picked up a rock.

He threw it far over the vacant highway and sagebrush into a black rock outcropping.

"Touchdown," Danny said. "Thrown by this coming fall's star quarterback."

Will forced a smile. "Thanks, but Jason will be the quarterback as long as his dad is the coach."

"You've gotta be optimistic, man. Maybe he'll get hit by a truck."

"Jason or his dad?"

"In an ideal world? Both."

Will let out a short laugh, and Danny laughed too.

"Maybe they'll just move," Will said. "I'm actually not sure that football is what I want to do. I was thinking about not continuing this fall, unless maybe you're reconsidering joining."

"Pssssh, no. I don't need to be coming off the field on a stretcher."

Will grinned. "Oh c'mon, you're always talking about history's great warriors. American football is about as close as you could get to donning a suit of armor and facing adversaries on a battlefield in hand-to-hand combat."

"Oh please, not even close." Danny's face lit up. "Back in the day—"

Will relaxed, hoping one of Danny's history rants might distract him from his thoughts, but he also wondered if the information would ever have any relevance to his life.

"If you won a war, you didn't just get bragging rights, maybe a trophy, or just money—you got to define how the world *is*. Culture, religion, language, commerce—*everything* that exists is because the victors wanted it that way or allowed it to be that way. And what's on the line if you lose? Not just dying, but things that many people consider worse—being sold into slavery, your family members getting raped, hostile religious takeover, your culture abolished, and shackles on your freedom to think."

"The stakes just aren't high enough for you?" Will mused.

"I'm just saying they're hardly similar. Unlike sports, there are no real rules in war. If a nation is fighting with any rule other than *winning at all costs*, they aren't really at war—they're just screwing around. If a horde of barbarians was going to pillage our community if Skyline High School lost a football game—or if the winner at the end of the season would be granted supreme world domination—then absolutely, I would sign up for football, but that isn't going to happen."

"A horde of barbarians in Idaho Falls. That would be the day, but I don't blame you for sticking with your tae kwon do and your sword-fighting academy."

"Ah, they're okay," Danny said. "Injury-prone too, I guess."

Will laughed. "You don't have to pretend they aren't fun just because my family can't afford them." He pressed his lips and let another rock fly. The stone connected with the same lava rock he had targeted before. He let out a deep breath and looked down the highway for seemingly the hundredth time, finally spotting the Barringtons' dark blue Suburban in the distance.

When Danny's sister Celeste pulled up, a wisp of blond hair skirted the concerned look she gave the two of them. She gracefully exited the vehicle, wearing an unbuttoned white blouse over a purple shirt. Will was sure her designer jeans cost more than his entire wardrobe. After noticing her for a split second, he glanced away. Will had liked her for years but didn't want to be like the other guys at school who gawked at her. More importantly, he didn't want to mess up his friendship with Danny.

"So, I don't know if I want my friends hearing it," Celeste

said, nodding back to the Suburban, "but what exactly did you do to get left out here?"

"Nothing! They were just jerks," Danny said.

She gave her brother a dubious look. "You weren't shooting your mouth off?"

"No, actually," Will interjected, "Danny didn't do anything wrong. The other guys were trying to pick a fight, and it wasn't safe to ride home with them. I'm glad you came."

"*You're* welcome." She continued to look suspiciously at Danny.

"No, I swear," Danny protested, "they were actually way madder at Will than they were at me."

"I don't believe it. He's too nice." She appraised Will and gently removed a bit of sagebrush from his dark brown hair. "Rough day, huh?"

"Nice?" Danny threw up his hands. "You have no idea! Actually, it's not like it was his fault, though. They were calling him a terrorist again—"

Will cut him off. "Yeah, it's been quite a morning. Celeste, I'm sure you don't want to be standing out here in the heat. Let's go."

He left his bag of gear on the side of the road, knowing he never planned to use it again.

Danny gave Will a worried look and paused as if about to say something, but just picked up the bag for him.

"Uh—thanks." Will didn't want to make a conversation of it.

Danny seemed lost in thought as he loaded their gear into the Suburban.

They greeted Celeste's two girl friends and two guy friends as they took seats in the back.

"We're starving," Danny said. "Let's stop to get some food on the way home."

"Coming to pick you guys up in the middle of nowhere wasn't how we wanted to spend the day," Celeste said.

"C'mon," Danny implored. "I have a deep biological need for a bacon cheeseburger, a chocolate shake, and a ridiculous mountain of fries."

"Your needs can be addressed on someone else's time," Celeste said.

"Ahhh! You are literally trying to kill us."

A girl with dark hair turned from the front seat and asked, "Do you want some water? You guys must be really hot."

"Yeah, thanks. A lot of people say we're hot," Danny tried to keep a straight face.

Celeste's two guy friends laughed.

Maya smiled and shook her head. "What made them leave you out here?"

"We left them," Will said. "It just wasn't feasible going with drivers who were a neurotic mess."

"Which is why we asked for *Mom* to pick us up," Danny said.

"Hey! You're welcome," Celeste retorted.

Will couldn't help but smile at the sibling rivalry he had witnessed for years between the blond twins. Celeste was three minutes older than Danny, which seemed to play into both of them constantly trying to one-up each other.

They hadn't driven a mile before a jostling noise came from the Suburban's front-right tire.

"Danny!" Celeste exclaimed as she pulled the vehicle to the side of the road.

"What? You think I telepathically flattened the tire?"

"No, but if it wasn't for you, we wouldn't be stuck out here!"

"It's a good thing Dad taught you how to change a flat."

In Idaho, the legal driving age was fifteen. Celeste and

Danny had been driving for a year, and they often squabbled over whose turn it was to take the wheel.

"We'll get it, Celeste," Will said, shooting Danny a look. "Don't worry about it."

They all climbed out of the Suburban, and Will could tell Danny was bothered by his sister's initial attempts to oversee them as they worked.

"Hey guys, check that out!" Jamal said, pointing off into the distance.

Will gaped at the unexpected sight behind them—a helicopter hovering far away above a red speck on the horizon. The faint sounds of propellers and gunfire were steadily becoming more noticeable. Flashes of light spat from the side of the chopper, and the car veered from side to side in response.

"Wow, this is awesome! That's a gunship!" Danny exclaimed.

"Do you think they're making a movie?" Summer asked.

Will frowned. "I don't see any film crews. It might be some kind of drug bust."

"Someone is going to get killed," Cody said, his face turning pale.

Summer gripped Jamal's arm, and they all stood transfixed.

The car skidded to a stop long before reaching them. The helicopter soared past it and began to turn around. A man emerged from the red vehicle's roof with a large cylinder over his shoulder. The helicopter opened fire just as a flash of light appeared from the back of the launcher. A rocket connected with the side of the chopper, igniting it into a ball of flames.

Will's jaw dropped, and the others let out exclamations of shock as they watched the helicopter plummet toward the sports car.

"It's gonna hit the car!" Celeste exclaimed.

The car screeched forward, narrowly avoiding the burning

mass of steel slamming into the road. The propeller spat pieces of asphalt and machine into the air.

"We should get out of sight!" Danny said as he climbed down the embankment. "They might shoot at us!"

Will and two others joined him—the rest seemed frozen in place.

The sound of another helicopter approached from the opposite direction.

As the red car sped past the Suburban, the new chopper blasted a storm of rockets, tearing up the highway ahead. The explosions shook the ground, and those still standing on the edge of the road recoiled and shielded their faces. Will ducked down as bits of debris shot over the embankment.

The rockets left craters in the road. The car swerved, but one of the front tires caught the edge of a crater, and the vehicle flipped. It toppled over and over until it lay upside down in a cloud of dust about fifty yards from the Suburban, on the opposite side of the highway.

Summer screamed, and others were coughing.

The helicopter began circling the overturned car.

"We have to get out of here," Celeste hissed. "Get the tire on!"

Will was already on it, even though the road was blocked in both directions.

The helicopter sprayed dirt as it descended to a clear section of the desert floor on the same side of the highway as the sports car. As it touched down, four men jumped out with their guns pointed at the vehicle. They managed to open the driver's-side door and pulled out a man in a white dress shirt with dark hair and an olive complexion. They tore an object from the back of his belt, then forced him to kneel with his hands behind his head.

Will felt perplexed as an eerie sense of recognition set in.

"No—that can't be," Danny said, speaking louder over the thumping helicopter blades.

"He looks like—" Maya said.

"There's no way," Danny said.

A soldier stood behind the kneeling man and pointed a gun at his head.

Maya gasped and pulled her head down.

The other men in camouflage forced a second individual out of the car, pulling him to his feet. One of the soldiers struck the man across the face, causing him to collide into the overturned car.

"That's—that's my uncle!" Will glanced back at Danny and shifted uneasily, trembling with panic.

"It might not be," Danny said.

"That *is* Chase," Will insisted as one of the militants punched the man in the stomach.

Diesel engines barreled closer behind them, and Will's fear for his uncle intensified at the sight of the military-looking vehicles.

———

Madoc Morgan sat in the passenger seat of a Humvee, heading toward Dr. Donovan and President Torres. He had shed his suit for a black shirt, camo pants, and combat boots. His blood was boiling over the losses and setbacks his men had experienced. *I'll make them suffer for it,* he thought.

He passed the downed helicopter and neared the overturned sports car and the landed chopper. It angered him even more to see the cluster of teenagers pointing their phones at the scene.

He spoke into the radio. "This is Commander Morgan. Why are the witnesses near the Suburban still alive?"

A voice answered, "Sir, our focus has been on apprehending the targets. They've proved to be unpredictably resourceful."

"Those kids are filming with their phones! Stay with the targets. I'll send someone in to kill the witnesses."

A deep voice in the back seat spoke. "Let me do it."

Morgan turned around to look at the large, bald Russian. He had a neck tattoo depicting a bloody trident and wore a depraved grin that even Morgan found a little unsettling.

"All right, Voskonov. Make it quick."

4

Three large vehicles painted in desert camouflage and a green civilian Hummer quickly encircled the overturned sports car. Camouflaged men with automatic rifles spilled out. A large bald man with a neck tattoo jogged toward the Suburban, leveling a black assault rifle.

"Let's get out of here!" Celeste said.

Will and the others frantically piled into the Suburban. Just as the doors closed, the large man paused to fire.

Celeste started the engine as he began to shoot.

They screamed as bullets tore apart the tires on the driver's side of the Suburban. The vehicle jerked down to the left.

"Everyone, keep your heads down!" Will shouted as he pulled Cody to the floor next to him and the other trembling bodies.

Celeste slammed into reverse, and they moved backward despite the shredded tires. The man laughed and fired into the front of the vehicle. Bullets tore through the metal, stopping the engine. Black smoke billowed from beneath the hood as they came to a woeful halt.

Summer was sobbing. The gun fired again, and the windows shattered as bullets blasted through them. Bits of glass spilled across Will as he shielded his face with his arm. The pause in the gunfire was filled with the man's laughter.

"We have to get out *now*!" Will said.

He pushed past the others and shoved open the right-side door, and he and Danny sprawled out. Maya burst out the passenger door and Celeste quickly climbed after her.

The sound of their attacker's boots crunched toward them, and they tumbled down onto the roadside embankment, which extended about six feet from the surface of the road.

Will began to panic. Maya was running into the desert, and though the Suburban was still between her and the man's line of fire, she would be exposed soon. Celeste was trying to move Summer, who was in hysterics. Cody's leg was drenched in blood, a large piece of glass protruding from his thigh. Danny and Jamal looked petrified in place.

Will longed for a place to hide—there was none. He saw the large, L-shaped lug wrench from changing the tire. His heart raced as he grabbed Danny's shoulder, pointed in the direction of the man, and made several hand signals. Danny's eyes widened, but he nodded.

"Go ahead and run," the man shouted in a Russian accent. "More fun for me."

Will and Danny moved up the bank of dirt. Will crouched behind the front wheel, Danny behind the back wheel.

Danny spun around the side of the Suburban and threw a rock. "Idiot!" he yelled, then scrambled back.

The rock bounced off the man's broad chest, and he fired into the back of the vehicle.

Will sprang up and threw the lug wrench at the man's face.

The tool hit him in the forehead, and he recoiled backward before swooning and collapsing on the asphalt.

No one else was coming.

"Run!" Will hissed. He slid down the embankment and sprinted into the desert. His legs churned beneath him, and he hurdled one sagebrush after another. When he came to a four-foot ledge in the lava rock, he jumped down, crouching behind the black rock for protection.

Taking in his surroundings, Will saw Maya with her bright red shirt still running ahead of him. *They'll see her easily. I have to get out of the path between her and their line of sight.* His gray shirt and jeans didn't clash nearly as much with the rocks and dirt. He could make it.

Will peeked back over the ledge and tensed with frustration. *Why aren't they running?*

Celeste knelt over Cody, tying off something on his blood-soaked leg. Danny looked like he was trying to hurry her. Jamal was attempting to keep Summer quiet and pull her away from the smoking vehicle and broken glass. Will dug his fingers into the rock and ducked back down.

So stupid! I don't want to die like this! I just need to watch out for myself. He looked for his next place to run.

A pang of guilt hit him in his chest as he realized how he would feel if Danny died. Will glanced back over the ledge. They hadn't made any progress. He ducked back down, every muscle in his body tensing in indecision.

Unlike me, Danny has a good life ahead of him—I'm the reason they're all out here. But I didn't choose this. And Chase is family! I hate this.

He continued to hesitate, then punched the dirt in resolve and climbed back over the ledge, running low to the ground back toward the Suburban.

Celeste's hands glistened crimson as she tied off her white, now-reddening blouse with a stick to tighten the tourniquet. Danny's hand was clamped over Cody's mouth as the boy writhed in pain. As he arrived, Will remembered that Celeste wanted to be a physician like her father.

Celeste looked into Cody's stricken face. "This can save your life. If we can get you to an operating room in a few hours, they'll probably be able to save your leg too."

Danny and Celeste helped Cody up.

Will pressed himself against the embankment next to the road and peered over the edge. One of the Humvees blocked his view from the shouting on the other side. "Danny, they're going to see this guy's body. Help me pull him down here," Will said in a hushed tone.

Danny grimaced. "Wha—Okay."

They crawled over the embankment. Will hit the man in the leg, but there was no response.

"Do you think he's dead?" Danny asked.

Will felt a deep ache in his heart at the thought that he might have killed someone, no matter how monstrous they were. There was a faint rise and fall of the man's chest.

Will shook his head. "I think he's unconscious. Just grab his leg."

"What if he wakes up?" Danny hissed.

"I don't want to kill him," Will whispered. "We'll just hit him again."

Danny nodded. Will picked up the gun, and they strained to pull the man over the embankment like a giant rag doll.

Jamal was making progress helping Summer and Cody walk away, but Celeste was waiting for Danny and Will.

"Go!" Danny urged in a low, harsh voice.

"I can't go without *you!*" she said.

Will stayed pressed to the embankment, his fingers clenching in the coarse earth as he peered at the Humvees.

"Come on, Will!" Danny pleaded.

Will shook his head. "That's my uncle."

"He's mixed up with some bad guys. We have to get away!"

Will tried to clear his mind—thinking of the objects ahead of him like chess pieces, with capabilities and weaknesses. Then he thought about his uncle being one of his only living family members.

He couldn't focus. Going through his options, he hopelessly bit his lip.

"Um, um, um. Danny, I need your knife."

"For what?"

"For when I go over there."

"A knife? You think you're going to *Peter Pan* over there with a pocketknife?"

"What on earth are you thinking?" Celeste said. "Come on, Danny, let's go! We can't wait for him."

Her words stung, but Will didn't hesitate. Searching the man's body, he found a knife secured to his leg. "Never mind. This one's better."

Will hefted the man's limbs and continued searching. He found three grenades, exhaled, and handed the rifle to Danny. "If you see this guy get up, shoot him. If anyone comes after you, shoot them. Go!"

"You're not taking the gun?" Danny asked.

"No, there's only one. You'll probably need it."

"Will, this is *suicide*!" Danny protested.

"Hey, I'm not going to drag you into this one too." He pushed Danny away.

"This isn't paintball! This isn't some game. We got lucky with this creep."

Will shook his head and blinked back the water forming in his eyes. "I know. I'll buy you some time. Go." He turned and moved along the embankment, closer to the men and vehicles.

———

Dr. Donovan and President Torres knelt as Madoc Morgan glowered over them. He cuffed Chase across the face with the butt of his handgun. "Where is it?"

Chase recoiled and spat blood out of his mouth. "I blew it up."

"We know it can't be destroyed. We've been spying on you for months."

"Oh, you meant Black Hammer. I thought you were referring to one of your minions."

One of the men kicked him in the side. Morgan drew his hand back to give another pistol whip, then paused.

"Have you found it?" Morgan called to his men.

"Not yet! We're prying open the trunk."

"Hurry! The National Guard will be on us soon."

"If you really have to see inside, I can get it open for you," Chase said while starting to stand up.

"You're not touching anything!" Morgan said. He continued to train his gun at Chase's face.

One of the men aimed at the trunk and opened fire. Shells flew from the gun as the bullets tore apart the lock.

"Commander, we found something!" one of the militants said as he ran to Morgan with a long black carrying case.

A broad smile crossed Morgan's face as he accepted the case. "Black Hammer is inside, isn't it?" he said to Chase.

"Oh, that? It's just a clarinet."

"A clarinet? In a biometric locking carbon-fiber case?"

"Yeah, something for you to waste your time with while the authorities arrive."

Morgan set the case on the ground and fired into its locking mechanism several times. A thin mist of smoke hissed from the bullet holes. Then he knelt reverently and pried it open. A broad smile climbed his face to his high cheekbones. Standing, he hoisted the open case into the air. "It's ours!"

His soldiers roared in celebration. Several men fired their guns into the air. Chase and the president exchanged frightened glances.

Morgan closed the lid and held it under his arm. He pointed his handgun at Chase. "So, this is your last chance to join us."

"If this is your version of wining and dining, you suck at it."

The commander frowned. "Your arrogance today has caused a lot of unnecessary deaths."

"Look, say whatever you want, but I would literally rather die than help you."

Morgan moved his gun from Chase to Torres. "Maybe, but do you want to be responsible for the death of the president of the United States?"

Chase shrugged. "We get a new one every few years."

"I'm done with you," Morgan said as he trained the gun back on Chase.

Will's arms trembled as he awkwardly held the knife and three grenades. Hopefully, real grenades worked the same way they did in movies. He recalled that simply pulling the pin didn't activate the grenade. There was a handle on each one, and as long as the handle was held after the pin was pulled, the grenade would remain inactive—but as soon as the handle was released, it would automatically spring off, and the grenade would explode seconds later.

He could see Chase and the president kneeling in the dirt. The attention of all of the men was on a case that one of them was kneeling over. *That's what they're after.* He surveyed the layout of the men and the vehicles. Going clockwise around the cluster of men, the green civilian Hummer was by the red sports car to his right. A large military-looking truck partially blocked his view and was the closest vehicle to him. Continuing around the uneven circle, the two Humvees were parked next to each other. The helicopter was the farthest away.

The man holding the case seemed like he was in charge, pointing his gun at Chase. Will couldn't make out what was being said.

Will laid two grenades on the bank of rubble in front of him. Then he clenched one, compressing the handle in his right hand and gripping the pin with his left hand. He was scared—maybe the man would let Chase and the president go since they had what they wanted. Will thought about what the shrapnel might do to the men in camouflage and rethought his options. He swallowed hard, hoping he wouldn't have to intervene.

The man fired his gun, and Chase spun around and fell.

No! I'm too late! I waited too long!

For a second, though, he could see his uncle's body move on the ground. In a bolt of desperation, Will pulled the pin and threw the grenade. He quickly threw a second one and ran forward with the last in hand.

The clang of the grenade landing in the helicopter's open door caught the men's attention.

"Grenade!" someone yelled, and they all rushed for cover. Several scrambled behind the two Humvees just a moment before the second grenade rolled between the vehicles.

The helicopter exploded in a massive, deafening fireball. While shrapnel was still flying everywhere, the second grenade erupted between the Humvees. Particles of wheels, glass, and metal flashed through the air, and a massive cloud of smoke engulfed the area.

Will took cover behind the large military truck. His ears were ringing, and he was shaking worse than before. He held the knife blade down and stabbed it into the truck tire. Then he ran to the next tire and stabbed it as well. He peered around the truck into the cloud of dust until he saw the man in charge, lying on his stomach with one arm protectively over the case. Will's breathing was irregular. Dizziness and nausea threatened to overtake him, yet he still ran straight at the man.

Will kicked the case out from under the leader's arm. The man cursed as the case slid far from his reach, and the lid flew open. Suddenly, Will's world shifted, as if he were moving in slow motion. Everything around him was a blur, except for the object inside the case.

It was a curious dark rod about two and a half feet long with features of both a knight's mace and a king's scepter. Thin gold carvings extended along the black shaft from the top of the hilt to the bottom of the head, which bore flanged edges. The ridges were primarily black, with a hint of metallic blue, and formed a single prominent ring of points around the orb and a sharp, singular point at the top where the flanges met.

The weapon was strangely familiar. He was certain he'd seen it before, but it was more than that. He'd held it, known it, cared for it—and it for him. Will felt like it was an old friend who now beckoned him to extend a hand.

Men shouting focused him back on the immediate danger. He snatched the scepter out of the case and ran farther from the attackers. The moment his skin touched the hilt, he felt a wave of strength surge through him. His head was clearer, and though he had never been in more peril in his life, he had never felt more empowered.

Will ran past the sports car, where he saw Chase, now motionless, a red stain on his shirt. Several soldiers clambered to their feet. Will wanted to stop but knew he had to find cover. Scurrying behind the Hummer, he glanced inside and saw the keys.

He raised the last grenade to his mouth to pull the pin.

Startled, he almost dropped the scepter. A large red flame billowed two feet from the scepter's head. It weaved, danced, and mystically churned, entirely unlike a natural fire. Will didn't feel any heat coming from the flame, but he still held it away from his body, not knowing what it was. The red flame was tinged with streaks of white and yellow as it continued to swirl around the head of the mysterious orb. He realized the new sense of strength he felt was likely keeping his body from trembling. Jerking the pin out of the grenade with his teeth, he kept his fingers clamped around the activating handle like a vise.

"I have what all of you want!" Will yelled. "And if any of you shoot me, I'll drop this grenade, which I have already pulled the pin from, and this object will be destroyed." He held both the grenade and the scepter above the Hummer for display.

Will couldn't completely hide the fear in his voice, but he knew the object was somehow giving him additional courage. "If you want this back, you will allow me—and the people you attacked—to leave in this Hummer." He paused, trying to catch his breath. "When we pass over the hill in the distance, I'll drop it on the road." He didn't say anything about his friends in case something went wrong, but he planned to go back for anyone still near the Suburban.

Will expected to hear someone respond, but no one answered. He slowly held the scepter and the grenade in front of himself and walked out from behind the Hummer. Everyone was staring at him in shock. Most of the men had guns in hand, but no one aimed at Will.

The man in charge, the one who'd shot Chase, stowed his handgun and casually raised his hands. "Let's calm down," he said as he slowly walked toward Will.

"Stop!" shouted Will.

"All right, Will. I'm very impressed." He motioned to the settling smoke and debris around them. "Though I'm only somewhat surprised. Destiny has brought us together. My name is Madoc Morgan. It's a pleasure to meet you."

Will gasped. "How do you know my name?"

"Well, for one, you're the spitting image of your father," the man said with a calm smile.

Will was taken aback. No one but family members ever said that Will looked like his father in a positive tone.

"And two, no one but your uncle can activate Black Hammer, the object you're holding, and when he does, the flame is only about a third of that size, after using a room full of amplifiers in a laboratory."

"Will, don't—" Chase moaned. A militant struck him with the butt of a rifle.

"Why are you hurting him?" Will shouted.

"He killed a lot of people today—and needed to be stopped."

"I—I don't know anything about what happened." Emotions about his father flooded in. "But it doesn't matter to me. I want you to help him and—" Will could no longer see the other man from the sports car. *The president? Maybe he'd gotten away?* "And get him into the Hummer, and we'll leave, and drop this onto the road before we drive out of sight." He had a nagging feeling that regardless of what they negotiated, he couldn't part with the object.

"It doesn't matter what happened? He killed people—my friends. Will, do you know who that was with him? The man who apparently you let get away?"

Will didn't respond.

"That man has more blood on his hands than perhaps anyone else in the world—President Alan Torres. He was meeting your uncle with other conspirators in a laboratory today to see how the government could use the object you're holding to kill and suppress people. You've felt the effects of the government not caring about the people they hurt, their manipulation of the world from the shadows. You don't really think your father did what they say he did?"

Will's eyes widened, but he didn't respond.

"Will, we learned about you because of your uncle. I know that no one appreciates how brilliant you are. You've been treated so badly, and yet because of your blood in relation to the scepter you hold, you can make a bigger difference in the world than anyone else on the planet. I'm just a guy trying to put an end to suffering, but you're someone who could actually make it happen."

Will hesitated. "You shot my uncle!"

"You probably would have shot him sooner than I did if you knew what I know." Morgan slowly approached.

"Don't come any closer!"

"I don't want to hurt you. If I did, I'd have my gun drawn. I want to be on the same team. The world hasn't given you what you deserve. It has held you back and pushed you down. I can help give you a life beyond your wildest dreams, much more in line with your potential and what you deserve. Besides— neither of us wants you to blow yourself up."

"I'll give this back to you. Just let us leave!" Will took several steps back. Morgan was only a few feet away from him now.

"Let's all leave together. Let's just put the pin back in that grenade. Do you still have it?"

His fear was fading. The itch to know more was overwhelming. Could this man really have the answers to his problems?

Will's eyes flitted to the grenade, and Morgan leaped forward. He ripped the explosive out of Will's hand and flung it into the distance. "I'm just trying to help you!" Morgan said.

Will almost fell over, but he steadied himself against the

Hummer. He pointed the scepter at Morgan as a reluctant defense. The man didn't seem to be afraid of the billowing red light.

"No!" Chase gasped.

Morgan dove headfirst at the dancing waves.

Everything seemed to shift into slow motion again. Chase's desperate cry hung in the air, and the world around Will was a blur except for the eerie face before him. The man's body seemed to slow until his head connected with the orb of the scepter. As the red light neared the man's head, a bright flash enveloped the entire area around them. Everything fell silent. No shouting, no breeze, nothing. There was a sharp, thunderous clap. Just before the bright light blocked everything out, the corners of Morgan's lips began to rise into a faint smile, and Will knew he had done something seriously wrong.

5

———————

Will felt heavy, as if in a deep slumber. His dreams blurred with reality, and reality was slowly spattering onto him. He became vaguely aware that it was raining, and that he was drenched with water.

His eyelids peeled open. Clouds enshrouded the night sky, and Will could see almost nothing in the blackness. His senses seemed as though they were individually awakening, and he realized he was cold. Too incoherent to do anything about it, but cold.

Will tried to think of the last thing he could remember. The images hit him, sending him bolting upright, heart hammering, desperately looking around to make out anything in the rain and darkness.

He tried to remember what had happened—the shouting, the gunfire, the explosions, the faces. *Where is everyone else? Are they okay?* He remembered the people lying on the ground. *They were just hiding for cover because of the grenades. I didn't throw the grenades directly at anyone, but the shrapnel must have hit some people. I had to risk killing them to help my family.* As he relived the scene in his mind, he brought a hand to his chest and lurched to the side, emptying his stomach onto the wet grass.

His fingers gripped the long stems. *Grass? In the desert?* He sat with his fists pressed to his forehead. *Where am I?*

Will's thoughts moved to the people he cared about, and his nausea was replaced by fear. Thinking through the chain of events, he remembered the power he felt when he hoisted—that scepter. Some of his panic dissipated, and though he couldn't see the object, he sensed it near him. Just to test the accuracy of his senses, he reached out and blindly tapped the scepter, which was resting in the wet grass. His hand recoiled. *What is that thing? Why are they after it?*

He knew at least part of the answer—it was powerful. Slowly, he reached out again, his hand hovering over the handle. It felt like it was calling to him again, like it needed him to pick it up. He wanted the rush of confidence and certainty he felt when he hoisted it. Will's mouth started to salivate.

He swallowed, hesitating. *This thing is too dangerous to have, considering the type of people who are after it. I'll be about as safe with it as someone who stole all of the loot from a drug cartel. How big of a deal would it have to be to involve the president of the United States?*

He bit his lip. At least the scepter could provide some light. He nearly drew blood as his jaw tensed. The light might beckon the wrong kind of people—make him a target. And what had it done to him? What had happened after the flash? He pulled back his hand and shook his head, resentful.

Will realized he had been holding his breath. After a deep inhale, he eased himself up. He began cautiously walking around, looking for anything to orient himself in the rain.

A light flashed from behind, and he jumped. He whirled around to face the headlights shining directly at him. Will bolted to the side, but after a few splashing steps, he heard a door open.

"Will?"

It was Celeste's voice. He turned and stepped hesitantly toward the vehicle. "Celeste?"

"Yeah, it's me. Where's Danny?"

"Uh, I don't know." As Will walked to her, he could see the abundant green grass illuminated by the light. "Where are we?"

"I have no idea," she said. "I woke up on the ground and then stumbled into this. It was unlocked, and the keys were inside."

Will was startled to see that it was the same green civilian Hummer he'd been leaning against when . . . it happened. He whirled around, straining to see in the darkness.

"What?" Celeste said.

"This is their Hummer. The people from the helicopters. This is one of theirs."

"I know. What happened? I can't believe you were crazy enough to go over there. The last thing I remember is a big flash of light."

"It was all so fast, and that's the last thing I remember too. Wasn't Danny with you?"

"No. He followed after you!"

Will's pulse quickened. "Danny! Chase!" He almost called out again but realized he didn't know who else might be nearby.

"I don't know—I don't know what is going on," Will said. "Maybe—and I can't see why anyone would do this—but maybe after we went unconscious from the flash, someone found us, drugged us, and drove us out here."

"Why would someone do that?" Celeste asked.

"I just can't think of any other explanation."

"Do you think Danny or anyone else might be out here?"

"I have no idea." Will shook his head. "All of your friends were long gone before the . . . flash. As far as my uncle and the people who attacked him, I don't know. And they shot my uncle. I'm not even sure if he—if he's still alive."

"Well, let's look for them."

They rummaged through the Hummer for anything that might be helpful. The interior looked highly customized, with additional electronic panels added to the front and altered bench seating. In the trunk space, a third row of reversed bench seats had been added to fit as many people as possible.

Celeste found a satellite phone and fiddled with it for a minute. "It turns on, but any number I dial won't go through. My cell phone is back in the Suburban."

Will was punching buttons on the electronic panels. "They have a navigation system, but it says it can't locate us on the map. It says there's no signal."

"But both the phone and the navigation are linked to satellites. They should work anywhere. Right?"

Will shook his head in confusion. "None of this makes sense."

They scoured every inch of the vehicle, finding a first aid kit, a toolbox, a flashlight, and a small metal case with several hand-size C-4 explosives.

They nervously replaced the explosives. Will also saw a facedown penny on a floor mat and self-consciously shoved it into his pocket, trying to justify that doing so didn't take up any extra time.

The Hummer was in a grassy depression surrounded by several hills. They searched for several hours in the deluge with the small flashlight, softly calling out for Danny and Chase, afraid to draw unwanted attention to themselves.

Will kept thinking about returning to the scepter, but decided it was better if he distanced himself from it. Somehow, the object had linked to him, and he knew it could only get them into more trouble. Over and over again, he thought about telling Celeste about the scepter, but he wanted to protect her from it. He also tried to deny that he felt a sense of personal possession of the scepter. Pushing the thoughts aside, he determined to focus on finding his friend and uncle.

"I can't believe there isn't at least a road nearby," Will said. "I kind of want to drive around, but I think we might just get stuck or more lost."

"I don't want to stop looking," Celeste said, teeth chattering, "but I think I'm getting hypothermia. I'm going to be in trouble if I don't dry off. And I hate to say this, but they might not even be here, which might be a good thing. We are definitely not in the desert. We haven't seen a single sagebrush."

They climbed back into the Hummer and ran the heater. "We can only keep this on for so long, or we're going to kill the battery," Celeste said as she stretched her shirt in front of one of the heating vents. Her arms were shivering as they held the wet purple fabric. "Your shirt will probably dry faster if you take it off and put it over a vent."

Will tensed, then tried to think of why the suggestion made him uncomfortable. Celeste had seen him shirtless countless times in the Barringtons' swimming pool. However, hanging out with her with no shirt on just seemed weird. "Nah, I'll just do what you're doing."

Celeste raised an eyebrow, but she seemed too focused on trying to warm up to comment.

"Maybe Danny and my uncle are more comfortable right now. Maybe people from the government came by soon after the flash, and they went with them, and we're just the ones who ended up somewhere else."

Celeste frowned. "But if a SWAT team, or those bad guys,

saw Danny with a military rifle, rather than trying to talk with him, they might have—and Danny wouldn't have just left us."

Will looked away. "I know." He paused for a long moment. "I know he wouldn't leave. The second it's light, we'll keep looking, and we'll figure out where we are."

"Absolutely." Celeste took a deep breath. "I hope Cody is okay. I hope the tourniquet I made was good enough."

"I'm sure you did a great job," Will said. "I don't know anyone our age who would do better."

Celeste nodded, but still looked distressed. "My friends probably got away, but I hope none of them hate me."

Will wanted to say something reassuring, but her concern seemed so unlikely and distant from his thoughts that the words just hung in the air.

"I know our families must be worried sick," Celeste said.

"Yeah," Will agreed, not wanting to verbalize the pain of thinking about how this must be taking a toll on his mom.

They sat submerged in their own thoughts as the rain continued to spatter against the windows. Will noticed his reflection on the metallic interior trim. His dark hair was a wild mess, and his brilliant blue eyes were still bloodshot from the smoke and debris.

He didn't linger on the reflection. *At least I can still see.* Will wished he could see Danny and Chase alive and well; he had to force alternative images out of his mind.

After a while, Will asked, "How long do you think we should let the heater run? We want to be able to drive out of here."

"I'm still freezing. Just a few more minutes."

Will noticed streaks of water on Celeste's cheeks, but in the dim cabin light, he couldn't tell if they were tears or rainwater. He almost asked if she was okay but stopped. Of course they weren't *okay,* and she was still shivering.

He looked out the window into the darkness, exhaled, then turned back. "If you want to use me to warm up, that's all right."

"Excuse me?"

Will shrugged. "I don't think you're going to stop shivering before the battery dies. So, I just figured I'd offer. If it's too awkward, forget about it, but either way, if we want to make sure we can drive tomorrow, we should shut it off soon."

She gave him a scrutinizing look, then cut off the engine and stayed on her side.

Will leaned his head against the window and looked out into the night. He was consumed with worry about his uncle, Danny, and the stress he must be putting his mom and grandparents through. Hopefully, it would stop raining before dawn. Maybe it was better that Celeste turned down his offer. He felt colder on the inside than on the outside, like he needed to shut off any desire for interacting with other people—like he'd needed to do so many times for emotional survival.

Then Will felt hands and arms wrapping around him. He froze in place. Celeste pressed herself against his side.

He realized he wasn't breathing. Her hands moved firmly up and down his right arm.

Will hesitated, then put his left arm around her. She felt somewhat warm, making him realize just how cold he was too.

He thought about how long he had secretly liked Celeste, but then tried to push the thoughts away. *This is survival—this means nothing. She doesn't like me any better than she did yesterday, last year, or the years before.*

He couldn't remember the last time anyone had embraced him like this. Hugs from his mom with her paralysis or from his aged grandparents were welcome but always felt a little awkward. He knew he had been like a glacier on the inside, with iced-over emotions built up to protect himself from the outside world. Now he felt those walls might be cracking.

Celeste's shivering eventually stopped, but Will still tried to make his chest rise and fall normally. *After everything that happened today, I can't believe this is making me so nervous.*

As she relaxed and nestled her head against his chest, he relaxed as well.

More hours passed, and though Will was wide awake, Celeste seemed as though she might have drifted into sleep. He wondered if he should wake her up or continue to hold her as she slept. Will was grateful for her warmth—physically. He was torn, wondering whether the emotional warmth was just making him vulnerable.

He imagined government officials or reporters looking for them and taking pictures of the two of them together at dawn. *One more thing for them to publish about me.* The situation brought back the memory of a conversation at the Barringtons' dinner table.

Dr. Barrington had mentioned something about needing to work more hours so they would have enough money set aside. Mrs. Barrington asked why, and he said, "So that you all have enough money after I go to jail."

"What?" Mrs. Barrington exclaimed.

"Yeah, with all of these boys coming to our house wanting to talk to Celeste, some who she doesn't even know, I swear I'm going to end up killing one of them!"

Mrs. Barrington and Celeste let out exclamations of shock and objection, and their strong reactions made Danny laugh.

"You know what I'm going to do?" Dr. Barrington said. "The next boy who comes by here asking for Celeste, I'll tell him what I would do if someone ever mistreated my daughter. I'll tell him that I would take such a person out into an abandoned warehouse, tack his hardware to the floor, and light the place on fire. Then I'd leave him with a rusty knife and tell him he could either cut it off—or burn."

"Daddy, you're horrible." Celeste rolled her eyes.

Dr. Barrington laughed. Danny laughed so hard he fell out of his chair.

Will smiled at the memory of Danny's laughter, then cringed to think of what terms he would be on with their father if a picture of Will and Celeste holding each other in a vehicle in the middle of nowhere became an international headline. *Also, where would that put me with Danny? Danny is one of the reasons I stifled having a crush on her years ago—that and the fact she's so far out of my league. Their parents must be pulling out all the stops trying to find them.*

Celeste stirred. "Will, do you want to get in the back seat?"

Will's eyes shot open. "Uh, why?"

Her head still rested on his chest. "I'm falling asleep, and there isn't enough space up here for both of us."

"I'm not going to be able to sleep, but okay."

"Actually, it's all wet up here. I'll take the back," she said.

Celeste climbed over the seats. They didn't speak again. Will almost looked back but continued staring forward, thinking it would feel intrusive. He realized he was looking in the direction of the scepter. He could sense it reaching out to him—or was it just that he was drawn to it, just like the men seeking it in the desert, as if it were some powerful drug?

I don't need it. He wrestled with what voids he might have in his life that would allow the dark weapon to appeal to him. *Fear? Wanting to feel more in control? More important?* He shivered, but not because of the cold. He knew there were other voids in his life that he'd long pretended didn't exist. His eyes glanced back in Celeste's direction.

His skin felt colder without her next to him. Will repeatedly tensed and relaxed his arms and legs, hoping it would help him warm up and maybe relieve some of his stress. He only stopped when he was too tired to continue.

Will regretted not having dried out his clothes better when the heater was running. He took his shirt off and draped it over the seat.

He was so exhausted, his eyelids growing heavy. His last thoughts before sleep overcame him drifted to the scepter. *But it's just trouble—and it's going to get us killed.*

6

———

"Will, wake up. The sun is coming up." Celeste nudged his shoulder.

Will sat up abruptly. His head ached, and he vigorously rubbed his eyes. "Have you seen anything?"

"Nothing past the fog," she said. "But this wild grass is so green—we definitely aren't anywhere close to home."

Will peered through the fog but could only see the base of the green hills around them. His attention was again drawn to the direction of the object, but he shook his head, trying to push away the temptation. "We need to find a road."

Celeste was already out the door.

Will reached for his shirt, but it was still damp, so he left it behind. The smell of the morning air caught him off guard. It was moist and salty, nothing like the air in eastern Idaho. His eyebrows scrunched together. "It smells different."

"I know. I don't get it," Celeste said. "It smells like we're near the ocean."

"Are you sure? I've never been to the ocean."

"I'm sure of the scent, but we can't be. The nearest coast is too far away. I don't know what else would make that smell, though."

"Let's follow the tire tracks back to the road." Will dashed behind the vehicle.

"Where are the tracks?" Celeste asked. "Maybe the rain—but those are tracks from our feet last night!"

They circled several times. Will crouched behind the back wheels and felt along the grass. "There are no indentations! Not even a bent blade of grass."

He squeezed his eyes shut. *I was touching this Hummer when the flash happened—while holding that object. That man knew something would happen. He wanted something to happen.*

"We've gotta check this place out." He started running up one of the hills into the fog, desperate for anything to orient him.

When he reached the top, he braced both hands on top of his head and turned in every direction, slack-jawed. He slowly sat down, too dumbfounded to act, not caring that the ground was wet.

"What is it?" Celeste said as she caught up to him. "What the—what's going on?"

Will nodded to the valley below. "There's your ocean. And the rest is—well, I'm kind of freaking out."

Through breaks in the fog, smaller rolling green hills emerged, flattening into a valley that stretched to the distant ocean shore. A river on their right wound down to the larger water, and a forest bordered the valley on their left.

There were three small houses in the distance with a dirt path winding to a village near the mouth of the river. The houses almost looked more like huts, with thatched roofs and smoke coming from one of the chimneys. Next to one of the houses was a crude stone enclosure with a few sheep milling around inside. The roofs in the village were also thatched, except for the stone spire of a small church.

There was no modern road in sight.

"How did we get here? And where is here?" Celeste held her hand to her mouth. She knelt next to him, and they watched people down below, hunched over, working the rough farmland. "This is some kind of sick joke. Someone drugged us and dropped us off outside a freaking reenactment village."

"Then it's an elaborate joke," Will said. "Those look like legit thatched roofs, and no one in America would farm like that. I think even the Amish communities are more advanced. And the ocean? We're nowhere near home."

"Okay," Celeste said, pressing her fingers to her temples. "Where *could* we be?"

"I haven't traveled much. You tell me."

"I've never been *here*! The landscape looks like scenes from movies of—the British Isles? And that looks like the Middle Ages. That Hummer doesn't look like it's been driven here at all, but I don't know how it could have been . . . dropped there."

"I've gotta get that weapon," Will muttered.

"What weapon?"

"I don't know what happened, but there was this glowing object that they all wanted, and light came from it . . . I think it might have something to do with us being here. I was leaning against the Hummer when it happened."

"What? Why didn't you tell me about that?"

"I didn't want to talk about what happened, probably not any more than you. It's black and looks like a knight's mace, or a scepter."

"A knight's mace? And you think that could send us here? That's crazy. What else happened? What else aren't you telling me?"

Will pressed his fists to the side of his head, the headache still lingering. *I know I should tell her everything, but I don't even know if I could explain it, or if she would even understand.* He certainly wasn't going to tell her that he felt a mental connection with the scepter. Will let out a deep breath and remembered thinking about how he felt like he'd lived within walls of ice to protect himself from most people. He wanted to put some trust in Celeste.

"I'm not sure how we were transported here, but I can try to tell you what I do know."

"Where is this mace, or scepter thing?" she demanded.

"It's in the grass, not far from the Hummer." Will hesitated. "I'll show it to you when we go back down."

"But even if something could transport us here, why just you and me? There were other people closer to you. Wouldn't they have been sent too?"

"What if they woke up spaced far apart in the rain like we did and then wandered in different directions in the dark? There are hills all around here. You woke up closer to the Hummer than I did, but I was actually touching it when it happened."

"I don't know," Celeste sounded skeptical. "Before we even consider an object time-traveling us, I want to go down and try talking to the people in those houses. Hopefully, we'll be able to understand each other."

"If they aren't just actors, they're going to think we're witches or something."

"It's our best way to figure out what's going on."

"Not if they try to burn us alive."

They spun toward a noise from an area where the fog was still dense. Will and Celeste moved down the hill until they were just peering above the grassy summit. The sound grew louder. They could hear horses' hooves steadily moving in their direction, soon accompanied by the footsteps of many people trudging across the wet grass. A horse snorted, and a man coughed. Will looked around for a place to hide. There were no trees nearby, and the nearest cover was the Hummer.

Silhouettes materialized out of the fog. Several men on horseback and others on foot moved toward them. The figures brandished swords, spears, and other weapons that were difficult to make out through the mist. Celeste whirled around and collided into Will, sending him flailing backward into a patch of mud. He rolled several times in the cold, thick sludge. The mud felt freezing against his bare torso. He stumbled to his feet and continued after Celeste.

She was almost to the Hummer. Will started to go after her, but he couldn't resist running to where the scepter lay. He felt a protective ownership of the black rod but rationalized that they might need it again.

He couldn't see the scepter in the grass, but he knew approximately where it was, both from memory and somehow sensing it. Celeste was already in the driver's seat of the Hummer, and he remembered how she'd encouraged Danny to leave without him in the desert.

Will found it, snatching it by the shaft from the ground. The scepter was thoroughly covered in mud and blades of grass. No light came from it, and Will wondered if it was broken, or if maybe it only lit when held by the handle. He felt some relief in possessing it again, and he sprinted back to Celeste.

Will climbed in the passenger side. "Maybe we should try to find a different place to hide? They might be coming here because of the Hummer."

"This can go a lot faster than the horses, and I am not staying here." Celeste poised to start the ignition. "I don't want to make any noise, though, in case they aren't coming down here."

"This is like horrible déjà vu," Will blurted in frustration.

"At least they won't be able to see us through these thickly tinted windows."

A lone man on a horse arrived at the summit and looked down upon them. He and the large black horse were completely clad in armor with blue and red trappings. The knight studied the scene for a moment, then turned and motioned with his lance. Other men on horseback and on foot appeared on the ridge and charged down the slope.

Celeste started the engine and floored the acceleration. The vehicle roared, glaring its headlight eyes at the men through the low misty morning light. Mud spit wildly from beneath the tires and high into the air, but the Hummer didn't move.

"A dragon!" someone shouted.

Several horses bucked their riders at the sound of the engine, and one man fell to the ground. The knight's large horse was unshaken, charging down the slope, the warrior's lance leveled at the vehicle.

Men on horse and foot continued to spill over the hill.

Celeste let off the gas and pressed it again. This time, the Hummer lurched forward, spraying mud and grass as she maneuvered to turn around. Will and Celeste jumped as the lance thudded into the vehicle's side.

"Go!" Will urged.

"I'm trying!" She continued to turn the wheel.

"For St. George!" a man shouted from outside.

More men reached the Hummer as Celeste again slammed on the gas. They hacked at the backside, undeterred by the spraying mud.

Arrows pelted the side of the vehicle as Will and Celeste sped across the uneven terrain. A group of men blocked their escape. One of them threw a spear straight at the center of the windshield.

Will gripped both sides of his seat and clenched his teeth.

Celeste swerved, and the spear smashed off a side mirror. They barreled onward, but a solid line of men on foot blocked their way with weapons ready.

Celeste grimaced but didn't slow down. "I don't want to run over anyone."

"Don't stop!" Will cringed and braced for impact.

Celeste tensed even more, still holding speed.

The line of men parted at the last moment, and the Hummer was hammered with a thunder of weapons. One man grabbed on to the luggage racks and pulled himself on top of the roof. Despite the jostling of the Hummer over uneven ground, the man held on and repeatedly beat into the roof with his axe.

Will stared in horror as the axe blade began making progress through the roof. Celeste swerved the vehicle back and forth. The man slipped off the roof but managed to hang on to the luggage rack. Holding his weapon in the other hand, he swung it hard into Will's window.

Will ducked as the axe smashed into the glass. The bullet-proof window didn't break, but a frosted array of spiderwebs now spread across it. The man began pulling himself back up. Will unlocked the door, pulled the handle, and kicked with both feet. The door only opened a few inches, but the force was enough to send the man tumbling into the grass.

"Good," Celeste said. She was gripping the steering wheel so firmly her knuckles were completely blanched.

Will glanced back to see the horsemen still following them. "Where are you going to go?"

"We're trapped by the river on our right and the forest on our left," she said in frustration. "We can't stay out in the open. I think we should follow the dirt path to the village and see if we can cut through to the other side. There might be a road going away—if not, we can drive along the beach."

Will looked around at the landscape. "This is insane, but I don't see a better idea. We have to get away from those maniacs and ditch the Hummer. The tire tracks will be easy to follow."

They reached the wheel-rutted road and continued speeding toward the village. The horsemen fell farther behind, and someone blew a ram's horn.

"I think they're trying to alert the village. They're probably worried this strange thing is going to attack the people living there," Will said.

Disheveled peasant men emerged onto the roadway outside the village with crude weapons. They looked horrified, but despite their lack of armor, they still stood guarding their homes.

Celeste pulled off the road to the right. "I'm going to try to pull through an opening between the buildings."

The peasants ran along the perimeter of the village. Many of the spaces between buildings had low stone walls with livestock. Will turned to see the horsemen catching up to them. The riders split into three groups—one went straight for the Hummer, one went toward the edge of the river, and the other entered the village at the roadway entrance.

"They're trying to trap us!" Will said, looking back over the seat.

"Great," Celeste said through clenched teeth. "I'm going a different route."

She veered off and smashed into a low stone wall, and the Hummer clambered over the rubble. Sheep scattered, bleating wildly, and Celeste veered away from the cornered animals. She gunned the engine, blasting through another stone wall and into the dirt street.

Women and children shrieked as they scurried into their homes. Celeste maneuvered the vehicle between the buildings, and people fled to get out of the way. The knight in red and blue dashed toward them from between two houses and impaled the wheel with his lance. The vehicle continued off-kilter, and the shaft was ripped from the rider's hand. Celeste sped down the street, trying to stay ahead of the knight. They came to a large cart that was blocking their way. Celeste didn't hesitate. Flooring the gas pedal, she smashed the cart into a splintering array of wood and vegetables.

The path was forcing them closer and closer to the river, with no clear opportunities to turn and escape to the beach. A boy rushed out of a blacksmith's shop ahead of them. He had a frightened yet determined look and was holding a blacksmith's hammer, which he threw straight at the windshield. Will and Celeste winced as it connected, creating a web of cracks.

The road opened near the riverbanks, where several horsemen were waiting for them, struggling to calm their frenzied mounts.

"Strike the wheels!" the knight yelled.

They were surrounded. Celeste tried to break past the line of horsemen while looking through an unobscured corner of the windshield. The warriors maneuvered out of the way and thrust their weapons into the tires. There were popping sounds as the vehicle jolted forward.

7

———————

Celeste continued to accelerate, but the wheels spat mud, grass, and pieces of shredded tire.

"Bloody chariot of Satan!" a man shouted.

Celeste frantically tried to move in reverse, and then forward, but the wheels just continued to spin in the soft turf. Smoke rose from each of the deepening ruts as the warriors at all four corners of the vehicle beat viciously.

Finally, Celeste let off the gas, though she still desperately gripped the steering wheel. She and Will both knew the Hummer wasn't going anywhere. More men with weapons were converging on them, joining the attack on the vehicle.

"Thy foul eyes will curse this land no more!" one of the men cried as he smashed out the headlights with an axe.

The heavy blows sent horrifying echoes through the Hummer. Celeste slid away from the steering wheel. She was shaking. Bits of weapons made their way through the vehicle's armor, and the seals around the windows loosened.

Celeste's voice shook. "Maybe we should just let them know we're in here. That we're just people!"

"What do you think the betting odds are on them killing people joyriding in 'Satan's Chariot'?"

A man leaped onto the hood and repeatedly stabbed downward with a spear. "We shall destroy thee in the name of our Lord God!"

Will reached over and honked the horn. The man slipped and fell off the hood.

"Bloody hell!" someone yelled, and the group beat the vehicle with even more ferocity.

Celeste dug her fingernails into Will's arm. "Will!" she hissed. "That wasn't necessary!"

"It took out one guy. I don't know what else to do!" he whispered back.

"Let's burn it!" yelled a man, approaching with a torch. Others scurried to pile wood and straw around the Hummer.

The smell of smoke seeped into the vehicle.

"We can't stay in here," he hissed. "Let's go out my door and try to make a break for the river."

"Too risky," Celeste retorted. "But we have to get out. There are explosives in the back! Let's tell them we're inside and take our chances reasoning with them."

"Reasoning with them?" Will said in disbelief, gesturing at the wild-faced man beating on the windshield.

"They're scared of the vehicle because they've never seen one before, but we're just people. Talking to them is our best hope."

"But I probably look like something that wandered out of hell," Will said, wiping at the mud on his face.

"Then I'll go first." She pressed her lips together, still hesitating.

The smoke thickened amid the crackling flames, and men still surrounded them, thundering away at the Hummer with their weapons.

"I'm going out the back," she said. "Maybe it will make us seem more like prisoners than the demons driving it—or controlling it, or whatever." She pulled the release handle for the hatch, but it didn't open.

"We can go back there and kick it," Will said.

They climbed over the seats. Part of Will wanted to wield the scepter as a weapon, but he knew it would be hopeless to try to fight all of these men. The fear of them stealing it irrationally weighed on his mind. The scepter was covered in mud and grass, and he put his T-shirt over it to further disguise it from looking like a weapon or something of value.

Celeste shouted from inside the vehicle, "You saved us! You saved us from this horrible beast!"

The beating continued, but one man said, "I heard a woman's voice inside."

"'Tis a deception!" another man yelled.

"No! It's no deception!" Celeste cried. "You have slain this beast and have saved our lives. Thank you! You have set us free!"

The beating slowed as the men studied the vehicle. They still held their weapons raised as the fire around the Hummer grew.

"I think I can climb out now. Do not hurt us! We are innocent and harmless!"

"Come forth then!" the knight ordered.

Will and Celeste kicked at the damaged door until it opened enough for her to slip through.

The men in rustic medieval farm clothing gathered behind the soldiers around the back of the vehicle, and all gaped at Celeste.

"She's beautiful!" one of them exclaimed.

Will followed after her, and one of the men raised a sword to strike him.

"No!" Celeste cried as she held out her hand. "He is good. You have saved both of us!"

At five-foot-seven, Celeste stood taller than many of the men. Her blond hair, though disheveled, still bore the sheen of careful maintenance as it rested behind her shoulders. A lock curled down, accenting her symmetrical, almond-shaped face, green eyes, and radiant skin. A subtle gold necklace rested around her neck. Her complexion was in stark contrast to everyone surrounding them, whose features seemed weather-beaten and, in many cases, malnourished. Her white, ortho-dontically straightened teeth were an anomaly among the gaping mouths around them, displaying crooked rows of yellow, brown, and vacant spaces. Her royal-purple shirt stood prominently apart from the dirty grays and browns worn by the others present, except for the red and blue trappings of the knight and several other horsemen.

Celeste's designer jeans may as well have been from a different planet. They accented her athletic figure from seasons of soccer and running track. Like the hems of her jeans, her black-and-white running shoes were dirty but still appeared more comfortable than the assortment of coarse leather footwear standing around them.

"She's the tallest woman I've yet seen," one of the men said.

Will cautiously moved to his feet, rising four inches taller than Celeste, bearing smears of grass and mud across his bare chest and mud-caked jeans.

"Who are you, and why are you wearing such strange attire?" the knight demanded. Many of the men seemed to have lost interest in the crackling flames around the beaten Hummer.

"I will explain everything!" she promised. "First, you must know that on this foul creature's dying breath, it murmured that it would send a great wave of fire burning anyone standing nearby. We must move away, or we will all be burned."

She started away from the Hummer, but the men roughly grabbed their arms to keep them from running.

"I assure you, we are good people, and that I am trying to help you by keeping us all away from the fire!" A trace of panic entered her voice.

The men continued to guard them, and they moved back from the fire.

"We must move much farther away!" Celeste insisted. "It will send a great cloud of fire. If anyone is nearby, they could be hurt or killed!"

"Trickery!" a man cried. "We can't trust her word!"

"We won't let it escape," the knight said. "Stand back and stand ready."

Will was blown away by how well Celeste was handling the situation and felt grateful that she was there.

As they continued to move back, the Hummer exploded. People screamed, and several horses reared with pawing hooves, shrieking and bolting in fear. A man pressed a hand to his bearded jaw where a flying piece of metal cut him. Other warriors roared in triumph as they watched the burning pillar of fire and smoke.

"I told you I was trying to help you! We are not bad people."

The cheers of excitement died as the flames reduced to a low crackle. Black smoke continued to churn from the debris. The wild-eyed men turned their attention back to Celeste and Will.

The knight stood menacingly before them. He was a mountain of a man, a little taller than Will and much bigger than the malnourished-looking villagers. His broad shoulders and chest appeared even larger with the layer of gray-plated armor. Sweat drenched his dark brown locks of hair, which extended to the level of his thick jaw. "Tell me truthfully—who are you?" His massive hand pointed a sword at them, and he gave Will a look as though hoping he might try something foolish.

"Stop!" A new voice rang out, as clear as the call of a trumpet.

The men lowered their weapons and dropped to one knee, averting their eyes to the ground. They parted to allow a man on a black stallion to approach. His polished armor gleamed in the morning mist. Even to Will's untrained eye, it was clear that the armor was of noticeably higher craftsmanship than the knight's or any of the other men's. His helmet was topped with a plume of red feathers, and his visor was artfully worked to resemble a lion's head.

When he lifted his visor, Will gave a start. He couldn't have been more than sixteen or seventeen.

"Unhand her. I wish to speak to the maid," the young man on horseback said. "Surely, this beautiful woman can mean no harm. Please, my lady, speak freely, and tell us why you are thus dressed."

Celeste hesitated. "I was stripped of my gown, and this was what I had left to cover myself."

"Still, your clothing is clearly foreign—as is your accent," the young man replied. "Why are you wearing purple? Only royals wear purple."

Celeste glanced at Will before mustering confidence in her voice. "Yes—I am a princess."

"From where?" the young man demanded.

"America. My father is the king of America."

Will almost choked.

"I've never heard of such a place."

Will interjected, "It's far across the ocean. We were attacked and taken prisoner by that." He squared his shoulders and pointed to the burning remains of the Hummer.

Every eye turned to him. The glares seemed to communicate that he had committed some kind of social taboo by speaking without first being addressed.

"Is he your slave?" the young man asked, nodding at Will.

"No," Will said indignantly.

Celeste looked at Will. He was shirtless, smeared with mud and grass from head to toe, but not thick enough to completely hide the bruises on his arms and chest gifted to him from the day before. Will wondered if his eyes still looked bloodshot. "No, he's one of our servants."

"He's filthy," the young man said.

Will tensed but said nothing so as not to blow the cover she was making up.

"Yes, it was quite an ordeal. He is a royal servant, though, and my father will handsomely reward you for our rescue and safekeeping. I have reason to believe that my brother may also be in this land. Assistance in finding him will bring you great riches."

"Great riches I already have," he said with an amused smile, then dismounted. "Forgive me for not introducing myself. I am Sir Edmund FitzAlan, son of Sir Richard FitzAlan, Earl of Arundel. If your safekeeping would gain your ladyship's and your father's favor, I shall gladly be of assistance."

Edmund reached for her hand, and Celeste allowed him to kiss it. "Thank you, Sir Edmund. We will be forever in your debt."

Will appraised Edmund; they were about the same size. The youth had fair skin with just a touch of rosiness. Light brown hair showed at the edges of his helmet, and his light eyes glinted with pomp.

"Strange folk were seen last night," Edmund said. "They robbed and murdered over a dozen people here in Littlehampton. Might they be from your land?"

"They may likely be the evil men who set that abhorrent thing upon us," Celeste said, sounding like she was trying to mimic Edmund's manner of speech. "If so, they are enemies of my father, and may be holding my brother and other men of my father's house hostage."

"My men have been searching for the murderers, and will continue the search." Edmund looked back at his men and grinned. "I do hope it is the group I lead who finds them. It appears we missed out on the excitement of the morning." He nodded to the smoldering metal skeleton.

Several men replied with an enthusiastic, "Yes, my lord!"

"Meanwhile, you must stay in my father's castle, where we can make you quite comfortable. 'Tis a shame that you've had such a dreadful experience."

"We would appreciate that very much," Celeste said. "Please be careful with those you might find from our land. The bad ones may have powerful weapons, while my brother and perhaps others are innocent."

"We're not afraid of any weapon," Edmund said curtly.

Celeste opened her mouth to reply but stayed silent.

"But this I could do for your brother," he continued. "If any men promptly surrender, we'll bring them to my castle for you to identify. I see that as reasonable."

"Very reasonable," Celeste agreed.

He turned to his men and raised his voice. "No harm to anyone who surrenders—even though it detracts from the fervor of the hunt."

There were nods and murmurs of assent.

"Perhaps I should leave the hunt to you while I seek a different venture?" He winked at his men, then looked at Celeste.

There were chuckles, and someone said, "Aye, my lord."

"Allow me to help you onto my horse, my lady." Edmund

extended his hand and assisted Celeste onto his steed, then joined behind her.

"What of the lad?" asked the knight, looking at Will.

"What of him?" Edmund said. "No one will want to ride with him in his condition. He looks filthier than a village dung collector." The men laughed.

"My name is William, and this is not how I normally look."

Edmund ignored him as he surveyed the charred remnants of the Hummer. "Cast the remains into the river. It will wash out to sea."

Several of his men hurried to follow his orders.

"In truth, what was that wheeled contraption?" Edmund asked, turning to Celeste. "It seemed to be armored in metal."

"A cursed wagon, powered by a dragon's heart." She was clearly thinking on her feet. "The wheels and metal scales were surely bestowed upon it in the forges of hell. We shall ever be in your debt for heroically saving our lives."

Edmund's eyes beamed as he gazed at Celeste. "Fair lady, the pleasure of beholding your smile is payment enough."

Celeste blushed.

Will found the interaction between Edmund and Celeste cringeworthy, but he kept his poker face and tried to think of what a medieval servant would be expected to act like. *Certainly much more . . . subservient.* He held back the frown that wanted to greet the thought; he couldn't let the young noble get under his skin. As he took in the blood-hungry men around him, all brandishing mechanisms of death, he knew that Edmund's infatuation with Celeste was the only thing keeping him alive.

8

———————

Edmund turned his mount to depart, and Celeste motioned for Will to follow. He maintained his composure, bracing himself for how fast and far he might have to run to attempt to keep up with the horses.

"My lord," the knight said, "I do not think the servant should be unaccompanied. Not until more is known about these strange folk."

"What have you in mind?" Edmund said.

"Let him ride with my squire to accompany the lady back to the castle. I think it wise not to let these foreigners be unaccounted for," the knight said.

It was immediately clear to Will who the squire was. There was a teenage boy on horseback alongside the other horsemen, and his head and shoulders seemed to deflate at the suggestion. Will had noticed the boy earlier, eagerly caught up in the frenzy of the encounter. He still held his sword ready rather than sheathing it like some of the others. He quickly righted himself in the saddle and looked intently to Sir Edmund.

"Very well," Edmund said, accepting the counsel, but

clearly not interested in giving Will more than a moment's thought.

"Yes, my lord," said the squire, who urged his horse forward. He gave a jealous glance to all the men who would continue the search for the ruffians, then turned to Will. "No tricks."

"Of course not," Will said, holding out his empty hands, already having placed the scepter through the back of his belt with the top portion wrapped in his T-shirt and the rest masked with a thin coat of mud.

The squire reluctantly sheathed his sword and extended a hand down to Will. "Get up, then."

Will clasped the hand and climbed on behind the squire. The saddle only had room for one, so Will sat on the horse's sweat-slicked back. He repositioned the scepter to make it less uncomfortable. He enjoyed riding horses, but it had been a few years since his grandfather sold his due to his advancing age and needing to pay Will's mom's medical bills.

The squire stayed turned in the saddle, eyeing Will cautiously. "Don't try nothing," he said. "I don't like this, and I don't trust you."

"I understand. I'd probably feel the same way if I were you, and I'm grateful for your help."

Edmund and five horsemen were already riding away from the river's edge toward a village street.

The squire grunted and urged his steed to follow. "You're fortunate Sir Roland don't miss a thing. Now don't do anything stupid while we're riding—witchcraft or nothing."

"I wouldn't know how," Will said. "I'm a normal person."

The boy looked back with a half grin. "Good. I'd run you through otherwise." He dug his heels into the horse to hurry it forward.

Will tried to position himself to keep from falling and reduce the pinching from the sharp row of points around the scepter's head. He wished for something thicker than the T-shirt, like a mace-carrying casing he saw on one of the men's belts.

He gripped the squire's thick, dark brown leather jacket, which extended to his elbows, with a beige long-sleeve shirt underneath. The thick leather seemed like it was layered and held together with rows of large stitching. Will thought it might help avoid cuts, but it wasn't near the armored protection worn by many other horsemen.

Peasants stood in the streets outside their homes, watching him—some with interest, others with loathing, and a few with fear. Will noticed a girl about ten years old pulling herself through the dirt outside the doorway of a small stone house with an uneven thatched roof. Her legs were withered, and she held herself up with her hands. She wore a frayed gray dress, stained a darker brown from frequent contact with the earth. Their eyes met, and the girl winced and looked away.

Will felt self-conscious for making her uncomfortable, so he looked away as well. He thought of his mother and how difficult it would be for her to live here, and for him and his grandparents to care for her in these austere conditions. His mom could move her arms but not well enough that she could ever walk with her hands. He felt a pang of guilt for making her worry, then realized that if they were truly back in time, she hadn't even been born yet. The thought took a moment before it could sink in. He tried to focus on what he would need to do to get through today and if there was anything he could do to help Chase and Danny if they were here.

They continued to ride among the gray-brown stone houses until they caught up with Edmund's men.

"Seems our lord may be taking a slower pace on account of your lady," the squire said with a knowing glance back at Will while keeping his horse behind the others.

"I'm sure she appreciates his attention." Will forced a courteous tone. How long would he need to play the part of a dutiful servant? *As long as I need to for us to get through this.*

"I'm surprised he's allowing the two of you back to his castle," the squire said, "even though the lord is clearly taken by her beauty. And whether you be innocent or not, there'll be many who suspect you evil. And again, don't try nothing stupid. The only reason you're on my horse is because I'm more afraid of disobeying Sir Edmund and Sir Roland than riding horseback with a demon."

"And just what does a demon look like? Because I've never seen one," Will said.

The squire glanced back and grinned. "Then tell me what that thing you were in was. How should we know you two weren't the soul propelling the contraption?"

"As for what it was, I believe her ladyship's description to Sir Edmund was accurate. I'm William, by the way. What's your name?"

"Garrett."

"Thanks again, Garrett."

"Once I've completed my training, I'll be Sir Garrett. This morning was a thrill, but you've cost me the opportunity to fight the murderers from last night. To make up for it, I'll tell people I tamed the man inside the beast."

Will was still wrapping his head around the concept of being seen as an adult at sixteen. "So long as it keeps people from wanting to shove sharp objects into me."

Garrett laughed. "I can't make promises on that account."

They continued up the open green countryside as the land gradually elevated away from the coast. Will looked past the back of Garrett's gray helmet, the squire's unkempt red-brown hair protruding beneath the rim, to survey the unfamiliar countryside.

Will was accustomed to pine mountain forests or sage-brush-scattered desert. Now he took in rolling green hills lined with deciduous trees. The humidity from the morning fog was dissipating in the sun's warmth, and Will assumed it must be sometime in the spring.

A massive castle came into view, looming above the forest. They neared a village outside the castle walls as they followed the river that wove through the town and down to the ocean.

As soon as Will's nerves settled a little more, his thoughts were pulled to the scepter. He wanted to activate it again when he found a moment alone, but part of him was afraid to find out what would happen if he did.

Guards opened the castle gates upon seeing Edmund. He rode across the expansive courtyard, while Garrett and the other horsemen rode along the inside of the castle wall in the opposite direction.

"Where are they going?" Will said, his voice tinged with concern.

"Sir Edmund isn't going to walk from the stables. A servant will return his horse for him," Garrett explained.

Will continued to gaze in Celeste's direction. He wanted to shout something and was surprised that Celeste didn't even look back. She sat with Edmund's arms around her as he held the reins. *Is she enjoying that? Did she forget about me?*

At the stables, the horsemen dismounted and spoke excitedly of the morning's exploits as several servants gathered to listen.

Will stayed out of the conversation and helped brush down Garrett's chestnut-brown mare. His grandfather had been somewhat of a cowboy, and Will knew how to care for horses. Will missed riding whenever he wanted and briefly thought about how his family sold their small farmhouse and moved into town due to the declining health of his mom and grandparents. Will wished he could just relax and enjoy caring for the beautiful animal as he kept his wary eyes on the men around him.

One of the horsemen pointed at him. "That's one of them that 'twas inside it!"

Another horseman drew a dagger at his waist and approached Will. He appeared to be in his twenties and had a crooked nose, likely from a poorly healed break. "I still think lettin'im live's a bad omen."

"I know I sound different," Will said, backing up. The man was more difficult to understand than the higher-born individuals, and Will tried to make his voice sound a little more similar to Garrett's. "But I'm just a person, not that much different than the rest of you."

"Your words mean nothin'," said the young man holding the dagger inches away from Will's bare abdomen. "But we've a loyalty t'our lord, and you best remember that you live at 'is will."

"Then long live Sir Edmund," Will said.

"And long live 'is father, Sir Richard FitzAlan," said the man with the dagger. "If you're still 'ere when the lord'n lady return from Rome, there could be different plans for you."

"Won't likely be anytime soon," Garrett snorted. "Let him be, Hector."

Hector continued to level the dagger. "We take protecting our lord and his family quite seriously, and we don't know a thing about this place you say you hail from. Best not do anything to make us suspect you've malice toward our lord."

"I would never do such a thing," Will said, standing his ground. "And I don't think he would want you brandishing weapons at his guest."

"Guest?" Hector seemed to consider the word. "Then we expect you to behave as one." He sheathed the dagger.

"What did the woman look like?" a servant asked.

Will was grateful for the shift in conversation. Most of the horsemen and servants appeared to be under thirty. Will thought that two of the horsemen were likely older, though it was difficult for him to estimate their age. Even through their chain mail, he could tell their bodies were lean and muscular, but their faces appeared as coarse as weathered rock from pox, sun, wind, and war.

The stable looked like a small barn made of dark timbers and a thatched roof. Will continued to help care for the horses, trying to stay out of the way so as not to draw additional attention to himself. He thought of the many other tasks a servant would be expected to know how to do—his lack of knowledge could be life-threatening.

The men dispersed as the work in the stable was completed.

"I have some things to attend to," Garrett said. "Can you stay put? I'll see about finding you a fresh set of clothing."

"I need to meet with Lady Celeste. Where is she?"

"Being tended to by maidservants, I'm sure."

"I need to speak with her, now," Will insisted.

"If she wishes to speak with you, she'll summon you." Garrett studied him.

Will again felt frustrated by the status she'd given him. "I want to request an audience with her."

"While she's being cared for by the maidservants? After her travail this morning?" Garrett asked in mild astonishment.

"I . . . I'll wait." Will groaned inwardly, knowing he was walking on thin ice.

"Course you will." Garrett slapped his shoulder. "None of us would go about demanding time from Sir Edmund. Now just stay here until we find something to do with you." The squire closed the stable door behind him.

Will exhaled and walked straight to where he saw a scrap of leather on the ground. The row of points around the scepter's black head still poked into his back if he bent the wrong way. He set to work wrapping the leather around the scepter's head to make a crude variation of the covers he'd seen several warriors use for their maces. He left a thin sheen of dirt on the scepter to mask the intricately carved gold lettering on the black shaft. With the dirt and such a crudely put-together cover for the head, he hoped people might be less likely to assume it had any value.

Once the covering was wrapped in place, he set the scepter down and looked at what remained in a barrel of water used for transporting water to the horses. The cold liquid bit at his skin as he cupped it with his hands and raised it to his face.

"Are you William?" a girl's voice asked from behind him.

The voice startled Will, and he turned around to see a teenager holding a stack of clothing and peering through the stable doorway.

"Hello, yes. That's me," he said, quickly wiping water from his eyes.

The girl stepped hesitantly into the stable. Her dark brown hair flowed onto her shoulders, and she wore a flattering cream-colored dress with a laced bodice the color of her hair.

The girl paused as she slowly looked Will up and down, her eyes lingering on his bare chest.

9

____

Will looked down at his hardened abs and wondered if she was staring at something besides the dirt and bruises. He looked back up at her, and their eyes met. She grinned playfully.

"Uh, hi. Thank you for bringing the clothes."

"Hello, I'm Emma. My apologies. If I had known better, I would have seen to you having warm water."

"What makes you say that?"

"They described you as a filthy warlock, but honestly, under all of that dirt . . . you might be handsome."

"Well, I'm not a warlock. Not any more than you or anyone else here."

She smiled. "You certainly don't look underfed."

Will laughed. "Are you calling me fat?"

"Don't laugh. There are many outside these walls who starve."

"Sorry."

She approached him. "Hold out your hands."

Will raised an eyebrow. "Why?"

"I want to see the type of work they're accustomed to."

"I think I'll pass," he said.

"Are you afraid? Hiding something?"

Will smiled reluctantly. "Of course not."

He held out his hands, and she examined them. "You're no field worker. I suppose I could believe that you're a royal servant."

"But not a royal myself?"

She crinkled her nose. "Not looking like this. Here, I'll set the clothes aside. I don't want to soil them by handing them to you."

"Thanks."

"Now, give me your trousers so I can take them to wash."

Will didn't move, and she held out her hand expectantly.

"Uh, how about I bring them to you?"

"Why go to the trouble when you could just give them to me now?" Emma asked with a quizzical expression.

"I'm just used to a little more privacy, that's all."

"Privacy? I guess I *could* picture you as a royal."

"Seriously, though, it's not a big deal. I can bring them to you."

"I'm afraid I must insist. I would be reprimanded if someone discovered I made our guest, even a servant, carry soiled linen across the courtyard. But if you would feel more comfortable, I'll avert my eyes." She turned away and waited.

Will looked around. Apart from getting into a stall with a horse, there wasn't much to stand behind. He kept the penny from his pocket, worrying that the year on it could cause trouble, and tore off his remaining clothes. Then he jumped into the barrel and took a sharp gasp as the icy water encompassed him.

Emma giggled. "You are a funny one! You must be freezing."

Will looked back at her with his teeth gritted together, forcing them not to chatter. "No, this is perfect."

Emma let out an amused laugh and gathered his clothing. She walked to the stable door, but looked back at him before she opened it. "You'll have to tell me about being a servant in a royal palace sometime."

"Okay," Will said, trying to keep his voice even, despite the cold water.

"What does that mean?"

"It means I'll tell you about it."

She smiled as she left the stable.

Will did his best to bathe in the dirty water, which left him shivering as he climbed out. As he examined the clothing, he longed for something modern to wear. He slipped on what looked like thick boxer shorts. There was no elastic band, and they wouldn't stay up. He put on baggy wool pantyhose over the underwear. The hose had no elastic, and it also slid down if he moved.

He found a short rope as well as a belt with a dagger attached to a thin, looped chain. He tied the cord tight around the hose and scratchy underwear, so they stayed in place. The waist of the hose looked like it could be wrapped over the rope if less leg room was needed, but the fabric was barely long enough to reach his waistline, and he secured the thin rope tighter than he would have if he had more fabric to spare.

The shirt was a little snug, but the blue tunic that went over it was roomy enough. If his mom saw him wearing it, she would probably mention that it matched his eyes. The fabric quality seemed better than what many in the village were wearing, but surely nothing compared to the apparel of the noble family.

Will remembered seeing most of the servants wearing daggers around their waists, so he put on the belt and dagger. The shoes had pointed toes with little padding on the soles and no arch support. Last, he added the scepter to his belt, in the same place where he had seen the soldiers wear their maces.

He double-checked his clothing, hoping that he'd put it on correctly, and went to the doorway of the stable. *Just how long does Garrett expect me to wait in here? He said he left to get clothes for me. Now that he sent them to me, is he even going to come back?* Will studied the courtyard. There was a large flat area surrounded by enormous walls and towers. A tower to the left was by far the highest due to being perched on top of a hundred-foot-high grassy hill that looked man-made due to it conically jutting above the flat ground surrounding it.

Will observed the comings and goings of plainly dressed servants and soldiers in chain mail for about an hour. He tried to get a sense of what it might be like to live in their shoes—not being able to relate to them could get him killed.

I'm not waiting any longer. For all I know, they've forgotten about me. Maybe if I go up one of the towers, I could get a better idea of where we are and where other people from our time might have gone.

He strode into the courtyard and entered the nearest open door at the base of a tower. A staircase spiraled upward, dimly illuminated only by arrowslits in the stone wall. He glanced over his shoulder to verify that no one was following him before stepping inside.

Will's hand traced the rounded wall as he quietly moved up the stairs, which were narrow at the center of the spiral and widened out at the perimeter. He desired to draw the scepter and wield it as a soldier storming the castle, but he resisted the urge, unsure how people might react to him with a drawn weapon. More than that, he wanted to keep the scepter as secret as possible.

Exiting the stairwell, he approached the battlements on the castle wall walk. There was no railing or barrier on the edge looking down into the courtyard far below, and the thought of falling made him walk close to the low parapet wall. Will watched for any nearby guards and thought of how accustomed they must be to walking next to the sheer drop-off every day.

He stood close to the parapet wall and felt more secure as he rested his hands on the coarse sandstone. Then he looked through the spacing between the crenel stones atop the wall meant for protecting archers firing at invaders below. The village of Arundel was just outside the walls, its streets below lined with small, thatched-roof houses and shops. Among them, townsfolk moved about their daily affairs. Beyond the houses, the green hills and trees extended down until they met the ocean far away and the village of Littlehampton, where the Hummer had been subdued by Edmund's men.

Will studied the individuals—many were hunched, underfed, and unclean. Everyone seemed relatively young; Will figured not many people made it to old age. There were farmers and some merchants, but nowhere did he see anyone who looked remotely like they were from his time.

"Hey, you!" a deep voice shouted. "What are you doing up here?"

10

___

Will spun around. A guard was hurrying toward him on the wall walk.

"Just looking at the view. I'm a guest of Sir Edmund."

The man grabbed Will's tunic. "You're foreign. What are you doing up here alone?"

"Throw him off the wall, Dennis! He's a witch!" yelled a voice below.

"No! No, I'm not," Will said. "I hate witches too! I say burn them all!"

Laughter came from below, and Will saw that it was the squire, Garrett.

Garrett shouted again, "Dennis! Let him be. He's not an invader. Send him down, and I'll look after him."

After Will came down, Garrett said, "I can't fault you for wanting to explore the castle a bit. There'd be something wrong with you if it didn't catch your interest. Are my garments to your liking?"

"Yes," Will lied. "These are your clothes?"

"Aye, Edmund might be closer to your size, but we weren't about to dress a servant in his finery."

"I understand. Thank you." Will pointed up to the castle ramparts. "I was hoping to get a view of the area to figure out where my uncle or the princess's brother might be."

"Well, I'll take you up to the highest tower." The squire looked off into the distance. "I want a castle of my own one day, and walking these walls is something I don't tire of."

Garrett led Will up to the tower built on the tall grassy mound. "Before all the stone walls and towers, it used to be just this hill and a wooden tower on top. Later, the wooden tower was replaced with stone, and then all the rest was built and beset with grandeur from the riches of the earls."

"How long did that take to build?"

"Oh, it's been added to a number of times over the last three hundred years or so. Its building was ordered by your namesake."

"My namesake?"

Garrett looked taken aback. "King William. William the Conqueror, of course."

"Oh, right. There have been many Williams."

"But none like him. Invaded England and dethroned our king—they called him William the Bastard before that."

"At least you got a castle out of it."

Garrett raised an eyebrow. "You *are* foreign. Many castles were commissioned by him. Almost all the large ones."

The squire turned and put his hands firmly on the battlements, looking down into the valley, forests, and farmland. "This is part of my dream. When I become a knight, I want to become one of the truly great ones. Earning money from tournaments helps. Sir Roland has won many of those. He's one of the best there is. But the real fortune is abroad. I've never been more than a day's ride from here, but I intend to one day fight in France. When I get a number of nobles and knights to surrender to me, I'll take them for ransom, collect a heap of gold, and really make something of myself."

Garrett pointed to the peasants working a field. "I'd hate to be one of them. They've no hope for anything—maybe for something better after they're dead. Meager food, crude work, living in bits of thatch held together and patched by their own dung. Lucky to live to twenty, maybe thirty. But not me. Most knights, you know, they do well—they're knights. But I want to come by enough gold to commission a castle of my own. Of course, it likely wouldn't be one this grand. The earl is one of the richest men in the world. But something my own, made of stone, something I can pass on."

"Sometimes I wish that I had such a clear . . . plan for my future."

Garrett smirked. "You could always be a gong farmer."

"I think I'll pass."

"Do you have them where you're from?"

"If we do, they're called something else."

"You know, the man who goes door to door, collecting everyone's dung?"

Will grimaced.

Garrett scoffed. "You and your royal palace. The gong farmer! Collects all the dung to be used for mending houses and fertilizing crops. But if he doesn't do his job well, he gets buried up to his neck in it for a day."

Will made a face. "That's awful."

"In truth, it's not so terrible a trade. He'll get his living and won't starve, unlike some other folk. Come, I'll show you some more of the castle."

They left the round tower and descended the steep wall walk to enter the main portion of the castle. Will thought about his place in this new setting. *As scary as this is, at least I have a clean slate—even if I have to pretend to be Celeste's servant. No one is thinking of me as "terrorist boy."* He mused over the strange way his wish had been granted—he had found a place where no one knew who he was. Will tried to think of other ways he could find gratitude in this desperate situation, but thoughts of Danny and Chase occupied center stage.

"Garrett, when will we receive word regarding the other people who may be from our land? My friend and my uncle?"

"Not likely until this evening. Several search parties are out. All you can do is wait."

Will pressed his lips together, holding back his frustration. *I don't even know if they're here, but I feel like I have to do something.* They walked through castle corridors and approached a doorway, where a loud clamor arose from the other side, and the aroma of food wafted toward them.

"Mmm. That'll be the feast cooking for tonight, to celebrate our victory this morning and to welcome the princess," Garrett said.

As they came closer to the door, Will felt heat blasting out of the room. Garrett stepped inside and shouted, "You're all going to incur the wrath of the king!"

"Oh, shut your trap, Garrett," a man said.

Will peered around the stone doorway and soon withdrew from the wave of heat smarting his eyes and the startling scene inside.

The ovens blazed, and judging from the heat and smoke, there wasn't much ventilation. The male servants hurried about as sheets of perspiration dripped down their stark-naked bodies.

Garrett laughed. "You know the king just passed a law that you've got to cover up when cooking!"

"I'd like to see *you* working in this heat," another man said.

"I'd rather die on the battlefield than suffer this," Garrett said.

Someone threw a wooden spoon at Garrett, and he ducked back into the corridor. He smiled. "Are folks required to wear clothes when working in the kitchen where you're from?"

"Uh, yes." Will suppressed a smile. "However, nudity in the workplace is a constant problem. They can hardly keep it under control."

"Can't say I blame them—it's awfully hot."

"Well, where I come from, they'll pluck your toenails out for such an offense."

"That's a bit much just for being overheated," Garrett said.

"Compared to the punishment they give the gong farmer here?"

"That's because he didn't do his job, not because he was just trying to cool himself. What do they do in your land if a person is idle in their work?"

"They lose their job."

"That's it?"

"Yeah."

"No physical punishment? They care more about people being dressed than whether or not they do their job?"

Will shook his head. "It's a shame."

"You won't be able to keep the peace long that way," Garrett scoffed. "Say, tomorrow I'm training with Sir Roland. He told me it's going to be quite brutal. It would be nice to have someone to help carry the weapons and armor about." He smiled. "Less for me to do. Care to join us? You might also learn a thing or two about fighting."

"Normally I would, but I should help with the search if they haven't found anyone."

"Sir Edmund will have many men looking tomorrow if they

don't find them today. Also, you'd need permission to join the search, and to borrow a horse."

"I'm sure I can convince them."

"But if you can't?"

Will thought about how much he would like to be able to defend himself or use the scepter as a mace, but he also felt conflicted about how fighting always seemed to lead him into trouble. "I would like to, but I suppose I'll need leave of Lady Celeste and Sir Edmund. We'll see what they say."

Even as he spoke the words, he thought, *It doesn't matter what they say, I'm going to be in that search party if they aren't found.*

11

That evening, Will followed Garrett into the great hall for the celebratory feast. The squire was caught up in a boisterous conversation with several men, and Will took a moment alone to study their surroundings. He looked for entryways to escape through if things became dangerous. Garrett could only protect him from so much, and suspicious eyes had met him all day.

The laughter and revelry reverberated from the stone walls and floor, and a fire blazed in a large hearth along a sidewall. The room was also dimly illuminated by candlesticks on the tables and a rustic chandelier hanging from the high ceiling. The tables were arranged in a U shape with two rows running the length of the hall and a platform at one end with the head table.

Will wasn't sure where he was meant to sit, so he looked around the room for Celeste. Both she and Edmund were absent, and he wondered if they were together. He listened in on Garrett's conversation as he watched for Celeste, but it was difficult to follow through the local accents and noise of the room.

Finally, Celeste entered. She wore a flowing white gown that looked like it was made of silk with a thin golden belt. Her hair was elaborately braided above her neck, and several blond locks trailed downward to complement her face. She wore a jeweled circlet across her forehead as well as a jeweled necklace. Two plainly dressed women, seemingly in their twenties, accompanied her.

The clamor in the room died down as she diverted the attention of those in the room.

Will pushed through the crowd to get to her and said in a low voice, "It's good to finally see you. What have you found out?"

"We'll talk more after," she whispered, glancing around. Then she straightened. "Are you well?"

Will scrunched his eyebrows. "Yes, fine, perfect health. Other than my clothes itching and my pantyhose sliding down. Let's go talk somewhere, now."

"Appearances, William," she said, glancing around again. "Sir Edmund has been very gracious." She gestured to her hair and gown. "What do you think?"

The words that came to mind were *stunning, amazing,* and *hot.* "I would say you were going for . . . an elven princess look."

She smiled and stretched her arm out. A white sleeve trailed down. Will also saw a small, gold-handled dagger fastened to her waist. "The dress is made out of samite, a type of silk. I'm lucky the sleeves and gown are meant to be flowing, or else it wouldn't fit," she said.

Will smiled. "It's much more appropriate than those shameless trousers. Did it take you all afternoon to get ready?"

"As would be expected of a lady," Celeste said.

Will looked at the intricacies of the braids arranged up in her hair. "It's a good thing you had different servants to help."

"Would m'lady care to sit?" said a manservant, gesturing to the head table.

"My servant will be joining me. He is also Sir Edmund's guest," Celeste said.

The man hesitated, then nodded.

The servant seated them at the table while the nearby chairs for Edmund and his men were still empty.

"How are things with Edmund?" Will asked.

Celeste smiled. "Not bad—he's actually pleasant to talk to. His parents are on a pilgrimage to Rome and will be gone for several months. He's in charge of the whole earldom in his father's absence."

"In charge of all this? How old is he?"

"He's seventeen. Pretty impressive, right?"

"Sure. He's certainly head over heels for you."

Celeste blushed and flitted a strand of hair from her face. "I don't know. I'm just good at talking with people."

"Yeah—*and* you're the only female he's seen that isn't malnourished, has all of her teeth, and has bathed within a month."

"No, I'm not." She looked around the room and spotted Emma. "She's pretty."

Will shifted uncomfortably in his seat. "Yeah, I guess so."

Emma, noticing their attention, sent a friendly wave and a wink at Will.

"She certainly has an eye for you," Celeste remarked. It was difficult for Will to read her tone.

Will glanced at the square wooden plate in front of him and adjusted it. "She's nice. I talked to her earlier. She's one of the servants. By the way, thanks a lot for placing me so far down the social food chain."

Celeste leaned in and whispered, "Down? You looked like a farm animal. I was just trying to help you, and I had to make something up on the spot."

"We need to get on the same page, and figure out who else from home is here, and what we're going to do about it."

"Not now."

There was a cheer near the entrance, and everyone stood as Edmund entered wearing extravagant red, blue, and gold robes. He was clean-shaven and appeared freshly bathed, his golden-brown hair combed back. He cheerfully greeted several of his men as he made his way to the head table.

Will noted Celeste's enthusiastic smile.

"You look remarkably beautiful, Princess." Edmund took both of Celeste's hands and kissed them. "I'm glad we could provide you with a gown that could attempt to match your natural elegance."

Celeste beamed. "Thank you. We are grateful for your hospitality."

"Ah, I see William the Bastard will be sitting with us," Edmund said, not attempting to hide the annoyance in his voice.

"Conqueror. William the Conqueror," Will corrected coolly. It was exceedingly obvious to him that birth status was even more important here than it was back home, and he continued to notice the trickle-down influence of that fact on even the smallest things. The insults Will overheard from soldiers were usually disparaging terms regarding the conditions of a person's birth, or who their parents were. *At least I'm not overshadowed by the reputation I had in the future. I'm not going to let this guy get under my skin.*

"Oh, are you a Norman invader, William?" Edmund said.

"I can't be—I'm not Norman," Will said.

"Good. Our king is at war with France. I would have to have you run through." He gestured for the room to take their seats.

"Sir Edmund," Celeste said, "I do apologize for having to impose upon you in this way, but have your brave riders returned with any news of my brother or others from our land?"

"No arrests as of yet. They stole horses, and word was given to us that they may have fled my land. Messengers were sent to neighboring lords, and my men will continue the search tomorrow. We can't have criminals roaming the countryside."

"Please remember to tell them, some of the foreigners are innocent," Celeste said.

"So I have informed my men."

"My lord, I would like to help with the search," Will said.

"As would I," Celeste added.

Edmund frowned and took a draw at his goblet, "It wouldn't be proper for a lady, and William, I'm not sure you would be of much help."

"We can identify them," Will asserted.

"Anyone could identify them if they have your accents. Besides, these men bested you already, and I doubt you're much of a fighter anyway."

"I can hold my own."

Celeste elbowed Will.

"Well then, tell me, William," Edmund said, "you're a servant—what exactly is it you do? Wait on the princess like a handmaid?"

The other men at the table laughed.

Will locked eyes with Edmund. "I do whatever the king needs me to do."

"You have a close connection to the king?"

"He trusts me to get things done."

"And your father, is he also a servant?"

"No, my father was a warrior."

"Was? Sorry to hear that. A foot soldier? A man-at-arms?"

Will knew he was treading dangerous ground and decided to go with a simplified version of the truth. "Army Delta Force, a group of elite soldiers that are sent to do what may seem impossible."

"Never heard of it," said Sir Roland, the knight who'd led the charge earlier that morning. "And yet you're only a servant, not in training to be a warrior yourself?"

"He is a *royal* servant," Celeste said.

"I'm also in training," Will said.

"To be what? A garrisoned soldier?" Roland asked.

Will hesitated. "I—"

"He doesn't know," Edmund interrupted.

"Playing with swords doesn't constitute training. I was going to train my squire tomorrow, but we're joining the search instead," Roland said.

"I would be happy to help you," Will attempted again.

Sir Roland grunted his disinterest and bit a piece of meat from a bone.

"Sir Edmund," Celeste pleaded, "I care deeply for my brother. I know it wouldn't normally be customary for a lady, but I would very much like to join the search for him, if there is any chance he might be in your land."

"It's just not appropriate for a woman. Now look, my men are quite capable, and I'm afraid you would just slow them down. Also, I would like you to join me for a walk through our gardens tomorrow."

Celeste looked deflated. "That would be nice. Were you planning to invite William as well?"

"For heaven's sake, no," Edmund said. "Roland, just take the servant with you. You might see if his foreign training amounts to anything."

"Yes, my lord." Roland pointed his massive hand at Will. "Listen, I don't need any trouble from you."

"Of course not," Will said. "You won't regret it."

He and Celeste did their best to watch how the others were eating. The feast included pheasant, deer, turnips, peas, thick slices of bread, and honeycomb. Everyone ate with their fingers and used daggers to cut the meat. The plates were square with a round indentation in the middle for the food and a smaller indentation in the corner for the salt. People kept one pinky apart from the meat when they held it so the finger wouldn't be soiled in meat drippings and could be used to dab the collection of salt and spread it onto their food.

Will followed the other's style of eating with a pinky up and wondered if the shape of the plates had anything to do with the term "square meal." He was famished, and to his relief, the food wasn't bad.

While people were finishing eating, Edmund said offhand, "It's a shame that our jester is ill, and we have no minstrels available."

Celeste's face lit up, and she whispered to Will, "We should build as much good rapport with them as we can."

Will felt somewhat confused. "Of course."

"William can play the guitar—I mean, or the mandolin, as you may call it," Celeste said to Edmund. "I was thinking if you had something like that, maybe he could play it."

Will felt his pulse race. He was surprised she'd remembered. Edmund looked confused, and Celeste made hand gestures as if strumming a guitar.

"A lute? You're a minstrel, William?"

Will's face blanched. "I've never played a lute." He'd purchased a guitar from a thrift store a few years back and played it occasionally. He wasn't particularly talented—he could play basic chords and pick out simple melodies but had never played in public. Celeste only knew he had a guitar because Danny had asked for one for his birthday after Will got his. However, Danny hadn't played after the first month of owning it.

"But you've played something similar?" Edmund looked amused, seeming to enjoy Will's discomfort.

"Possibly similar, and not well."

Edmund's smile broadened. "Well, if you're horrible, you may entertain us just as much as if you're good. Roger, fetch the lute! The servant of the princess is a minstrel, and he may even prove to be a jester!"

Will could feel the blood draining from his head. "I'm not good," he hissed at Celeste.

She gave him a worried smile. "It's okay, just do your best. They'll love you."

"You play the piano. Why are you bringing me up?"

She leaned in. "I've been thinking of anything we can do to make them like us. The piano hasn't been invented yet."

"Neither has the guitar, apparently," he whispered, then tightened his lips in frustration. First, Celeste was portraying him as a servant, and now he had to pretend to be a minstrel too?

The servant handed Will the instrument. The neck was bent at a 90-degree angle, and the body was pear-shaped. "Here's the quill," the man said, giving Will what looked like part of a feather shaft.

"It will take a while for me to become familiar with it," Will said.

"Very well, stand over there to tune it, but hurry, we have no other entertainment," Edmund said. Several others shouted encouragement.

Will walked to the other side of the room in a daze. He ran the quill across each of the four strings and alternated his fingers to different positions on the neck. *This isn't like a guitar.* He continued to test the positioning of his fingers on the strings and became more familiar with the general layout of simple notes.

"Begin for us, minstrel! We're done waiting!" Edmund shouted. The others in the room shouted and clapped.

Will tried to keep his breathing steady as he walked to the center of the great hall. No one here was trying to harm him, yet his heart was still pounding. He had no idea what he was going to play, or what the repercussions would be if he chickened out.

"Well, start then!" someone cheered from the crowd.

"In a moment. I'm thinking of what you all might enjoy the most." He nervously played through a series of notes, trying to think of a song they might not find too bizarre but that would also be enjoyable for this boisterous crowd. All of the songs that came to mind struck out.

"Play on, William. Something lively!" Celeste called.

Will tensed. He wondered if there was a song that could wipe the smile off her face. He needed her to stop pushing him into awkward role-playing situations.

He began a simple melody and plucked through the whole song before starting while humming to mask his mistakes. He watched Celeste intently and knew she recognized the tune when her jaw dropped and she began shaking her head.

No! she mouthed repeatedly.

Will smiled and continued playing through the song.

"William, this is a rather dull song. Perhaps you should select another," Celeste called.

Edmund held up his hand. "Nay, play on."

Will began to sing, and he watched Celeste become paler with each line of "Puff the Magic Dragon," a song that chronicled a seaside dragon and a boy who dearly loved him.

Will watched the people in the room become uneasy as he sang the chorus about the dragon frolicking through the mist. Celeste looked completely terrified as she gazed around, observing the general discomfort. Then Will wildly strayed from the words of Peter, Paul, and Mary.

The wicked little boy bore the devil's name.
He set his horrid dragon on a man and royal dame.
The warriors of Arundel braved its metal shell.
They saved the land and sent the beast burning back to hell.

The room exploded with cheers of approval, and Celeste seemed to relax a little.

Vanquished, the dead dragon washed out to sea.
Sir Edmund of Arundel set the man and princess free.
Vanquished, the dead dragon washed out to sea.
Sir Edmund of Arundel set the man and princess free.

The great hall applauded. Edmund smiled and nodded approvingly. "And you said you couldn't perform. Sing it again!"

Will felt a wave of relief, reassuring himself he could remember the words the same way as he had improvised. He sang the song three more times, encouraging the group to join him.

Celeste appeared much more relaxed. Will smiled as another idea formed.

"In truth, my friends, you can see that I am not all that skilled. If you want real entertainment, m'lady is an exceptional dancer!"

Celeste's eyes widened, looking as though she wanted to run from the room. A roar of approval filled the hall. *Just building rapport. She can dance much better than I can play a lute.*

"I apologize," Celeste stammered. "I am not well enough for that."

The room shouted encouragement, and Celeste turned bright red.

"We can all dance," Edmund said. "Clear the tables."

Celeste looked to him in gratitude.

Will watched as she took Edmund by the hand. He struggled to decide how he felt about her. Even though he was frustrated, he still admired many of her personality traits, and he resented males who only seemed to see her superficially. The glowing smile she gave Edmund made Will look away.

People were filling the center of the room as the tables were moved. Lost in thought, Will felt a hand on his arm. He spun around and was relieved to see that it was Emma.

"I didn't mean to startle you," she said. "You performed well."

"Oh, it's good to see you. Thank you."

"Will you join us in dancing?" she said, moving a stray lock of dark hair behind her ear.

"Only if you show me how you dance here," Will said. "I really have no idea."

Emma smiled. "I would be glad to."

She grabbed his hand and led him to join the others. Will felt tense over the prospect of making cultural blunders, but then he took a deep breath and decided to just let himself have fun.

Emma flashed him another smile, and he smiled back.

Will glanced in Celeste's direction. She was looking his way with her eyebrows knit together in concern. When she caught his eye, she quickly looked away and said something to Edmund.

The group formed a large circle, holding hands. Before they started singing, Emma said, "You'll have to teach us one of your dances sometime."

A chill ran down Will's spine. "Sometime." His brain raced with a myriad of modern dances and then tried to think of which ones might not in some way be offensive in medieval Christendom. He thought about the prospect of living in the Middle Ages for the rest of his life and trying to explain who he was to Emma or anyone else without feeling like he needed to lie either for self-preservation or to prevent a massive alteration of history.

The group sang, and he slowly joined in as he learned the words. He and Emma took several steps to the right and kicked, then several to the left and kicked. There were more steps, and he tried to keep up. Celeste was across the circle from him—she seemed to anticipate the dance moves well, and she gave a laugh to something Edmund said. Will couldn't tell how much she liked Edmund or how much she was playing him, but he knew that the game they were in was a dangerous one.

12

<hr>

After the banquet, Edmund wanted to escort Celeste to her chambers. She insisted that Will come as well so he could know where she was staying. Edmund seemed annoyed, but he consented. When they arrived outside the chamber door, Edmund wished Celeste a good night and nodded for Will to follow him.

"I wish to speak to William privately," Celeste said.

Edmund frowned. "My lady, it seems improper for him to enter your private chamber at night."

"It would. However, I assure you I solely wish to speak to him."

"Yes, but it still seems immoderate," Edmund said.

"Believe me, Edmund, it's all right—William is a eunuch."

Edmund's eyes bulged out as he looked Will up and down.

Will wasn't sure what a eunuch was, and he forced himself not to say anything, though he felt increasingly irritated.

"Well, in that case," Edmund said, "I suppose there is no problem with it." He made a pained expression. "And that would explain a few things. I've heard that some eunuchs can sing well." He chuckled and walked down the corridor.

Celeste pulled Will into the chamber and closed the door. "Will, we have to talk about—"

"What's a eunuch?" Will demanded.

"It really doesn't matter. I just had to tell him that so—"

"What—is—a—eunuch?" he said intently, emphasizing each word.

"Uh, it's a servant in the olden days who looked after the women."

"That alone doesn't sound so bad. What else?"

She blushed and couldn't meet his eyes. "That's really what it is . . . a male servant who looked after the women."

"And what does that have to do with *singing* well?" Will felt his blood beginning to boil.

"Uh, well, uh, eunuchs—were castrated. That's why they were trusted with the women."

"You told him I was castrated!"

"Shh, I did it so I could talk to you privately."

"There are a million other ways two people can have a private conversation without castrating one of them. First, you call me your servant, then I'm a minstrel, and now I'm castrated!"

"You're the one singing a potentially dangerous song and trying to get me to dance in front of everyone."

"Which is nothing in comparison. What is wrong with you?" he said, shaking his head.

Neither of them spoke for a moment.

Celeste broke the silence. "I've just been trying to sound believable and make them like me—I mean us. Maybe I could have come up with better answers with enough time, but standing there thinking over simple questions for a long time takes away our believability, and I haven't seen you coming up with better quick answers. I'm sorry I threw you under the bus. Everything you've seen me do out there is just bravado. I'm terrified."

"Fair enough. I'm scared too. I feel like we're trying to tread water and just drowning each other instead of actually swimming. But still, why performing music?"

"I wanted them to like us. I imagined you were good, so I thought you would enjoy it. I mean, you were good."

"Is there anything else you've imagined about me that I should know about?" Will asked, raising an eyebrow.

She smiled and looked away again. "No, and I didn't tell them anything specific about us when you weren't around so we wouldn't have to worry about contradictions."

"Thanks. Neither have I."

They spoke for a while about details that needed to match in their backstories as lost foreigners from a place called America.

"We have to figure out if Danny and my uncle are here and get home. But what do we do about those guys in camouflage who attacked us?" Will asked.

"Our best bet is to let Edmund's men try to capture those men. If things get screwed up here with history, couldn't that mean our families wouldn't be born? And what would happen to us?"

Will shook his head. "I've worried about that too."

"Do you think my other friends are here?" Celeste asked quietly.

He thought about them, and about the president, who probably ran like mad as soon as he had the chance. "I don't think so. They were so far away, but I can't be sure of anything."

"Do you think the mace can take us home?"

"Again, I'm not sure. We have to account for the people from our time before we try."

"Yeah. I'm in this situation because I went to pick up you and Danny—and then wouldn't leave without him when he went after you. As much as he and I fight, I can't just abandon him. It's a twin thing. I wish we knew for sure if he was here or not, so we weren't just running in circles. And I'm still mad that they won't let me join the search."

"At least you'll have a magical time in the gardens with Edmund," Will said.

"Hey, I'm just keeping us alive."

"You're flirting with him a lot. That could be risky."

Celeste glanced away. "Let me worry about him. He's really nice. We shouldn't upset things with him."

"You mean he's being really nice to you."

"Try to see things from his perspective. He's in charge of everyone, and most of the soldiers are older than him. He has to come across as strong and confident."

"You don't have to be a jerk to do that."

"He could have you executed on a whim. Don't pick a fight with him."

Will let out a dry laugh. "I don't think I've ever picked a fight. They seem to pick me."

"I know—but we need to be on the best possible terms with him. His father is one of the richest men in Europe. With Edmund in charge of things while his parents are in Rome, he's extremely powerful."

"So I've heard." Will sighed. "How do you see yourself being on 'the best possible terms' with him?"

Celeste huffed. "I'll worry about that."

"He did give you a nice bedroom." Will nodded to the white canopy over the four-poster bed. "It looks a lot better than sleeping on the ground."

"Or in a car."

Will walked to the other side of the room, past a large tapestry of well-dressed people conversing in an extravagant garden. He stopped at a wooden seat and lid. A small box of scented squares of linen lay next to it. Will lifted the lid and looked down the exterior wall of the castle.

"You even have your own private bathroom," Will said, setting the cover back down. "You know, I'd stay the night with you here—but I'm not really a eunuch."

"What?"

"You can tell them that the word means something else where we're from. I don't want to imagine what would happen if they found out otherwise that I had body parts I wasn't supposed to have. For the sake of keeping up appearances, I'm going to go."

"Already?"

He started to move to the door, but Celeste intercepted him, gently holding his forearms. "Please wait?"

Will felt his pulse race. "For what?"

"It's just that there are so many things we *could* and *should* talk about."

"Probably—but I don't want your boyfriend taking my head off if someone finds out I'm not castrated and I lingered here at night."

Celeste blushed. "Just stay a little longer. And he's not my boyfriend."

Will swallowed. He didn't want to leave. "If he finds out you feel that way, all the more reason to behead me."

"All right." She put her arms around him in a hug. "Just please be safe."

The hug surprised Will, and as she withdrew, he said, "Yes, Your Majesty."

Celeste playfully slugged his arm. "Enough of that."

"I'll try to gain some respect from them tomorrow. You can work on keeping Edmund happy."

"Okay, good luck." She unlatched the door and opened it for him.

"But try not to make him too happy."

Celeste shook her head and gave him a gentle push out the door. "Good night, Will."

"Good night, Celeste."

As soon as she closed the door, Will began looking for a vacant room in the dark stone corridor so he could finally better examine the weapon. He knew it would have been easier to do in Celeste's room, but he was worried about what she might think about his connection to the scepter.

I'll tell her after I understand it better.

He planned to sleep in the great hall with the other servants, but he couldn't wait any longer to study the weapon. There wouldn't be much time, though. Someone, particularly Emma, might notice his absence.

Will tested the thick oaken door of an unlit room, holding his breath as it creaked open. He verified that the small room was empty, then slowly closed the door behind him.

A stone window frame showed the crystal-clear night sky with a dazzling array of stars far beyond what would have been visible in the light pollution of a modern city. He stood at the window and detached the head from the leather protector at his waist. The light from the nearly full moon and stars was just enough to see the object, and he wiped away some of the dirt he'd left on it, uncovering two thumb-size depressions on the hilt.

He pressed on one of the depressions, and the eerie red swirling light leaped from the head of the scepter. A boost of confidence swept over him. When he released his thumb, the waves of light withdrew back into the spiked orb. Will cautiously looked down to the moonlit forest outside the walls, but he couldn't see anyone. Still, he moved away from the window before pressing his thumb to the same indentation again.

The red, twisting waves of light appeared again, and he waved it back and forth as trails of flamelike waves followed the scepter's head. He hesitantly reached out his hand to the ring of spiked protrusions until his fingers were just touching the red light. It didn't feel hot, but he sensed an energy from it.

Will didn't want to completely touch the head for fear that it would transport him somewhere else in time, and he further examined the hilt. His thumb was currently on a dark red depression. Next to it was a faint white depression of the same size.

He moved his thumb to press the white indentation and felt a surge of strength through his arm and into his body. A much smaller white flame of energy tightly circled around the head of the scepter now.

Something seemed wrong, but he couldn't identify it. He released his thumb, and the breeze outside and the sound of crickets chirping seemed normal again. Will pressed once more, and the sounds slowed down. He did it several times, listening to the sounds speed and slow. Not dramatically, but enough that it was noticeable.

Does this thing actually slow down time, or just my perception of time? Or is it speeding me up compared to what is going on around me? He reveled in the possible implications. *That might mean if I were fighting with it, I could move faster than everything around me. But it might just be enough to be noticeably faster, not by any means freezing time.*

He gave the scepter a wide swing and accidentally hit a candlestick holder. The small metal object shot across the room and smashed into the wall with much greater force than Will would have anticipated.

Letting the light out, he stood frozen in place, hoping no one would come to investigate the sound.

I have to be more careful. If I were actually moving faster relative to the passage of time around me, the increased speed would result in more momentum and damage. He felt along the hilt and determined that it would be fairly easy to maintain a grip without choosing to depress the white or red sections, mostly a matter of whether he positioned his thumb upward or not. *It must have just been luck, good or bad, that I had my hand on the red portion in the desert.*

He thought about telling Celeste. The desire to possess the weapon resonated through him. *It wanted me to find it.* Will thought of the fight in the desert and how eager the militants had been to take it from Chase. He wondered if his uncle, or the other people who carried it, felt the same unspoken connection with the scepter. *I would be protecting Celeste by not getting her yearning for it. The man in the desert said it was meant for me.*

He debated whether he should hide it or take it with him in the morning. *I don't think anyone else should examine this—it could just get us into more trouble.* Then he debated whether or not he would be safer carrying it for self-defense and risking other people taking an interest in it.

Even if I use this to defend myself against someone, people will think I'm a sorcerer and they'll want to band together to kill me. He smiled. A sorcerer—that actually sounded pretty cool.

—————

After Will drifted to sleep, he entered a series of vivid dreams beyond the clarity of anything he had experienced before.

He was in a dark forge, and he could feel the heat from the fire radiating on his face as he withdrew the scepter from the flames in a glowing array of light. He hoisted a giant smith's hammer and beat again and again on the incompletely formed metal, guiding it into what it would be. Sparks lit up the rock walls of the isolated forge. He saw that the hands crafting the scepter with the hammer and anvil were not his—they were coarse and stained with soot. In another thunderous crash of the hammer and light, he found himself in a forest.

The trees were so tall, Will couldn't see the tops. The canopy permitted gleams of light to shine down in thin rays and dance on the green and blue leaves. He breathed in the pure air and took in the vibrant tufts of red grass, then looked at his hands.

They were the hands of the person who forged the scepter, and he wore a brass-colored armband with strange characters written on it. The scepter was fixed to his belt. He was about to draw it until he noticed water lapping on the white shore beyond the trees.

He ran through the trees and across the white sand to the vast lake of crystal-blue water to see his reflection. The face of the youth staring back at him bore fair, symmetrical features, a scar on his cheek, and disheveled auburn hair. He felt the scar, and something reflecting in the water distracted him. He slowly looked up and saw two sources of light shining in the water.

His eyes followed the sources up into the sky, and he fell back on his hands. Two large moons shone down on him.

Will awoke with a start and looked around the dark, great hall. It took a long time for him to orient to where he was. Anxiety filled his chest as he remembered how far he was from home. The other servants were all asleep, and several were snoring. Part of him wanted to get rid of the scepter. *But it's mine.*

He checked the cord of rope he used for a belt to make sure it was still tied to his wrist and to the scepter hidden beneath his bedroll. *This is an obsession! This isn't healthy!* Will reached to untie the rope from his wrist but stopped—he had to keep it safe. They might need it to get home.

He had to keep anyone else from taking it.

13

The firelight danced in Madoc Morgan's eyes as he and his men sat around a small campfire deep in the forest. "You know, we would achieve greatness like you've never imagined if we stayed here."

"Sir, with respect," said Skinner, an American with a close-cropped military haircut and many combat close calls under his belt, "it's too unpredictable. It's an absolute curse that we're here, and we'll only be more cursed if we stay and try to chase wild ambitions. We need to get those two kids up at the castle, along with that strange object, and make the boy get us out of here."

Several heads nodded.

"That isn't how Black Hammer works," Morgan said, contemplating how best to help his brothers understand. "I was the one it touched when activated. It read my soul, and it brought us here because it determined this is where I have the greatest potential to fulfill my deepest desires. If we're united in our brotherhood's goals, then this is where all of us have our greatest potential."

"Perhaps, sir. I still say it's cursed," Skinner said, his anxious eyes darting from Morgan to the others around the fire. "The scientists could never time travel with it. Just teleport. Right? They said it took Donovan and whoever he touched with it to where that person had the potential for something they wanted—but never time travel, and never in a big group. We don't know what is going on!"

"We know exactly what is going on," Morgan said confidently, thinking of the reconnaissance work he and his men had done in the nearby villages. They'd grouped up the night they arrived using radios; unfortunately, the batteries would be dead soon. "We're sitting around a campfire, in England, in June 1345. Remember, I've ravenously studied history to learn from the rise and fall of empires. The chaos of the Dark Ages has always fascinated me. I'm confident we were sent here because Black Hammer connected my historical knowledge to my desire to fulfill our brotherhood's goals. Hopefully, we're wise enough to take advantage of the gift we've been given. All of us wanted to reshape society and establish a new world order. Is that not correct?"

There were murmurs of agreement.

"Is this time and place not more fertile for fulfilling our destiny than the modern day?" Morgan asked.

"Hold on there," Johnson said in a Southern drawl. He bore a short brown beard and was the group's demolitions and explosives expert. "Our conquests have always been in the shadows—the modern shadows. Sir, respectfully, it seems like you're forgetting what we agreed to. We said we were going to use Black Hammer to instantly travel to the location of any head of state, right? To be able to assassinate them at our whim or manipulate them into giving us anything we wanted. This whole 'hunker down and forget what we were working on' is a fantasy."

"This is a bigger opportunity than we've ever had before," Morgan said. Dark shadows curled across his face with the flickering of the firelight. "We wanted to shape the world, in the three-pronged tenants of the Dreizack Trident—those who rule, those who obey, and those who die. Right now, civilization is still in its malleable childhood. Deep mental change and domination of humanity were not as possible in our time as they are now. This is a reality we can control, a reality that we have experienced, a reality that we can win."

"Experienced? Now don't go starting with your reincarnation speech again," Johnson drawled.

"I won't give you the speech," Morgan said, "but I'll ask you to take the sword you stole by the hilt. Go ahead, take it. Tell me that the weight of the sword in your hand doesn't resonate deep down into your core, into your very being."

"Commander, we have families back home," said Romano, a Colombian with dark hair, graying at the temples. "What I have fought for was to give them a better life. If we go and try to change history, they'll never be born. We'll never be born!"

"We're alive now. This is our new life," Morgan said.

"But they won't have one!" Romano shouted back. "We built a great life for ourselves in the shadows. Who could need more money than what we have? I saw this Black Hammer operation as an insurance policy to protect ourselves."

"You don't need an insurance policy here." Morgan smiled. "You've had years of experience as an international arms dealer. Your skills with weapons and trade would practically make you a god here. I respect your concern for family. The order of the Imperial Dreizack is my family. All of us are family, and I see each of you as brothers."

Romano leaped to his feet, spit coming from his mouth as he yelled, "Who are you to speak of the importance of family? You killed your parents to get to where you are!"

A man next to Romano jerked him to his seat.

Morgan stayed calm. "My father was a monster, and my mother supported him. They were no family to me—you are. I have never betrayed a brother committed to our values."

"What about the ones we left for dead in Idaho?" said Wolf, a German sniper bearing a muscular face and buzzed blond hair.

"It's a tragedy—and they wouldn't want their sacrifice to be meaningless," Morgan said.

"Maybe a tragedy that could have been avoided with better leadership," Wolf said, his hand inching toward the German HK P12 handgun in his holster.

"You were the one most in favor of the INL plan!" said Dekker, a broad-shouldered Dutchman with a coarse blond beard. He placed his hand on his own sidearm and shook his head at Wolf.

Wolf's hand paused. "Yes, and I actually want to stay here and bless the world with the values of our brotherhood. However, sometimes it's not the target or the rifle that's the problem."

Morgan stood. "All right, young buck. Let's get this out of your system! You want to challenge me?"

The German sniper leaped up and raised his fists.

"Lay him out, Commander!" Dekker shouted.

Morgan had extensive martial arts training in addition to special-ops experience as a Marine Raider prior to the CIA. There were countless ways he could kill someone.

Wolf threw a quick punch, but Morgan dodged it, caught his arm, and slammed him to the ground, pinning him with his face near the fire.

"Stop! Stop it!" yelled Koppel, the German combat medic.

"Are you ready to die?" Morgan seethed.

Wolf gritted his teeth and shook his head.

"Most leaders in my position would kill you, and they wouldn't be wrong."

Wolf started breathing rapidly, his eyes squeezed shut, sweat dripping down his face. The rest of the group didn't dare interfere.

Morgan inched Wolf's face closer to the fire. "But instead, I'm inclined to save you. I let you live, and your life is mine."

"Yes, Commander," Wolf breathed. "I'm so sorry to have questioned you."

"Get up." Morgan pulled Wolf to his feet. "We're all a family, and we don't have manpower to waste."

"Thank you, sir." He darted back to his place on a log.

Koppel let out a deep sigh of relief. "If any of you get injured, there's only so much I can do to help you." The medic repositioned his dark-rimmed, circular glasses. "That's another problem with being here. With our combat experiences, almost all of us would be dead if it weren't for modern medicine and surgery. And Commander, as you said earlier, the Black Plague is going to sweep across Europe in a few years. This place is a death trap."

"Tell me, Doc," Morgan said. "Isn't the bubonic plague caused by bacteria?"

"Yes, sir."

"How hard would it be for you to grow penicillin or other antibiotics?"

"It's a mold culture—not really that difficult."

"What do you think the price of that would be in a city stricken with the plague?" Morgan grinned.

"*Unbezahlbar!*" Koppel's exclaimed in German. "Priceless! You spoke of building armies with gunpowder weapons, but in a few years, cities would surrender just for a cure to the disease. I mean, you're right. From an 'achieving your potential' standpoint, this place would be ripe for the picking."

"Precisely," Morgan said, trying to contain his excitement that some of the men were beginning to grasp his vision. "We still need the guns and the armies, but as you say, there are all kinds of ways our modern knowledge can be weaponized."

"Maybe," Skinner said, his leg subtly bouncing up and down. "I'm just not comfortable trying to play with the future."

"It may have already changed. You need to accept that your relatives and anyone you used to know are gone," Morgan said, glancing at Romano with a sympathetic smile. "Don't be so superstitious, Skinner. That's another frailty we can exploit here. Our knowledge and technology will be seen as supernatural, and we can spin that however we want. We can rule people as the pharaohs did by being worshiped as deities—making obedience simpler. People here are waiting for the return of Jesus Christ, which is part of what fueled their desire for the Crusades. Just add a beard, and I can fulfill their longing by proclaiming myself to be their long-awaited Messiah. Most people can't read the Bible, so we can redefine Christianity however we like."

"Madoc Bloody Morgan, the King of Pirates, now turned Jesus Christ." Johnson whistled. "This is too much to take in."

"You doubt me?" Morgan's eyes quietly bored into the other man's.

Johnson looked away and sighed. "Sir, actually, knowing you, I think you'd have a shot. But seriously, why care if people think you're a god, or if you have lots of gold—if you live with no electricity, no indoor plumbing, and no internet?"

"Oh, you're so soft!" Voskonov scoffed. The large Russian still had a blood-crusted wound on his bald head from where Will had thrown a wrench at him. "None of us entered our various fields of military training to be pampered!"

"Sure," Johnson said. "But after each deployment or

mission, we planned to come back to a place with good cookin' and TV."

"There are so many helpless peasants here," Voskonov said. "You could assign one to be your personal bidet. I'm not one to be as motivated by grand plans, but to have power over each individual person. Each kill, each woman I take, and so on—I savor. This place is, you may say, a playground."

"Agreed!" Dekker exclaimed.

Morgan nodded. "You'll have more than your fill of plunder and havoc."

"I'm also in agreement with our commander regarding the boy," Voskonov said. He pointed to the gash on his forehead. "He gave me this. I wish to kill him. Burn the boats behind us. Total commitment to staying in this new life."

"I'm drawn to fighting in the old ways. Most of us have training in this—our commander especially," Dekker said, giving Morgan a deep, respectful nod. "But we need to train more. Also, Johnson, Rashad, and I are the only ones here with proper beards." He gave his own coarse blond tuft a tug. "The rest of you look like princesses compared to the locals. You need to let your hair grow."

"We look like giants compared to the locals!" Voskonov thumped his chest with both fists.

Morgan intently gauged the commitment in the faces of his men. "Beards for all of us is a good idea. We need to do everything we can to blend in, and we certainly need to train rigorously. Do *not* use any more bullets. Unless you are sure you'll die otherwise, do not use a single one. We don't know what we'll be up against before we're able to make more. With the men from the earldom hunting us, and people from our time being wild cards, anything can happen. We have to be ten steps ahead of the game and eliminate any modern loose ends who are here. No matter what course of action we take, they can't live. We are a brotherhood, and I would like to see all of you commit to making an empire here—the likes of which the world has never seen."

"We are all with you," Wolf said. He leaned forward, glaring at the others, almost daring them to dissent.

Rashad spoke hesitantly, "Sir, there is one thing."

"Go ahead," Morgan said.

"Being important rulers sounds great for you guys, but I'm Arab! Everyone is going to want to kill me. Romano could get away with saying he's Spanish or Italian, but not me!"

"We'll say you're with us, and you'll have our protection," Morgan said.

"I am committed to the order," Rashad said, "but you have to acknowledge this would be a dismal existence for me."

"Who do you think would be better at ruling the Middle East, me or you?" Morgan asked.

"Uh—I look more the part, and speak the language."

"Exactly. And after we conquer the world and give people technology and luxuries beyond their imagination, with you in charge of all the lands occupied by the Moors, who would be known for all time as the greatest military leader in your homeland?"

Rashad nodded. "I see what you mean."

Morgan gestured to all of them in a sweeping motion, his chest puffed out. "Open your minds like Rashad. What has the word *power* meant to you? Has it meant money—to buy what you want? Has it meant authority—to tell someone what to do? But think of this. For a person to decide, *this is how I choose the world to be for thousands of years*—that is power."

14

———————

Celeste awoke to a knock at the door. It was barely light outside. Remembering where she was, she tried to calm her nerves.

"M'lady," said a female voice, "I'm sorry to wake you, but I have good news."

Celeste leaped out of bed and flew to the door. "Is it my brother?"

"No, m'lady. But your servant's uncle arrived at daybreak. He says he knows where your brother is!"

She swung open the door. "Really? Is my brother all right?"

The pretty servant who had danced with Will stood outside the door.

"I believe so, m'lady," Emma said.

"Please take me to him. Wait—I suppose I need to change first." She sighed at the obligatory delay.

"Would m'lady like assistance?"

Celeste gave a smile and reminded herself to stay in character even though she would rather put formalities on hold and rush to reunite with a family member. "Yes, come in."

"Yes, m'lady."

As Emma helped Celeste with her dress, she said, "William departed this morning. A bit unfortunate they missed each other."

Celeste wished she could just text Will. "Has Edmund spoken with William's uncle?"

"Oh, no. His lordship wouldn't have us disturbing him at this early hour, though he would want us to make the man comfortable. I hope I didn't err in waking your ladyship. Only, I thought—"

"You did the right thing. Thank you."

"The man was invited in several times, but he insisted on waiting at the gatehouse. I'm told he's quite eager to take you and your servant to your brother."

"Do you know when the search party will return?"

"No, m'lady. Near nightfall, I suppose, unless William finds your brother beforehand."

"I understand you've spoken with William a number of times. Is he—is he getting along well with the servants here?"

"Oh, yes, m'lady. He's quite charming."

"Hmm," Celeste murmured. "Good."

"Pardon my asking, m'lady, but do you know if he has a woman back in your land?"

The question caught Celeste off guard, and the subtle tapping of her foot stilled. "I . . . don't think so." She saw Emma smile in the reflection of the mirror. Her reaction bothered Celeste, but she pushed the feeling aside. "Is the dress good enough? Are we ready to go?"

"Yes, m'lady."

"Great. Thank you." Celeste walked quickly through the castle corridors with Emma hastening to keep up. They entered the misty courtyard covered by a gray sky. Celeste kept telling herself to appear ladylike and not go too fast.

They entered the gatehouse, where a man was speaking with the guards. Celeste was relieved to see someone who looked like they were from home. His modern business haircut, though disheveled, was the first giveaway. The man also didn't have the same worn and malnourished look that shrouded many of the people here. He was tall, with high cheekbones, and wore a beige medieval tunic with dark brown trousers and a sword at his hip.

"Hello, you must be Princess Celeste. The whole countryside has been talking about you," the man said with a smile and wink.

"Yes—they said you know where my brother is?"

"I do. He's all right, and I can take you to him. What an ordeal we've all been through! I'm so sorry that you and your family were dragged into this. Do you want to wait for Will to come back, or would you like to go to your brother now?"

Celeste had trouble identifying why she felt uneasy. This man's accent was American. She tried to remember the scene in the desert. She was sure Will's uncle had light brown hair. This man's was dark brown.

"You're Will's uncle?"

"Yes, Chase Donovan, at your service."

"Um, let's wait until Will gets back. It will save the need for extra trips."

"That's fine. I really look forward to seeing him. I feel terrible about this whole situation."

"Which of my brothers did you find, Justin or Trevor?"

The man's expression changed, and Celeste knew he could sense her skepticism. Then Celeste pictured the man before her, wearing a black T-shirt and camo pants. She glanced down and saw the toes of the man's combat boots sticking out below the dark medieval trousers. *This is the man who was standing over Will's uncle with a gun!*

"He said his name is Daniel," the man said, "and that he's your brother. You seem frightened, my dear—are you all right?"

Celeste backed up and turned to run. The man rushed forward and grabbed her. In the same instant, seven figures sprang up from the grass outside the castle gatehouse. The men wore local grass and foliage integrated into the back of their modern military clothing, making them blend in perfectly with the terrain outside the castle wall. They bore medieval weapons and shields. One drew a bow and arrow, and they swiftly attacked the two guards.

"To Commander Morgan!" shouted one of the large commandos, axe in hand.

"Help! Guards!" Emma screamed.

Weapons clashed, and the guards shouted to alarm the others. Morgan pulled Celeste out of the gatehouse. She dug her feet into the ground, but she wasn't strong enough. A tempest of fear swept through her. She felt like she was going to black out. Amid her terror, one thought stood out. *He knew Danny's name! Maybe they got him!* She focused her fear into intense anger and bit hard into the man's arm.

He cursed, and his grip loosened. Celeste jerked free and ran back to the courtyard. She heard the body of a guard fall to the ground behind her.

"Guards!" Celeste shouted. "Intruders!"

Two castle guards rushed past her, and the clanging of metal intensified. She remembered Edmund telling her that the castle was only garrisoned by fifteen full-time guards. He explained that the walls and towers were the primary defense against invaders and that fifteen men could man the battlements until reinforcements were summoned. But the intruders were already inside.

She wasn't sure where to run. Looking to the highest and most secured tower atop the tall grassy hill, she saw an archer poised on the ramparts. Celeste was grateful for her background in track and soccer—if only she weren't wearing a dress and uncomfortable leather shoes as she ran up the steep stone steps.

"Celeste, stop!" shouted an attacker not far behind her.

A guard opened the door and waved her inside. "M'lady, you'll be safe in here." His face was young, and Celeste could see the grave concern in his eyes.

He sealed the door behind Celeste, and she tried to catch her breath.

One of the intruders kicked the door, but it held firm.

"Tape the C-4," a voice on the other side of the door said. "Blow it open."

"Get away from the door! Get away from the door!" Celeste shouted.

The guard ignored her, bearing his sword at the ready, his focus intense. She pulled at his arm, but he shook her away.

Celeste frantically looked around for where to go. The tower itself was wide and stout with no ceiling, just open sky. Stairs against the side of the tower wall led to the wall walk, where another guard was raining arrows at the men below—but the arrows only made dull thuds as they hit the men's shields.

"Please come with me! Their weapons will kill you if you don't get away from the door!" Celeste shouted at the young guard as she ran up the stairs.

The door exploded inward. Celeste slipped on the smooth stone steps and barely caught herself from falling. The guard lay unconscious on the ground while men protecting themselves with shields spilled through the doorway.

An arrow whizzed from above and struck one of the intruders in the shoulder. The man moved for cover, and her assailants reassembled their shield wall. One of them picked up the largest remaining section of the oaken door and added it to their protective barrier as they made their way up the stairs.

Celeste backed behind the archer. He had an arrow fully drawn back but no clear shot at the men on the other side of the makeshift barrier. The archer ran around the perimeter of the tower to get an angle on the exposed section of the group.

An arrow shot out of the small barred window of the oaken door and struck the archer in the chest. He gasped, reaching for something to hold on to, only to reel his arms as he fell to the inner portion of the tower with a sickening crunch.

"Stay there, Celeste. We won't hurt you!" one of the men yelled.

She dashed to the other side of the tower wall walk. The assailants reached the top and split up to go around the perimeter to corner her.

Her heart raced, and she felt lightheaded as she looked to the ground twenty feet below at the bodies of the two guards. There was a cart beneath her with straw in it, but Celeste thought it was too small to easily land in, and the straw alone might not be enough to break her fall.

"Don't do it!" one of the men demanded.

Celeste glanced up. It would only be seconds before they reached her. She held her breath—and jumped.

Her dress billowed behind her, and air rushed through her outstretched hands. She bent her knees, hoping her legs wouldn't break, and pain shot through her ankle on impact. The cart jolted and tipped forward but stayed upright. She climbed out, and one of the men was about to make the same jump. Gritting her teeth, Celeste angrily tipped the cart over.

"Go ahead and jump—it's not that far!" she called.

The men cussed at her as she limped as fast as she could out the open doorway. She ducked as a shield smashed into the wall behind her. Eight castle guards ran up the stairs toward her.

Celeste winced as she lowered herself onto the grassy hill leading to the courtyard. Then she lay down, folded her arms across her chest, and squeezed her eyes shut as she let herself roll wildly down the steep hill. When she came to a stop at the bottom, she tried to orient herself.

A servant yelled, "What in the name of St. George?"

Celeste gasped as she saw a black rope extending down the outside of the tower wall and the modern soldiers running down it commando style. The guards made it to the top of the tower as the last man reached the ground and pulled the rope after him. Then they came charging down the hill.

Celeste cringed, knowing she could only go so fast with her injury but that her life might depend on her muscling through the pain. She ran as fast as she was able toward the main body of the castle and hobbled up a spiraling staircase, bracing her hand against the wall to compensate for her leg, wishing for a good place to hide.

She heard the men enter the stairwell. They were gaining on her.

When she reached the top, she found a long, spacious room with a high ceiling. The walls were lined with tapestries, vases, and suits of armor. A large stained-glass window took up the center of one of the walls. Celeste knew there was no way she could outrun them down the length of the room, so she limped to hide behind one of the tapestries along the wall. But before she could reach it, the men burst through the doorway.

Celeste maneuvered around a table with a lit oil lamp that must have been forgotten by a servant in the panic of the morning. The man they called Commander Morgan kicked the table over, and the lamp shattered, lighting the table on fire.

"Halt, and surrender!" Edmund bellowed from the other

side of the long room. He brandished a large sword with a gold-encrusted hilt and a shield displaying his family coat of arms.

The modern men assessed the lone threat while Celeste hurried to him.

"Yield your weapons now, and I'll see that you receive quick executions!" Edmund demanded. A part of Celeste was impressed by his confidence to stand alone against the group of men, but she was terrified for both of their sakes.

Morgan motioned to a man who had an arrow drawn back. "Shoot him, and let's get the girl."

Edmund deflected the arrow with his shield.

"Cowards! The eight of you don't dare face me?" Edmund banged his sword against his shield and moved toward the intruders. The fire on the ground grew and spread to a nearby tapestry.

Celeste pulled on Edmund's tunic. "Let's get out of here, Edmund!"

"Hold your arrows," Morgan ordered as a smile climbed his cheeks. "The kid is mine." He approached with his flame-bladed sword ready. The blade resembled snakelike waves rather than being a straight piece of metal. Edmund charged, pulling away from Celeste.

Morgan met him in the center of the room, and their swords clashed. They exchanged blow after blow, with neither one gaining the advantage. Guards soon began spilling into the room behind Celeste.

"To Sir Edmund!" shouted one of the guards, and they rushed at Morgan. Morgan's men also moved forward through the spreading smoke.

The guards protectively broke between Edmund and Morgan and began fighting.

"Out of my way! Stand aside!" shouted Edmund. But the

guards ignored his demand and deftly swung their blades at the intruders.

Celeste made her way to the back of the room. Her injured leg buckled beneath her, and she fell to the floor.

The guards were better with medieval weapons, and they pressed the modern men back. The invaders were taking injuries but were still on their feet.

"Use the guns!" Morgan shouted over the din of chaos. "Use the guns!"

Several men drew handguns and fired in single shots. The crack of the gunfire reverberated from the walls of the large chamber until the few guards remaining drew back in astonishment.

Morgan's eyes burned into Celeste's as he charged at her through the smoke.

Her hands shook as she drew the dagger at her waist and held it out at him. Morgan sneered, knocking it out of her hand with his sword, then yanked her up from the floor and spun her around. His cold blade pressed against her throat.

"Stop, or the girl dies!" Morgan yelled.

"Hold!" Edmund shouted to his men. He approached Morgan and held his sword point several feet away from the man's face. "If you harm her, I will eviscerate you! And none of the blasts from your small cannons will fell me until I've slain you," he seethed.

"I'll kill her unless you do precisely what I say."

Edmund was red with anger. "What do you want? Gold?"

Morgan's men laughed, sending a shiver through Celeste.

"No, Edmund," he scoffed. "Nothing like that. We want the boy Will and a black scepter he stole from us."

"What boy? I have nothing to do with this, and neither does she," Edmund spat.

Morgan marched Celeste across the room with the sword to

her neck. "The boy Celeste arrived with. The object also resembles a mace."

"William? I know nothing about this," Edmund said. "He's not here in the castle, and this assault on my men and the princess is entirely unnecessary."

"We need both William and the mace," Morgan insisted. "In exchange, we'll release her. We'll wait at the castle gate to make the trade. Go get William and bring him back. Remember our capabilities with what you call 'small cannons.' You won't survive a blast from them any better than your men."

"Perhaps," Edmund said. "But you are not leaving this room alive unless you release the princess."

A man wearing glasses moved close to Morgan and Celeste and whispered in a German accent, "Commander, they might assemble a small army while we wait for the boy—I'm concerned about our bullet count."

Morgan gritted his teeth and nodded to his men. "Group up at the window." He locked eyes with Edmund. "Since you seem stubborn in your negotiations, you force my hand. You're making this much more difficult. Bring William to me, and the mace, at noon two days from now, at Stonehenge."

Stonehenge? Celeste thought. Images of being sacrificed on an altar flashed through her mind. She twisted to get away, but Morgan held her tighter. She caught her breath as he repositioned the blade against her neck.

The large Russian man, the one who had attacked Celeste and her friends, smashed the stained-glass window with his battle axe, and smoke drifted out through the new opening. The others prepared a rope.

"Stop!" shouted Edmund.

"Approach at the henge's natural entrance from the northeast," Morgan said, joining the others at the window. "We want the boy and the mace. If you bring an army—we kill Celeste. If anyone tries to follow us—we kill her. Do as we say, and her ladyship will be returned to you unharmed. Also, tell William we have a sniper rifle and not to try anything stupid. Is that clear?"

"Wait for him to return today," Edmund demanded. "To travel to the Giant's Ring is unnecessary. It's so far from here."

"It's inconvenient, but from there, we'll be able to see anyone coming miles away." Morgan's voice was cold.

"We're ready, Commander," Wolf said.

"Then move out," Morgan said, and his men began descending the rope.

Celeste's heart raced at the thought of going out the high window with these horrid men.

"You're all cowards!" Edmund shouted. "Without your strange weapons, my men would have gutted every one of you!"

"Just bring what we asked for. Are we agreed?" Morgan said.

"I accept, but if she is harmed in any way, there will be no closet or corner that will hide you from my wrath," Edmund said. "You're weak, and feeble, and you hide behind your cannons. Any one of my men could beat any one of yours in single combat. If you are ever seen in my lands again, I'll see that you experience a horrible death. Broken on the Catherine Wheel! Hung, drawn, and quartered!"

Morgan smiled. "We'll be back, with more men and our *intelligently* designed weapons. We'll lay waste to your entire earldom."

Edmund balked. "Our forces and the king's would make quick work of any mercenaries you tried to drum up."

"Don't be so sure that the king will be on your side," Morgan said with a sinister grin.

15

Celeste tried to pull away in disgust as soon as she and Morgan reached the ground. The base of the castle was shrouded with fog, and shouts of guards came from above them.

Morgan hurried her into the cover of the trees and forced her to the ground.

"Any of you need to tie off wounds before we get out of here?" Morgan asked.

Celeste braced her hands against the dried leaves on the forest floor and quietly took in the cuts most of the men had on their arms and legs. She knew how to address the wounds, but she would rather see them die than help them. The men wore modern body armor on their torsos, and several of them had slash marks across the front sections. Celeste scowled, knowing that without the body armor, they might not have been able to capture her.

"I'm pretty cut up, but I can make it to our rally point," a man with a German accent said. The others stated they were ready.

"Then let's go." Morgan turned to Celeste. "We have to hurry, and you're coming with us. You can either do this the easy way, or the hard way."

Celeste glowered at him. "Wow, I didn't know I would get a smorgasbord of options. But seriously, who picks the hard way?"

"Only people who are masochistic. Just shut up and run fast."

He held the scruff of her dress as they hurried through the woods. Pain shot through her leg as she hobbled through the trees.

"Voskonov, carry her," Morgan said.

Celeste shuddered at the thought of the large Russian touching her. A dark wound on his forehead, likely from the wrench Will threw, added to the foreboding specter of the thick bald head with hungry eyes and bloody trident tattoo on his neck.

She trembled as he scooped her up like a sack of potatoes, and they continued to run through the woods.

He tossed her onto the ground when they reached a clearing with horses tethered to the trees.

"It looks like y'all had some fun!" said a man with a short-trimmed brown beard and a thick Southern accent. "So much for being a quick grab-and-go with little to no combat. No boy or Black Hammer?"

"No. Shut your face, Johnson, and get out some bandages," Voskonov snarled.

The man with glasses and a German accent began tending to the men's injuries.

"We should have used the guns earlier," a man with dark hair muttered in a Spanish accent as he wrapped his shoulder.

Morgan eyed him, and a burly man with a blond beard spoke. He had a European accent that Celeste had trouble identifying. "We all made it. Conserving our ammo may have saved our lives tomorrow or the next day. Did you expect we would conquer the world without engaging in some hand-to-hand combat?"

Conquer the world? Celeste thought. *These guys are crazy!* She stood and slowly edged away from the group, warily considering escaping into the woods while cursing her sprained ankle. She froze when she noticed Morgan looking at her as if reading her mind.

"Celeste, you're going to be riding with one of these men. Don't even think about running away. You can't imagine the pain I will inflict upon you if you try, and if we can't easily exchange you, we'll be forced to ambush your friends along the roadway. In which case they could be ... seriously injured."

The man's voice made Celeste's skin crawl. "Fine, but I want my own horse," she said, holding her head high.

"Sorry, sweetie. We don't have an extra horse," said an American with a buzz cut and shifty eyes.

"Two of you can share," she shot back. "I could ride in the middle of the group, even with the reins tied to another horse. You could easily see me, and I wouldn't be able to ride off."

"It's not happening," Morgan said as he readied some gear on a horse.

"She could ride with me," Voskonov said with a creepy smile.

Celeste cringed. Her reaction made the Dreizack laugh. The burly man with the blond beard slapped Voskonov on the back.

"Nah, I call dibs," the Southerner said.

"It doesn't matter who she rides with," Morgan said. "Get your gear together and let's move out."

Celeste felt ill. She turned around and wished she could disappear. She was angry that she wasn't able to physically defend herself. For most of her life, she had gotten what she wanted through words, but now she wished she knew how to fight. Celeste forced back tears and tried to think of how she could gain even the smallest amount of independence.

She shook her head at the idea that came to her. Her resentment of the men deepened as she thought through what she would do to herself. Celeste shuddered and turned away from the group, then stuck her fingers in the back of her mouth. She squeezed her eyes shut as she pressed down hard and forced herself to gag, vomiting all over the front of her dress.

"Disgusting!" exclaimed an Arab man, and the other Dreizack added a myriad of insults.

Celeste turned back to face them, wiping her hands on the back of her dress. She took in all of the sour expressions.

"Sorry about that. This ancient food must not agree with me. So, who was I going to be riding with?"

16

—————

Will was exhausted. He'd been in the saddle before dawn, following Sir Roland and his men as they criss-crossed the countryside. When they stopped at the occasional farmstead or hamlet to ask questions, he noticed that Roland seemed far more interested in the group of men who'd ravaged Littlehampton than in finding Danny and Chase. Will caught many of the men eyeing him occasionally, but there was little conversation due to the brisk pace of the horses.

The steeds were frothing at the mouth, and the group stopped beside a stream to let the horses drink. Several men stretched out on the grass to rest while Will helped Garrett check the horses' shoes.

One of the animal's legs spasmed as Will inspected the nails driven through its iron shoe, tipping Will off balance from his kneeling position. The hilt of the scepter pressed against the grassy earth, dislodging it out of the makeshift case on his belt.

Will gasped and scrambled to pick it up, hoping no one would notice the exposed dark head. A shadow stood over him, and Will snatched the scepter off the ground and sprang to his feet, holding it defensively.

"Ho there, I'm no enemy of yours, Master William," Sir Roland said with a look of mild amusement.

"You just startled me." Will tried to look casual as he recased the weapon.

"Nothing wrong with always being on the ready, considering the lot we're looking for. That mace will better serve you if you learn a proper stance."

"Well, I would like it to serve me well," Will said.

"Then you need to get your feet positioned in a firm foundation—so you can strike with power. You can't fire a catapult from a rowboat. You have to stand strong, and wield your weapon with purpose." The knight demonstrated, drawing his own sword. "If your adversary thinks you know how to handle yourself, they may be more hesitant to fight—which is likely the best you can hope for without more training."

"Thank you, sir," Will said. He found himself liking the knight more and more.

Church bells sounded in the far distance.

"There's smoke! Smoke from Arundel," Garrett exclaimed.

"Likely a thatched roof in the village," a man-at-arms suggested.

"It might be coming from the castle," Roland said, his dark brows furrowing. "In either case, we have a duty to return. Mount up!"

The ride to the castle was frantic. They charged through the woods and across streams. Will's and Garrett's horses were laden with supplies and much slower than the rest. They soon lost sight of Roland and the other horsemen in the trees.

When they could see the castle in the distance, Garrett pointed and exclaimed, "Look there!" It was clear the smoke was coming from a section of the castle. "I pray it is only an accidental fire."

Will's thoughts went to Celeste, and he tried not to imagine the worst. The fire wasn't even near her chambers or the gardens, and he assured himself that she was safe. However, the more he thought about her well-being, the more urgently he prodded the horse.

The smoke had faded by the time Will and Garrett neared the castle gate. Edmund and several guards were standing outside, completely disheveled and covered with soot. Roland was on foot, speaking with them.

As they rode up, Will felt everyone's eyes riveted on him. His heart sank into his stomach. "What happened?" he asked.

His question was ignored, and Edmund marched toward Will, pointing a finger at him. "You! Off my horse!"

"Wh-what's going on?"

Edmund reached to tear Will out of the saddle, but Will dismounted off the other side. "They told me to ride this one."

Edmund stepped to Will and swung a fist at his face.

The punch knocked him off balance, and he looked beyond Edmund for intervention but saw in the hardness of the men's faces that there would be none.

"What happened?" Will shouted. "Where is Celeste?"

Edmund moved to strike him again, and Will dodged to the side and shoved him. "Where is Celeste?" he demanded.

"William! You're out of line!" Roland bellowed.

"I haven't done anything!"

Edmund grabbed him, and the two grappled to the ground.

Rough hands tore them apart. Will struggled to his feet with two men pinning back his arms, while another tore the scepter from his belt. "No, that's mine! It's mine!" he shouted.

"Is it? I understand you robbed it from the men who

kidnapped your princess," Edmund said, looking ready to launch another attack at Will.

The words slammed into Will like a spear to the chest.

"What? What happened? I didn't rob anyone!"

A guard curtly summarized what had happened.

When he was finished, Will said, "The mace belongs to my uncle, and I found it in the grass after those men attacked us."

One of Edmund's men-at-arms wiped flecks of dirt from the scepter and admired its workmanship. "My lord. Would you like to assess the object's value before returning it for this woman? We've known her but a day."

Edmund didn't give the scepter a glance. "Whatever its value, she's worth it." He glared at Will. "And he's certainly worth turning over."

"Let's get this straight," Will said, squaring his shoulders and staring back into Edmund's eyes. "You're going to trust the word of men who murdered people in your town, attacked your castle, and killed your soldiers above Princess Celeste's word? She told you they were criminals. She also said you could trust me."

Edmund was undeterred. "Of course I don't trust them— but I know what I want and the only way to get it."

17

———————

Two men-at-arms had a viselike grip on Will, and several more accompanied them as they took him inside the castle to the dungeon. Emma and several other servants watched from the courtyard on the other side of the gatehouse entrance.

Emma's face twisted in pain and grief as she looked at Will. *Is she that worried about me?* He gave a faint smile, trying to show encouragement. He wasn't sure what reaction, if any, he expected, but she looked even more stricken. Her eyes flashed to Edmund, and the look of grief was replaced by fear. When her gaze returned to Will, she shook her head and mouthed, "I can't." Then she reluctantly turned and walked away.

Will felt shaken by the reach of Edmund's influence. Apparently, if the lord decided that someone was bad news, they were suddenly off limits. Will realized how much Emma stood to lose by being friends with him now. Certainly, her income and lodging, and there likely weren't other people employing servants in the area, which could mean starvation. Edmund had the authority to execute, but Will wondered if he would go that far for someone merely being his friend. Regardless, it was clear he should expect no allies here.

The cell they locked him in had just enough space on the ground for Will to sit with his legs extended. There was no comfortable position on the uneven stone floor. Fragments of withered straw indicated that a prior occupant might have been made comfortable, but Will wasn't given the luxury. Even though the cell was small, he was sure they wouldn't hesitate to stuff as many people inside as possible.

As the hours passed, a rusted pot filled. Will grew ever more cautious about not accidentally bumping it over. He wondered if it was only meant for feces or—even worse—only his food or water. His mind worked over what might happen in the coming days and how he could try to escape. His preoccupation made him forget his hunger and thirst, but he felt famished as the light in the cell faded with the setting sun.

Will leaned his head back against the coarse wall and thought about the words the man in charge said to him in the desert before the flash—that they had great potential together. *I don't trust him,* Will thought. *He's a murderer. I wish I had never seen that thing.* He felt a deep connection with the object to his very soul. But it still wasn't worth it. He wished he had never picked it up.

I could get away between here and Stonehenge. If I meet with those men, it will be because I chose to. Will swallowed and pressed his fist to his mouth.

He thought about what social responsibility he might have to prevent the men from doing something stupid that could alter history, then shook his head. *What could I even do? It might be altered already.*

He remembered what Celeste had said to Danny in the

desert before he went to approach the vehicles with the grenades. She'd begged her twin brother to abandon Will and leave with her. *If I had been the one who needed the tourniquet on my leg, instead of Cody, would she have even stopped? There is no question that if I show up at Stonehenge, I'll be risking my life for hers.*

But Celeste has been my ally in this.

He let his head rest back against the stone. *If nothing else, she's my best friend's sister. But Danny? I don't know if he's here, if he's alive, or if they'll still let Celeste live if I go meet them.*

Will drifted off and found himself again in the realm of vivid dreams. He was in the front line of a great army. He looked at those around him. They were his friends, although they weren't faces Will recognized. They exchanged brave words of encouragement in a language that Will didn't understand, yet he felt supported—part of a unified family of warriors.

He bore a shield and the scepter and looked ahead to an ominous cloud of darkness approaching from the sky and the ground before him. There was apprehension in the ranks. Will realized that the darkness was thick with the enemy, so thick with dark figures it was blocking out the light ahead, storming at them from the air.

Grotesque faces stared back at him, enemies bearing swords, clubs, and javelins.

His army's horns sounded the charge to attack. He surged forward with the scepter in a blaze of white light, striking and blasting enemy after enemy, beating them back, smashing them down.

Will noticed that no one was at his side. *Have my friends fallen?* He glanced behind to see that his army had marched several paces back. Watching him fight alone, without compassion, intentionally waiting, abandoning him to be slaughtered.

He cried out in anguish, swinging wildly, ferociously, trying to keep back the cloud of weapons around him. Will did not know who the greater enemy was—the host of darkness or those he had considered friends. With blow after blow, he became angrier, and he screamed, and he screamed, and he screamed.

"William! William! Wake up!" Someone was shaking his shoulder.

Will was drenched in sweat, and it took a while for him to realize where he was. Garrett knelt on the other side of the bars. He had a lantern that sent ominous shadows from the prison bars across the small cell. He was still grasping Will's shoulder through a gap.

"No one cares if I die," Will stammered.

"Well, you're a bit daft—and ugly—but I wouldn't go so far as to say that. You've simply had a bad dream."

"No, no, it's true." Will took a deep breath.

"What in the name of St. George were you dreaming about?"

"Being abandoned." Will hesitated. "Why are you here?"

"Well, I saw the look on your face when they said they would lock you away. That look reminded me of the way I felt after my family died from the fever. I know what it's like to feel alone. I just figured I'd bring you some food and keep you company."

Will was silent for a moment. "Thank you. I really mean that. Thank you, Garrett. But what about Edmund? Won't he be angry with you?"

"Oh, maybe I'll get locked in here too," he said with a wry smile. "I'd just say I was protecting his lordship's interests by keeping you from starving. Don't worry yourself about it. You were shouting in a strange tongue. What was it?"

"A different language?"

"Yes, I've never heard anything like it."

Will pressed a fist to his forehead. "I wish I knew."

Time travel, foreign languages, dreams, and imprisonment —of all the feelings he could experience, Will was unsettled that his drive to get the scepter back was one of the strongest.

18

Celeste tried to keep herself from shivering as she rode atop her own horse through the dark, icy fog. Wearing a dress forced her to ride sidesaddle since she wanted to be as modest as possible. She understood it was customary for women here, anyway. Morgan had estimated that they would reach Stonehenge before sunrise. During their journey, Celeste had been as bristly and unappealing as possible while still complying with what they told her to do. She felt lucky that they kept their hands off her.

Her hatred for them grew when they had returned to camp, boasting of their raid on a farming settlement. The only silver lining was that they'd acquired another horse, so she didn't have to listen to Johnson and Skinner cuss at her because the two men were sharing.

She had intently listened in on their conversations and was relieved to find out that the Dreizack had never seen Danny or Will's uncle, and that Morgan had learned Danny's name from inquiring in the town of Arundel about Will and the ongoing search parties. Today, Edmund was supposed to arrive at noon with Will and the object the men wanted. She felt torn about whether or not she hoped they would come. *No sense in all of us dying.* In case they did make the journey, she had cleaned herself up in the cold water of the creek the last time the group made camp, wishing she could look and feel more like herself.

The light of the moon emanated through the surrounding fog, and they pressed forward across the grassy plain.

"There it is!" declared Morgan, pointing ahead. Great columns of stone were barely visible through the mist, illuminated by moonlight on the flat expanse.

They continued forward and reached a shallow grassy ditch encircling Stonehenge. They crossed it and dismounted next to the giant pillars. Celeste walked inside the stone circle and ran her hand across the moss and lichen covering one of the great rocks. Long grass grew among the pillars, making the prehistoric site seem forgotten in time. In other circumstances, she might have found being there at dawn to be deeply moving, but as a captive of a brotherhood of power-hungry lunatics, the location felt eerily foreboding.

Some of the men gazed up at the pillars and arches in awe, but the reverence didn't last.

Voskonov sat down on one of the fallen pillars and spat. "Stupid waste of time, hauling these huge rocks out here."

"If they hadn't, you wouldn't have anything to sit on," Skinner cracked.

"These things are as old as the pyramids in Egypt," Morgan said. "Understanding this site, and many others like it, provides us with strategic advantages."

"Yeah—but no one really knows why it was built," Johnson said.

"Actually, I have a pretty good idea," Morgan countered. "That's the entrance." He pointed to a flat passage through the ditch that encircled the henge, which was also the direction from which Edmund was supposed to approach. "It points northeast and marks the exact point of the sunrise on the summer solstice. During the Ice Age, annual freezing and thawing caused a straight, deeply grooved path to form here. People living in this area clearly found significance in the path's perfect alignment with the sunrise on the longest day of the year."

"Sir, I've heard that much before, and I understand the location's advantages for today, but it doesn't seem like there's much else to it." Johnson shrugged.

Morgan smiled. "You have to dig deeper to get to the hidden treasures. Up the river from here, archeologists found old wooden post holes in the same configuration as Stonehenge. They think the wooden site was used to celebrate life, and on the eve of the summer solstice, people would travel down the river to this place to honor the dead. And that's where my knowledge comes in handy—I know what is in those mounds." He nodded to the many small rises in the grass dotting the plain around them.

"What?" Johnson asked.

"They aren't naturally occurring. They're burial sites—with treasure."

"Really?" Wolf said, mouth agape, as he stopped cleaning his sniper rifle.

"It's just a backup plan. If we can't get the king to use his wealth to manufacture our weapons and use his men for our armies, we can come back here, spend a lot of time digging up treasure, transport it to Scotland, and fund our manufacturing there. The Scots hate the English, and it wouldn't be hard to build an army to invade England—but that's a lot of extra work."

Celeste looked away and pretended not to be listening. *He wouldn't talk about this in front of me if he was going to let me go.*

"But first things first," Morgan said. "Let's set a security perimeter. The odds are high that those fools will try to stage an attack. They would have to have a massive army to be able to surround us before we saw them coming. But even then, not massive enough that we couldn't punch through a weak spot in their lines. Wolf, you're up top. The rest of you, spread out evenly on the ground. Celeste, go sit out on that stone at the entrance of the circular ditch. We'll want them to be able to see you."

"You mean you want me to be good bait," she muttered.

"Don't you want to be freed?" Morgan asked.

"You're going to let that happen?" Celeste wheeled around. "You're going to let me leave?"

"Of course. That was the deal." He gave her an empathetic look.

She held his gaze for a moment, then turned back to the northeast to wait on the designated rock. Hugging her knees, she looked out into the fog-filled distance and waited.

Romano called, "Hey girl, do you think your boyfriend will show up?"

"Boyfriend?" Celeste said. "Edmund will."

"No, the modern boy you were with—Will Donovan."

Celeste hesitated. "If they make him."

Hours passed, and it was difficult for her to know the time of day because the sky was trapped in an eerie shroud of haze. Celeste spent the time debating over what she should say or do if people came and what she should do if they didn't.

"I see a rider coming from the northeast!" Wolf shouted, looking through the scope of his gun.

Celeste's heart began to race, but she still couldn't see anyone through the mist. She stood and took several deep breaths.

"How many?" Morgan asked.

Wolf hesitated. "So far, just one."

"Who is it?" Celeste called.

"Shut your mouth," Voskonov growled from somewhere behind her.

"Yeah, it's the kid," Wolf nodded. "Alone. But he's got something across his lap. Three feet long or so."

"Is it Black Hammer?" Morgan said.

"Can't tell. It's wrapped in something."

Celeste tensed. *Oh, please, Will. Don't get yourself killed too.*

"Keep him in your crosshairs," Morgan said calmly. "The rest of you, keep your eyes on your respective horizons."

Finally, Will emerged from the fog. He rode steadily forward on a black horse, its hooves kicking up clods of grassy earth. Will was wearing a brown cloak with the hood down and a sword at his side. His face was stony and determined.

"Go ahead, girl," Morgan said from behind her. "Go greet him."

She ran forward. Will dismounted and drew her into a hug.

"Are you okay?" he asked.

"I'm . . . I can't believe you came alone."

"Well, I could only stick around Edmund for so long."

Celeste gave a faint laugh and blinked back a tear.

"I don't think they're going to let us go," she whispered. "They've been talking about tricking the King of England, and making him do what they want."

"Which is what?"

"Making weapons, gunpowder, and medicine. Taking over the world. Killing the king when they don't need him anymore. But Will, they've been talking about it in front of me. Why would they do that if—"

"Bring it here, Will," Morgan called out. "Nothing stupid. I have a lot of guns on you."

Will looked earnestly at Celeste. "Get on the horse, and ride back the way I came. Edmund and his men are there waiting for you. I convinced him that this was the only way to guarantee you'd be safe."

She gasped. "What about you?"

"I can't come with you."

"Will, no!" she said in a hushed tone.

Will gave her a conflicted look and opened his mouth to speak.

"Now, boy!" Morgan said. "And do it slowly."

"No grenades to save you this time," Dekker said.

Will removed the bundle from the saddle and helped Celeste onto the horse.

"I didn't say anything about putting the girl on the horse," Morgan said. "Do you want her to get shot?"

"You left Arundel before you and I could negotiate terms," Will said.

Morgan drew his pistol and cocked it. "This is not a negotiation. Hand it over now, or both of you die."

Will walked forward and handed him the bundle. "If you do that, you'll never see the scepter again."

Morgan tore away the cloth, revealing the shaft of a farming scythe with part of the rusted metal head broken off. Celeste's heart sank, and her hand clenched harder onto the reins.

"I want to give it to you. I'm going to give it to you—but our terms are changing. I'm going to become your new collateral. Her for me—she goes, and the scepter is yours."

"You've got some stones, kid," Morgan said. "But that's unacceptable. I need to see the scepter."

Will shook his head. "If you were in my shoes, you might have a few trust issues right now. No, it's her for me. If you so much as harm her, you'll get nothing. Take it or leave it."

Morgan seemed calm, all but for the muscles tensing in his

jaw as he eyed Celeste. She cringed but couldn't look away from him and his handgun.

"Fine," Morgan said. "But you're on thin ice. Where is it?"

Will waved for Celeste to leave. "Go! Don't worry."

Celeste made a concerned face, trying to wordlessly ask, "How can you say that?"

"Please, hurry!" Will begged.

She prodded the horse forward but couldn't take her eyes from Will. The last she could see of him as the mist started to obscure her view was Morgan pointing his gun at Will's forehead. She steadied herself in the saddle as she tried to blink back tears, then urged the horse onward.

19

The cold eye of the gun stared back at Will, but he forced himself not to back down. Behind the weapon was the man with a devil's smile who said he could give Will a better life. The man whom the men from Arundel spoke of as "Commander Morgan."

"There's something I need to tell you that I didn't want to say in front of her," Will said. "You know all about that thing, the scepter. You said you knew that I'm somehow linked to it. I have been bullied all my life. No more. I want to be one of the bullies. I want to know what is going on, and I want to join you." Will yearned to learn everything he could about the scepter, but he kept telling himself that helping Celeste and stopping these men were the priorities.

Highly trained or not, Morgan couldn't contain his surprise, and Will suppressed a smile.

A giant of a man cursed behind him in Russian.

"You killed three of our brothers with grenades," snapped an American with a militant haircut.

"And you shot my uncle and tried to kill me and my

friends," Will fired back. "But that is all in the past—or future —or whatever. This is now!"

The Russian man stepped forward with his fist drawn back. "And I'll finish what I should have then!"

Morgan held up a hand, and the brute stopped in his tracks.

"Back in the desert, you said we had a lot of potential to work together," said Will. "It's a big world—you could use one more smart guy."

Morgan continued to train his gun on Will. "Times have changed, and we don't need your help anymore."

"You said that only my uncle and I could activate it."

Morgan's lips tightened.

Will pressed on. "What did you need me for anyway? To torture me into making it work?"

"Might be," Morgan said nonchalantly. "If we still wanted to go somewhere. Maybe we want to stay here."

Will's blood ran cold, and he tried to keep his voice confident. "Well, any important warriors here have teenage squires. If you want to appear as someone important, you'll need at least one squire. The last thing you want to do is come across as a bunch of random guys on a camping trip."

"But if joining us was your plan, why not bring it with you? Why the ruse?" Morgan asked.

"I needed to know that Celeste would be safe. I've known her all my life."

"A little sentimental for our group, kid. No one is safe from us." Morgan shifted to the side so he was no longer blocking Will's view of a man with bright blond hair lying across one of the high stone arches. He was poised, looking through the scope of a sniper rifle aimed in Celeste's direction.

Will's face blanched. "No!"

"You were saying we needed another smart guy?" Morgan smiled.

"I'll take you to it now! All of you."

"That's more like it."

Will hoped the man would take his rifle sights off of Celeste, but the sniper remained ready with his finger on the trigger.

———

Celeste continued to ride forward into the fog, not knowing if she had passed Edmund in the haze. She could no longer see Stonehenge behind her, and she felt lost.

A voice shouted from her right, and about a dozen men on horses trotted toward her.

"Celeste!" Edmund called out. He raced ahead of the other horsemen. "I'm so relieved to see you! Are you all right? Did they hurt you?"

"I'm fine, thank you. What are you doing to help William?"

Edmund reined his horse beside hers. He reached out and gently held the back of her hands as she held the reins. "I have just felt awful ever since those vermin took you. Would you like to stop and take a rest?"

Celeste furrowed her brow in frustration. "No, we don't have time."

The servant girl, Emma, rode up beside her holding a satchel ready. She looked concerned and glanced between Edmund and Celeste, waiting for a command to provide assistance.

Edmund was confused. "Your servant didn't want us to tarry after him."

"What?" Celeste exclaimed.

The other horsemen gathered around. "M'lady," Sir Roland said, "it is what William insisted."

"But they'll kill him!"

Edmund gently reached out and placed his hand on her back. "M'lady, I was going to bring an army to surround the Giant's Ring and force them to surrender you, but William stated, quite disrespectfully I might add, that they would kill you and use ambush techniques that would kill any men who accompanied him. He said they have gunpowder weapons far beyond the ability of even what we witnessed. I eventually decided to exchange him for you prior to giving them the mace."

"Then we are going to where he hid the mace to make sure they release him alive," Celeste demanded.

"I suggested that," Roland said, "but he said it would risk getting him and others killed."

Garrett spoke up. "M'lady, William was very sure he could persuade the men to let him live. He said he would know how to reason with them."

Celeste huffed in exasperation. She remembered that Will's *stupendous* ability to get along with others had caused her to have to drive out into the desert to pick up him and Danny in the first place.

Thinking of her twin brother sent a hollow pang of dread through her chest. Danny might be dead. He and Will had always been a part of her life.

She turned and looked squarely at Edmund. "Is the mace hidden in an area where we could ambush from—before they could use their gunpowder weapons?"

"Yes, but—"

"Let's go there then. Those men are killers. They aren't going to let him go alive. He's wrong if he thinks he can convince them otherwise."

Edmund wore a sour expression.

"Sir Edmund," Celeste pleaded, "William is like a family

member. If you save him, I will promise my hand to you in marriage."

Emma's hand flew to her mouth.

Celeste couldn't believe she had said it—it just came out. *But what am I supposed to say now? Just kidding?*

Edmund's eyebrows raised, and he began to smile. "That would have to be arranged through your father's court, but if it matters that much to you, it would be our honor to be of assistance." His smile grew bigger. "I was wanting to kill those mongrels anyway."

20

———————

The Dreizack made Will ride Celeste's former horse as they followed at gunpoint. Will led them to one of several dense stands of trees on the open plain. He had selected this area because he knew he could approach it from the back end without anyone at Stonehenge seeing him.

"I hid the scepter in the hollow of a tree in the center of that wooded area. I'll go get it."

"Wait," Morgan said. "Dekker, go in with him to retrieve it. Keep a gun on him. I don't want him touching it."

"Certainly, Commander," said the man with a blond beard and European accent.

"You can trust me," Will said, looking at Morgan. "You'll get the scepter. Besides, you wanted me to use it for you before."

"Not anymore, Donovan," Morgan said. "And trust is earned."

Will dismounted the horse and walked across the grass and into the trees. Now that no one could see his face, he felt the confident mask he was trying to wear wavering.

Will climbed over a mossy log and stepped through the

dense wall of trees. He reached a large beech tree with a narrow hollow in the center. "It's in there."

Dekker retrieved the scepter. "Okay, boy. Get going," he said, motioning with his gun.

Will's body tensed. He didn't want this man to carry it, and not just out of fear of how they might use it.

Slowly, they made their way back through the trees to Morgan. Will felt a deep pang of guilt for giving up the scepter. It felt like part of him. *I don't see any other way to figure out what these guys are doing without getting close to them. I hope they're buying all of this.*

Dekker graciously offered the hilt of the scepter to Morgan. "All yours, Commander."

Morgan took it with hungry eyes. After examining it, he thrust it skyward, and his men cheered.

He lowered the weapon and pressed the red impression on the hilt several times. Nothing happened. He touched the white portion, and the white light swirled from the head of the scepter, the same as it had for Will.

"Amazing!" Morgan said.

Will was sure that the man could also feel the same surge of energy that he had.

Morgan moved the scepter through the air, and from Will's perspective, the casual movements jumpily sped by, almost like a video played at a faster speed.

Morgan looked at Will with a devious smile—then swung the scepter down at his head.

Will put his arms up as a meager defense.

Morgan stopped midswing, and the rest of the men laughed.

"That's what you did to me the last time I saw you," Morgan said.

"Not quite like that. I held it out, and you jumped into it."

"I still don't see why I should let you live. I've grown to like it here."

"Sir, we might need him as a backup plan," a man with a Spanish accent pleaded.

"I don't need a backup plan," Morgan said, "but maybe I could use a squire. I might give you a chance, Donovan. But remember—trust is earned."

———

Meanwhile, Celeste and the other riders galloped in a wide circle to remain out of sight as they approached the stand of trees. They stopped behind a shallow rise in the land, just high enough to block their horses from the view of the location where Will had deposited the scepter.

"Several of us are going to go into the trees on foot," Roland said. "We'll ambush them at the tree line, then retreat into the trees, where they would have to dismount to engage us. Then I'll sound my horn, and the rest of you come around and attack them on horseback. We'll have them trapped at the tree line."

"I'll lead the charge on horseback," Edmund said.

"Very well," Roland agreed. "Garrett, you'll stay with the two women."

Garrett was already off his horse with his sword drawn. He pressed his lips in frustration. "Sir—you know I can fight."

"I know," Roland said. "That's why I'll have you protect the princess."

"Yes, sir," Garrett accepted reluctantly.

Roland and five others crept over the hill and quickly made their way to the trees.

"He trains me to be a knight, yet he holds me back from real fighting every chance he gets," Garrett said, almost to himself.

"He must care about you," Celeste said.

"Sorry to trouble you, m'lady. Yes. We're all we have left of my mother—his sister."

"I'm sorry to hear that."

"Thank you, m'lady."

Celeste dug her fingers into the leather saddle as she waited.

Emma eased her horse closer to Celeste's. "M'lady, would you like any food or drink? Anything to make you more comfortable?"

Celeste let out a nervous breath. "Thank you, Emma, but I don't think I could possibly eat or drink anything at the moment."

"When you're ready, I'm here for you."

Celeste nodded. "What did you think of these plans?"

Emma glanced at Edmund and the other riders, then hesitated. "I would say you are all very brave."

Celeste wished Emma felt more at liberty to speak her mind and fixed her eyes on the crest of the low hill. After what felt like a year, Roland and the others appeared. Celeste desperately scanned the group for Will.

"They came and left before we arrived," Roland said.

"Then what took so long?" Edmund asked.

"We thoroughly studied the tracks on the ground. William is still alive."

Celeste exhaled in relief. "Can we follow their tracks?"

"They have a head start on us, and judging by the sky, it will be raining soon. It is doubtful that we could track and catch them."

"But I know where they're going!"

"Where?" Edmund asked.

Celeste answered, "They're going to Windsor Castle to try and seek an audience with the king. They want to provide new weapon technology to him in exchange for an alliance—and a share in the plunder of all Christendom."

"Are you sure of this?" Roland asked.

"I'm completely sure. They talked about it the entire time I was with them. I don't think they were planning on letting me leave alive. They let me go because they wanted that object so badly. They want to change the entire world and make everyone their subjects."

The men exchanged glances. "If what you say is true," Roland said, "then this is a greater problem than helping William. Sir Edmund, the king should be warned of what type of men these are before they reach him."

Edmund nodded. "I would be able to obtain an audience with the king. He and my father have fought together in battle. The king also owes my father money from loans for royal military campaigns." He paused. "But—the king is an ambitious man, with a declared desire to conquer France and Scotland. If he ultimately makes an alliance with these men in order to obtain grand weapons, it could become politically dangerous for me to speak against them."

"Well, whether you get to the king first or not, you could just tell him the truth," Celeste said.

Roland shook his head. "It may not be that simple. Is it true what William told us, that their small cannons can fire many times—with greater accuracy at a distance than archers?"

"It's true. After those men make enough bullets, the projectiles that come out of their guns—or cannons, as you say—they alone could defeat a large army."

"And they can shoot accurately over a mile?" Edmund said.

"The larger guns, yes."

"I don't believe it," said a man-at-arms.

"I swear it's true. I've seen such weapons used many times,"

Celeste said. "They plan to help the king make many of these—for full armies."

"As much as I want to kill them," Edmund said slowly, "it would seem wrong to deny the king of the opportunity to improve his troops."

"My lord," Sir Roland said, "I know your father has been an ally of the king. But if the king had such powerful weapons in large numbers—what need would he have for an alliance with Arundel? Especially when he owes your father a great deal of gold?"

"The king is—ambitious." Edmund frowned. "But he has never wronged us."

"My lord, has it not been wrong that he has not paid back your father?" Roland asked.

One of the men-at-arms spoke up. "Also, my lord, when the leader of those men took the princess, he said he would come back to Arundel with an army and not to expect the king to be on our side."

"If the king had these weapons, what would keep him from taking the rest of your father's wealth for himself?" Roland asked.

"I know," Edmund said gravely. "I wish my father were not abroad so I could speak with him on the matter. But if those men are on their way to meet with the king, I must decide now."

Everyone was silent as he looked at the ground, deep in thought.

Finally, Edmund looked up with a grim expression. "I don't see that we have much choice. We must ride them down."

21

No more dreams came to Will. He had abandoned the scepter, and so it seemed to have abandoned him.

He clenched his cloak around himself in the cold early-morning darkness as he stood a distance from the circle of the Dreizack. They were debating what to do with him, occasionally looking in his direction. Will knew that several wanted him dead, a few alive, and that their leader, Madoc "Bloody" Morgan, seemed undecided. It was really only his decision that mattered.

They had been traveling at an arduous pace for two days and nights, only taking breaks as required for the horses. Will struggled to keep pace with these men who were conditioned to perform on little sleep, but to a small degree, he earned their tolerance.

Instead of going to Windsor Castle, they were now heading to the Tower of London after learning from a traveling merchant from the town of New Windsor that the king was away from his usual residence. Morgan was intent on getting to the king as quickly as possible, fearing that Celeste's knowledge might reach him first.

Will asked Morgan several times about the scepter and the Dreizack's plans, but to no avail. The man remained closed off. Will's initial intent to get answers and potentially try to stop these men was overshadowed by the need to survive.

The debate seemed to end, and Morgan left the group and walked toward Will with a handgun drawn at his side. Will quietly stood his ground, not looking away from Morgan—even though his heart raced and he wanted to run.

"We are going to arrive in London today," Morgan said. "And I need to decide whether or not we're keeping you before we get there."

"What do you need me to do?" Will asked, trying to sound sincere and confident.

"I need to know where your heart is. We don't have any downtime, so we'll talk as we ride."

Will's horse walked next to Morgan's, while the others rode in front and behind them. Their steeds were weary from the strenuous ninety-mile journey and moved at a much slower pace.

"You look nervous. Do you want to go back to what was your home in the future?" Morgan asked, his eyes surgically dissecting Will.

Will debated how he should play his cards. Selecting the best words would be hard enough—making his tone and body language match what he was saying would be even harder. He felt like an undercover spy being questioned by the enemy, and he didn't want to find out what the enemy did to spies. "Everyone hated me in the future because of my reputation. This medieval life is really rough, but in a way, it's a clean slate."

"You don't miss your mom or your modern toys and electronics?"

"Well, sure I do. I wouldn't be normal if I didn't. But I didn't feel like I had a future there. I might be able to have a future here with the Dreizack."

"You think you had a hard life?" Morgan sneered.

Will shifted in the saddle. "In some ways."

"Lots of people have had it worse than you. Look around. I'm not sure how strong you are, or how much you can handle."

Will swallowed hard, but he saw an opportunity to turn the focus away from himself. "How did you get to be as strong as you are?"

"You wouldn't understand."

"I can try."

"You think you had it hard because people didn't like you? My father regularly beat me. When he wasn't beating me, he was busy orchestrating several international crime rings. He was good at keeping himself legally disconnected from the enterprises, and he appeared like the perfect model citizen to the outside world. I hated him. I left home the second I could and joined the Marines. I loved the skills and brotherhood of the Marine Raiders. But let's be honest, the pay sucked, and even though I left home, I couldn't shake the pent-up emotions I had from growing up."

"That sounds horrible," Will said, relieved that Morgan was opening up to him.

"It was. I decided that my pain would go away if I killed my father. On my way home from a deployment, I purchased this." He whirled open a white-opaque porcelain butterfly knife. "It was easier to get through security. I returned to our house and stabbed my father without hesitation. I didn't realize my mother was home. When she saw me standing over him, she was horrified. I tried to talk to her, hoping she might even feel relieved, but she rushed to her phone. In that moment, I made a choice—I killed my mother and made it look like a murder-suicide."

Will was aghast but tried not to show it. There was no way he could ever harm his mother.

Morgan continued, "My younger brother and I inherited everything, and we spent the next decade quietly building on my father's empire, determined to be far more successful than he was. We had many separate organizations that didn't know they were connected, and we ran enterprises and staged attacks for staggering profits. I've never considered myself a criminal because I created so many jobs and indirectly fed many families. The people we killed were usually destroying communities."

"That's awesome that you could make a difference for so many people," Will said, hoping it would keep Morgan talking.

"I had to make a lot of sacrifices. What sacrifices are you willing to make?"

Will felt ill. "Like what?"

"Would you be willing to kill a friend or family member if they stood in the way of doing what was right?"

Will leaned back in the saddle and hesitated. *Isn't that the worst job interview question ever?* "I can't pretend that it would be easy, but they say the ends justify the means, so if the ends were important enough—then you have to do what you have to do." As he said it, he felt like a part of him was dying inside.

"Part of the reason I told you that," Morgan said, "is so you realize that if I would kill my own mother because she stood in the way of my future . . . What do you think I would do to some random punk kid?"

"No kidding. I don't want to find out."

"You know, like the media and the public, I hated your family—my brother was killed in your father's bombing."

"I-I'm really sorry to hear that."

"His loss crushed me. No matter how much wealth I acquired after that, it couldn't satiate my thirst. I formed the Dreizack with the intention to one day emerge from the shadows and bring order and peace to our chaotic world. I wanted to stay ahead of what the US government was doing and learn more about my brother's death—so I became part of the CIA. Getting a security clearance wasn't a problem because I learned from my father how to keep my record clean. My CIA access to information furthered my ability to recruit members for the Dreizack, and when I learned about Project Black Hammer, I pulled all the strings I could to get affiliated with it. But before that, I learned about your father's bombing." Morgan paused, scrutinizing Will.

"What did you find out?"

"He didn't do it."

Will blinked several times. "What?"

"I wouldn't believe that your father knowingly transported a bomb into that hotel any more than I would believe someone telling me that a mall cop arrested Michael Donovan for shoplifting pink lip gloss. Your father could have made a much better bomb. The trail of bomb-making material to his SUV and house was sloppy and seemed like it was planted. And if he wanted to, he easily could have pulled it off without dying or getting caught. I don't think he knew there was a bomb in the crate he was transporting. There was actually a recorded statement from a CIA employee who said how much Michael was looking forward to spending time with his son that weekend."

Will thought of a picture his mother kept of his parents with him as a smiling baby, perched on his father's shoulders. "Why—why wouldn't they have told us that?" Will felt like his whole life's paradigm was being turned upside down. His mom and other family members had always said there was nothing to indicate that his dad would ever commit any kind of terrorist act, especially with the amount of compassion he showed others and the number of rescue missions he had been on with Delta Force followed by his service in the CIA.

Will often doubted what they said because of the supporting evidence showing his father's guilt. He was sure those who loved Michael were in denial. *But Morgan hated my father, and what he learned was enough to change his mind.*

"Because the government did it, and covered it up," Morgan said.

"But the explosion killed a lot of government officials," Will countered. So many people had strong emotions about his father, and Will didn't want his own emotions to get in the way of facts.

"It was a way for them to get rid of a lot of people who were against what they were up to. It's sick and horrible. Michael risked his life many times to save others, and I have no doubt that he was set up. He was a great man—the world really missed out on something exceptional when it lost Michael Donovan."

"Why didn't *you* expose them to the world?"

Morgan made a pained smile. "What, as a whistleblower? Because I didn't have a death wish! I didn't want to merely shed light on a corrupt government—I wanted to topple it."

"I see."

"Do you want to go back to the corrupt world we came from, or do you want to use our knowledge to reshape humanity from the ground up, and avoid centuries of war, disease, and rot?"

Will felt that if what Morgan said was true, it would completely change his perspective of the modern free world. He felt his desire to oppose the Dreizack wavering. No matter what, though, he needed to sound convincing. He tried to push away thoughts of people he cared about in the future. "I don't feel like I owe our future world anything—it could be a lot better in many ways."

"If you prove yourself, you could become like my squire—my apprentice. You're younger than the rest of us, and our legacy can only continue with a future generation of rulers. You would be respected and honored beyond your wildest dreams."

"I can't think of a bigger thrill."

"Neither can I."

Will was growing scared, scared that inside, a part of him was agreeing with Morgan.

22

———————

As they continued to ride, church bells tolled in the distance. "We're getting closer," Morgan said. The group picked up their pace. The trees became sparser, and in the distance, they could see the steeple of a church and a group of white buildings with dark brown timber frames topped with thatched roofs. Just beyond the buildings was a wide river with a large, faded white stone bridge extending across it.

On the other side of the river lay medieval London, with many more church spires pointing skyward, rising above the cramped housing. One structure stood out from them all.

"Is that it?" Johnson pointed across the river to their right. The large castle was near the banks on the opposite side, looming high above the buildings nearby. Its two outer walls bore large turrets and surrounded a much taller, bright white keep with its own grand turrets at each corner.

"That—is the Tower of London," Morgan said. "It's amazing to see it like this. In our time, the large keep was aged and no longer painted white."

"This whole time, I've been picturing just a tower," Skinner said.

"It's called the *Tower* of London," Morgan said, "because after William the Conqueror invaded England, he built the castle not only for defense but to *tower* over and intimidate the citizens of London. The large central keep is also known as the White Tower."

Will looked across the horizon and took in how much the castle overshadowed the smaller, tightly packed buildings around it. The visual difference was stark—whoever resided in the looming white tower was unquestionably in charge.

The stench of human and animal waste filled Will's nostrils as they neared the buildings. He braced himself, hoping the city interior wouldn't be worse. They continued along the street leading to the bridge, and people stopped to stare at the group of men on horseback.

"Is this *the* London Bridge?" Johnson asked, nodding to the immense whitewashed stone bridge with narrow, tightly packed three-story buildings built along both sides, leaving a central lane for travelers to cross.

"One of them," Morgan said. "They eventually fell down just like in the nursery rhyme."

"Do we ever need to worry about that?" Wolf asked.

"No. The first Roman bridge was destroyed in a Viking raid. The second was destroyed by a tornado. The third burned down. This one will last several centuries."

They slowed to a stop at the ominous gatehouse guarding the entrance to the bridge. Long spears jutted out from the top of the gatehouse's battlements, displaying impaled, rotting heads. The hollow eye sockets stared back at them in frozen terror.

Rashad turned on his horse to face Morgan and pointed to

the impaled heads. "Commander, I hope your sales pitch goes well."

They paid the bridge toll and continued onward. Most of the lower floors of the buildings lining the bridge were shops. The merchants, who assumed that men riding horses must have money, shouted solicitations to admire their wares. The Dreizack ignored them and continued across the crowded bridge.

Sailboats and rowboats glided up and down the River Thames. Will assumed the brown hue of the river was from sewage and debris. When they neared the end of the bridge, the fetid odor intensified, growing much worse than before. It was a stench so overwhelming, no amount of holding his breath could keep it from assaulting Will's senses.

The absence of plumbing accounted for the mass accumulation of human waste, and the smell was amplified by putrefying fish remains and animal entrails. The collection of refuse, perpetually fermenting in the soupy mud, pooled in the streets. Will focused all of his attention on not puking as his saddle steadily plodded up and down, and he cringed as he saw two cat-size rats fighting over an unidentifiable animal carcass.

"I can taste it in my mouth!" Johnson drawled.

In spite of the smell, the streets were packed with people. More merchants lined the roads, while others inspected their wares or traveled past. Many gave the Dreizack curious looks as they went by. A group of children was playing in the street. One boy had a hand-size, reddish-yellow sore festering on his neck. The raw, open skin made Will wince, even though the child didn't seem to give it a second thought.

As they neared the edge of the moat, there was a deep animal roar. Will's horse skidded to the side, and its head fixated on the direction of the noise. Will held the reins steady while looking for the source of the extremely out-of-place sound.

"That can't have been—" Dekker muttered.

"A lion, probably," Morgan said. "The Tower of London is famous for its Royal Menagerie of exotic animals, including large animals from Africa. That's probably the zoo." He pointed to a stout stone tower in the middle of the moat, with a causeway extending to it on both sides of the moat. "I remember reading somewhere that peasants who didn't have enough money to pay the entrance fee could gain admittance by bringing stray animals to feed the big cats."

Will petted his horse's neck and coaxed it forward.

The guards outside the first gatehouse warily tightened the grip on their poleaxes as they watched the group of strange men on horseback approaching. The Dreizack wore medieval cloaks with the hoods drawn back. Under the cloaks, they kept their modern military combat apparel, including body armor and combat boots. Several carried assault rifles strapped over their shoulders, and Wolf had his long sniper rifle. All of them had swords or axes at their belts. They were also letting their facial hair grow in. Morgan now had thick black stubble shadowing his face.

"Halt. State your business," one of the guards demanded.

"I am Sir Madoc Morgan, and these are my elite warriors and craftsmen. We seek an audience with the king so that we might provide His Grace with advanced gunpowder weapons."

"Gunpowder weapons are just noisemakers," another guard scoffed.

"The weapons we have are lethal—and accurate at a distance."

"Well, let's have a look then," said the first guard.

Morgan unslung the M4 rifle from behind his back and held it out for the guards to see.

They laughed. "I've seen cannons three times that size which weren't worth taking into battle. You must be daft if you think we'd trouble the king for this."

"Let me help you understand," Morgan said as he dismounted his horse, and the others followed suit.

Morgan pointed the rifle across the street at a merchant shop with a large clay pot among its wares. "Let's say that red pot was a French knight."

Will stood holding the reins of both his and Morgan's horses steady as Morgan fired a single shot. The pot exploded into pieces, and the horses reared their heads and pulled against the reins. Animals inside the Royal Menagerie noisily clambered. The shop merchant looked frightened and bewildered. Several people in the street gasped and distanced themselves from the shop.

Now it was the Dreizack's turn to laugh, but Morgan motioned for them to stop.

"I beg your pardon, sir," a guard said. "I've never seen anything quite like that."

"Sir Madoc," said the other guard, slowly approaching, "may I have a closer look at your weapon?"

"A look? I'll let you keep it." Morgan held out the rifle for the guard to take.

The guard's eyes widened, and he stretched out his hands. Before he could lay his fingers on the rifle, Morgan pulled it back.

"That is, after you grant us an audience with the king, and he approves of us manufacturing these weapons for all of his men—then yes, you may have one."

The guards exchanged glances, and one of them said, "I'll see that His Grace knows you're here." He turned and ran back down the causeway, shouting to more guards at the main castle gate.

After hours of waiting and having their weapons confiscated, they were led into the court. King Edward III sat on his throne at the far end of a large room with white-painted walls decorated with red and gold tapestries. Will noted that being able to keep something white was an obvious status symbol in a land where it seemed difficult to maintain cleanliness. A circular wooden chandelier hung from the high ceiling, ornamented with gold and bearing a ring of candles. The gold-encrusted white throne looked down on the room.

Will imagined that the king would be old, heavyset, and slouched—possibly being hand fed. He couldn't have been more wrong. Edward appeared to be in his thirties and the model of health and fitness. He had a warrior's build, and a light brown beard framed his face. He sat with his shoulders squared and feet planted in front of him, exuding confidence and strength even at rest. The fingers of his sword hand subtly tapped up and down on the throne's armrest in rapid succession. Will couldn't tell if the king was eager to meet with them, eager to have the meeting over with, or if he might just want to be out of the castle and in the thick of battle. Even if he wasn't seated on a throne elevated several steps above the rest, dressed in fine robes, Will was sure that if he were to walk into a room without any fanfare, he would still naturally exude a commanding presence.

A well-dressed young man, about Will's age, stood at the foot of the stairs to the right-hand side of the king. Will assumed he was Prince Edward because he was the spitting image of his father, minus the beard. Morgan had told the group earlier that the prince would become a legendary warrior, later to be known as the Black Prince.

There were several other men present besides the soldiers. Will assumed they were advisers. He glanced back as he heard the guards sealing the doors behind them.

Morgan walked ahead of the rest of the group and knelt before the king. The other Dreizack and Will also knelt. Will resented kneeling to anyone, but he didn't want to discover the consequences of not following suit.

"My liege," Morgan said.

"Rise," said the king with a naturally bold voice. "We presume the importance of your visit will merit the sense of urgency you implied. State your purpose."

"Yes, sire. My name is Sir Madoc Morgan. We are warriors and inventors, and have developed gunpowder weaponry that your lordship will find useful in your conquest of the Scots and French." His voice was also strong, and when he rose, his manner projected a sense of certainty that seemed an unspoken communication to the king that he was also a leader and warrior.

"So, you're merchants. Your accent is strange—where do you hail from?" Edward said.

"A land far across the ocean, settled by your subjects, and we wish to be of service to the Royal Crown. As to being a merchant—"

"Madoc Morgan?" the king interrupted. "As in Madoc, the Welsh Prince?"

"Yes, Your Grace," Morgan said, keeping his face neutral. Will had overheard Morgan mention to his men that he might be able to leverage his name to draw a correlation to the fabled explorer—making their story about being from an unknown land more believable. He also said there was a risk of this correlation creating trouble, and the Dreizack had debated whether Morgan should go by a different first name. This brought up commentary from Johnson about them regarding their commander as "Madoc Bloody Morgan, the King of Pirates" because of the famous pirate Bloody Morgan, and Madoc's passion to rule and plunder.

"Morgan is also a Welsh name. Are you one of Prince Madoc's descendants?" the king said, his eyes scrutinizing.

"How astute of you, Your Grace," Morgan said.

"So, is it true that he reached land sailing west two hundred years ago?"

"Yes, Your Grace," Morgan said.

"If this is true, then anyone on land he settled would owe fealty to me, as well as you and your men," the king said.

"Of course, Your Grace. This is part of the reason we have come. You can trust our allegiance to you."

"And them? Where are they from?" the king pointed to Romano and Rashad.

"They live in the same region. I assure you, all of us are faithful Christians, and loyal to the Crown. As to being a merchant—I am a noble, a military commander, and a visionary, not a simple merchant. We have not come here to merely exchange goods, but with a desire to help you manufacture advanced gunpowder weapons and to fight in your campaigns."

"You aren't dressed like nobility or a soldier," the king said.

"Your Grace, we prefer combat agility in our travels to fine raiment. A demonstration of our weaponry and fighting capabilities will validate this."

The king motioned for one of his advisers to come forward, who held an unloaded M4 automatic rifle.

Edward carefully inspected it while his son and advisers peered from the base of the steps. The king examined each component of the gun and looked down the barrel curiously, then handed it to his son.

"The opening for your cannon is very small," the king sighed. "While the unique metalwork is of some interest, it could only project a small pebble. It appears useless to breach a castle wall or gate."

"Quite so, Your Grace. That particular weapon would not be

used to breach a wall, but the range, accuracy, and repeating firing capacity far exceed the capabilities of any archer."

The king frowned. "That may be the case for your land, but I have the best bowmen the world has ever seen, and much larger cannons in my army. The cannons served to scare the Scots, but such weapons are so short-ranged and inaccurate that I don't see them as a prominent component of warfare— other than possibly destroying fortifications. We can see how your weapons stand compared to my archers. However, if you've only come to insult my military strength and waste my time, you'll find yourselves facing serious repercussions."

23

The Dreizack gathered their weapons, and the group went up to the roof of the White Tower, the central keep and highest portion of the castle. The keep had a broad roof surrounded by defensive parapets and small towers in each of the four corners. Will stood on the fringe of the group of men, keeping away from the edge of the wall and the ninety-foot drop below. He was gravely concerned that what was happening could alter the course of history, not to mention cut their lives short if they became enemies of the king. He debated his options and decided to continue pretending to be in league with Morgan for the sake of knowing what was going on at the seat of power.

"They're ready," Morgan said as he looked out across the River Thames. It was about a quarter mile from the White Tower to the opposite bank of the river, where Skinner and Johnson stood with several of the king's guards. They were on undeveloped marshland with four spears stabbed straight into the ground and iron helmets placed on the top of the spear shafts.

"You truly think you'll strike those helmets?" the archer chided. He was enormously muscular and casually held a longbow six feet in length at his side, almost as if it were an extension of his own body.

"First, we'll just see how close you can get—and how quickly you can loose your arrows," Morgan said.

"Certainly much faster than you." The archer brushed his shoulder-length golden hair to the side. "I could fire a thousand arrows in the time it takes to prepare a single shot from the cannons I've seen."

"Yes, but we certainly wouldn't waste His Grace's time by demonstrating weapons like those he has seen. Do you believe you'll be able to reach the helmets?"

"I could shoot beyond the helmets on a clear day—but there's a headwind. I can't say that they'll reach."

"Just see how close you can come," Morgan said. "The men on the opposite bank will take note."

The archer nocked an arrow to his bow and muttered, "Bloody waste of arrows."

"Your Grace, is this your best archer?" Morgan asked.

The archer stiffened.

"He'll suffice," the king said.

"Don't worry about arrows. I'll repay you for them," Morgan said with a wink.

The man drew the arrow back in a quick, fluid motion. His muscles bulged against the massive pull of the large bow. After loosing the first arrow, he drew back and sent off three more with lightning reflexes—the last arrow released while the first was still in the air.

The shafts sailed in perfect alignment with the helmets on the opposite shore. Two disappeared into the river near the far bank, and the others barely reached land, displaying their white goose feather fletchings above the tall grass.

Men on the tower and on the riverbank applauded. The archer looked to the king for approval, and the king gave a nod.

"Considering the wind, that is an exceptional distance for an attack on our enemy," King Edward said. "We anticipate our bowmen to be very effective against the French. Show us your *pebble cannon.*"

"Yes, my king," Morgan motioned for one of the king's advisers to bring the MSG90 sniper rifle. "I will have my marksmen demonstrate for you."

Will felt more nervous, and he parted his lips to speak, but no words came.

"Thank you." Wolf bore a smug smile and positioned the gun so the king could see him loading it. "These are my projectiles. We call them bullets."

Wolf took a knee and propped the sniper rifle on the rim of the wall. Everyone pressed themselves against the exterior wall, straining their eyes to see the small iron helmets in the distance.

For the sniper, this distance was trivial. He took aim and opened fire in four short bursts. One by one, the helmets shot off the tops of the spears, while the spears themselves jerked backward. A torrent of ravens cried out and flew from the courtyard. As the sound of the last shot hung in the air, the medieval men were speechless—their world had just been flipped upside down. Then they let out shouts of amazement.

"That has to be a trick!" one of the king's advisers said. "We'll see if the helmets were truly struck."

Wolf glanced back and frowned, then pointed his rifle to the sky and shot a raven in midflight.

The king's men on the opposite bank examining the helmets shouted and pointed with excitement.

Edward pointed at the rifle's scope. "This improves your aim?"

"Yes, Your Grace." Wolf flipped on the safety and placed the rifle into the king's outstretched hands.

The king raised his eyebrows upon first looking through the scope.

"Please be careful, sire," Morgan warned. "The weapons can be very dangerous if used by someone who has not had extensive training."

The king examined the weapon for a moment longer before handing it back to Wolf.

"Father, we knew the future was with long-range weapons!" the prince said excitedly. He pointed across the river. "With this accuracy, we could kill all the crossbowmen in a French castle before even coming in range of their bolts!"

King Edward eyed the opposite bank with his brows knit together. "And nearby cities might even surrender without conflict once they learned we had such weapons." He appraised Morgan a moment, then walked to him and firmly clapped him on the shoulder. "Madoc, Madoc, Madoc. This is quite impressive." He paused. "But in truth—what are you asking for in return?"

Morgan looked at him sincerely. "Only for the opportunity to serve you, my king."

The king scoffed. "Be more specific."

"We want to help you establish a specialized blacksmith shop for mass-producing these rifles. I highly recommend this be done at the Tower of London or an equally secure place. We want to rigorously train your men in using the rifles, then lead those troops on whatever campaigns you desire."

"You're not asking for payment?"

"A share of future plunder. And I owe your archer here four arrows," Morgan said with a smile.

The king and the other men laughed.

The archer looked conflicted, but then said, "Permit me one of the rifles you make, and we'll forget about it."

"There is one thing," the king said. "I, my son, and the knights of my order command God's English troops. I would be pleased to give you and your men titles, land, and perhaps lesser military leadership. However, that leadership would be under the command of men I have known for years."

"I understand your caution," Morgan said. "You and your son will ever maintain full command of all Englishmen. I cannot stress enough the technicality and potential danger of working with these weapons in a large group. You can have whomever you wish to command your swordsmen, bowmen, and so on—but I must insist on full command of all rifle legions. I'm afraid, for us, this point is not negotiable."

The king sternly gazed into Morgan's eyes. "I could take your weapons as a minuscule part of centuries of unpaid taxes from your land and imprison you and your men if you don't cooperate in manufacturing and training."

Morgan didn't flinch. "Your Grace, you certainly could, and you could even kill us if it suits you. However, my generous terms are the only way you'll be using these weapons to conquer cities. None of you even know how to make the ammunition if you decided to take them."

The king's expression hardened as he considered Morgan's words. "One thing I require of all men leading my troops is commitment. You commit to taking French cities for me, and we'll continue to have something to talk about."

"Of course, Your Grace. And there is no reason to stop with France," Morgan said.

The king's expression softened into a smile. "You'll tell me more. I see a potential arrangement." He clapped Morgan on the shoulder again and extended his hand. Morgan shook it with a calm smile.

Will felt his heart sink. He realized his mom, his grandparents, and everyone he knew might never be born. He looked at his hands. *I'm still here.* He'd overheard Morgan speaking with his men about the physics of time and space and how he believed that even if they were never born in the future, they would continue living in this time. *This probably changes everything—the future of the world! What do I do now?*

He felt weary as he watched others talk about where they could obtain large quantities of materials for gunpowder and how they could protect the rifle smithy along with the royal mint in the Tower of London. All of the men appeared relieved that they were moving closer to becoming allies.

Will watched in silence, though he wanted to alarm the king and his men. *You can't trust them—they're just manipulating you! They're going to eventually kill you and your son!*

"You must be hungry," Edward said. "We'll eat and drink in celebration as we discuss terms. You'll tell me more about your concepts for battle."

"Your Grace, we would enjoy that very much," Morgan said.

The group moved toward the door back into the keep. Will stayed at the rear of the group and shuffled in the direction the others were going. When he was about to pass through the doorway, a firm hand grabbed his shoulder, and he looked up to see Morgan eyeing him.

"I'll meet up with the rest of you," Morgan said to the group. "I need to stay a moment and have a word with my squire."

24

Once the others were gone from the roof of the tower, Morgan said, "So, William. There's something we need to talk about." He put his arm around Will and began walking him toward the edge of the tower wall. Will kicked himself for probably letting his poker face crack while he watched the Dreizack make arrangements with the king and his men.

They reached the edge of the wall overlooking the distant courtyard below, and Morgan maintained his firm grip around Will's shoulder. He swallowed as he considered the long drop.

"You seem a little shaken," Morgan said sternly. "I thought you would be pleased."

"I'm feeling very positive now—but for a moment, I was awestruck by the magnitude of what we're doing. The sheer possibilities overcame me. It's just so overwhelmingly exciting." He took a glance at the courtyard far below.

Morgan continued to scrutinize him. "You're too far in to back out now, or even falter."

"Yes, sir." Will swore that if he survived this moment, he would never let his guard down again. He had no doubt that

Morgan could easily push him from the wall and explain an unfortunate mishap. "I'm completely committed to this. Your showmanship was amazing."

A smile teased at the corner of Morgan's mouth. "That was a lot of fun for me. When we go back to join the others, if anyone asks you any questions, just refer them to me. And if you have any questions or concerns, get them out now."

Will thought of all the questions that had been burning in his mind. He decided that those about his relationship with the scepter should wait for when Morgan trusted him more. "I don't really understand how you—how we plan to govern people. If I did, I would feel more like I was part of the team."

Morgan sighed. "Think of all the civilizations, nations, or governments you're familiar with."

"Okay."

"Ours will be better than that."

Will smiled. "Can you be more specific?"

"Yes, but first, put yourself in context. You have more potential than nearly anyone I've met. Are you going to waste it? Your father was a remarkable person who dedicated his life to service and saving lives. You have that same kind of capacity. Right now, you have the greatest opportunity to help do that."

Morgan pointed across the city. "All of the poverty you have seen here—human waste lining the streets, peasants using their own feces to patch their houses together—this is the high end of luxury compared to what is scheduled to occur in Europe during the next decade. Millions of people are going to die from the Black Plague, and the streets will be strewn with heaps of rotting corpses . . . if we don't warn them how the disease spreads and make antibiotics. Approximately one out of every three people you've met here will die if we don't do anything—and that will be on us."

Will's heart sank as he thought of Emma, Garrett, Roland,

and the many others he had interacted with; one-third of them dying soon in agony.

Morgan continued, "But that's just a problem facing Europe in the near future. The rest of the world is a complete disaster. Standing on the top of this royal castle, you are looking at the current peak of the world's humanity and civility. From here, you can see symbols of high class—the royal mint, the royal zoo, a grand castle. The English have always had a reputation for sophistication, and Britain from our future time was about as courteous and polite as you can get."

Morgan gestured to the tower they were standing on. "But what else is here at the center of human decency? The king's own father, King Edward II—don't mention this to anyone, I'm sure it's a taboo topic—was murdered here by having a metal pipe inserted up his rectum and a burning hot spike pushed through the pipe and stabbing into his internal organs—because he was suspected of having a male lover."

Will shuddered. "That's horribly cruel."

"Welcome to the 1300s. And things don't change anytime soon. This castle is the site of gruesome murder, torture, and frequent execution for centuries. Remember all of the heads on spears at the entrance of London Bridge?"

Will nodded.

"Those people were likely taken into the castle by boat via that water gate, infamously known as Traitor's Gate." He pointed to the outer wall facing the river, where there was a narrow-gated entrance for boats from the river to pass into the moat, with a small harbor beneath the tower containing the king's residence. "Then they would be taken into the castle torture chambers to face a wide array of contraptions before their execution. Many don't survive the torture, but they are beheaded all the same. The others are likely beheaded just outside the castle walls for the delight of a cheering crowd.

King Henry VIII has two of his wives beheaded at a whim inside the castle courtyard right over there. Later, Queen Bloody Mary orders a killing spree across the country against her religious opposition."

Will could almost hear the screams of people he imagined being tortured and executed. The thought was gut-wrenching when added to the image of the decaying bodies lining the streets from plagues and thousands of family members wailing in sorrow.

"This island is a bloodbath for centuries. But compared to the rest of the world, it's just that—a nice, calm bath. Here, no one is eating the executed nobles or peasants. Meanwhile, there are groups of people on every continent practicing cannibalism. Right now, the Aztecs are sacrificing thousands of poor souls by ripping out each person's heart while they are still alive —and in many cases eating the victim's body. Yet, compared to much of the world right now, the Aztecs are a highly sophisticated civilization!"

Morgan continued, "The Dreizack can bring about peace, order, health, prosperity, safety and prevent the suffering of billions. You get to be a part of it, Will. You'll be able to be a ruler. Not only will you have the chance to vastly help humanity—you'll be unimaginably wealthy, and forever revered as a historical icon. Can you see how fantastic this is going to be?"

"Yes." Will couldn't deny that Morgan's vision was inspiring. "I mean, we would be celebrities, and with our knowledge we could spare the world of so many tragedies and injustices." He paused and bit his lip. "So, when we rule, would we give people civil rights?"

Morgan leaned back against the wall and gave Will an odd look. "Well, yes. Maybe not the slanted American misconception of civil rights, but yes, we would create a society where people could be happy and well provided for."

"What do you mean by slanted?"

"Will, you're a smart guy. Let's be logical. You want us to pass out muskets to each group of cannibals we encounter just so we can say they have the right to bear arms?"

Will shook his head. "I suppose not."

"And as soon as you have a nation where people think they have the right to free speech, you have blood in the streets over differences of politics, religion, and any number of grievances. Gutenberg is scheduled to make his famous printing press about a hundred years from now, adding dynamite to the fire. Uncensored words have enabled every major revolution that has taken place. And then there is the freedom of religion. Don't get me wrong, I'm not for an atheist state. Religion boosts morale and makes enforcing laws much easier. I just don't think religion should be a free-for-all. The pharaohs understood things well, and it's a shame that few empires have been able to replicate it. The most effective state religion is one where the government leaders are seen as an extension of deity, worthy of worship."

Will's head reeled trying to imagine what horrendous lies he was being asked to support so people could be subjected to such mental domination. "Okay," he said, trying not to sound fazed.

"And other items in the Bill of Rights, like the right to a fair trial by a jury of your peers. Seriously, who would want that? When you look at a jury, you're looking at a group of people too stupid to be able to talk their way out of doing jury duty. The only way you would want those guys determining your fate is if you were guilty and hoping for a free pass. Now how are you supposed to maintain order with a system like that? Most modern criminal justice systems are completely ineffective.

Inmates are glamorized on TV and given fine room and board in an iron-barred resort at the working taxpayer's expense. You're then left with a society that isn't afraid of defying the law and where the prisoners get better treatment than military veterans."

Will nodded to placate Morgan while trying to sort out what he did and didn't agree with. He had always been so focused on his own problems that he hadn't given much thought to the concepts that Morgan was firing through.

"At the end of the day, people don't really want all of these frivolously labeled *rights*. They want food in their bellies, they want safe communities, and they don't want to worry about tomorrow. People would rather have a government that would actually care for them than a cartoonish organization that they can boss around."

"How will you get people to change their culture and enforce all of this?" Will said.

"Just like the Romans—rule with an iron fist. You make people happy to obey and terrified to disobey. Kill people who object—for the safety of everyone, of course. Also, we'll have an open slave trade of prisoners who commit crimes rather than wasting funds on prisons. We'll also allow them to be subject to punishments that many might consider worse than death."

Will jerked his head up to look at Morgan, trying not to show expression. "Like what?"

"Just about anything, as long as it doesn't make them inoperable to work."

Will had to look away as he took in the gravity of what he was pretending to support.

"You have a problem with that?"

"I'm just trying to wrap my mind around scenarios worse than death." Will paused as the ramifications of the terrible concepts sank in. In some regards, the man had made valid points, but collectively his agenda felt so wrong. He could sense Morgan waiting for an answer, and he thought about what he wanted to hear. "We'll all be gods, and can do whatever we want."

Morgan grinned. "Exactly. And everyone will love us for it."

25

———————

Throughout the banquet, Will couldn't help imagining the face of each English person present covered with black, poxed boils and lying dead out in the London streets. *In a couple of years, many of these people will be stacked corpses if nothing changes. The soldiers, servants, nobles, and especially the people outside the castle. The merchants, the families—and the kids.*

Morgan seemed to calculate everyone as he encouraged them to talk. However, as time passed, he deferred discussing plans while the alcohol flowed around him. The king seemed to enjoy himself, but Will also thought that he seemed somewhat guarded throughout the evening and less merry than his men.

Will listened intently to the conversations, but people had stopped talking about anything substantive a while ago and were now leaving the great hall. He wanted to get some fresh air and better process everything that was going on, so he also excused himself. He walked through the castle until he found an isolated stone window peering out into the night sky of the old city. The sound of people in the streets was quieting down, and Will felt a guilty sense of comfort in not being able to see or hear them.

If I help change the future, all of those people won't die. He tried to force away the mental image of thousands of people weeping over dead loved ones in the street. *If I stop Morgan, their sorrow is inevitable. If I help him, instead of growing up resented—I could be a historical legend.*

He cringed. *But a legend for what? Being part of the foundation of a reign of actual terror?* He thought of all the people he knew in modern times who might not be born. If they were born, what would they look like as brainwashed victims worshiping generations of future Dreizack rulers?

He felt his stomach turn, and he leaned his arms on the window ledge. Was it even possible to go back home now that the king had seen modern guns? *But people here are already slowly shifting toward making guns. This isn't a new idea, and the king doesn't know how to make these yet.*

That might change starting tomorrow. He mulled over the plans he'd overheard about traveling south tomorrow to obtain supplies for making gunpowder and building a smithy for manufacturing at the Tower of London.

Will withdrew the penny from a small leather pouch on his belt. He had looked at it many times when he was alone, as the one thing that tied him to home. He'd thought about discarding it before—it seemed to just make him homesick. The tails-up, old, unlucky penny dated 2006. One year short of a lucky seven. He felt the indentations of Lincoln's profile on the penny and remembered how the president had helped free people from slavery. *What am I going to do about Morgan's conquest with slavery? What if I let the Dreizack begin their quest for world domination and then wait until they age and die? They would still do a lot of evil, but maybe if I'm left in charge, I could change everything and prevent centuries of other injustices and atrocities.*

He thought about how his paradigm of his father had shifted based on what Morgan told him. *Would my father support Madoc Morgan for decades out of hope of being a good influence after Morgan died? Would he refuse to sacrifice his life to save millions, if not billions, of people so that he could be born?* Will thought about his father's military service and how family members described him. Will knew that at least the answer to the second question was *no*.

He thought again about his mother and grandparents. *Even if there is a chance that the Dreizack haven't permanently altered the future, and my family might still be able to be born—can I imagine my mom or grandparents saying, "Go ahead and let one out of every three people on a continent die from the plague, let slavery abound, let the Holocaust happen, and let every other atrocity of the last seven hundred years proceed—just so I can be born."*

He couldn't imagine their voices saying anything like that. *Yet—Morgan's utopia is worse than the future I grew up in. Is there a way to keep him from having power and also save millions of people?*

Morgan had assigned Will to stay in a room with Skinner. There was only one bed, and Skinner told Will there was no way he was sharing it. Will had been sleeping on a bedroll for several days and didn't mind rolling one out on the floor.

Throughout the night, Will intentionally coughed, sniffled, wheezed, and moaned. Skinner periodically yelled at him to be quiet. Will apologized but continued to make the sounds even louder, acting as though he was trying to stifle them.

"I'll cut your lungs out if you don't shut up!" the man shouted. But Will knew he wouldn't actually kill him—not without Morgan's approval.

At the first sign of dawn, Will got up and groaned. "If it's all right, I'm going to step out and get some fresh air. I feel really awful. I'm not going to be able to eat breakfast."

Skinner grumbled as he rolled over in bed. "Fine, get. You should have left last night."

Will was about to walk out when Skinner sat up and said, "Wait, Commander Morgan doesn't want you running off anywhere." He slowly reached up and cradled his head, wincing from the headache brought on by a night of drinking.

"Of course not," Will said. "I'll just be in the courtyard, out in the open, where everyone can see me. I just need to get out of this stuffy room."

Skinner frowned while groggily processing the information. "I don't want you here at all, but I'm not getting up, and Commander Morgan doesn't want you to be unaccounted for."

"I won't be 'unaccounted for.' I'll be in the courtyard. If I were going to run off, I would have done that while you were sleeping."

"Trying to sleep!"

Will put one hand over his abdomen, held up his other hand apologetically, and gagged as if he were about to throw up.

"Just get out! And don't leave the courtyard. I swear, if I get sick, I'm going to tear your arm off and beat you with it!"

"Thank you, sir." Will nodded, and before Skinner could change his mind, he slipped out of the room. After closing the door, he made a loud, hacking cough that ended in a series of gags. He heard Skinner curse and throw something against the door. Will would have smiled if he hadn't been so fixated on what he was going to attempt.

He moved out into the misty gray morning air. The king's residence wasn't in the White Tower; it was in another tower above the small harbor in the moat. Will was told that nobility rarely traveled through the streets in London because it was more difficult to protect them and they could travel faster on the calm river than they could in the crowded thoroughfares. When the king traveled to the castle, his boat would pass through a water gate in the long stone wharf wall that separated the river from the moat. Once the boat was in the moat, it could pass through another water gate in the tower containing the king's residence. Then the boat would dock in a small, shallow harbor inside the castle walls.

Will reached a doorway to the tower and carefully went up the stairs. He knew he couldn't just go knocking on doors. *That would probably get me beheaded. I'm going to have to trust someone to get me access to the king.* His first intention was to find the servant who brought food to the king. Hopefully, they would allow him to deliver his message.

Will reached the top of the stairs, but he froze when he heard footsteps moving toward him in the corridor. Part of him wanted to hide until he could see who it was, but the only place he could go was back down. The footsteps were getting closer. He would have to run from this person—or let them see him.

Will stepped into the hallway and was surprised to see the lord chancellor, who'd spoken with the Dreizack the night before.

"'Tis odd of you to be here." The chancellor frowned.

"I need to relay an urgent message to the king."

"You? At this morning hour? If it was so important, why wouldn't your master or one of his men deliver it?"

Will paused. "It's regarding the king's safety, and I'm the only one who knows."

The chancellor raised an eyebrow. "Well, out with it then."

"It is for the king's ears only."

"I am the eyes and ears of the king. He does not have time for everyone in the realm to impose upon him. Tell me, and I will relay the message if it has any substance."

"I'm afraid I cannot. It is of such imminent importance and urgency that I can only tell the king."

The chancellor's face resembled a cold granite wall as he stared at Will. "I will tell the king that you have a message. He will determine whether to see you. He may also command that you first confide in me so that I may determine if the matter merits His Grace's time."

Will nodded. "Thank you. I promise it will merit his time."

"You should not thank me. You may incur repercussions from the king if your message is deemed to lack sufficient merit."

The words sent a shiver down Will's spine. The chancellor commanded him to wait in a spacious room nearby, where the white walls were accented with exposed dark timbers. Small red flowers were painted in rows on sections of the wall. The positioning of the wooden furniture made it appear that the room was used for small social gatherings.

"Sit here, and don't touch anything," the chancellor commanded as he pointed to a wooden chair.

As Will waited, he continued to rehash what he was about to do. He wasn't sure how much patience the king would have for him—if he were allowed to see Edward at all. He wondered what Celeste would do and hoped she was okay.

The view from a nearby window was obscured with bleak gray fog, and Will felt that his outlook on what was about to happen was equally cloudy.

He finally heard footsteps coming down the corridor. The chancellor entered and waved impatiently for Will to follow. "Come, lad."

Will stood. "Will the king speak with me?"

"Yes, but this had better be substantive. If it is not, and the king or your master don't kill you, I just might."

The chancellor quickly walked away, and Will kept pace alongside him.

Will replied, "It would be treason for me to say nothing."

"We shall see."

They reached a large door with two guards standing outside it. Will wondered if the guards were always outside the king's chambers or if they were there because of him.

The chancellor knocked on the door. "Your Grace, the youth is here."

"Enter," a voice commanded from inside.

The chancellor opened the door, and he and Will stepped inside. The trappings of the room spoke loudly of the king's pomp and power. The walls were painted with elaborate floral designs. A pristine white fireplace emanated a warm glow from the hearth, and the wall above displayed a coat of arms with four sections.

Will had overheard Morgan explaining the coat of arms before they arrived in London. Two of the quadrants diagonal from each other had images of three lions, representing the three regions ruled by Edward III—England, Normandy, and Aquitaine. The other two quadrants bore French fleurs-de-lis, representing the Kingdom of France, which he did not rule, but felt entitled to enough that he preemptively incorporated it into his coat of arms.

Will couldn't help but notice that the white fireplace, while technically the least clean object in the king's residence, was cleaner than anything owned by most of the people he ruled.

A large bed with tall timber posts and a long red curtain that could be drawn around it stood in one corner of the room. In the other corner was a doorless entrance into a small oratory room with a tall, stained-glass window looking down on a table bearing two large candlesticks and a golden crucifix standing in the center.

At the center of the bedchamber, the king sat at an ornately carved white table with gold leaf incorporated into the woodwork. There were three other chairs on the opposite side of the table, giving Will the impression that the king was accustomed to conducting business here. Will felt the posturing of such meetings further added to the king's projected air of superiority. To a person who traveled from far away to meet with Edward while still in his bedchamber, the meeting location surely would drive home the sentiment of coming to "kiss the ring."

The king's posture and facial expression would have conveyed that he was relaxed—except for his eyes. They were meticulously assessing Will.

"This is Sir Madoc's squire," the chancellor said. "His name is William."

The king nodded. "You may go."

Will stepped forward and knelt. "Sire, thank you for—"

"Rise," Edward said. "What is it that is so secretive that my lord chancellor or your master could not have relayed to me?"

"My lord, my loyalty is to you above all else, and it is my humble duty to inform you that on multiple occasions, Madoc Morgan has said that he intends to kill you after he uses your royal funds to build an army for himself."

"Truthfully? What precisely did he say?" Edward's brow furrowed.

Will continued, "As soon as he leads your troops bearing gunpowder weapons on a conquest of France, he anticipates using funds from plundering to develop even more sophisticated weapons than what he will build for you. He'll use those weapons to turn and take all of England."

The king leaned back. "You heard him say all of this?"

"Yes."

Edward stared deep into Will's eyes, weighing his words.

His face seemed shadowed with concern. "And—how did he say he would kill me?"

Will maintained his gaze. "He wasn't specific, but he is capable of many forms of assassination."

The king looked away for a long moment. Then his pensive expression softened, and he shook his head. "My poor boy, I'm afraid you've had a misunderstanding."

Will felt like he might sink through the floor. "Sire, he and his men discussed their plans in front of me on multiple occasions."

"Your master understands the way our kingdom works. He would not replace me as king whether I was murdered or died of natural causes. There is a noble line of succession of those who will come after me, of which he is not a part. He knows this."

Will began to speak, but the king decisively waved for him to be silent. "As to the idea that he could make his own army— no one is allowed to raise troops or develop weapons without my permission. He could not raise so much as a small gathering without my approval, and to do so would be an act of treason. He also knows this. I intend to supply him with fabulous wealth and power for his service. With all the wealth of Europe and the Holy Land on the horizon, starting a war with his only ally would be foolish." King Edward paused and steepled his hands. "Tell me, what quarrel do you have with Sir Madoc? He appears to be feeding you well."

"Sire, I have no quarrel with him. It is my duty to report what I have heard—"

"So, apart from his desire to take my kingdom, he is a perfect man and has done you no wrong?"

"He enjoys murder and cruelty. He is a gifted liar, and he has no chivalry. He is not a nobleman, and only just started calling himself 'Sir Madoc.'"

The king frowned. "I can see your disdain for him. It's written on your face."

"I hate what he plans on doing to people, far apart from what is necessary to establish order. You think you can contain him—he's not someone who shares power."

The king pressed his lips together, then exhaled. "You hate what he enjoys doing to people? You mean things such as taking you far away from your homeland so that he could serve me, holding a girl hostage whom you fancied in order to save the life of his men, maintaining in good keeping a mace which you long for, and of course, attacking your uncle?"

Will stood speechless. The room that at first seemed large now felt like it was closing in on him.

The king smiled and gave a laugh. "Of course, I might sympathize with your desire to seek revenge, but when doing so interferes with the destiny of England and maligns an important ally of God's chosen king—it's simply treason."

"No, Your Grace—"

"Would you not say so, Sir Madoc?" The king turned to look toward the small oratory room.

Will watched in horror as Madoc Bloody Morgan stepped from around the corner and into the doorway. Fire smoldered in his eyes, and the pale white blade protruded from a clenched fist at his side. "Yes, Your Grace. I would consider it high treason—of the grossest kind."

26

———————

The king took in the look on Will's face. "Young squire, Sir Madoc told me yesterday of your occasional fits of insanity and your inclination to make absurd outbursts. He told me of what you've said in your sleep. You mentioned some of it, but I hoped to hear your beliefs about Sir Madoc and all of his men being wizards, and how you could travel through the air if only you could bear his mace." He gave a sad smile. "I asked why he kept you in his service, and he said you were otherwise very capable. He also spoke at length of his fatherly concern for your well-being. Well, we can clearly see how you have repaid his goodness. Tell me, Madoc, what do you think of your squire now?"

"As you said so well, Your Grace—he's a traitor." He slowly walked toward Will. "William Donovan, what a disappointment."

"Coming from you, I'll take that as a compliment."

"Coming from me? A soon-to-be distinguished agent of the king, in the greatest of world conquests? Part of my pity for you was because of what happened to your father. I probably have more in common with him than anyone you've ever met. I can't believe how you would turn on me." He took a step closer. "This castle is renowned for its sophisticated torture devices. I think you should make their acquaintance."

"I will not endorse the torture of this confused youth," the king said. "I believe he intended well, but is touched with insanity. However, I cannot let someone go about spreading disparaging lies, especially someone who knows so much about our campaign." The king briefly made a pained expression. "Young squire—I'm afraid there is only one way to ensure that your treasonous words are never spread. Guards!"

Will felt as though a dark wind had swept his soul from his body. He had no words now. No plan. His throat felt as dry as scorched earth.

The door burst open, and the two armored men stepped in.

"Lock him up. He is to be executed for treason." The king dismissively waved his hand and turned to speak with Morgan as if Will were just an unpleasant task to be crossed off.

Will didn't internalize the words Edward said to Morgan, only the dismissive tone and his relaxed posture. The man had just decided that Will would die with about as much emotion as disposing of an inconvenient rodent. Molten resentment welled up inside of him. *He can't just casually decide that I should die. How many innocent lives have been lost so that people like these two can chase wealth and power?*

A hard hand slapped the back of his head. "C'mon. Get movin', boy," one of the guards said. But Will refused to break his seething, rebellious glare at the king. Anger's fire gave him renewed strength.

"I said get!" The guard kicked Will hard in the thigh. The other guard drew his sword.

Will's eyes flitted to the blade and back at the king. "You

aren't going to use a sword in here. You'd stain the poor king's rugs."

This drew Edward's attention, and he turned back to Will. "I hoped you would appreciate my mercy in sparing you from torture. Your sacrifice is necessary for the betterment of the realm."

One of the soldiers grabbed Will from behind, pinning down his arms.

Will looked dead into the king's eyes, and he worked to control the emotion in his voice. "I hope you remember me right before Bloody Morgan has you beheaded."

Edward leaped to his feet and moved toward Will, but before the king could close the distance, Will swung his fist down into the guard's groin. The man gasped and loosened his grip. Will ducked under his arms and fled out the open door.

"Stop him!" the king commanded.

Will sprinted forward and heard swords scraping the throats of scabbards as men ran after him. The hallway soon ended, and as he rounded the corner, his pointed peasant shoes slipped on the smooth stone floor and he collided into the wall.

"You're dead!" Morgan yelled as he closed in.

Will managed to stay on his feet and continued to run. His heart lurched as he saw that the hallway ended in a closed door. He prayed it would open as he wrenched the metal handle.

The door swung wide. Will burst through and ran outside the tower onto a short causeway between the outer and inner wall. Continuing the mad dash, he heard the guard and Morgan shouting behind him and saw guards on other towers running toward Will.

"Kill him! Kill him!" Morgan shouted.

Will ran inside the tower on the other side of the causeway. He had no idea where to go. He was now farther inside the castle, making escape more difficult. Disorientation overwhelmed him, but he knew he needed to get to an outer gate or to the moat. The wharf wall would trap him from being able to swim from the moat to the river, and he would have to get to the other side of the castle in order to swim to the city.

He desperately looked for an exit from the tower and ran up a stairwell. The shouts from the guard bit after him. He found a door and ran out onto a long stretch of wall walk. The inner wall was much higher than the outer, and in his peripheral vision, he could see the guards converging toward the tower ahead of him. The chances of getting to the other side of the castle looked grim.

Shouts came from all around the castle grounds, and footsteps pounded close behind him. Will was too terrified to look back, and he churned his legs as fast as they could move.

Two guards stepped onto the wall walk ahead of him, one with a sword and shield, the other with a long poleaxe.

"Finish him off!" the guard behind Will yelled.

The faces of the men ahead of him lit up with sadistic smiles. *I can't stop. They're going to enjoy killing me, and they don't even know why they're supposed to do it.* They charged toward Will with their weapons raised.

He glanced at the ground far below. The fall might be survivable, but he wouldn't be able to walk. Armed soldiers on both sides of the wall jeered up at him.

In a few more sprinting strides, he would collide with the sharp weapons of the men in front of him.

Will sprang to the side, placed one foot onto the wall's battlements, and jumped toward the guards ahead of him, with half of his body over the edge of the wall and the other half over the long drop below.

He felt the tip of a sword tear through the back of his tunic. His back arched, but he didn't take his eyes off his target. The man with the sword and shield in front of him swung his sword across his body into the space where Will had been. Will heard the guard behind him let out a blood-chilling scream. In midair, Will grabbed the top of the man's shield and pulled himself back toward the edge of the wall walk with all his strength, kicking both feet into the chest of the man with the poleaxe. The guard released the weapon, flailing his arms as he fell from the wall. Will felt a release of tension on the shield as its owner screamed while diving headfirst to the ground on the opposite side.

Will thudded onto his back, knocking the wind out of him. Then he lurched the shield over his head, gasping for air. A blow didn't come. He peered around the shield only to see the guard behind him lying motionless in a pool of blood. Will cringed. *What happened? Where is Morgan?* It took him a moment to piece together that the guard in front of him had connected with the throat of one behind.

He looked around. The sound of yelling from around the castle rang in his ears. The castle guards had just seen three of their friends go down. For a moment, Will pitied them. He recognized one of the voices yelling and looked back to the water gate tower, where Morgan was standing, waving his arms and barking orders. *He must not have wanted me to move to any new sections of the castle without seeing where I went—always the head of the snake.*

Will was still breathing heavily, frantic for options. An arrow collided with the battlements beside his head, and he crouched into a ball behind the shield. Several more arrows ricocheted against the stone near him. His shield jolted as an arrow pierced it. He couldn't stay here—he had to keep moving forward.

Looking up at the tower ahead of him, Will saw a man with a drawn bow step onto the ramparts. Will positioned the shield between himself and the archer. His whole body tensed. He knew his side and back were now exposed to arrows from the more distant archers, but he was out of ideas. He took in the sounds of men shouting threats, Morgan barking orders, running footsteps—and the grinding sound of a gate rising.

Will's ears perked up. The sound of the gate was coming from near Morgan, the area of the water gate. A second arrow pierced his shield, and another hissed by as it nearly grazed the back of his neck. Will was soaked in sweat. He glanced over the battlements at the water gate, but it wasn't moving. He was confused. Where else could the sound be coming from? Then he realized it was the wharf water gate between the river and the moat. *They're letting someone in or out of the moat by boat!*

Will leaped to his feet and turned back toward the water gate—back to Morgan. He kept the shield covering his back, scooped up a sword, and ran in a semicrouched position to make himself a smaller target. Arrows continued to whiz past him, and one glanced off the shield. He continued in a full-out run onto the causeway between the inner and outer walls. Morgan still stood at the top of the water gate tower, murderous intent engraved on his face, his eyes piercing Will like javelins.

He caused all of this. The death of the guards. The death of everyone since before we came here. The death and suffering of millions to come. Now he stands at the top of the tower, blocking my freedom. Will knew his only path to escape meant facing Morgan.

He entered the water gate tower and headed to the roof. Will felt leery as he entered the top of the tower but knew he couldn't slow down. *He knows I'm coming. I don't hear him shouting for guards to converge on this tower. He's waiting for me.*

Will positioned the shield in front of himself and swung the sword around the corner, hoping to connect with Morgan.

The sword clanged off the stone wall. Then there was an

explosive sound, and Will jolted as a bullet passed through his shield and grazed his forearm. The pain was excruciating and sent Will spinning off balance, but as he circled, he hurled the sword at Morgan.

The blade whipped through the air at Morgan's chest. The man dropped down to avoid the weapon, and Will made a mad dash for the tower's edge facing the moat. He released the shield and threw himself headfirst over the side of the wall.

There was another gunshot, and the bullet tore through the edge of the loose fabric of his tunic. His arms and legs flailed as his face accelerated toward the water. He caught a glance of the nobleman's boat entering through the water gate in front of him. They would close the gate any second. He winced and extended his arms, hoping to avoid breaking his neck on the bottom of the moat.

Will exploded into the cold, murky water, and his arms crumpled as his hands met with soft mud and weeds. He pushed away and felt the mud slide between his fingers as he propelled his arms and legs toward the dim light of the gateway. His body cried in pain as it met the resistance of the water against his battered limbs. The bullet wound in his arm had missed the bone, but it still felt like a searing-hot iron. Will tried to block out the pain, knowing that Morgan would shoot him if he surfaced and was probably already ordering the wharf water gate closed.

His shoes came off as he kicked through the water, and he could faintly hear the clanking of the gate. He swam harder as his lungs begged for air, hoping not to be impaled by the crashing spikes.

Will felt the whoosh of the gate plunging through the water just behind his feet as he entered the clearer water of the river. His lungs felt like they were going to burst, and he couldn't hold his breath any longer. He gave a few more kicks to get around the edge of the wharf wall and out of sight of people in the nobleman's boat. Then he swam upward, trying to make as little noise as possible as his face broke the surface.

He looked to the top of the wharf, unsure if someone had seen him through the muddy water. Men were shouting, still looking for him in the moat. His chest continued to heave for air as he swam along the side of the wall and farther away from the gate. The wharf wall was slick with green-brown moss, and he couldn't cling to a single indentation in the weathered stone. He took in the expanse of the river and felt stranded. Even if he had the energy, there was no way he could swim across without being seen.

Will looked down the length of the wall toward the city. *There has to be some point where I can climb out of the water. It's only a matter of time before someone looks over this side of the wall.*

"We will not stop looking for him until we find him or his body!" Will heard Morgan shout. He felt his adrenaline fading. He held up his arm and looked at the bleeding wound. *Well, that's going to get infected—if they don't kill me first.*

Eventually, Will reached the small boat dock in the wharf wall, but he hesitated to climb out. He thought about waiting until dark, but even if the guards didn't search that area, he would certainly draw attention from everyone using the dock. He peeked up to see the top of the wharf. There were several small buildings, but he would be exposed for a moment before he could get to them. The men on the castle towers still seemed to be focused on the moat. A small sailboat slowly passed him on the river, and the three men aboard were looking back at him. *I've gotta go.*

Will climbed onto the top of the wharf and walked away from the castle. He fought the urge to run, knowing it would only draw attention. His bare feet hurt as he stepped across the uneven stone. He knew he was leaving a trail of water and hoped no one from the castle would notice. His arm and back stung, and surely the back of his brown tunic displayed a gash and a dark red stain.

"There he is! That's him!" someone yelled from the castle. Will felt as though a torrent of ice shards had pierced through his wet body. He fought the urge to bolt away. Maybe if he didn't seem concerned about their shouting, they might not think he was the person they were after.

"Go! Go! To the gate. After him!"

Will ran.

27

Will's bare feet slipped out from under him on the wet, mossy stone, and he crashed to the ground. Sharp pain shot through his body as he landed directly on the cut on his back. He jerked onto his side, and every muscle from his fingers to his toes tensed in agony. His vision blurred with pain as he bared his teeth in a silent scream. He could still hear shouting. It was getting closer. No way to escape. He'd done his best, and now he felt broken.

But Will lifted his eyes—it seemed like the refuge of the city buildings was so far away. *I'm not giving up. I'm not giving them another win.*

"Stop him! The boy's a criminal!" a guard yelled from the castle wall.

Will winced and mustered his remaining reserves to stand. He pressed forward to the city, but two large boatmen approached him.

"Ho there, stop, lad!" one of the men said.

Will was still trying to catch his breath, but he knew his only hope of escape was past these two men.

One of the boatmen reached out to grab him. Will shoved the man's arms away and ran as fast as his bare feet could carry him. He heard the two men behind him, but he didn't dare look back as he raced to the city cobblestone and darted into the streets.

He heard hooves galloping on the stone bridge spanning the moat from the castle to the Lion Tower, and then from the tower to the city. They'd send everyone after him, and the citizens wouldn't have a reason not to point to where he went.

Will rounded a street corner, looking for another place to turn—anything to throw the riders off course. The sound of hooves was growing closer, and he looked back to see a commoner pointing toward him. Will's face contorted in pain as he propelled himself down the street.

There was nowhere for him to turn, and a bustling crowd blocked the way ahead.

"Get out of the way! Get out of the way!" he yelled as he collided with people, knocking several to the ground.

"Watch it, you bloody dalcop!" someone yelled after him.

"Raggabrash!" cried another.

Other commoners hurled insults after Will as he barreled up the street. Several men looked like they were thinking about stopping him. For all they knew, he was a thief knocking people over while fleeing the law. Will moved with such frantic speed that no one was ambitious enough to intervene, but the people still jeered after him.

"Filthy rubbish!"

"Thief!"

"They're gonna kill you!" a woman cackled. It wasn't the words, but the amusement in her voice that struck Will to the core—that someone he didn't even know would think him getting killed was amusing.

Someone threw a rock at Will's head. It missed, but another thudded into the back of his shoulder. He fell to his knees, and several people laughed.

Shaking himself, Will got up and forced himself to run to another street. He turned again in the ancient city's disarrayed labyrinth of roads. He was surprised that he no longer heard horses but knew there was no way he could hide anytime soon due to the help the soldiers would receive from the city's residents.

He continued to weave from street to street until he couldn't run any longer and finally hobbled to a walk. Hopefully, the slower gait would make him stand out less to someone going about their daily routine. Will made sure no one was looking when he turned onto another street, longing for a place to hide. He saw a dark, narrow space between two buildings, just big enough for him to slip through. After looking around to see that no one was watching, he reluctantly went inside.

Will collapsed onto his knees behind a pile of refuse. His mouth felt like a parched desert, and a filthy puddle seemed to taunt him. He was desperate for something to drink, but the stench made the water unpalatable.

I failed. The fate of the world depended on me, and I failed. He thought about the guard lying in a pool of blood on the castle wall walk and the crunching sounds the other two men had made when they hit the ground. He squeezed his eyes shut as if doing so might erase the memory. He thought about the promise he'd made to his mother seemingly millions of years ago—that he wouldn't get into fights—and smirked. *I guess I broke that one.* Then he choked. *I'll never see her again. I'll never see anyone again. The horrific things I've imagined are going to happen. I no longer have the option to improve the world after the Dreizack conquer it.*

With his adrenaline dying off, the pain from his wounds screamed at him. The skin on his left forearm was torn open from being grazed by the bullet, and bits of mud and moss nestled in the exposed flesh. He flicked at several wet pieces of dark green, which just caused more pain. What was the point? There was no way he could keep it from getting infected.

The cut on his back throbbed, though it didn't feel like it had reached bone. His ribs were bruised from landing on the wall, his knees sore from falling. Not to mention the rock to the back of his shoulder. He struggled to find the least painful position to sit in.

Will regretted trying to be a spy in the Dreizack ranks and giving up the scepter to Morgan. He wondered if Celeste was all right and thought about what lay in store for her. *She'll probably marry that prick.* He felt his reasons to keep trying, to keep going, unraveling.

Best-case scenario, I live the life of a peasant fugitive in the Dark Ages and watch as the Dreizack pillage humanity. If they catch me, I'm dead—and if Morgan can have his way, he'll make it slow.

He thought about the occasions before time traveling when his desire to live wore thin. There had been so much going on recently that those feelings had been kept at bay. *I've always had some purpose since we were attacked in the desert. I was helping people—or failing to help people.* He tried to think of how he could be of any benefit to anyone and winced in pain as he shifted his weight.

His eyes fell, coming to rest on the dagger at his waist. *What was it they said about defeated soldiers? They slit their own bellies when failure was certain?* He looked away from the dagger to the putrid puddle of water.

But seriously—what do I have to live for? However they decide to kill me will be worse. Is this dagger the only friend I have left?

He swallowed and thought about how long it would be

until nightfall. There was no way of obtaining clean food or water. He thought about the fate that awaited him once he left hiding. More and more, the dagger seemed like the easier option.

Frowning in disgust, he squeezed his eyes shut and tried to think of anything that he would want to live for—anything he could appreciate about being alive. It felt like a long time before he realized how frantic Morgan must be without finding Will or his body. A wry smile visited Will's mouth as he thought of Morgan's face pulled taut, dark brows drawn together in worry, barking orders at his men, and them anxiously doing their best to appease him. Will imagined Morgan unable to sleep, restlessly pacing a stone floor, wondering whom Will might tell about their plans. He also imagined the king being unsettled and remembering Will's face—knowing that Will's life was much more than a trifle to flit away.

Just being alive was a small victory—even if each breath was merely a nuisance to his enemies. *I made it this far and can keep trying to evade them. I just have to find an enemy of the king who would also have motives for stopping the Dreizack. Options would include nearly everyone in Scotland and France. I'm not out of this fight, and the reason I can easily imagine Morgan being frantic is because he knows I'm not out of it yet.*

He tried to reassure himself by acknowledging that each of his wounds could have been much worse. He thought about what his mom would want him to do, and even though she wasn't alive, he knew he was loved. No matter what anyone did or said, she had loved him enough to give him life, and she hadn't done that just for him to end it in a gutter.

His thoughts were interrupted by someone whistling in the street. The sound was growing closer. Will pressed himself behind the refuse between him and the street and kept as still as possible. The person was only a few feet away from him now

—he realized he recognized the melody. *Who in the world would be whistling that?*

He waited for the person to pass, and the music became fainter. Then he peeked over the refuse and crept forward to peer into the street. *Who in the world would be whistling the theme to* Star Wars?

A man wearing a cloak was walking away from him. He held a crossbow in one hand. The hood was down, showing sandy, light brown hair.

Will felt himself well with hope. "Uncle Chase?"

The man spun around. His tired face, its light brown stubble now grown in, filled with relief. "Will!" he breathed.

Chase ran back to him, and they embraced. Will motioned for his uncle to follow him into the confined hiding space.

"I've been so worried about you!" Chase said, keeping his voice low.

"I've been worried about you too. I wasn't sure if you were here—or even alive."

"We saw you yesterday on top of the White Tower. We've tried to get to you but weren't expecting you to be chased out of the castle."

"We?" Will asked.

Chase grinned. "Yeah, wait a moment." He cautiously looked out into the street, then made three whistles.

A boy came running around a corner. A boy Will had thought he would never see again. He wore dingy peasant clothes and a sword at his hip.

When Danny finally saw his friend, his face broke into a huge smile. He ran into the alley and nearly tackled Will in an embrace.

Will fought the urge to laugh out loud when Danny first reached him, but he nearly bit through his own lip as he tried not to cry out in pain.

Danny quickly let go as Will grimaced.

"Are you okay?" he asked in a hushed tone.

"Never better," Will lied.

"What happened to your arm?" Chase whispered in alarm.

"Oh, it's just a flesh wound," Will smiled, knowing Danny would get the reference to the movie *Monty Python and The Holy Grail*, grateful he was once again among friends.

"No, it isn't. Your arm's off," Danny said, though his voice was void of humor as he gazed at the open line of red skin from where the bullet had grazed.

"I'll worry about it when we're out of this place. Where can we go that's safe?"

"Probably nowhere right now," Chase said, his voice dropping even lower. "The whole garrison is looking for you. What happened in the castle?"

"I'll tell you," Will said, "but I'm dying to know what happened to you guys first."

"All right, I'll go first," Chase said, "but only because you're injured. After the Dreizack attacked the president, I woke up in the rain—dazed and my shoulder bleeding. I don't know if Madoc wanted to torture me into submission or just kill me slowly. I was near Madoc and several of his men, but I got away. They heard me, and I think Madoc guessed that it might have been me in the darkness. He shouted after me that they'd already killed you. I was so relieved to see you alive! Anyway, after tending well enough to my wound that I didn't bleed to death, I found this kid at dawn, gawking around Littlehampton like an American tourist."

"Oh, you only ID'd me because of my modern clothes," Danny said.

"We didn't know if you were alive or not, and we knew we needed to stop the Dreizack from altering history. So I cauterized my wounds, and we made our way here, hoping the king could raise a large enough army to outnumber however many bullets the Dreizack had."

"I already tried to convince the king to stop the Dreizack," Will said. "It didn't go over well."

"No kidding," Danny mused.

"We tried multiple times to get the guards to let us meet with him, but they wouldn't allow it. Finally, we were given a time for a week from now. We heard the gunshots yesterday and returned to the castle to see you alone with Madoc Morgan on top of the keep. We've been waiting outside ever since for an opportunity to get to you."

"I wish we could have talked before this morning," Will said.

"Well, at least we were able to help you some," Chase said.

Will looked confused, and Chase continued, "Who do you think shot the men who were pursuing you?"

"Really? I didn't realize they had been shot. I wondered what happened to them."

Chase held up his crossbow. "I took them out with this while hiding on one of the thatched roofs. I built this bow to have two platforms, and two cords so I can load and fire two arrows. The small pulleys on the side make it more like a modern compound bow, so I don't have to use an extra instrument to wind it, while still getting just as much power per shot. I can fire eight arrows with this in the time it takes a person to fire a current crossbow twice."

"Wow—thank you. I was sure they were going to get me."

"Well, I guess I owed you one anyway from when we were back in the desert."

Will shook his head. "That seems like forever ago."

"I made the bow in a blacksmith's workshop here in London. He let me use some of his materials to make it after I showed him some basic ways he could improve his craft. It was hard for the scientist in me not to give him more tips because we need to minimize having a futuristic influence. We must stop the Dreizack from doing anything with the king that could interrupt the course of history and prevent us from having a home to return to—if it isn't already too late."

There were footsteps in the street. Chase waved for them to be quiet, then peered around the corner. He relaxed. "Psst, Stephen, over here."

A middle-aged man with a thick brown beard streaked with gray and strong, broad shoulders joined them in the alley. Two skinny young men were close behind. "There's hardly any space," the middle-aged man said. When he saw Will, his thick gray eyebrows rose. "Oh, do I finally have the pleasure of meeting Will?"

"Yes. Hello," Will said, taking in the new faces.

"This is Stephen," Chase said. "And this is Nicholas and Geoffrey. They've been a great help to us."

The young men gave simple greetings, and Nicholas smiled kindly with a missing front tooth. They both had wisps of facial hair that could hardly be called beards. Geoffrey nervously looked back over his shoulder, and even in the dim light, Will could see deep pox scars running the length of his face and neck.

"It's the least we could do after your uncle fought off heathens raiding our village," Stephen said.

"What?" Will said.

"Yeah," Danny said. "A raiding party attacked the town we stopped at for the night."

Stephen added, "Lucky they were there, or we would have lost everything. Several houses were set ablaze, and I was in the thick of the fighting. Then your uncle sees the brutes attacking our women and intervenes with a small gunpowder weapon. The thunder drew the attention of the others, and he killed enough of 'em that our lads could deal with the rest."

"Really?" Will said.

Chase nodded. "I used up all the shots in the gunpowder weapon, though."

"We're forever grateful to him, and Danny here, and promised to help them in their endeavor as a token of gratitude and brotherhood. I was a soldier for many years, and my sword is pledged to him for the time being."

"Oh, hey," Danny said. "Guess who we ran into here?"

Will started to get his hopes up. "Who?"

"Guess."

"Did you see Celeste?"

"Yeah!" Danny said. "We saw her and her entourage approaching the castle a few hours after the bad guys did their demonstration with the guns yesterday."

"Really? I didn't think they would bother to come."

"Well, they did. And she promised to marry this Edmund guy, and told them I was the Crown Prince of America or some crap like that."

Will took a step back. "She's engaged?"

"Yeah, she told me she promised to marry him so they would try to help you."

"She did that—for me?"

"It surprised me too," Danny said. "She seems a little different—almost nicer, and yet tougher at the same time. But I'm not surprised at all that she's found a way to be the center of attention."

"Where is she?" Will asked eagerly.

"They're all at an inn," Chase said. "Once we told Sir Edmund about the situation, he seemed deeply alarmed. He's concerned that Madoc and the king will work together and take his future inheritance. He and his men are trying to keep a low profile in London until they decide what to do."

Will shook his head. "No one could convince the king not to develop advanced gunpowder weapons."

"That's what Edmund and his men think. We should join them, but first, we need to disguise you in one of our cloaks."

28

———————

They snuck Will into the back of the inn. He felt uneasy not knowing where he stood with the men from Arundel. And how did Celeste really feel about Edmund?

"Psst, Celeste!" Danny whispered as one of Edmund's men permitted them to enter the room. "We found him!"

Celeste, Garrett, and Emma leaped to their feet with excitement. Edmund and the other men remained seated, but they gave Will their full attention.

Will glanced from Edmund to Celeste and made a small bow. "M'lady. M'lord."

Celeste stopped short of embracing Will, a little surprised at his formality, and then she also glanced at Edmund. "It's a great relief to see you."

"Thank you," Will said, "for trying to help. I didn't think any of you would come—and congratulations on your engagement."

Edmund nodded. "I want to know everything that occurred when you were with those heathens."

"Of course, sir," Will said. "There's much to tell."

Emma smiled and looked like she wanted to say something but hesitated and stayed where she was. Will remembered how she kept a distance from him because he and Edmund were at odds.

Garrett wrapped his arm around Will's shoulder. "Good to see you alive, my friend!"

Will gasped in pain.

"Are you all right?" Celeste exclaimed.

"Great to see you too, Garrett—I'll be fine."

"His arm's messed up, and his back. Show them," Danny urged.

Will sighed and removed the cloak.

"That's going to get infected!" Celeste said, clearly struggling to keep her voice down. "What did they do to you?"

"They tried to kill me, that's all." Will let out a faint laugh.

Celeste sat him in a chair and closely inspected his wounds.

"We'll have to clean it and sear the flesh closed," Chase said.

"With what?" Will asked.

"We'll heat a piece of metal in the fire and then burn the skin to seal it off. It's your best chance at preventing infection from spreading through your body."

Will winced. "Can't you just clean it and place some herbs on it or something instead?"

Sir Roland let out a guffaw and shook his head. "Herbs? Son, I've seen wounds smaller than these kill a man. You have but two options. Hot steel or cold steel. You do as the man says and sear the flesh closed, or you cut off the limb. If you want cold steel, better to get it over with before a fever sets in. As for your back, I'm afraid there's just one option if you want to live."

"I'll take the hot steel," Will said, trying to sound brave.

"I'll make preparations," Garrett said. He and Emma hurried to get supplies.

"Make space on the bed, and Will, take off your tunic," Celeste said.

"Thank you." Will started to remove the garment, grimacing as he brought it over his head. Celeste helped him pull it the rest of the way off, and he lay down on a dry cloak spread across the bed. Garrett worked a hot poker in the small fireplace. Will tried not to move as Celeste picked out debris and cleaned it with ale and a cloth.

"Oh, William," Emma said with a pained expression as Celeste worked on his back. Her expression worried him, but he didn't want to show any fear.

"Tell us what transpired with the king," Edmund said.

Will saw the red-hot tip of the iron drawn from the embers. He tensed, then forced a smile. "Sure—but I feel like I'm being interrogated."

Danny let out a dry laugh.

"We're going to have to do this a number of times. Both wounds are longer than the amount of metal we can heat at once," Chase said.

Will didn't want to appear weak to a single person in the room. He took a deep breath. "I'm ready. Go ahead."

The branding burn on his back was worse than any pain he had experienced in his life. He could feel, hear, and smell his own flesh sizzling. His fists clenched into the cloak he was lying on, and his whole body trembled. The odor was horrible.

"I'm sorry, bud," Chase said in a pained, sympathetic tone. "We'll probably need to do that about six more times to ensure we cover everything."

Will breathed heavily. "Is that all?"

"While the iron reheats, tell us what happened," Edmund said.

"I yield, my lord. I submit. I'll tell you everything! Stop the torture."

Edmund held a slightly amused yet patient expression as he waited for Will to catch his breath.

Will was relieved to see Edmund coming across less arrogantly than before. Hopefully, it might last. He began unloading the story, stopping to answer the questions from Edmund and the others.

"Will, are you ready?" Chase asked.

"Yeah," Will said, and his whole body tensed.

Celeste sat on the bed next to him. She tenderly took the hand of his uninjured right arm in both of hers.

Will appreciated the kindness, but he was worried he would hurt her if he clenched down hard in pain. He gave her hand a light squeeze, then let go to grip the cloak. Turning his head away from the others, he bit down into the coarse wool as the hot iron cooked a thin line on his skin.

"Let him finish his account before you continue," Edmund said.

"God be praised for your mercy, my lord," Will said, and he continued to detail his experience.

The group pummeled him with questions, and he told them everything he knew about the Dreizack's plans with the king—everything he could without revealing that they were all from the future.

"Sir Edmund," said one of the men-at-arms, "I believe it best to test Arundel's ties to the Crown and tell the king of these men."

"His Grace ordered the lad be executed for the very act," Sir Roland said. "Of course, William isn't highborn, but Sir Edmund, presenting yourself as an enemy to the king's most valued ally could place a target on Arundel."

"Is there any way we could oppose them without there being ties back to Arundel?" Edmund asked, his voice intent.

"Are you sure of the road they're taking to gather supplies?" Roland asked.

"Yes," Will said. "They said they're taking the only road to the south."

Roland looked to Edmund. "We could ambush these foreign men on their journey."

Edmund frowned.

"That would be treason," one of the men-at-arms said.

"Perhaps." Edmund leaned back in his chair. "But it would certainly be treason to let these men slay our king after abusing his good graces—and I will not shame my father by making his house an enemy of the Crown. Also, these men expressly intend to tarnish all Christendom. And though, if discovered, we would be denounced and executed, how could we sit idly by and do nothing? I wish my father were not away to Rome—and that this heavy matter would lie upon his shoulders. But alas, as the future Earl of Arundel, how can I also not think to protect our lands when this beast Morgan said he will join forces with the king and come against us?"

"You have my support for an ambush," Will said. "I'm completely committed to stopping them. Whatever it takes."

29

––––––––

The small band of those who opposed the Dreizack made a well-concealed camp in the dense forest near the old Roman road that extended south from London. It was the only road to the region where the Dreizack and the king planned to obtain their supplies. Several days had passed, and Will's wounds were still tender to the touch but had avoided infection so far. He and the others worked to make preparations to ambush the Dreizack and destroy any supplies they were transporting back to London.

The setting sun was casting its final rays through the trees above as Will, Danny, and Garrett wearily returned from a rigorous day of combat training with Roland and Edmund's men.

"The two of you made improvements. Now you're just completely helpless, instead of utterly and completely helpless," Garrett teased.

"Hey, watch out," Danny replied. "This was just day one. We're going to get a lot better."

Celeste wasn't permitted to participate in the group training, so she had watched them all day while mimicking their moves. She approached them eagerly. "Can one of you practice with me what Roland taught you?"

A look of concern crossed Danny's face. "Edmund and Roland don't want you training."

Will added, "They don't want Danny and me fighting on the ground during the assault, either. They're just letting us train with them for physical conditioning and self-defense. We're going to be archers, and we should practice with the bows before it's dark."

Celeste's face reddened. "You don't think I could use self-defense training? I was the one who was kidnapped! I'm the one who they would do horrible things to if I was caught. It was completely humiliating not knowing how to fight like everyone else. I know where Edmund and Roland get their mindsets from, but I would think that you two would understand."

"I get it," Danny said, rubbing the back of his neck. "I'm just worried that if you train, you'll want to be near the fighting. I was just—I was worried sick about you before. And I don't want anything to happen to you again."

"And you don't think I wouldn't want anything to happen to you or anyone else here? It's ridiculous for you to think that I shouldn't be helping and at least be able to defend myself!"

Danny shifted uneasily. "You always want to be front and center. If you get trained, I think you would do something . . . overly ambitious."

"That isn't true, and it isn't fair," Celeste said. "What about you, Will?"

"I kind of feel the same about not being able to fight as well as other people here. I think you should be able to train. I think we need all the help we can get."

"She's not your sister! You wouldn't care what happened to her if she charged headlong into a group of soldiers."

"I would care—a lot," Will said.

Celeste stared at him, seeming to try to gauge the depth of his words.

Garrett broke in to relieve the tension. "She's a fiery one. With a sword in her hand, God help us all. She might shame the lot of us in training."

Will nodded. "After the beating I just took from Sir Roland, I don't think I could be any more shamed. I really want to learn how to fight with a mace, and he's going to hammer me until I have the technique right."

Emma was nearby, toiling over a kettle. Celeste turned to her. "Emma, do you think I should be able to learn to fight if I want?"

She gave a pained smile. "I wouldn't be one to tell her ladyship what not to do."

"No, what do you really think?" Celeste asked.

Emma took in a deep breath. "I can only speak from my position." She paused and looked away. "No amount of training would make me as strong as Sir Roland—and most women would be jealous to have so many gallant men willing to defend her."

"Thanks for being honest, and I appreciate that, but I think all of you are missing my point. I don't want to feel completely dependent. I know I can contribute, and I can learn any technique as well as Daniel and William, especially archery."

"You would be of no help as an archer," Roland said, walking up behind them. "You don't have the strength to pull back a war bow."

They turned uneasily at the sound of Roland's deep voice.

"I'll get stronger! I just need you to give me a chance."

Several of the others walked up to join the group. Chase spoke up. "I can modify the bows so they have more force while requiring less draw strength, similar to the crossbow I made with pulleys."

"That would seem necessary," Edmund said. "But as a true warrior, I should be able to defend my love. I failed once, and I shan't fail again. It would be a slight to me for her to train."

"No, it wouldn't," Celeste pleaded. "And you didn't fail before. You brought me back unharmed. If you approve of me training, it would show that you respect me. Besides, what is a lady supposed to do when everyone else is training?"

"Resting. Enjoying herself," Edmund said.

"I would enjoy learning new skills, and I would rest easier if I had them. I would feel even more appreciated by you if you supported my wishes."

"My lord." Roland cleared his throat. "Whether or not she is capable of training, she would be a constant distraction to the men if she trained alongside them."

Edmund hesitated, and Will cut in. "My lord, you wouldn't want to bear the company of an unhappy fiancée. I can teach her what I learn."

"Please!" Celeste said.

"If it would help you feel more at peace," Edmund agreed reluctantly. "But m'lady, know that I would lay down my life for you."

Celeste blushed and looked at him with genuine appreciation. "Thank you. I do know that."

The beaming gaze Celeste gave Edmund made Will look away. He thought about the feedback Sir Roland had given him earlier and the skills he needed to develop.

The group continued to deliberate on their plans until it grew too dark for Celeste and Will to train that night. Emma sat close to Will on a fallen tree as the group debated. She was no longer hesitant to interact with him since Edmund had stopped treating him like an enemy. Emma stayed quiet during the conversation, and her head eventually rested onto Will's shoulder.

Will's pulse quickened. Emma was a wonderful person; if it weren't for Celeste, he wouldn't feel so conflicted. But Celeste was engaged. Regardless, he knew he couldn't afford to let himself get distracted.

As the group dispersed, Chase pulled Will, Danny, and Celeste aside. "We need to talk alone. I volunteered to take watch at the roadside tonight. Come join me after the others are asleep."

30

The night sky was lit with a dazzling canopy of stars peeking down through the tops of the trees. Will, Celeste, and Danny crept through the woods and crossed the dilapidated, wheel-rutted road with tufts of grass growing through the remnants of the old Roman stones. Chase stood and looked warily past them.

"Were you followed?" he whispered.

"I don't think so," Will replied quietly.

His uncle continued to look back across the road. "The night sky is light enough that we should be able to see anyone coming across the road from camp. If we keep our voices down, I don't think anyone could come within earshot without us knowing. How are all of you holding up?" He gestured for them to join him on a couple of old fallen logs facing the road.

"All right," Danny said, "but I'm dying for something better to eat."

"Hard bread, dried meat, and old pease pottage—food of the gods," Will jested, before shifting his tone. "There are a ton of things I want to talk about."

"Me too," Chase said. "We need to talk about if and how it's possible to get home."

"First," Will said, "could you tell us how we got here? What the scepter is? I really need to know." His desire to get the scepter back stirred.

Chase sighed. "Yeah, that's fair. I've told Danny part of it. I was debating telling the rest to just Will, but if something happens to us, it's best for all of us to know. But you have to swear that this information never leaves the four of us. Is that agreed?"

They agreed, and Chase took a deep breath. "It actually starts with Will's dad."

Will began to feel uncomfortable.

"When my brother died, I was just fifteen. Soon after, I received a box that Michael wanted delivered to me if something happened to him. It had a strange black vial with thin gold lettering on it, in characters I didn't recognize. Characters in no known human language—like what's written on the scepter. A map was also in the box and a letter from Michael. He said that the vial had an elixir in it that he received from someone he fully trusted, and that I should drink it and use the map to obtain an object of great importance."

Chase continued, "He said that he already drank a different vial of the same elixir to verify that it was safe and that he felt like his mind was sharper and his reflexes faster. He said the *being*—he used that word, which kind of concerned me—said that he also wanted Will to drink it, and that he had already given it to Will."

"That sounds creepy," Celeste said.

"That's what I thought. I mean, normally I would have trusted my big brother. I always had, but there was footage of him crating a bomb into a hotel and blowing himself up, along with many other people. I didn't know what to do. Did this elixir make him go crazy?"

Will cut in, "Actually, Morgan was in the CIA, and he researched the bombing and said that my dad didn't do it. The government framed him. They murdered him, and we had to live with the consequences."

"I doubt Michael did it, at least not intentionally—but you know you can't trust anything Madoc Morgan said. He was trying to manipulate you."

"I think he was telling the truth about that, though."

"You never know with him. But at that time, I didn't drink the elixir. I waited. Will was just a baby, and as he grew, he was a very bright toddler and developed coordination at an above-average rate."

Will started to feel self-conscious, unsure where this was going.

"The budding scientist in me wanted to make sure there was nothing tainted about my vial, so I gave half of it to our aging dog. The dog regained some of its youthful energy and started learning new tricks. After two years, I drank the other half of the vial."

"So that's why Will is so quick," Danny said.

"Probably."

Chase gave the information time to sink in, and Will felt everyone waiting for him to respond. There were so many memories and emotions crashing in on him at once. "What do you think was in the liquid?" he asked.

"Ah, so this is where things get . . . interesting. I was already poised to have a great career in science like my father, and after drinking the liquid, I found that my mind was sharper, and I felt more motivated. I still didn't follow the map yet because it led to a cave all the way in Africa. After a few years passed, the government made me a good offer, and I negotiated to have a facility built for me at the Idaho National Laboratory, where my father once was the director, but the government had some strings attached to the deal. I knew the research I did would always cause the government to want to keep an eye on me, so if I wanted to go to this cave, I needed to go before I started working with them."

He continued, "The cave was in the wall of a cliff in the Great Rift Valley in Kenya—a region where some of the earliest human remains have been found. I had to rappel down a cliff face to get to it, and then pry away a stone sealing the entrance. When I entered the passage, I was blown away by what was inside. There were murals depicting a person, or what looked like a person, engaging in wars wielding what looked like a mace with a glowing head. There were constellations and star charts that were clearly depictions of planets and suns, but I didn't recognize the constellations. Then a mural showed this individual leaving his planet and traveling through the stars to arrive at a circle with *Earth's* continents on it."

Will thought of the dreams he'd had and grew eager with anticipation.

"I went farther down the passage, and it opened up into a large room with iridescent waves of blue light illuminating the walls, just bright enough to see without my flashlight. In the center of the room was an upright sarcophagus that looked like the individual depicted in the murals. I'm pretty sure this was his tomb and that his body was inside the sarcophagus. The figure of the individual had his arms extended, and he was holding the scepter, almost as if offering it with both hands—and I took it."

"Are you sure he was from another planet?" Celeste asked.

"The murals distinctly showed him leaving a series of other

planets and coming to this one. What the truth is, I'm not 100 percent sure, but that's what it depicted."

"Did the individual in the mural have auburn hair?" Will asked hesitantly.

"Yeah!" Chase said. "How did you know?"

"I think I had some dreams about some of what you mentioned. But they were just crazy dreams."

"You'll have to tell me more about that. Back home, I experimented with the scepter. I found that events around me slowed down somewhat if the white light was ignited, making me move slightly faster than the time transpiring around me, and that when the red flame was ignited, if I touched it to a small animal, the animal would—no kidding—disappear. I did a number of tests with mice and found that they teleported to where there was an abundance of what they wanted most—food, water, mates. I tried it on myself, and it caused me to disappear and reappear somewhere that showed a lot of potential for what I wanted in the moment."

Chase grinned. "That made for some . . . awkward situations. Especially since I was barely conscious when I arrived. Not like the complete knockout we had when we came here, though. I never time traveled, and I could only take lightweight objects I was touching with me."

"So you could just teleport anywhere you wanted?" Will said.

"Not with a high degree of predictability at first, and someone from work found out about it, and it got back to higher-ups in the government who wanted to know how they could maximize its powers for their interests. Their thinking was that if I could figure out how to take other people with me, I could take a tactical unit of Special Forces to go after any hidden enemy in the world. They named the project Black Hammer."

Will nodded. "That seems like a reason Morgan would go after it."

"Yeah, but I wasn't worried about the repercussions at first. I was so excited to be developing my power with the object. I built a series of amplifiers in a lab and got to a point where I could teleport with one other person to where whoever was touched by the head of the scepter had the most potential to achieve what they wanted. My touch was the only thing that would activate the red portion of the scepter, whereas anyone could activate the white portion. We tested my blood and found that I had genetic material incorporated into each of my cells that wasn't like, well, any other species on Earth."

"Is that because of the liquid?" Will asked.

"I'm pretty sure. And also, I think it's the reason the scepter might respond more to you than to me. I only got half a dose. I did some trace samplings of the inside of the vial, and it was—a type of blood."

"Blood?" Will said. He braced his hands on the log he was sitting on. He already struggled with his identity. He glanced at Celeste, whose eyebrows knit together as she also tried to process everything.

Will took a deep breath. "So who was this guy, this being, that gave my dad the vials?"

"I don't know—only that Michael trusted him."

Will looked down. "You guys promised not to tell anyone—"

"That you're an alien," Danny smiled.

"I'm not an alien." Will was unamused.

"Will, we've known you a long time," Celeste said. "We know who you are."

He sent her an appreciative glance, but the comment wasn't enough to lift the sudden weight that had dropped on him.

"Don't think of it as being alien. Think of it as being super-human," Chase said.

Will gave a wry smile. "But my whole life, all I've wanted is for people to see me as normal."

"Will, everyone is unique. There is no such thing as normal," Celeste offered.

"Sure." Will forced a pained smile as he thought about what growing up would have been like if people saw him as the son of a terrorist *and* as an alien.

"Something extremely important about you, Will," said Chase, his voice sounding deeply concerned, "is that if there is any chance of us being able to get home, you have to be alive to use the scepter. You shouldn't be near any fighting. I don't even want you training because you could get seriously injured."

Will's head jerked up. "Wait—I get the logic behind that, and I'm grateful for your concern. But . . . what if you need me?"

"If something happens to you, we're all stuck here. If you want to help us, you need to stay alive."

"I get it," Will said. "But I think the even bigger priority is stopping the Dreizack."

"There are other ways you can help the group," Celeste said. "But your uncle is right. We can't get home without you."

Will exhaled. He debated telling them what had been on his mind for the last few days. *Here it goes.* "This might come as a complete shock to all of you. You might think it's outrageous, and you might even hate me for it. But the odds are high that we can't go back home. Have you thought about all of the people who suffer from plagues, genocides, slavery, tyranny, and the sheer absence of human rights that abound for the next seven hundred years? If we can't go home, I've started to feel an obligation to try to prevent it."

"Even if we couldn't go home, I wouldn't try to alter the future," Chase said, sounding wary.

"Don't you think not doing something would be pretty hard-hearted?" Will asked.

"No. If we tamper with history, there is no way of knowing that even worse atrocities won't happen."

"Worse atrocities? If any of you could hypothetically travel back home with things unchanged, you could say to a Holocaust survivor, 'You know, if I could go back in time and prevent genocides from happening, I wouldn't because I would be afraid that something worse might happen.'"

"Whoa! That's completely unfair," Chase said. "I'd never be that insensitive. In your example, though, what if someone like Hitler actually took over the world and no one could put a stop to his mass killings? Things can always be worse. That's not something I think we should risk."

"Someone like Hitler is about to take over the world," Will insisted. "And no matter what we do, there is an element of risk. What if we stopped the Dreizack and theoretically returned to the future with no drastic changes? The future world constantly has wars—who's to say people wouldn't wipe each other out a few years after we got back? Wouldn't it be better to help create a more peaceful world?"

"You listened to Madoc too much. Now you're starting to sound like him," Chase said.

"Some of his views are like truth laced with poison—but if you take away the poison, you're left with truth," Will said.

"Either way, you're left with the views of a freakin' megalomaniac," Danny said.

"No—because I don't want power over anyone. I just don't want so many people to suffer. My whole life, people have assumed I stood for something wrong. I've made a lot of mistakes, and for once I just want to do what's right. Sentencing all of those people to agony—just doesn't seem right."

"I get it." Celeste shook her head. "But I'm not comfortable with what you're proposing."

"Okay—please just think about it for a moment. You all

know we could peacefully acquire massive amounts of wealth using our knowledge of modern technology. We could use that influence to carry out a monumental worldwide movement to prevent centuries of suffering. If we introduced germ theory alone, we could save millions of lives. If the world had a more empathetic platform to build its societies on, it might prevent the mindsets that have our future world in an endless cycle of wars."

"But Will, we would never be born," Celeste said. "You almost sound as if this should be our plan A."

"I don't know if we would be born, but we would have lived here. I don't fully understand the physics of it, but do you think we would just, *poof*, disappear if too many things change?"

"I don't think so," Chase said. "But, in our version of history, we know how things turn out. The only guarantee we have of the planet being somewhat stable seven hundred years from now is to stop being so reckless."

Will let out a dry laugh. "Stable planet? You're almost proving my point. Pollution on our future planet probably irreversibly threatens human life. Don't you think the world would benefit from a heads-up on that?"

"I think I know what this is partially about, but I don't know if you want me to say it," Danny said hesitantly.

"Go ahead."

"Well, I know you're actually concerned about other people, but—I think a deeper issue is that you hated life in our time."

The words struck Will like a blow to the face. "Like it's so much better here."

"Since we've met up in London, you haven't seemed—depressed," Danny said.

Will flinched. "That's not really fair. All of you had much better lives than me in the future."

"But I don't have any life here!" Celeste said. "Everyone in this time period sees women as subhuman."

"Well, if we stayed," Danny said, "you'd have a better life than the others they treat as subhuman."

Celeste slugged him in the arm.

"Let's stay quiet," Chase whispered. "Celeste has faced a lot of challenges that us guys haven't had to deal with."

"Which won't change for women anytime soon—unless we do something," Will said. "And come on, do you really trust future governments? After what they might have done to my dad? After them getting us into this mess in the first place?"

"No, I got us into this mess—and so did Madoc Morgan," Chase said.

"Listen," Danny said. "I'm the history fanatic, and I've enjoyed this knights-and-castles adventure. You've gotta understand that any government or organization made up of people isn't going to be perfect. But the constitution is a good thing. Modern human rights are a good thing. We shouldn't risk losing the good things people have sacrificed for."

"I still can't shake the feeling that we would be abandoning people," Will said. "But we can talk about it later."

"What we need to agree on now is that the king needs to be stopped from making modern weapons." Chase looked at each of them. "Gunpowder weapons already exist here, and merely having seen better ones may not have a lasting impact on the future. The other lives we've impacted may be lost in the plague anyway. I still think there's a slim chance of getting home."

"I 100 percent agree with stopping Morgan and the king," Will said.

"They might take weeks or months to gather supplies and travel back to London," Chase said. "We can spend that time preparing a roadside ambush and training. Everyone except Will."

"No. You want me to stay alive? Then you should want me to be able to defend myself. I'll be careful, but you should want me to train harder than anyone has ever trained at anything. Because that is exactly what I intend to do."

31

The next day, Will and the others took a break after training since dawn. His shoulders were getting an intense workout from swinging a sword overhead for hours, and he felt it.

Emma approached him, carrying a pail of water and a ladle.

"Care for a drink?" she asked.

"Yes. Thank you."

She brought the ladle to his lips. The cold spring water felt revitalizing, and some spilled down his chin and onto his chest.

"Oh, my apologies," Emma said.

"No need to apologize. It feels fantastic."

"Would you care for more?"

"Absolutely."

"In your mouth?" she asked, smiling.

"You could pour it right on me."

She laughed and dripped a ladleful of water around his neck and shoulders.

"Hey, are we going to get some of that?" one of the men-at-arms asked.

"Sure, Hector." Emma handed the pail and ladle to him.

"Thanks again," Will said.

"You're welcome. Do you have a few minutes?" Emma nodded away from the group.

The others were stretching, finding places to sit down, or waiting for the pail of spring water. "Yeah, sure."

They walked through the trees, and Emma said, "You fight well. It's impressive to watch when I'm not caught up preparing meals."

Will grinned. "Saying I fight well would be very generous."

She laughed. "You're improving quickly." Her voice was that of the girl Will had first met at Arundel. Confident, fun, sweet, unrestrained.

"I wish you could be more like this when Edmund is nearby." Will paused. "Has he ever . . . mistreated you?"

Her eyes shot up. "Never. His lordship and his family have been very good to me."

Will searched her face. "It just worries me that—it's almost as if you're afraid he'd kill you if you say the wrong thing or make a mistake."

She gave a pained smile. "The FitzAlans have been most kind, but if I lost my position, I might as well be dead. My family died in the same fever that took Garrett's family."

"I'm so sorry to hear that."

She nodded. "I was spoken for, but he died too. Now I'm nearly an old maid."

"No—how old are you?"

"Sixteen."

"I'm sixteen. That isn't old."

She forced a smile. "Things may be different where you're from. Can I ask you something?"

"Of course. Go ahead."

"What is a eunuch—in your land?" she asked in a hushed tone.

Will let out a laugh. "What did you hear?"

She seemed a little embarrassed. "Just that you were a eunuch, but that it means something else where you're from."

"It just means a highly trusted servant, nothing more."

"Servant in general, or servant who oversees the women?"

"Uh, servant in general. I've assisted multiple members of the royal family."

"Do eunuchs marry?"

"Uh—yeah. I don't even think it's the best word to use since the meaning is so different." The marriage of American eunuchs wasn't a backstory item he and Celeste had established, and he'd have to tell her and the others about this conversation. Emma had always seemed genuinely interested in their foreign land, and it would be difficult to continue to lie to those beautiful brown eyes.

"How young do people get married here?" Will asked, wanting to shift the conversation away from himself.

"My friends married when they were twelve."

Will's eyes widened. "Oh."

"There have been other men interested in me, but I don't want to set my heart on a path that doesn't have a chance of ending well."

"Ending well?"

She sighed. "Someone like Garrett is going to become a knight and would only marry a lady. Someone like Edmund would be an unthinkable match, and his men are all married or not the marrying type. Of course, there are other men in Arundel and Littlehampton, but no one I've felt a closeness to. I've been told I'm too proud for my own good. Many women fall for a traveling nobleman or soldier only to be left alone caring for a baby. I've sworn that would never happen to me," she said, her jaw set as she looked into the distance.

"That makes sense," Will said. He never wanted to hurt Emma. Garrett and the others only seemed superficially inquisitive about America. Will knew that if he grew close to Emma, she would enjoy listening to him talk for hours about his foreign land. She had volunteered to join the group going to get Celeste at Stonehenge so that she could care for her ladyship's needs. Will thought that part of her reason for volunteering was the opportunity to travel farther than she ever had in her life. If it was just him, he might be able to juggle a fantasy world of half-truths with her, but the need to have everything corroborated with the other three from his time could get them into serious trouble. Regardless of how likable Emma was, he dreaded needing to lie to her, whereas he usually looked forward to talking with Celeste.

Will chose his words carefully. "If I were to have a romantic relationship now, I think I'd be so mentally distracted, I would get my head taken off in training. That, or I'd be so focused on preparing to attack the Dreizack that I would end up hurting the person I cared about. It really isn't something I could currently wrap my head around."

She looked disappointed. "I see. Of course. What do you desire to do after?"

"After? After we win or we're dead—it seems too far away to think about." He was worried about hurting her feelings and tried not to sound too dismissive.

"Yes, but sometimes thinking of what comes after adversity helps us pass through it." Her eyes searched Will's.

"You're right. I'm glad we have such a good group to support each other. I think the others would enjoy your true personality. Celeste and Daniel won't judge you. I know that formalities are often needed, but I don't think Edmund would have you beheaded for being such a nice person."

She gave a half smile.

"Hey, William!" Danny's voice rang through the trees. "We're starting up again!"

"I better get back. It was good talking with you." He gave her a friendly smile, before turning to join the others.

That night, after the group ate the venison stew Emma prepared, she sat with Will and the others their age, but this time didn't put her head on his shoulder or do anything else flirtatious.

Will wondered if what he'd told Emma was really true—that if he had romantic feelings for someone, it would just get one of them hurt. *If that someone is Celeste, as long as Sir Edmund is around, it's definitely true.*

32

———————

The days of training and preparation were long and rigorous. They occasionally sent men-at-arms into London to get supplies and see if Morgan's group had returned another way. There had been no sign of them, and the group kept hope that the Dreizack and the king's men would still return on the Roman road even though two months had passed.

Will held the sparring mace and short sword as he took a fighting stance that had become natural after rigorously training every day in the forest. He had shown more sheer, dogged determination to learn and improve than anyone else. Sir Roland stood across from him, bearing a sparring sword and shield. The knight had relentlessly trained the group while they waited. For Will, the fundamentals of stance, footwork, blocking, and striking were becoming instinctive. Roland continued to teach them more advanced moves, and Will was a quick learner.

Will's upper body muscles had grown stronger from heaving steel weaponry day after day. The mace and sword that had once felt a little awkward in his hands now felt like an extension of his arms as he positioned them between himself and Roland.

The others in the group stood around them in a clearing surrounded by dense forest. Each was taking a turn at a brief sparring bout with the great knight, who seemed to have endless stamina. None so far that day had landed a blow on him, and Will was determined to be the first. He still wasn't nearly as strong as Roland and was going to rely heavily on his instincts and reflexes.

Will feinted with his sword and swung the mace in from a different angle. Roland parried the attack and brought his sword down to strike. Will deflected the blade with his short sword, and the two exchanged blow after blow, with neither striking the other's body. They circled, and the relaxed expression on Roland's face hardened in concentration. The weapons rang out several more times. Then the tip of Roland's sword tapped the leather doublet protecting Will's chest.

Will heaved a deep breath and forced himself not to show how frustrated he was.

"I can tell you've been listening while I've trained you," Roland said, and he nodded to the circle of spectators. "Next person."

"Thank you, sir," Will said as he stepped out of the ring, and Danny took his place.

"Try kicking me again, and I'll break your leg," Roland grunted.

"Yes, sir." Danny smiled sheepishly. One of the first times he'd faced Roland, Danny braced his sword against the knight's and then did a roundhouse kick into Roland's side, after which the man sent Danny sprawling onto his back.

Garrett greeted Will at the edge of the circle. "That was

quite a compliment, coming from Sir Roland," he said in an enthusiastic but hushed tone. "You've really come a long way."

"Oh, thanks," Will said. "I still want to be better."

"Certainly," the squire said. "Sir Roland wouldn't bother training us if we felt differently."

Emma still left drinking water for them but no longer greeted Will at the end of training. They had grown to be good friends, and she was usually close to camp, trying to keep up with the food preparation.

Will glanced around the outside of the circle, hoping Celeste had been watching. However, he wasn't surprised to see her in her usual distant spot, intently focused on her archery. She wore a gray doublet over a white shirt and dark brown trousers. She insisted on wearing male clothing because a gown was impractical for training. Emma seemed to think that it was odd but refused to openly comment. Edmund's men were surprised when he supported Celeste's wardrobe request, but after his consent was given, they said nothing. Celeste also wanted to cut her hair short to appear more like a male from a distance, but Edmund wouldn't go that far.

Her skill with a bow had become increasingly more advanced. Will and Danny also trained in archery, but Celeste was putting in more time, and she exceeded Danny in accuracy. She and Will were on about the same level, which Danny attributed to Will's naturally good throwing aim. When they were alone, Danny cracked a joke about it being because Will had alien blood, but he could clearly see the joke bothered Will, and he hadn't brought up the subject again.

The sparring exchange between Roland and Danny was brief, with Roland landing multiple blows. He gave Danny a few stern words of advice, and then a man-at-arms replaced Danny in the circle.

When the group finished for the day, Will walked toward

Celeste to carry on the long-established routine of the two of them sparring together in the evening—but Edmund was now talking amiably with her.

Will waited a distance away as Edmund said something to make Celeste laugh. She gestured to the tight cluster of arrows she had landed at the center of the target, and Edmund made an approving statement. Will turned, not needing to see the rest. He sheathed his sword and spun the training mace in the air, catching it by the handle. For the thousandth time, he wished it were the scepter. He grappled with how much he missed the object, still unsure if longing for it was good.

Will finally grew tired of waiting and started back to camp. He stopped when he heard Celeste call, "William!"

He turned to see Edmund walking toward him on the way back to join the others.

"Do not harm her," Edmund said, a phrase that he repeated so frequently that Will only responded with a nod.

When Will reached Celeste, she said, "You still want to train tonight, right?"

"Of course. If you still want to."

She grinned. "When have I not wanted to?"

"Never." He smiled. "You seem to enjoy swinging a sword at me."

"And you at me?"

"Well, Edmund won't have you hung from a tree if I get maimed."

Celeste frowned. "I wouldn't let him hang you—and don't you dare hold back on me."

Will laughed. "How could I? I don't want you to take my head off."

They walked deeper into the forest so they could be out of sight of the others. Their first few times training together were nearly drowned out by jeers and shouts of amusement. It didn't surprise anyone when the two distanced themselves far from the group when practicing.

They walked beneath the thick green foliage of oak trees, taking care to step over the green ferns and tree roots rising amid the grass and old leaves of the forest floor.

"How are things with Edmund?" Will asked.

"He's been great," Celeste said off-handedly.

"Great?"

"Sure."

"Great like we currently don't have anything to worry about, or great like you want to marry him?"

"Considering all of the superstitions and prejudices he was brought up with, he's a good person."

"Well, of course he's good to you."

"And you too," she asserted. "We wouldn't even have a shot at taking on the Dreizack without his help. Without him, we probably would have been killed the day we got here."

"You're right, but that doesn't answer my question. It's okay if you don't want to talk about it, though."

"I bet that would make you happy if I married him," she said curtly. "That would mean you got your way, and we never went back home."

Will wanted to avoid arguing, but he decided to give her an honest response. "It wouldn't make me happy if you married Edmund."

"Why?"

"Because—because other than you, he treats everyone like they're completely inferior. He only treats you like you're marginally inferior. It's none of my business, but do you really think he'll continue to be as nice when you're married, and he isn't trying to win you over?"

"It is none of your business—but he is a gentleman. He's

even completely respected the premarital physical boundaries I requested. I think he would continue to be kind to his lady."

Will shook his head and muttered, "You had to *request* them—instead of *set* them. I've had my fill of talking about Edmund."

"Will, you know I would rather go home than stay here." There was a tinge of anger in her voice. "But you still haven't committed to going home if we get the chance."

"I don't like making promises if I don't know I can keep them."

"Let's just train already." There was an edge in her voice.

"As her ladyship wishes," Will said.

"Stop that."

"As you wish." Will's eyes were distant, and he held the sparring sword ready, waiting for Celeste.

Her mouth twitched with a hint of frustration as she positioned herself in a fighting stance and leveled her sword at him.

There was a moment of tension as they both unflinchingly looked at each other. Then Celeste swung her sword ferociously.

Will stepped back, blocking the blow, and hustled to block attack after attack that Celeste skillfully launched at him. He knew she would be mad if he didn't give her his best, and he returned a series of strikes that Celeste parried.

Celeste hammered at Will and his sword with all her might. She bared her teeth with each swing, and Will backed up for fear of one of them getting hurt by her sudden, unbridled intensity. He parried several more blows, then used a disarming technique to send her sword to the ground in a crackling of dried leaves.

"I think we should take a br—" Will started to say, but Celeste drew the dagger at her waist and lunged at him.

His eyes widened, and he held out his hands defensively. Unlike the sparring blade, the dagger was razor sharp.

She dove and tackled him. Will gasped as they tumbled backward and rolled down a twenty-foot dirt embankment, colliding several times with large roots protruding from the soil.

In spite of the rough and painful spill, Celeste managed to keep hold of Will. As they came to a stop, she locked her arm around Will's neck and latched on to his back as they both lay in a scatter of leaves.

Will felt a sharp point at his throat. "Stop!" he commanded.

"I win," she whispered in his ear.

"You're insane!" he shouted.

Celeste withdrew the tip of a dead leaf from his neck and released her arms and one leg from clamping around him.

Will quickly clambered to his feet. "You could have killed one of us!"

"By rolling down a hill?" Celeste grinned. "I dropped the dagger before I tackled you."

Will cursed himself for not noticing. She seemed to have taken a play out of his own book. "You're going to get someone killed. This isn't a game."

Celeste was quickly on her feet, her face concerned. "How are we supposed to help each other by going easy on each other? You have to stay alive if we have any chance of using the scepter. I'm trying to help you, and yet you seem irrational enough to talk about how you'll be near any real fighting, when just now, you panicked at the sight of an actual blade!"

"I panicked because I didn't want you to get hurt either. I haven't trained for *not hurting someone* lunging at me with a knife. There are things I could have done if we were actually fighting."

"But you froze up." Celeste sounded more worried than accusatory.

"I was just shocked that you would actually try to stab me."

"You still don't trust me?"

"You could make it a lot easier. Let's just try to be on the same team."

Celeste made a sly smile. "You want to be on the same team? Teams share the same goals. Teammates are honest with each other. So, if you held the scepter in your hand with the red flame ignited, and you touched yourself with it—would it take us back home? Are we really on the same team?"

"Assuming we've stopped the Dreizack?"

"Sure. Where does Will Donovan have the greatest potential? Where does he want to go?"

"I've thought about that a lot," Will said softly. "Chase said it isn't so much a matter of telling it where you want to go, but the scepter assessing you to the very core. I want people to accept me for being me—no labels attached. I also want to help people."

"I know exactly where I would want the scepter to send me. To my living room, in my home, with my mom and dad, and all my brothers and sisters around me."

"I admit to envying you and Danny," Will said. "But I'll be honest with you—I can't shake the feeling that I would be abandoning so many people to awful fates if I went back to our time."

"You need to accept the safest course. As long as humans exist, there will be suffering, and as long as humans exist, they will find happiness. You will never change that. I've sometimes wondered—if the scepter sends you to where you want to be, why did we wake up near each other when we arrived? To me, it would have made more sense for you to wake up right next to

Morgan and the other sociopaths. You and the other marauders of time travel."

Will paused for a long moment, maintaining her gaze without flinching. He wasn't the same person he had been back on the modern summer break, when the pettiest of things mattered. Crushes, bullies, it all seemed minuscule now. When he spoke, he said words that his past self would not have been able to utter. His voice was even and unshaken.

"You know why I think I woke up nearer to you than to the Dreizack? It's because I liked you—and not as a friend. We weren't even really friends. To you, I was just your twin brother's friend. I'm nothing like Morgan or the Dreizack. And if you think I'm a sociopath, then you have no idea who I am."

It was Celeste's turn to be taken aback. After soaking in his words, she said, "Why didn't you just tell me you liked me?"

"Would it have mattered?" Will said, relaxing his tone. "Besides, now you're engaged—that's definitely drama we don't need."

"I got engaged to save you! I did that because I cared about you!"

"And I'm grateful for that. I really am. But if we never get the scepter back, and time travel isn't an option—you'd still marry Edmund?"

"It's complicated," she said, looking away.

"M'lady! Are you well?" Edmund's voice called. "I heard shouting."

Will and Celeste exchanged looks of fear.

Celeste shuddered and called back in Edmund's direction. "I'm fine. We're down here."

It took a while before the sound of fast-moving footsteps across leaves reached the top of the embankment.

Edmund stood towering above them. "What did he do to you?" he demanded with both hands on his hips.

"We were sparring up where you are, and then I was clumsy, and caused us both to fall," Celeste said.

"Your servant let you fall?" Edmund made his way over the tree roots down to them.

Will bit his lip as he struggled not to say anything.

"It was my fault, really," she said.

"Hmm," Edmund said. "And what were you shouting about?"

"I believe I upset William. He thought I was actually trying to kill him, and I was trying to convince him of the contrary."

"You needn't convince him of anything. He's your servant." Edmund looked at Will with disapproval and shook his head. "You really shouldn't be training with him anyway. If you still want to continue to learn, allow me. I've trained in swordsmanship since I could walk."

Celeste's mouth hung open for a moment. "I do want to continue training."

"Then from now on, allow me. Your servant really isn't qualified."

"Maybe we should have a bout sometime. So far, you've avoided sparring with me," Will said casually.

"With you? It would be an ill use of my time. You've trained for scarcely two months."

"But I've trained relentlessly, and I've learned from one of the best. Maybe you're afraid I might win."

"You're looking at one of the best," Edmund said reproachfully.

Will couldn't disagree, and he knew he was letting his irritation with Edmund get the better of him. Though not as muscular as Roland, Edmund was fit and tall for his time period. He was agile and had perfect sword-fighting form. Edmund could deftly maneuver his weapon around an opponent's, and his men had marveled several times that Morgan was a skilled enough swordsman that Edmund hadn't killed him in the first second of single combat.

"Whoa, hold on," Celeste interrupted. "You two don't need to quarrel. I can train with whoever is available."

"Oh, but I am intrigued by William's proposition," Edmund said with an eager grin. "We are training, after all. It seems a sparring match would be appropriate."

"You don't need to fight!" she insisted.

"It's just a quick sparring round," Will said calmly. "We have two training swords."

"Here?" Edmund mused. "We wouldn't have a match here. We shall return to the others and do it for all to see."

"There isn't enough daylight if we wait until then," Will said.

"Then we'll face each other at first light." Edmund smiled. "Let us go tell the others. I know it will amuse them."

They began walking back up the hill, and Celeste shot Will a look that said, *That was stupid.*

Will inwardly agreed. He wasn't worried about fighting Edmund so much as upsetting the group dynamic.

As they drew closer to the camp, Edmund began walking faster. He moved ahead of them, clearly eager to tell about Will's challenge.

Celeste stepped closer to Will for just long enough to say one thing in a hushed tone before separating and walking away. "You don't need to prove anything to me."

33

———————

Will heard exclamations of shock and then laughter from those in camp as Edmund declared that Will said he could beat him.

Will was reluctant to join the others, but he did so with his chin up. He calmly accepted the verbal jabs from the men-at-arms and the private lectures on social decorum from his friends. From all the feedback he'd received, he decided to let Sir Roland's gruff advice be what lingered with him. Prior to the group retiring for sleep, the knight took Will aside and said, "It would be wise of you to lose." Will took it as a huge compliment.

As he unrolled his bedroll between Danny and Garrett, he debated whether or not he would heed Roland's advice. He realized that, win or lose, there would be negative repercussions. He thought about embarrassing himself, and how much force Edmund might put into his blows.

Anxiety gripped him for a moment, and then he smiled inwardly. Fear of embarrassment and pain would have kept him awake at night in his previous life—but not tonight. He said goodnight to the others and positioned himself on the bedroll so he wasn't putting pressure on his bruised hip. Then he pulled the coarse blanket over himself and quickly fell asleep.

———

Will's eyes peeled open as light first crept into the forest. He rose, not wanting someone else to tell him to get up to face Edmund. He quietly rolled up his bedroll while the others slept and was startled when he saw that Edmund was already up and watching from the other side of the camp.

Edmund smiled to see Will's reaction. "Good morning," Edmund said quietly, so as not to wake the others. "We agreed on first light."

"We did. But I assume you want to wait until the others are awake?"

"Naturally."

Will walked over to him and extended his hand. "My lord, it will be an honor to spar with you. Thank you for the learning opportunity."

Edmund looked surprised, and he considered Will's hand for a moment before shaking it. "Think not that I'll be softer on you for this gesture or that it will sway my concentration."

Will smiled. "I hope not. It would be an insult to me if it did."

He had watched the noble train for two months, while Edmund had mostly ignored Will. He knew Edmund's signature attacks and was certain he could predict his moves well enough to win. However, Will recognized that Edmund was the better swordsman and would likely beat him if they fought as strangers.

"I may insult you with my sword, but I shan't insult you

with weakness." Edmund's demeanor softened, and as Will stood next to him in the absence of a group of people calling him "lord," he didn't seem so different from Will.

Will was about to respond when they heard galloping hooves distant in the forest. Edmund and Will exchanged glances, and both rushed to grab their weapons.

"Awake!" Edmund ordered. Roland was already up. The others slept with their weapons within arm's reach and hurried to their feet. Edmund and Will stood shoulder to shoulder as they faced the fast-approaching horseman. Their visibility was limited in the dim light of dawn, and a thick shroud of fog laced its fingers through the forest.

They lowered their weapons when they saw that the horseman was Stephen, the stout veteran soldier with a gray-tinged beard, whom Chase and Danny had befriended when defending their village.

Stephen brought the horse to an abrupt stop in front of them and quickly dismounted. His face was gaunt, and he panted as he tried to catch his breath. "They're coming!" he stammered. "They're coming!"

Edmund's face lit up, and he thrust his fist into the air. "It's about bloody time! Those sons of whores are going to get what is coming to them." Several others cheered, but the rest were quiet, concerned with the distraught look on Stephen's face.

"No, no, no, my lord," Stephen said. "It's not what we planned for—it's not what we planned for at all."

"Well, spit it out then," Roland said.

Stephen shook his head. "They've twenty wagons, and over five hundred men."

The words shocked Will to the core. Several of the men crossed themselves. "Sweet Jesus," muttered a man-at-arms. They thought there would be up to thirty men and were able to make preparations for close to a hundred, which would have been far more than enough to guard a few wagons, or even garrison a royal castle.

"Are you sure there're five hundred?" another man-at-arms challenged.

"Aye," Stephen blustered. "I could see their column from the hill. There's at least five hundred, maybe more. They'll reach our section of road in no more than twenty minutes."

"St. George, but the pains we've taken in preparing for this!" Edmund said. "We've only seen several small groups of soldiers leaving this way. Who are these extra men? A flock of farmers?"

"No, my lord. They're in full armor, men on horseback and on foot—they're professional soldiers."

"Mercenaries," Roland said.

"But an army of them?" Edmund added. "Why so many?"

"There's no way we could have known they would wait to transport so many supplies at once," Chase said. "The king and Morgan must be paranoid to hire so many men."

"We can't fight that many! It's certain death!" said Geoffrey, one of the thin young men from Stephen's village.

"I agree," said Nicholas, the other young man who'd come with them. "We helped you come this far, but there's no point in us dying for nothing."

"I'm not one to run from a fight!" Edmund said. "We have an ambush plan, and should carry it out no matter the odds."

"Sir Edmund," one of his men said hesitantly, "there are only seventeen of us. If we made such a foolhardy attack and somehow managed not to be killed—your father would have our heads for not advising against it."

"Bollocks!" Edmund kicked the dirt. "Perhaps there is something we can still do to stop them." He turned to Chase. "Any suggestions, engineer?"

Chase stood with his arms tightly folded and his mouth pursed. "Not for that many and with this little notice."

"I'd rather drink cold horse piss than turn tail and run," Roland said, "but if we want to kill these men, this is not the time and place. Perhaps we could attack them and try to destroy the contents of the wagons after their large escort is disbanded."

"You mean once the supplies are protected behind castle walls?" Will said.

"Will, trying to fight a group this big isn't a realistic option," Chase said. "We're outnumbered thirty to one."

"And they surely have more training than many of you," Roland argued. "There's no point in the lot of you getting butchered."

"But twenty wagons?" Will said. "They aren't going to build a small smithy. They're building a factory!"

"Have you a death wish, boy?" scoffed one of the men-at-arms.

"Will," Chase said. "We'll come up with a plan B. We'll figure something else out."

"He's right," Celeste said. "We can take action later."

"I get what you're saying," Will said, "but we can't assume that there won't be many more men guarding the castle than usual, right? Or that the knowledge of how to build advanced rifles won't spread quickly once the supplies reach London. So here's plan B: We wait until all of these supplies have reached the Tower of London, the Dreizack have taught the king's men how to make rifles, and we are going up against an army of men with guns."

"As bad as that may be," one of the men-at-arms said, "if we attack today, we'll all die, and they'll reach London all the same."

"Will," Danny said, "General Patton said that no one ever won a war by dying for their country—they won by making the other guy die for his. Trying to attack now is *suicide*. Come on,

Will—no."

"We'll make *them* die," Will said. "But remember the bigger picture, and that this isn't about any of us. Yes, if we don't attack, we'll all still be alive, and we'll wake up in the morning knowing that, at this pivotal moment in time, we did nothing." He took a deep breath. He hated being the center of attention, and he hated public speaking. *But I'm right about this.* "I'm carrying out the ambush plans we made—you're all welcome to join me."

"Now see here," Roland said. "After they've hacked you to death, they'll cut off your head and put it on a pike outside of London bridge, and they'll cut up your body into four sections, and send a piece to each of the four corners of the realm to show the world what happens to those who oppose the emissaries of the king."

Will swallowed but remained steady. "And after the Dreizack have taken away everything worthwhile from England and the rest of the world, at least there'll be proof that someone had the literal guts to object."

"You know you'll fail alone," Edmund said.

"Yes, I do. I'm asking you to reconsider—as the only hope for Arundel, England, America, and the world. Who would rather risk death than surrender to certain tyranny?"

"I get what you're saying," Danny said, unable to make eye contact with anyone. "This could be a major turning point—for everyone. Unless someone has a better idea. I don't see how I can't take this risk with you."

"Danny! No!" Celeste shouted.

"I have a key role in the plans," Garrett said. "You can't do it without me. I'll join you."

"You shall not," Roland said. "And if you defy me on this, you'll wish you had been drawn and quartered."

Celeste clenched her fists in frustration. "I don't want to

admit that we might not get a better opportunity—but once they train people to make guns from our land, that changes everything for everyone's future, whether we stop the Dreizack or not. And we can't risk that. And—Danny, Will, I can't lose you. If we do this, you'll need every bow you can get, and you have mine."

"My lady, this is foolishness!" Edmund said.

"Oh, look at this," one of the men-at-arms scoffed. "A group of children off for a frolic—your naivety will be your death."

Chase glared. "They have more courage than the rest of us —and unfortunately, they're right. I don't see there being a better chance."

Edmund angrily pointed at Chase. "But you just said it couldn't be done!"

"We have to try. We're outnumbered, but we do have preparations, and we have something else they don't. The soldiers on the road are there merely for profit. We're fighting for the futures of our families, our homelands, and everything we care about. I'm going to defend that section of road like it's a piece of my own country and the doorstep to my home. We've formed strong bonds of brotherhood. Please help us, and I swear so long as I live, I will not leave this fight until every one of you has made it to safety."

Stephen grabbed both Nicholas and Geoffrey by the shoulders. "You fought on our doorsteps. Now we'll fight on yours."

Geoffrey yanked his arm away, the pox scars reddening around his scraggly beard. "Not me. I'll watch the horses."

"Emma can do that. What are you going to do, watch them blink?" Stephen asked.

Geoffrey crossed his arms, tightly hugging himself, and took several steps back.

Edmund looked to his men. "When these men come back

to Arundel with their guns, what will we say to our kinsmen? That we had a chance to stop them, but we ran away?"

"If we attack here, we'll never be saying anything to our kinsmen," one of the men said.

"I would rather that than look them in the eyes before they're murdered, knowing that my men and I had lost heart. There is no more time for deliberation. I need to know if you will join me," Edmund said.

Roland placed his hand on Edmund's shoulder. "If you wish it. I'll fight with you, my lord—and you'll have Garrett's sword as well."

One of his men-at-arms nodded and said in a tone of reluctance, "My lord, you'll always have our swords."

"If we're going through with this, we can't delay," Chase said quickly. "It won't be sufficient, but I'll tell you what we can adapt."

———

As the small band began to split up to their respective posts, Edmund spoke to Will with an apologetic look on his face. "God be with you."

"And with you. I'll do my best to protect you and your men with my bow."

Edmund looked to Celeste. "Protect her."

"Of course—my lord," Will said.

Edmund clapped him on the shoulder, and they parted ways. The sudden turn of events made Will regret the resentment he'd felt toward Edmund.

They all hurriedly collected their items for the attack.

"Good luck, Garrett. Your support means a lot to me," Will said.

Garrett stopped hastily double-checking his pack and gave

Will a quick, firm hug. "Oh, I have the easy job. Aim true, Will. Aim true."

Emma's face was grim as she gave Will's arm a brief squeeze. "God be with you." The words rushed out of her mouth.

Will joined Celeste and Danny hurrying to the tree stands, where they would be shooting down at the road. No one spoke for a moment, then Will said, "I'm really grateful to you guys for—"

"Wanting a front-row seat to watch you crap yourself," Danny interrupted.

Will snorted. "Anyway, thanks for backing me up."

"I want both of you to know what you mean to me," Celeste said.

"Don't, Celeste." Danny shook his head. "It's too distracting. This isn't the time."

"This is the perfect time! To think of what is important to us."

"I'm fighting for you two, and everything else," Will said.

"I'm fighting for the whales," Danny said. "I doubt the Dreizack are environmentally friendly. C'mon, you'll get me all teary-eyed, and I won't be able to shoot."

Will might have laughed on a different occasion, but now none of them so much as smiled. He moved closer to Celeste and said in a low voice, "I'm sorry that you had to be here. Be careful. I don't want to lose you."

She gave him a pained look and interlocked her arm tightly with his as they hurried forward.

Chase caught up to them. "Will, I need to speak with you." He nodded to Danny and Celeste. "Go to your posts."

The twins continued, though they kept looking back at Will.

Chase's stern gaze beat down on him. "Stay in your tree

stand, and as soon as they break through our front line, get out of here."

"I'm not leaving without—"

Chase grabbed Will by the shoulders. "Don't be stupid. You're the only one who can control time travel, and you were never meant to be stuck in this mess anyway."

Will pulled away. "Look, I know, but—"

"Tell me you'll leave the tree stand and run to the horses—not if, but *when* they break our line." The pain in his uncle's voice was palpable.

Will returned his gaze, biting his lip. "You got it."

34

———————

Will, Danny, and Celeste waited high in three separate trees about thirty yards away from the road. They were concealed in foliage with rope ladders on the backside of the trees for them to escape.

Will gripped the thin wooded rail of the tree stand. No matter how much they practiced, he always felt uneasy looking straight down at the ground. He turned toward Celeste, who was on a stand in the tree to Will's right. She seemed deep in concentration as she waited for the soldiers to appear in the distance. To his left, Danny was hurriedly checking and rechecking his bowstring, arrows, and sword. Danny's nervousness made Will even more anxious, and he squeezed the railing harder with both hands. He lifted one hand and waved to his friend, who didn't notice him.

"Danny," Will hissed. "Danny."

Danny's head snapped up. Will waved a "hang loose" sign, with his thumb and pinky extended, and Danny nodded and returned the gesture.

There were four men in other tree stands farther up the

road. The rest were spread out along the ground behind a thick thorny hedge that separated the road from the forest. Several held crosses at their necks and were praying. Will found Chase and had painful flashbacks to when he helplessly watched his uncle get shot by Morgan in the desert. He looked to each of the other people he'd developed friendships with over the course of their preparation. He felt a pang in his gut as he worried about what would happen. Then he looked farther up the road to his left, where Garrett was hiding.

The squire was concealed beneath the ground in a box with a trapdoor, hidden under tall grass in a high point in the center of the old Roman road. Wheel ruts cut into the earth on both sides of the mound, concealing Garrett's box. He was lying down in the cramped space on his back, able to see through a thin slit in the direction the wagons would come from. His task was to reach through the trapdoor and hook a small animal-skin bag filled with an explosive concoction made by Chase onto the axles of the wagons as they passed. The wheel ruts in the road were so deep at that point in the road that the axle of a wagon would nearly touch the ground, allowing Garrett to place the skins without being seen by any footmen near the wagon. However, the squire only had five bags of explosives in the confined space.

Before he could see the enemy, Will could hear the distant sound of pounding feet and hooves. He watched the rise in the road for the first sign of movement, barely aware that he was digging creases into his fingers where he grasped the arrow nocked to the bowstring.

First visible on the horizon appeared a thicket of lances held in the air, followed by the armor-clad horsemen bearing them. Will felt himself begin to sweat despite the cold morning air. The sound of boots, hooves, wagons, and jostling armor grew louder as the ominous wave of plated men poured into view. Grim, metallic gray was the overwhelming color of the oncoming force—from their armor, helmets, and chain mail to their sharp mechanisms of death. Each wagon was heavily laden and surrounded by men on foot. This would not be the surgical ambush Chase had planned for.

Will watched the distant area where Garrett was concealed as the horses and footmen went over the high mound of turf. Will could barely see the animal-skin bag that hung from the first wagon axle after it passed over Garrett's position. The tree branches quivered as the endless tide of men continued to come into view. He glanced from the mass of men to his arrows and knew it wouldn't be long before he ran out.

Will continued to watch for the beige bags to be placed by Garrett. The improvised plan was for him to hook explosive charges on the front two wagons, the tenth wagon, and on the last two. Will bit his lip hard as he saw the second-to-last wagon move away from the mound without a charge. *Did Garrett drop it? He couldn't have lost count of the wagons.* Will exhaled as he saw the last pass the mound with a charge in place.

The front line of the soldiers continued past Will's position along the road. Will saw the familiar faces of Romano, Wolf, and Voskonov. He gripped the arrow nocked to his bowstring harder and searched for Morgan.

After about seventy men had passed his position, Will looked to his right to see a lone horseman galloping up the road toward the foreboding column of soldiers.

———

Sir Roland slowed his destrier as he reached the horsemen at the front of the column. He held out a large parchment of paper with a red wax seal and shouted, "Hold! I carry an urgent message!"

The horsemen didn't stop, and several lowered their lances at Roland.

"And who are you?" a man said, sizing up Roland and his large black warhorse.

"A messenger, charged with seeing that this letter reaches your leader."

The line of horses slowed, and they warily surveyed their surroundings.

"Let's have it then," one of the horsemen said, riding up to Roland and reaching for the letter.

"Are you in command?" Roland asked, ignoring the outstretched hand. He hoped that if Morgan were here, he could flush him out from the other men.

"No," the man said, "but I'll give it to him." The rest of the long column eventually halted.

"Why are we stopping?" demanded an annoyed voice.

A man with a blond beard maneuvered his horse between the first line of men and rode up to Roland. "What's going on?" Dekker demanded.

Romano and Koppel were close behind and reined their horses beside Dekker.

Roland tensed to control his anger as he looked at the three men, knowing they were likely responsible for the deaths of his friends at Arundel.

"Who is in command here?" Roland demanded. "I have an important message to deliver."

"We are," Dekker said, extending his hand to take the letter. Roland reluctantly gave it to him.

Dekker broke the red wax seal bearing a coat of arms. He quickly read the letter, then looked up. "Who is this from, and who are you?"

"As I said, a messenger."

"Let me see it," Romano said, and Dekker shoved the parchment into his hand.

Romano read it aloud. "For the hope of a free world, and for the friends whom you murdered."

Dekker drew his sword and pointed it at Roland. "I want names."

A cloaked figure emerged from the woods in front of the group, bearing a crossbow with two steel-tipped bolts. "After the pains you took to stalk my family, I'm surprised you didn't recognize the Donovan Crest on the seal," Chase said.

The faces of the Dreizack registered astonishment, and their hands darted for their handguns.

Chase loosed the crossbow bolts into Koppel and Romano, and they toppled from their horses.

"The crossbowman from the rooftop!" exclaimed one of the king's horsemen.

In one sweeping motion, Roland unsheathed his sword and swung it clean through Dekker's neck. *For Arundel!* he seethed inside.

The other horsemen converged on Roland, who spurred his stallion toward Chase. Then all hell broke loose.

Catapult arms with barrels of tar tied to the ends burst from the foliage and hammered down onto the roadway. The barrels shattered as they smashed into men and horses in the foremost third of the army. Several men were hit in the head, killing them instantly. Horses reared and shrieked. The black contents splattered across men, mounts, wagons, and earth.

At the same time, a large tree crashed across the roadway, blocking the soldiers from reaching Roland and Chase. Another tree fell about halfway to the back in the column of men, which was intended to block the escape of the caravan, but now only separated the army into two groups.

Roland and Chase fled into the forest as horsemen tried to maneuver around the fallen tree after them. Snares sprang up, swinging branches with rows of sharp spikes into the chests of the pursuers.

————

Will and the other archers in the trees had small candle boxes with metal casings that concealed the light from the roadway. They lit the tips of their arrows and shot the streaks of fire down into the tar. The sticky black sludge burst into flames.

Horses screeched and threw their riders to the ground. Men screamed as they cooked inside their own armor. The explosive charge on the front wagon ignited, blasting it into a flying array of burning splinters, assailing those nearby.

The second wagon was ablaze from splattered tar and the explosion of the first, but its own animal-skin bag still hadn't ignited. The archers sent fiery arrows hissing through the tree branches toward the wagon axle. White goose-feathered shafts protruded from the timbers and nearby soldiers.

The second wagon exploded, sending the men sprawling. The tenth wagon's charge was struck by an arrow from one of the men-at-arms, and it also hurled its contents in a billow of fire.

The acrid stench of burning wood, leather, hair, and flesh whirled from the road. Will held his breath for a moment, but knew there was no escaping the odor. Men in the forward column dove for cover from the raining arrows, and others raised their shields and charged toward the forest, hacking to break through the thick hedge lining the road.

Arrows flew into the men rushing the hedge, while Danny shouted disparaging words between arrows: "Go cry to your pox-faced mothers, you leprous goats!"

Weapons churned to break through the branches, and Edmund's men-at-arms hacked, chopped, and stabbed at those making progress. A man on the road hurled an axe over the burning hedge. It struck Hector, one of the men-at-arms, in the chest. Will's heart sank, and he sent an arrow into the man who threw the axe. Will felt queasy at the sight of the carnage below, but the adrenaline of the moment and his fear for his friends and family on the ground helped steady his nerves.

The wall of soldiers from the road thickened, and they made progress hacking through the defensive hedge. The first soldiers to break through were quickly cut down. But many more soon took their place, the thorns not deterring the armored men.

The small band of warriors was so outnumbered they could barely keep up with killing individuals who broke through. Three horsemen from the road charged their steeds through broken branches and began swinging weapons. Another man from Arundel fell. Archers in the trees began targeting the horsemen. Several arrows struck the backs of the horses, which let out cries of pain, throwing their riders off balance enough for the warriors on the ground to drag them from their mounts.

Stephen fought wildly in the mayhem, swinging a poleaxe. Flecks of blood spattered on his beard, and he drove the hammer-shaped back of the axe blade into the side of the horseman beating down on Nicholas's shield. The man cried out as the steel crushed into his armor, giving Nicholas the opportunity to silence him.

Roland charged his horse through the trees to drive off men fast approaching their flank. Few could navigate their horse as deftly as he could, and he used the advantage of his speed and height to deliver disabling blows to the men who challenged him.

Several of the soldiers tripped on thin hemp ropes strung between the trees by Chase and the others as a last-minute preparation. Soldiers with bulky helmets had difficulty seeing the thin ropes and were all the more prone to falling. However, men behind them took note and discarded their helmets as they charged at Roland. One man threw a spear at Roland's horse. The stallion let out a sharp cry of pain as the weapon drove into its chest between spaces in its armor.

The great warhorse buckled to its knees midstride, throwing Roland forward onto the ground. The soldiers converged on Roland as an easy target. The first to reach him was met with a crossbow bolt in the chest. Roland stabbed the next man in the groin, then got to his feet and nodded to Chase.

Chase moved through the fray to take a clear shot at the attacking soldiers. Four soldiers broke away to target him. He shot the first two—then fumbled to get more bolts into place. He was too late, and a man lunged at him with a sword. Chase moved, letting the sword pass between the arch and body of the crossbow, and spun it, wrenching the sword out of the man's hand. Then he kicked the soldier in the chest, sending him onto a burning patch of tar.

The next man swung a battle axe down at Chase, who barely had time to bring up the crossbow as a feeble defense. The wood splintered, and Chase stumbled backward. The man hoisted the axe overhead and swung it down. The axe sank into the dirt next to Chase's head as the man lurched forward, two arrows protruding from his back. Chase rolled to the side as the other man fell.

Chase drew his sword and slid it into a patch of burning tar. The tar stuck to the blade; orange flames and black smoke spit from the steel. He ran to aid Edmund and his men.

Edmund bared his teeth and viciously swung his blade. Several men-at-arms had fallen while protecting him. Soldiers from the road surrounded him and two men-at-arms, and Edmund frantically tried to beat away assailants.

Chase joined him and swung the sword in a broad stroke,

sending drops of burning tar into the faces of opposing warriors. They cried out and were swiftly cut down.

He had a moment to see if Will had obeyed him. "Will! Will! Get out of here! You were supposed to leave already!" Then his attention was drawn back to another oncoming man.

Will relaxed the tension of his bowstring and took in the mayhem around them. He turned to see Danny no longer firing arrows, his face blanched from the gore below, swooning as though he might pass out and fall from the tree.

"Danny! Danny! Sit down!"

Danny seemed to roll forward, then he slowly sat down, his head drooping between his knees in nausea and in shame.

Semiautomatic rifle fire sounded from the roadway, ripping through the tree branches, and one of the men-at-arms fell from the trees. Bullets smashed away the bark next to Celeste.

Will watched as she leaned from behind the tree and fired another arrow.

"No! Celeste, hide!" he shouted.

Undaunted, she quickly drew and released another arrow while partially concealing herself behind the tree trunk. A roar of gunfire sounded again, and bark splintered into her face. She clasped her hands to her eyes and braced herself against the tree.

Will felt sick with anxiety. *I can't leave them now!* He scanned the roadway and saw the muzzle flash where Skinner crouched behind a wagon. Will aimed, loosed an arrow, and watched as Skinner was hurled backward.

The king's men were hauling armfuls of supplies from the slowly burning wagons with white-feathered arrow shafts protruding from the sideboards. More soldiers were flooding into the forest to surround the small group of warriors.

The shouting, screaming, crackling flames, and sharp clanging of metal on metal were so loud that Will barely heard a voice bellowing, "Check the wagon axles! Check the wagon axles! They placed explosives!"

Will recognized the Southern accent. He couldn't spot Johnson in the tumult below, but he could see men checking the axles of the wagons. Will began to panic. If they removed the explosive charges from the last wagon, nothing would block the back of the column from retreating. One of the men-at-arms should have shot the bag, but arrows were no longer coming from their positions. He looked to the end of the column of soldiers on the other side of the fallen tree, where men on foot poured toward them around both sides of the blockade like a legion of angry fire ants.

Will could barely see the explosive bag on the wagon farthest back in the train. *I can't hit it from here.* Then he thought about those he cared about on the ground. He had to try. Will nocked a tar-tipped arrow and lit it from the candle. He pulled the arrow as far back as it would go and aimed high to compensate for the distance and the weight of the tar. He loosed the arrow and stood motionless as the streak of fire sailed over the men on the ground. It fell ten feet short of the wagon.

He saw Johnson run to inspect the wagon. The man reached to detach the explosive bag from the front axle. Will loosed a second arrow. Johnson removed the explosive and turned around. His eyes gaped open as the fiery arrow pierced the bag in his hands.

There was another boom and a pillaring flash of fire and black smoke. One of the wagon's wheels buckled, sending its contents tumbling onto the ground.

Will glanced at his few remaining arrows then to Danny and Celeste. They were both on their feet and shooting again. *I still can't leave them.* He nocked one of the precious remaining arrows to his bowstring. *Only five more left.* He really had six arrows—but one was meant for Morgan.

Members of the Dreizack shouted for the soldiers to remove the undamaged supplies from the wagons between the fallen trees and carry them to the back of the column.

Will looked beyond the fallen tree dividing the supply train from the wagons at the end. They were overflowing with supplies and turning around. The last wagon slumped smoldering in the center of the road. There was just enough space on one side of the road for the other wagons to go around it.

A knot twisted in Will's gut as the largest moved off the road to retreat through the narrow gap. He scrunched his eyebrows in confusion as Garrett climbed from his hiding place and ran toward the burning wagon. He was carrying the last explosive. Garrett must have realized that one burning wagon wouldn't be enough to block the space in the road from a retreat.

Garrett ran down the empty space of road, stumbling on the uneven ground.

A crushing realization hit Will—he recognized one of the riders in the retreating wagon. The haughty, sweeping gesture of the man's arm, the dark hair, his handgun—it was Morgan. His black beard was more grown in; Will remembered his men mentioning he might later proclaim himself as Jesus Christ returned. If anything, Will thought that the dark beard beneath the ferocious eyes made him look more demonic.

Will whipped up the steel point of his last arrow and took careful aim. The taut hemp bowstring pressed naturally into the leather tab covering his three callused fingers. The roar of violence below partially faded from his mind as he gauged the faint breeze and focused his concentration on the center of Morgan's chest. He took a deep breath in and exhaled halfway.

Garrett quickly closed the distance between himself and the burning wagon, then pulled his arm back to hurl the explosive. Morgan raised his gun and aimed at the squire. Will released his arrow and the shaft flew in perfect alignment, but before clearing the tree branches, it grazed a cluster of leaves.

The gun sounded twice, and Garrett's body jerked violently backward. As he fell, he lobbed the animal-skin bag upward into the sky.

"Garrett!" Will screamed, standing paralyzed as he watched his friend's body crumple to the earth. The pouch dropped down into the burning cart. Morgan leaped for cover into the thicket of trees opposite.

A moment passed, and then the burning remnants of the wagon exploded, sending angry streaks of fire, wood, and metal through the air. The explosion penetrated the adjacent wagon, heavily laden with barrels of processed gunpowder. The second explosion was larger and louder than all of the previous ones combined, thundering a deafening boom, swallowing everything nearby in a ball of fire.

The remaining wagons were in a tight line, ready to retreat through the same narrow space on the side of the road. One by one, each of their explosive contents erupted in a chain reaction.

Will had started to climb down from the tree when he saw Garrett topple backward, but now his ears were ringing, and he was barely aware that he was falling. The ground quickly met him like a battering ram.

He lay still, struggling to breathe. His consciousness was spinning, everything shrouded in the gray air and falling ash.

Maybe Garrett was somehow still alive. The thought pushed him off the ground, and he drew the sword and mace at his belt. Gritting his teeth, he staggered into the mayhem. Deep in his mind, he knew he should probably do what Chase said, but he was running on pure ragged emotion. He could feel the scepter's presence and wished he had the power and assurance of wielding it.

The soldiers reengaged in fighting, and Will was an exposed target.

His ears were still ringing as he made his way toward the now-burning section of the forest. Two soldiers rushed at him. In their faces was the same eagerness and hunger possessed by murderers who haunted Will's dreams. *They're trying to stop me from helping Garrett*, Will thought, and his senses sharpened.

Will deflected a sword with his mace and stabbed the man in the armpit. Another soldier swung a sword, and Will parried with his own, then crashed the mace into the side of the man's helmet.

He continued to run through the trees. Two more men moved in front of him to attack. Every second mattered if Garrett was still alive. Will charged toward the men. As they swung their swords to strike him, he dropped down and slid between their feet while raking his weapons across their unarmored shins.

The men fell, and Will moved on through the burning trees. Sparks kicked up as he ran onto the roadway where Garrett lay, his body covered in ashen debris. Will sensed that he was even closer to the scepter.

"Garrett! Garrett!" Will shouted, shaking the squire's shoulders.

Garrett grimaced, and his eyes slowly rolled open. "I told you that you needed me," he stammered. A brief hint of a smile crossed his lips.

"Garrett, you were brilliant! I'm going to get you out of here. You're going to be all right."

Garrett feebly pushed Will's hands away. "I can't make it through this. Get yourself going."

Part of Will wanted to go after what he felt was rightfully

his—he couldn't see anything on the other side of the smoke and flames, but he knew Morgan was nearby.

He snapped his attention back to Garrett. "I'm not leaving you!" Will struggled to pull him up and over his shoulders in a fireman's carry. He staggered forward, wondering just how far he could go. *As far as I have to.* Will planned to make a wide loop around the fighting to get back to the planned exit point.

Will moved into the trees as fast as he could. He felt Garrett's warm blood on his neck and shoulders. The storm of metal beating metal, men shouting, and flames roaring grew louder.

"Will," Garrett wheezed, "no one will hold it against you if you leave me."

"Not happening. Just quit bleeding on me, all right?"

He felt Garrett's ribs vibrate almost as if to laugh, which gave Will a spark of hope.

They reached the planned point of retreat, at the edge of a shallow ravine with a rocky creek bed at the bottom. The ravine was too rugged for horses to cross at this point, though it could slowly be crossed on foot. A zip line had been built going from one side to the other, and their horses were tethered on the opposite side of the ravine, making it difficult for any pursuers to keep up once the small band was safely across.

Will glanced back to see figures from the battle running toward him. He tried to keep Garrett from falling, and with one hand pulled a small, curved metal bar from his tunic and placed it over the zip line rope. His hands were drenched with blood, and he groaned. He couldn't get Garrett across.

"William!" a voice bellowed. Will turned to see Roland bounding toward him, with others from the group close behind.

"Give Garrett to me!" The man lifted Garrett from Will's shoulders and took him across on the zip line.

Chase was the next to reach the ridge.

"Who else is still on this side?" Will asked.

"You should have left a long time ago!" his uncle shouted.

"Have Danny and Celeste—"

Chase shoved Will to the zip line and thrust his hands onto the handle.

"Can you hold on?"

"Yes, but I'm not leaving without—"

"Then hold on!" Chase pushed Will off the edge of the ravine.

As he slid through the air, Will's fatigue and bloody hands made it more challenging to maintain his grip. He resented his uncle for not telling him if Danny and Celeste were safely across and assumed the question had a bad answer. Scanning the fast-approaching ridge ahead, he could only see Roland and Garrett.

35

———————

Danny and Celeste had climbed down from the trees to follow after Will, but they lost sight of him while trying to keep from getting killed. They were now lost and separated from the rest of the group.

"I think we should make our way back to the ravine and cross on foot," Danny whispered.

"We can't leave without Will!" Celeste hissed back.

"He's either hiding with Garrett, he made it back, or . . ."

Celeste scanned the forest around them, biting her lower lip.

Danny spoke again. "If he makes it back and we aren't there, he'll come back looking for us, which just puts him back in danger. And—do you realize what they'll do to you if they catch us?"

She whipped around, and her eyes angrily bore into his. "I think about that every hour of every day."

Danny winced and nodded.

"There are two of them down there!" a man near the road shouted.

The twins ducked behind the foliage. There was more shouting and the sound of soldiers moving in their direction. They peered up the hill and saw a dozen men on foot approaching.

Celeste slowly drew back the arrow nocked to her bowstring.

He grabbed her arm. "Are you kidding? Run!"

They bolted from the undergrowth and desperately dashed down the hill. There were whoops and shouts from the pursuers running down after them.

Danny and Celeste reached the edge of the ravine. It was shallow and rocky, but if they climbed down, there would be plenty of time for a host of weapons to be thrown at their heads and backs. They were nowhere near the zip line, and they looked for anyone nearby who could help.

Danny debated jumping down the jagged rocks—hoping not to be too injured to stand up again. Then he heard the metal from Celeste's sword scrape against the scabbard. He turned and drew his own.

Danny stepped in front of her and deflected the oncoming blow from the first soldier. The second soldier moved to attack Danny, but Celeste parried his blade.

The men were stronger, and the weary teens struggled to stay on their feet as they were backed closer to the edge, deflecting blow after blow.

Celeste's sword was knocked from her hand, and the man she was fighting locked his arm around her neck. She cried out and tried to fight free, but he held down her arms as well.

"No!" Danny yelled and heaved his sword at the head of the man he was fighting. The man deflected it and kicked Danny to the ground. As he fell, he dropped the blade, and the man slammed his foot into Danny's chest, pinning him down, then hoisted the sword to plunge it in a life-ending thrust.

Danny kicked upward into the man's groin. The soldier made a choking sound as he fell to the ground. Danny sprang to his feet, and though he bore no weapons, ran at the man holding Celeste.

Strong hands grabbed him from behind, and his arms were pinned behind his back. Danny kicked, but other men grabbed his legs. Pain shot through his arms as they were twisted so far that he thought they might break. He cried out in pain and devastation.

A man's voice behind him mused, "Isn't this a gift."

Bloody Morgan strode toward them, his eyes like the metal from a blacksmith's forge—recently hot with fire, now dark and smoldering. "I don't think you realize that you have given me the ideal situation for getting what I want."

He pointed the scepter's sharp peak between Danny's eyes. Morgan's voice held an icy calmness. "You're going to tell me everything I want to know. Everything."

Danny glared back, his facial muscles tensed, and his eyes fought to keep back tears.

"I know you think you're a tough boy, but you see, the ideal interrogation involves two people who care about each other." He paused. "We'll start in on Celeste, and you'll tell me every-thing. I assume your dead friends knew we were headed back to the Tower of London." He smiled. "It has some great torture devices, and I've been dying to try them out."

Danny spat at Morgan but was denied the satisfaction of even reaching his feet.

Morgan laughed and turned toward Celeste. He was about to speak when he heard the click of a gun's hammer drawing back.

"Madoc Morgan, reach for your gun, and it will be the last thing you do."

Morgan spun around, eyes blazing.

"You are hopelessly incompetent," Chase said. "First, you let your supplies get destroyed, then you just let me walk up on you. Weren't you paying attention when the Marines taught you to watch your six? But then again, you were never really a true Marine."

Chase stood on the hillside apart from the foliage, bearing a handgun. His opposite arm was a dark red, yet he still held on to a sword, partially resting it on the ground. His sand-brown hair was in disarray, his face smeared with ash and blood. Chase's gray-green eyes trained on Morgan like cold gun barrels.

One of the soldiers rushed toward Chase with a sword, but before the man could land a blow, Chase heaved his blade upward into the man's chest, his eyes never leaving Morgan.

"Hold!" Morgan shouted to his men.

Chase continued, "Word on the street is you're trying to take over the world. Probably not a good idea for someone who can't learn from past mistakes. What were you going to do first, invade Russia in the winter?"

Danny let out a harsh laugh.

"You're a fool, Donovan," Morgan seethed. "Now, all three of you will die whether you shoot me or not."

"Go ahead and draw the gun—make my day."

"You know you can't walk away from this."

"Maybe not, but those two will." He nodded to Danny and Celeste. "We're going to make a little swap. Those two walk away—and you get me."

Morgan snorted. "The great Dr. Donovan is going to trade himself for the commoners?"

"They're my friends, and my countrymen."

"Toss your gun down first," Morgan demanded.

"You know, I can't put my finger on why, but for some reason I don't trust you. Let them go!"

Morgan waved for the pair to be released.

Danny and Celeste stood free of the men holding them, but instead of running, they just stared back at Chase.

"Thank you," Celeste choked out, then turned toward the ravine.

A tear rolled down Danny's cheek as he stood looking back at Chase.

"Danny, go. It's going to be okay," Chase said.

Danny crinkled his eyebrows as if to say, *We know it isn't going to be.*

"Danny, go!"

He turned and went to where Celeste was waiting for him, and they hurriedly climbed down the rock face.

"Drop the gun," Morgan said.

"You know, I don't think I will," Chase said. "Not when I can take out the leader of this farce."

"If you shoot me, you know my men will kill you."

"Your men? Your men fight like they were trained by a clown."

Chase steadied the gun—and pulled the trigger. It clicked on empty, and a wry grin formed on Chase's mouth. He tossed the gun to the ground; it had been empty since his encounter in Stephen's village.

Morgan's chest heaved. The anger and frustration of the day rekindled. He left his handgun in his holster and ignited the white mystic light from the scepter's head.

"You must be out of bullets too," Chase mocked. He positioned his sword in both hands. "Also, good luck with your inferiority complex, knowing you can't wield the red power of Black Hammer."

Morgan rushed up the hill. The scepter made him appear to be moving at an exceptional sprint.

Chase grimaced and flung his sword at Morgan. Even in the

man's accelerated state, he still had to pause to account for the blade flying at his head, while at the same time, Chase dove at Morgan's legs.

Morgan deflected the blade and brought the handgrip of the scepter down into Chase's back.

Chase gasped, but his forward momentum was enough to knock Morgan off his feet, and the man lost his grip on the pale white depression on the scepter's hilt. The light extinguished, and he no longer had the advantage.

Chase clawed for the scepter as they wrestled on the ground for control. He got his thumb on the red depression of the scepter, and a faint light appeared. With increased motivation, he struggled to pull the scepter to his forehead, which without a room full of amplifiers, would only allow the person touched to teleport in the present time.

Morgan resisted and pulled the scepter to his own forehead.

They touched at the same moment, and there was a sharp flash of light. Both men were thrown on their backs several feet from the scepter, too dazed to continue fighting.

The soldiers surrounded Chase, and the last thing he saw was the handle of a sword crashing into the side of his head.

36

―――――

Will frantically tore strips of cloth to bandage Garrett while Roland carefully assessed his wounds. One bullet had gone through his chest and another through his abdomen. Garrett seemed to hover in and out of consciousness.

They were out of sight from the end of the zip line with Emma, Geoffrey, and the horses, waiting for others to arrive.

Roland bore an anguished expression. "Garrett, why did you let this happen to yourself?"

"I'm—I'm sorry. Where is everyone else?"

The knight's eyes were bloodshot. "They're coming."

Will knelt to place a cloth bandage on Garrett's wounds. Roland gave Will a pained look and discreetly shook his head.

Will fell back on his hands, his lips quivering.

Garrett had a moment of increased lucidity. "Did we stop them?" he breathed.

Roland swallowed hard. "Of course we did."

"We killed the leader?"

Roland hesitated.

Garrett groaned and rolled his head to the side. "Then was this for nothing?"

"No—you fought well! You protected Arundel."

Garrett winced. The answer clearly wasn't good enough for him. "There was so much I was going to do—travel to Normandy, be with a woman, find glory, get my castle." He grimaced. "Mostly, just be a knight—like you."

Roland's face filled with pain. "You're far better."

Garrett's face blanched as he struggled to look around. Edmund was behind them, leaning against a tree, staring back toward the ravine. The face of the seventeen-year-old seemed to have aged decades. All of his men-at-arms had died making sure he made it to safety. Long ago, they had all discarded anything that might tie them to Arundel, and Edmund stood in his common armor and tunic, spattered with ash and blood. Stephen knelt several feet behind Roland, similarly battered, covered with black soot, still holding the blood-stained poleaxe.

Emma was next to Will; she looked stricken with grief and seemed to share Will's helpless eagerness to do something for Garrett.

"Where is everyone else?" Garrett's eyes glistened. "They aren't coming back?" His head sank wearily back against the ground.

Will's emotions were eating him from the inside out. He wanted to say something to console Garrett, but he couldn't find any words. *He wouldn't be about to die if it wasn't for me. His friends wouldn't have died—or mine.* Will looked from Roland to Edmund and thought of the only possible thing that might help Garrett's emotional agony. He stood and walked directly to the earl's son.

"Sir Edmund, it would mean a great deal to Garrett—"

"Hold," Edmund said in a tired voice. "I believe I know your request, and I've been gathering my strength for it."

Will paused, debating whether to make him clarify.

Edmund walked past Will and gazed down on Garrett's face. "You were the first from Arundel to commit to this," he said in a pained tone.

Garrett looked up, his eyes confused. "My lord . . ."

"My men died in this fight. Good men," Edmund said. "If I had taken their council, they would be alive."

Edmund paused, and no one spoke.

He drew his blood-slickened sword. "However—because we committed to the attack, we may have forced our enemy to expend their foreign bullets. We destroyed much of their supplies to make more, and we killed many of the Dreizack. For the time being, they cannot attack my father's earldom. They cannot attack our homeland. They cannot attack the wives and children of my men. All of this because of your courage to fight and your bravery in the battle. How could I not dub thee a knight?"

Garrett's eyes faintly widened.

"My lord, that would mean a great deal to him," Roland said.

Will felt closer to Edmund than ever before, and he desperately hoped Garrett would feel some degree of comfort.

Edmund wiped his sword on his tunic.

Garrett's features relaxed, and he kept his eyes open.

Edmund gently tapped his sword on Garrett's shoulders, "It is my humble privilege that I hereby dub thee Sir Garrett of Arundel."

"Thank you, my lord," Garrett said.

"No, thank you, Sir Garrett," Edmund stepped back, allowing the others to be with him.

Garrett let out a painful breath. "Sir Roland, please don't be angry with me."

"No, no, Sir Garrett. How could I ever be angry with you?"

Garrett's features relaxed, and his eyes closed for the last time. Tears rolled freely down Will's cheeks.

Roland tenderly held Garrett's hand, and kept his gaze upon him until long after his last breath had faded away.

———

Will felt a wave of relief when he finally saw Danny and Celeste, but they seemed too downtrodden to show the same enthusiasm. Danny wouldn't speak nor look Will in the face. When Celeste told Will about Chase, he dropped to his knees.

Celeste knelt as well. Her voice was weary. "We have to give this up. I'm going back to Arundel."

Will looked at her out of the corner of his pained eyes. "I thought you said you didn't have a life here."

"A life in Arundel with Edmund is better than more of this."

The group took Garrett's body with them and fled farther away from the ravine before stopping for the night. They made a simple grave for Garrett with a wooden cross.

No campfire was lit, and most were silent except for an occasional exchange of terse words. Danny still wouldn't talk to or look at anyone.

Will needed someone to talk to, but all of his attempts were met with resentment. Even Emma seemed angry at Will. She had known many of the people who had died for years.

He walked away from the camp as night fell. As he paused at Garrett's grave, it racked him to know that the others couldn't be buried, and that their bodies, and Garrett's simple grave, would soon be forgotten in time. He continued deeper into the forest and collapsed on the ground.

This is all my fault, and not just the ambush. A deep pit sank in his stomach. People back home thought the world would have been better if he had never been born—perhaps they were right. *If it wasn't for me, we never would have time traveled here. Maybe me being alive has destroyed humanity—as an alien freak and truly a terrorist.* They told Garrett this was a victory, but it wouldn't take long for Morgan to rebuild and recruit.

He tried to remember how he had pulled himself out of emotional darkness in the alley in London. Thinking about revenge was futile. Finding things to be grateful for was onerous. He tried to think of his mother's love and the gift of life she had given him. *She'd probably regret it if she knew what I've caused. Everyone I care about would have been safer without me.*

It felt like he had been sitting there a long time before he slowly drew his dagger and contemplated pressing it to his abdomen.

He gripped the handle harder and touched the point to his center. Morgan was going to win. They didn't get all of the supplies, and there wouldn't be another chance. Danny had said long ago that the victors of wars shaped the world, and Morgan had won.

His mind was silent for a while. Was this what it came to? They would eventually find his body, the lowest of losers. Danny and Celeste might be unhappy with him now, but it pained him to imagine how much sorrow they would experience after finding his body lying here.

He thought for several minutes about how this choice would hurt people he loved. Then he slowly withdrew the dagger.

Morgan may beat the world, but he hasn't beaten me. I'm the one about to defeat me! I'm not going to give him or anyone else the victory of me killing myself. Regardless of what other people think—I matter to me, and I'm not a quitter. I'm going to be the victor of the war inside myself.

He stood and threw the dagger as far as he could over the trees. *Watch out, Bloody Morgan. I'm still coming for you.*

Will went back to the camp. He didn't expect that anyone would want to see him any more than they had before, but he found Danny sitting alone on a log looking at the ground, and Will sat next to him.

"Hey," Will said.

Danny didn't respond.

Will sat with him for an hour, just so Danny would know he wasn't alone. Will remembered the look on his friend's face when he nearly passed out in the tree stand after the first few minutes of combat. It seemed that now the adrenaline had worn off, processing the images that followed and the loss of brothers had pushed Danny to completely shut down. Will couldn't get the images of the men dying on the road out of his mind, either. Men who were simply hired to do a job, having no idea of Morgan's intentions.

Danny finally spoke. "I don't want to go to sleep—because I know what my dreams will be."

"Me too," Will said and rested his arm around Danny's shoulder. Danny let out several quiet sobs, and Will felt tears roll down his own cheeks.

Time went by, and eventually Danny took a deep breath. "The deodorant here also sucks." He nodded at Will's arm around him. "Maybe you should switch brands."

Will pulled his arm away, and his countenance relaxed. "It's better than your hamster-and-elderberry smell," he said, referencing a snippet of the French guard's taunt in *Monty Python and the Holy Grail*.

Danny's forlorn eyes continued to stare vacantly at the ground, but his lips bore a faint trace of amusement. Will felt some relief. He knew that his friend was still somewhere in there—deep inside.

37

The group spent the day after the battle arguing about what to do. Edmund was committed to not returning home until Morgan was dead, and plans went in his favor.

They traveled back to London during the night and instructed Geoffrey to establish accommodations for them in an obscure inn since no one at the battle had seen his face. Whenever outside the inn, they traveled in small numbers and kept their faces obscured by cloaks. Staying out of sight as much as possible, they spent several days surveying the Tower of London.

Then an announcement was issued from the castle that an enemy of the Crown was to be publicly executed in the morning—an enemy named Chase Donovan.

The small group sat huddled in the private room of the inn. Those remaining included Edmund, Roland, Stephen, Geoffrey, Emma, Celeste, Danny, and Will.

"The man saved my life in battle," Edmund said in a hushed tone, not wanting anyone outside the room to hear. "With enough money, I could negotiate his release." The loss of his men and the intensity of the battle had changed Edmund. The arrogance and haughtiness had faded away, and even though he was still in charge, he seemed to treat the others more like family than underlings.

"No, my lord," Roland whispered. "If it came to light that we were opposing the king, it would put your father at great risk when he returns. A ransom proposal likely wouldn't be accepted anyway, considering the king's new allies."

"Shall we let them kill Chase?" Edmund said with contempt.

"That's not an option," Will said.

Roland replied, "Chase saved my life as well, and I am also in his debt—but we have to think of another way. Perhaps we can intercept Chase on his way to the place of execution."

"We can't wait until then," Will said. "They announced his name. This reeks of a Madoc Morgan trap. He wants us to do something like that."

"They could set such a trap even if he weren't still alive," Geoffrey said.

Will's fingers curled into fists, even though he knew Geoffrey might be right.

"Show some respect," Stephen said.

Geoffrey leaned away. "Someone needed to say it."

"I care about him too," Celeste said. "But I don't want more of us dying."

"You don't care about him as much as Will and I do." Danny had a hard look in his eyes. "He and I went through a lot together. After what he did for us, you would give up on him?"

"No," Celeste said. "But he didn't sacrifice himself for us so we could turn around and get ourselves killed. He would probably be angry at us for trying."

"*I* have to do something." Will gave Danny a concerned look. The two had extensively talked about what happened at the ambush and in the tree stand. Even though Danny had shown increasing signs of vigor and resolve, Will still worried about his friend.

Danny's expression registered hurt, and he leaned forward, his face reddening with intensity. "I'm not giving up on him, and I will not falter if we attack."

"If he's alive, I think I know where they would keep him," Will said. "I saw where they keep the torture devices."

Celeste shuddered. "That's where Morgan would have him."

"Perhaps," Edmund said, "but if he is Morgan's bait, wouldn't they also have a snare prepared in the area where Chase is imprisoned?"

"Probably." Will remembered the look in Morgan's eyes when he had stepped from the king's oratory.

"I greatly respect the man as a fighter and an engineer," Roland said. "However, we may not get more than one chance to strike at the Dreizack while they're in London. We know that three remain. It will be easier when they're not waiting for us."

"Oh, come on!" Danny said. "We'll think of something."

"I really don't know about all of this," Geoffrey said. "Trespassing into the king's castle? Helping a condemned man? This is all treason."

"How dare you," Emma said. The group was a little taken aback. This was the first time she had interjected in a group debate. "Sir Edmund has been opposing Antichrists who have deceived the king. Our lord has been in the service of king and country. I may not be able to fight, but I'll not scurry off if there is anything I can do to help."

Will gave her a smile. He was glad she felt comfortable speaking her mind and hoped her words were another step in healing their friendship.

Edmund spoke. "We are acting in the king's best interests.

I've had to wrestle with my own conscience, but I believe thus far we've done the right thing."

"Listen here, Geoffrey," Stephen said. "There'll be no last-minute excuses of cowardice. We need to know if we can count on you."

Geoffrey's face blanched as he looked at the eyes in the room boring into him. He picked at one of the old pox scars on his cheek. "Yes, yes, of course. I see your reasoning more clearly. We would be trying to help the king, though he doesn't know it, and to help Chase, who is a friend."

"We'll need all the help we can get," Edmund said. "If you'll all join me, I say we attempt to rescue him."

38

Night fell, and Will, Danny, Celeste, Roland, Stephen, and Edmund waited, hiding in a row of shipping supplies on the river docks near the castle moat.

Roland held a spyglass, previously made by Chase for scouting the road prior to the ambush, and looked at the tall, pointed tower of All Hallows Church. Emma was hiding up there, and they were waiting for her to light a candle at the top of the belfry when there were no guards near the section of wall for them to sneak past.

Will crouched with his back against the low stone wall. He held four small explosive charges that Chase had taught them to make. They were smaller than what Garrett had used. Hopefully, they would be sufficient. Will thought through the plan over and over again, knowing that if any single part failed, they would all be killed.

Once Emma lit the candle, they would hurriedly carry the boat to the moat, try to row as quietly as possible to the castle's water gate beneath the king's residence, use the explosive charges to break an opening in the gate, rush up to the king's quarters, and hold him hostage there in exchange for Chase, Morgan, the remaining Dreizack, the scepter, and safe passage out of the city. Maybe they could make a clean exchange without anyone getting killed. Geoffrey was at the inn, ready with their horses and supplies in case something went wrong and they needed to move quickly to another part of the city.

"The lantern is lit. Let's move," Roland whispered.

Adrenaline surged through Will, and they picked up the rowboat and walked it around the building. He felt vulnerable in the exposed area and was eager to get to the moat and the dark shadows of the castle walls.

They were nearly to the water when owl hooting sounded behind them. Will's anxiety went up a notch. Emma was supposed to make owl-hooting sounds to alert them of incoming danger. The candlelight from the church tower was gone.

"Wait," Will whispered. The others slowed as they heard the owl sounds too.

Roland whipped up the spyglass and hissed, "There's still no one on that wall, but we should fall back."

They hurried the boat back into hiding and readied their weapons, anticipating someone approaching them—but there was no one.

"What do you think she saw?" Celeste asked.

Roland studied the plaza, and his face tensed into a snarl. "Geoffrey."

"Let me have a look," Stephen said, and Roland shoved the spyglass into his hand.

"I'll flail him," Stephen seethed. "He's talking with the guards at the gate."

Edmund cursed under his breath then, mouthed a silent scream.

Will clenched his fists and tried to keep his breathing steady.

"I knew we couldn't trust that idiot," Danny muttered.

"The guards are escorting him into the castle," Stephen whispered in disgust.

"Stephen, you know him best. What is he doing?" Edmund asked.

Will had never seen Stephen so angry, and the man took a moment to respond. "Clearly betraying us, but he's too big a coward to go into the castle with the guards unless he thinks he's going to get something—a reward in gold, most likely."

Edmund shook his head. "He could have stolen from us and fled at any time. He could have gone to the soldiers at any time. Why now?"

"If he stole from us and fled, he'd eventually have to face me back at home. If we're caught, he doesn't have to worry about any of us again. Perhaps he thinks he'll get a bigger reward if we're caught in the act. I'm only guessing, though. Geoffrey's a fool. I'm so sorry, my friends."

"You're not at fault," Edmund said. "Thank God for Emma."

"We still have to do something, or my uncle will die tomorrow," Will said.

Edmund shook his head. "I don't know what else to do. They'll know we were going to try to leverage the king, and if we don't try tonight, they'll anticipate a rescue attempt at the execution, and maybe even change locations—if he's still alive. And Morgan will know we're hunting him in London."

"Morgan will keep the scepter even more private," Celeste said.

"We can't return to anywhere we've lodged," Roland said, "or use any of our lookout sites in the city."

Edmund nodded. "We must leave London tonight."

Will felt like his world was collapsing in on him, and he braced himself against the stone and mortar of the wall.

"There's my idea," Danny said. "That I didn't tell Geoffrey about."

"If it's the one you explained to me, it's too far-fetched." Roland shook his head.

"I'd still like to hear it," Edmund said. "Quickly, explain."

"Once I read that there is a sally port tunnel going from the White Tower out into the city so that the king could come and go without being seen. But I don't know where the city entrance is."

"That doesn't help us," Edmund said.

"I read that the tunnel goes under the moat and also exits into the Lion Tower, so that if an intruder breached that point in the reinforcements, soldiers inside the castle could go from there to the Lion Tower, to surround the invaders or provide reinforcements to defend the moat."

Roland shook his head. "The problem is that you don't know where in the tower such a door would be. It would certainly be hidden—and there is no way for us to get to the tower, and over its wall, without being seen."

Will pressed his hand to his chin, desperately trying to work with the information to see if there was a solution. "The torture chambers are also in the White Tower. If we can think of a way to get to the tunnel, it might take us near Chase."

"I want to help Chase, but it's a bad idea," Roland said.

"Does anyone else have any better bad ideas?" Danny asked.

"Than creeping about in the lion cages for a hidden door?" Edmund scoffed. "We have to leave now."

Stephen shook his head. "Sorry, Danny, I don't see this one working."

"Wait!" Will held out a hand. "I think I know how we can

try to make it work."

After hashing through Will's plan, Roland sighed and rubbed his chin. "If we do that, we'll all be sopping wet and leaving puddle trails wherever we go. Not to mention being slower at fighting."

"Not if we take off our chain mail and clothes first and keep them concealed," Will said.

"What?" Celeste exclaimed.

Will shrugged. "He's right. We'd need dry clothes."

"Yeah," she said, "but that would make things really *awkward*."

"Propriety isn't a luxury we can afford," Danny said.

"No, I mean, I'd be blundering around trying not to see you guys."

"Everyone can just take off what you don't want wet," Will suggested.

"Guards are hastening from the castle!" Roland warned, focusing through the spyglass. "We must decide now. Either we retreat across the river by boat, never to return, or commit ourselves to this plan."

They tensed, looking at each other, then in the direction of the guards, no one wanting to commit everyone else to either fate.

"I'll not command any of you to make this attempt," Edmund said. "But I am in favor of it."

Celeste grabbed the edges of her chain mail and began to pull it off. "I'm not going to be the reason we hold back."

"But perhaps *you* should stay, m'lady," Edmund said. "This plan carries more risk than the other."

"I'm the only one carrying a bow, and I can't bear the thought of all of you trying to do this without my help."

Carrying explosives would be problematic for the new plan, and Will gave them to Stephen, who played his part by yelling

French and English obscenities at the guards and getting them to pursue him into the city.

The others hurriedly tied their chain mail, weapons, and clothes across a board, then placed the board on the crossbars of the boat. They flipped the boat upside down and carried it into the moat. The water smelled like an acrid bog. They kept their heads in the air pocket but couldn't completely submerge the boat.

"We have to let out more of the trapped air," Will said. "We need just enough to keep our gear dry and take a few breaths." With the adjustments, they were able to get the boat completely under the surface.

The Lion Tower was about twenty feet from the edge. Roland and Edmund had grown up next to the River Arun and the ocean and were good swimmers, as were the modern group. They part kicked, part swam along the bottom of the moat's soft floor until they felt the boat's bow gently bump into the base of the stone tower. Will bent underneath the rim and slowly peeked his head above the surface. He peered across the moat to the shore, then up to the rim of the tower. From their position in the water, the only way someone from the castle could see them would be to lean over the wall and look straight down. He was grateful for the sound of the lapping of the river water and the noise from the city masking the ripples they made. Their stealth was their survival.

He gently tapped the hull of the boat underwater, and the others slowly surfaced their heads. After catching their breath, they lifted the boat up and tilted it to let in more air until they could access the board bearing their clothing and weapons. They carefully removed it and slowly let the boat fill with water.

The wooden boat still wouldn't sink to the bottom. Will and Danny swam down to retrieve large rocks and gently placed them in the boat to overcome the wood's buoyancy until the timbers descended to the moat's floor.

Meanwhile, Edmund and Celeste worked to assemble a long, thin pole by tying arrows together. The tip of the first arrow was partially embedded into a rope with a slip knot, so once the pole of arrows extended high enough, the loop could rest around a stone on the wall's battlements. Will estimated it was about twenty-five feet from the water to the top, and they would need most of the shafts from Celeste's quiver.

"Careful," Celeste hissed. "If you get my arrows wet, they won't shoot as well."

After maneuvering the loop over a crenel stone on the top of the wall and pulling the length of arrows free from the rope, they slowly detached the shafts and replaced them into her quiver.

———

Roland pulled on the rope to test its security as he warily surveyed the tower wall and moat. He took a deep breath before looking back at his friends. "If anything happens to me, leave. Flee as fast as you can."

He took another deep breath, planted his feet against the wall, and began ascending the rope. His wet feet were slippery against the cold stone of the tower, and the climbing was slow going.

When he reached the top, he braced his hand on the rim of the wall. This drew the attention of the guard, who drove a poleaxe down at Roland. The knight's eyes widened, and he tried to move to the side, but the blade cut the edge of his shoulder. His face contorted as he shot up a hand to clamp onto the guard's throat.

Roland's feet slipped against the wall, and he desperately

held on to the top of the wall and the guard. The other man struggled to breathe, but Roland's grip kept him from crying out. The knight's muscles ached, but he waited until the guard was no longer moving.

Roland climbed over the wall and lay breathlessly on the wall walk. He looked around for another attacker but saw no one. He put a hand to his bleeding shoulder. Luckily, the cut wasn't deep.

Quietly, he pulled the guard's body away from the edge, listening closely for footsteps on stone or a weapon scraping out of a scabbard, but he only heard the constant evening noises from the city and the river. He signaled for the others to stay put, sank down onto the wall walk, and remained wary, continuing to look around.

A deep growl resonated from below. He tensed and peered into the darkness toward the rows of cages. He couldn't see the animal that had made the growl, but he wasn't looking forward to searching the tower for a trapdoor.

The clothes and weapons were pulled up first. Then Will climbed up the rope.

"I'll help the rest up," Roland whispered. "Start searching outside the cages on the floor and walls for any loose stones."

Will nodded, took his belongings, and slowly descended the stairs.

***

The tower was shaped in a semicircle and served as a halfway point across the moat between the land and the castle. It provided a secure place for the public to see the animals, when permitted, without allowing them all the way into the castle. Will heard some of the creatures stirring and hoped they wouldn't become unusually loud. He reached the stone floor and looked at the two entrances to the Lion Tower. *Someone could pass through either door at any moment.*

After donning his clothing and chain mail, he found a closet space that held food and supplies for the animals. He quietly moved the supplies and tested the stones for any sign of looseness. There was nothing.

Gazing at the wall of cages, Will shivered as multiple pairs of large eyes gleamed back at him from the darkness. Dried feces and urine on the stone floor stung Will's nostrils.

Danny was the next one up the wall and quietly made his way down to his friend.

"If there is a trapdoor," Will whispered, "I don't think it would be in this center area where the public could access it. My guess is that it would be in a cage that wouldn't be difficult to exit out of—from the tunnel."

Danny looked around at the different cages. There were lions, a leopard, a polar bear, exotic birds, zebras, and more. "Nah, it's in the lion cage."

"That wouldn't make any sense," Will said. "The king or someone else fleeing the castle would want the exit to be safe."

"No, if the king were trying to secretly exit the castle, he would go all the way to the end of the tunnel, to whatever building it lets out into. The purpose of this sally port would be for soldiers inside the castle to be able to move to a different defensive position if part of the castle was breached or to launch a surprise attack on someone besieging the castle's front gate. You've seen the royal coat of arms?"

"Yeah. It has a bunch of lions and Frenchy fleurs-de-lis."

"On a coat of arms, the beast's head, legs, and tail are symbolic. For hundreds of years, the English kings have displayed lions in the position of *passant guardant*—or 'passing guardian.' I'm telling you, the lions guard the door. Like us, no one is going to want to go in there. Soldiers exiting the tunnel could bring a hunk of meat for the lions and toss it into the cage before exiting."

"We didn't bring any meat."

"Well, there is the . . ." Danny nodded up to the wall walk where the guard was lying.

"We aren't going to feed someone to the lions," Will whispered.

"It sounds bad if you phrase it that way."

"That's because it is bad."

"Well, maybe we would feel better about him dying if it served a purpose."

"What? So, when someone dies, we should just take them to the zoo to feel better about it?"

"I couldn't have done it anyway. I would have asked you to do it."

Will sighed. "Well, I don't want to kill the lions just to inspect the cage."

"Whoa, sicko. You're contemplating murdering kitty cats."

"Someone should feed you to the freakin' lions," Will mumbled.

"Calm down, Mr. Spec-Ops."

Will slowly walked toward the lion cages. He swallowed as two big cats approached the bars. "Are you sure about this? If a lion was sitting on the trapdoor, how would they get it open?"

"If part of the ground was moving beneath you, wouldn't you move?"

Will nodded and surveyed the other cages. "*If* you're right, I think it would be in the cage with the lone big male. I saw some meaty bones and animal hides in the closet with the animal supplies. Maybe we could lure him out and into the empty cage?"

Danny shivered. "That's scary, but I don't see any quieter options."

Edmund walked down to join them.

"Any luck?" he whispered.

"We think if there's a door, it might be with the big guy," Danny said.

Edmund didn't respond at first as he looked around. "Are you mad?"

Danny quickly described the situation and plan, and Edmund cursed under his breath. "Fine then. Do it."

Will and Danny got the lion's attention with the bones, and it put its large paws against the bars as it tried to bite.

They withdrew the bones a few inches, and the beast continued to sniff at them.

Danny nervously lifted the latch on the gate. The big cat pushed it open eagerly and came toward them. Will and Danny kept their weapons ready and encouraged the lion with the scraps. They placed the crude bait inside the empty cage, but the lion stopped and looked around, more interested in its newfound freedom.

Will's heart raced as he slid the scruff of an animal hide across the stone floor and into the cell. The lion instinctively pounced on it as if it were prey. Edmund secured the door behind it.

"You best be right about this," Edmund whispered.

They waited for any signs of being overheard amid the sounds of the city. Then they crept into the empty lion cage and began testing the large stones in the floor for any looseness.

At the back of the cage, Will felt a shift between two of the stones. His heart pounded as he pulled out the stone and felt the cold steps descending into the blackness. *Jackpot!* He waved and pointed at the entrance to the others, who raised their arms in triumph.

Will felt the unseen steps with his hands and braced himself for the blindness that was about to swallow them.

39

They quietly hid the guard's body behind animal feed in the supply closet, then ventured into the abyss of the tunnel.

The damp stone passage was low enough that Will had to keep his head bent down and narrow enough that he could easily touch both walls. He felt anxious as they blindly moved forward, keeping one hand on the shoulder of the person in front of them so as not to stumble over each other.

Roland brought up the rear and soon gave several hard jerks on Danny's chain mail. Danny and the others stopped, then they heard it—the quick movement of multiple pairs of feet coming from where the tunnel exited into the city. The dim light from a torch streamed toward them.

"No. What do we do?" Danny whispered.

"Everyone, keep to the left wall," Roland instructed. "Celeste, when the one bearing a torch reaches us, strike him first. We're counting on you."

"I'll try not to let you down."

Everyone pressed themselves against the damp stone while

trying not to make a sound. Celeste was across from Will, and he could barely make out her silhouette in the approaching torchlight as she slowly fitted an arrow to her bowstring in the dark.

Soon the flame came into view, and the men stopped when they saw Celeste and Roland.

"Kill 'em," ordered the soldier bearing the torch.

The men converged, and Celeste's arrow buried into the chest of the torchbearer. He crumpled to his knees, dropping the torch.

The passage was lit in an eerie glow as the torch lay on the ground, momentarily disorienting the soldiers. Roland's eyes were more adjusted to the darkness, and he lunged forward, driving his dagger into the belly of one of the men. Another soldier swung his sword at Roland, but the knight stepped back, dodging it, and lunged forward again to finish the man. The body fell on the torch, extinguishing the light.

The last soldier turned and ran.

"No!" Roland said.

"Get down!" Celeste shouted.

As Roland dropped to the ground, Celeste let loose an arrow into the darkness. There was a brief cry of pain, and a pause, but the footsteps continued away.

"God's teeth!" Roland growled.

Will's heart raced. The guard would surely tell everyone they were down there.

They reassembled and stumbled through the passage as fast as they could until they reached a small set of stone stairs. Edmund pushed up on the ceiling, and a trapdoor gave way.

"It has clearly been in recent use," Edmund said as they clambered into an empty bedroom and wedged the door in the floor shut behind them. "Once that man returns from the city, the whole castle garrison will be on us."

"The room with the torture devices is in the basement of this tower," Will said. "I'll show you where."

"Right, I'll go first." Roland drew his dagger and a small, single-bladed francisca throwing axe from his belt. "We need to move as quietly as possible. William, stay close by to provide directions. The rest of you keep back, weapons ready and eyes sharp."

They swiftly moved through the corridors, pausing at each turn. When they reached the passage in the basement, Roland peeked around the corner and held up a hand for the group to stay put.

He motioned for them to move in closer, then whispered, "Six armed men are standing outside a door. They're surely guarding something, and given the location in the castle, it's most likely a prisoner. They'll see us a long time before we can get to them. I think we can overwhelm them, but there's a high risk that we'll suffer casualties." He made eye contact with each of them. "Is everyone committed to a swift, direct attack?"

They nodded.

"I have an idea," Danny whispered.

Roland held up a hand. "Quiet. I'm going to decide how we proceed."

"Will someone just trust me?" Danny removed his sword and scabbard.

"What are you doing?" Roland mouthed.

"Trust me—stay here and don't follow me."

Danny began to walk down the corridor. Celeste grabbed his arm, but he shook it off.

Roland looked at Will and tossed up his hands, mouthing, "What is he doing?"

Will bit his lip and motioned for the rest of the group to wait.

Danny walked toward the guards.

"Hey, what are you doing down here, boy?" one of them demanded.

Danny continued to approach them. "Hello, maybe you could help me out—I'm trying to find something good to steal. You know, like jewels or stuff."

"What nerve!" Several guards moved forward to grab Danny, not bothering to draw their weapons.

Danny raised his palms and dropped his jaw as if completely astonished that they could possibly be upset with him.

Just before one of the men grabbed his shoulders, Danny slapped the man's face. "Saucy blighter!" he yelled, then turned and sprinted back down the corridor.

"Hey, stop!" one shouted as four men pursued him.

Once Danny rounded the corner, Roland hissed, "Attack!"

The guards were quickly dispatched with a host of weapons.

The two remaining guards drew their swords and charged. "St. George!"

Roland threw his axe into the chest of one, and Edmund finished the other.

Will found the key in the pocket of one of the guards and fit it into the lock.

"We should have asked the last two to surrender," Celeste said.

"A bit late for that," Edmund muttered.

Danny removed a lantern from the hallway, and they stepped into the ominous dark room.

Will froze as the smell of dried blood and sweat hit him. The lantern cast grim shadows as it reflected off the sharp and grizzly torture devices throughout the room. He brought the back of his fist to his mouth. He continued to move in, apprehensive of what they might find.

There was a large inclined table with a tall body strapped to it, limbs stretched in all four directions.

"Will?" a voice breathed.

"Uncle Chase? Are you okay?" Will rushed forward and brushed the man's face.

Danny was close behind. He exhaled in relief. "We found him."

Chase's mouth twitched. "Like jewels or stuff?" A smile struggled to form on his parched lips. "You bloody peasant."

Will and Danny let out a dry laugh and hurriedly worked to untie him.

Chase's eyes rested on Will. "I'm glad you're alive but hoped that you wouldn't be foolish enough to try anything like this."

Will smiled. "It's great to see you too."

"Now then, let's get you off this rack," Edmund said. "Can you walk?"

"I think so." Chase groaned as they helped him sit up. "Not that I have much choice. It feels so much better to have the ropes off."

"Make haste," Roland said as he returned to the door to look down the corridor. "Someone likely heard the fighting."

Will and Danny helped Chase off the table, and he tensed in pain with his first awkward steps but was able to walk on his own toward the door.

"It makes me sick that they did this to you," Celeste said. "There's no way we could ever thank you enough. It should have been me and Danny imprisoned in here."

"No," Chase said. "You shouldn't have been the ones to pay for my sins."

"Don't be hard on yourself. You didn't intend for things to turn out this way. Do you know where the scepter is?" she asked.

"The scepter—" Chase grimaced and swallowed. "That's

part of the reason Morgan was torturing me. He wanted me to make amplifiers here for teleporting people. He wanted to travel anywhere in this present time with me bound in chains. After what they put me through, they're convinced I'll never build anything for them. They did experiments with my blood, which yielded no results. The last several times Morgan was down here, he wasn't wearing the scepter. He gloated that it was hidden where only he could access it and no one could find it in a hundred years. Also, I overheard him and his men talking —they used up the last of their modern ammunition defending themselves on the roadway."

"But how are we ever going to get home?" Celeste's eyes widened.

Chase shook his head, avoiding eye contact.

"I'm not certain," Roland said, "but we should likely take our chances with the tunnel."

"Do you think he meant more like 140 years?" Danny asked.

"What do you mean?" Chase looked perplexed.

Danny spoke rapidly. "You said Morgan didn't think anyone would find it in a hundred years. I'm trying to think of his views on that time frame. Let's say, in about 140 years, the reigning king passes away, leaving behind two young sons. Their uncle takes custody of the boys, who soon disappear while at the Tower of London. People suspect that their uncle had them killed after he declares himself king. And let's say the skeletons of the two boys were found here about three hundred years later. If there was any place in the castle I was confident would be undisturbed for a long time, it would be where the princes' bodies would be hidden."

"What the devil are you talking about?" Edmund asked.

"Uh, well, it's a fable, back where we're from," Danny said.

"What an odd place your America is."

"Where's the location?" Celeste asked.

"Under the stairs leading to the old chapel—but I'm not sure where it is."

"I know where it is," Will said. "It's here in the White Tower, just up the stairs."

"We don't have time for this," Edmund said. "I can buy a new scepter for you."

Celeste grabbed Edmund's arm. "It's not something that can be replaced and is extremely important to our people. Please, let's just check."

"It's just up the stairs," Will pleaded.

"Fine, fine," Edmund said. "We are in haste."

"Thank you." Chase nodded. He picked up a sword from one of the fallen men.

They hurried as quietly as they could to the dark stairwell near the chapel and began inspecting the stairs.

"This portion is loose," Celeste said and heaved off a large stone step.

The group quickly gathered around. There was a space dug out beneath the stairwell but nothing inside.

"Someone was keeping something there," Roland observed.

"The stone wasn't placed all the way back in, so it wasn't as secretive as it could be," Celeste said.

"There are markings in the dust about the length of the scepter," Will said. "Maybe Morgan came back and got it after hearing about our plans from Geoffrey, then went back to the water gate."

"I don't know," Danny said, "but I think we've pressed our luck enough and should get out of here."

"We won't have another opportunity in London," Celeste lamented.

"If we die wandering about the castle, we won't have opportunities for anything," Roland said.

"We leave now," Edmund said sternly.

They heard men shouting on the floors below them.

Roland looked down. "They know we're here."

They hurried toward a stairwell but found themselves cornered by soldiers. Roland bellowed, "Attack!" as he engaged them, and the others followed.

Metal crashed into metal. Then there was a scream and the sound of a wooden bow clattering to the ground.

The scream felt like ice stabbing into Will's heart. He jolted around to see a large man with one arm wrapped around Celeste, pinning her arms down. A slit of moonlight shone on Voskonov's monstrous face and the bloody trident tattoo on his neck.

<h1 style="text-align:center">40</h1>

Voskonov dragged Celeste deeper into the castle.

Everyone else was doing their best to fend off the soldiers. Will swallowed hard, barely deflecting an oncoming sword from impaling him, then shoved past to go after Celeste.

He looked around frantically. There were so many ways they could have gone. A faint scream came from the floor above, and Will bounded up the stairs. Finding an open door, he charged in.

Voskonov still had Celeste's arms pinned to her sides, her back to him with her quiver of arrows pressing into his chest. His massive paw was clamped around her mouth. She thrashed with her feet, and her eyebrows shot up when she saw Will.

"Let her go!" he demanded.

He swung his common mace down to crush Voskonov's head, but the Russian dodged to the side, grabbed Will's arm, and hurled him to the floor.

Will dropped the mace, and Voskonov kicked it clattering out the door. He tossed Celeste to the side and drew an axe at his belt.

"You're dead," he snarled as he closed in on Will. He abruptly stopped when Celeste punched him in the back of the head. He turned around, and his massive fist sent her sprawling to the ground.

Will stumbled to his feet and lurched back as a broad swing from the axe barely missed his midsection. Then he lunged forward and landed an uppercut to Voskonov's jaw. The blow surprised him, but a second later, he smirked and head-butted Will to the ground.

The stone floor jarred Will to the bones, and his vision blurred. He grimaced as he imagined the axe chopping into him.

The blow didn't come, and he opened his eyes to see a figure between him and Voskonov.

Celeste was brandishing her small dagger, shaking as she protected Will.

"Leave us alone!" she yelled.

Voskonov laughed as she swiped at him. He patted the blows away with the side of his axe, then reached out and grabbed her wrist.

Celeste took the dagger with her free hand, cutting into Voskonov's forearm.

He grunted and used the blunt end of his axe to shove her down. As she fell, she tried to pull the axe out of his hand but couldn't hold on. Her head struck the stone floor, and she didn't get up.

Will was back on his feet and charging at Voskonov with a three-pronged unlit candlestick from a table. Voskonov threw the axe at Will and nearly took off his head.

Will lunged with the candlestick, but the Russian kicked it out of his grasp. Will's hand recoiled in pain. Voskonov drew his dagger and rushed forward.

Desperate for anything that could be used as a weapon, Will scooped up a metal goblet and a square wooden plate. He deflected blow after blow with the wooden plate, then moved in and smashed Voskonov in the face with the goblet.

Voskonov yelled out, then picked up the oaken table and swung it into Will's chest.

Will toppled over, the entire weight of the heavy table pinning him to the ground. He watched in a daze as Voskonov impatiently strode forward, gripping his dagger. The man's terrible face had started the nightmare with the Dreizack so long ago, and now this monster from their dreams was going to be the specter that finished it.

Then Voskonov turned. Celeste had gotten back up, and she ran at him, bearing an arrow in each hand with the tips held downward.

She yelled as she jumped into the air and swung both arrow points down at him.

Voskonov grabbed her forearm and thrust upward with his dagger.

Celeste let out a gasp, and Voskonov made a choking sound. She held on to his head as he stumbled backward before slamming onto the stone floor.

Neither of them moved. Celeste lay facedown with a blood-stained dagger protruding up through the back of her chain mail; an arrow embedded in Voskonov's neck.

"Celeste! Celeste!" Will painfully breathed out as he struggled to move the table. "Celeste!"

Once he could get out from under the table, he still couldn't stand. He felt like he was broken. Like the world was broken.

Celeste groaned and barely moved.

Will scrambled over to her.

She turned onto her side and winced as she pulled out the

dagger. It clattered to the floor, and she held her hand against her side.

"How bad is it?" Will asked.

She removed her hand to see the area of chain mail where the narrow dagger had penetrated through the edge of the links, but it had only cut her on the side of her ribs. There was blood on her hand. "It's just a scratch."

"That's more than a scratch! Let me help you."

She half smiled. "Oh, so now you want to help me?" She struggled to push herself to her knees, holding one hand under her arm.

"You know, you could have responded a little faster," he said.

"I needed a few seconds." Her eyes found his. "You were shouting my name a lot."

"I would have missed you," Will said. They locked eyes for a moment, and Will tenderly brought his hand to her face. The fighting in the hallway sounded as if it was upon them. Despite their exhaustion, they stood and gathered their weapons.

They left the room to see Danny wildly swinging and shouting at an attacker. He deflected a blow and did a martial arts kick into the man's chest, then ran to reach Will and Celeste.

Relief washed over his face as he strained to speak through heavy breathing. He clapped both of them on the shoulder. "Have a good vacation?"

"Smashing," Will said. They hurried back to Roland and the others, who were being backed down the narrow corridor.

"Up the stairs!" Roland commanded.

They obeyed. The clockwise stairwell put right-handed fighters at a disadvantage if they had the lower ground. It also enabled Roland and the others to strike at upper bodies while their opponents could only attempt to strike at legs.

Roland and Edmund stayed at the rear, beating back the attackers, but there were so many they were driven higher and higher up.

"Keep the stairs above us clear!" Roland shouted.

The others ran up and emerged into the starlight atop the White Tower.

"How are we going to get back down?" Celeste asked.

Will ran to the edge of the roof and looked over. "More are coming into the Tower! The king and his son have swords and are entering as well."

"What?" Danny exclaimed. "Fighting them would be like fighting the undead!"

"What do you mean?" Celeste asked.

"They're both legendary warriors—vital to European history. We'd have trouble fighting either of them—and while they're trying to kill us, we have to make sure they aren't harmed. We're on top of one of the world's most infamous prisons, and now we're trapped."

"Let's bolt the other three corner tower entrances," Chase urged, his adrenaline seeming to compensate for his injuries, "and then defend the top of the keep as if we were trying to defend it from a besieging army. Hurry! Before anyone else comes up!"

They split up to run across the roof to the other three tower turrets at the corners of the keep.

As Will ran toward the opposite turret, a dark figure emerged. The silhouette jarred him. He knew that tall phantom all too well.

"You're too slow," Madoc Morgan scoffed.

Will skidded to a stop, wishing that Celeste still had her bow. Morgan was holding the scepter, the spikes dark, as he walked toward Will.

The din of fighting in the stairwell behind them grew closer. Chase, Celeste, and Danny rushed to join him.

"I see you gave the prisoner some fresh air," Morgan said.

"I'm going to kill you for what you did," Chase seethed.

"We found your pathetic storage place for the scepter," Danny said. "Where the princes were found."

"I wouldn't say it's pathetic," Morgan said. "The skeletons they eventually find there will probably be yours and Will's."

"You're sick!" Celeste said.

"And you're fools if you think you're going to live."

The four friends charged at Morgan.

The mystic white flame of the scepter ignited, and in what seemed like a flash of lightning, Morgan struck the sword out of Chase's hand and swung the scepter back again to crush his skull. Will was barely fast enough to redirect the weapon with his common mace.

Chase moved to tackle Morgan, but the commander was too fast, shoving Chase into Celeste and Danny. All three toppled to the ground.

"My real quarrel is with you, isn't it—traitor," Morgan said, pointing the scepter at Will.

"I was never your ally. I was playing you the whole time," Will said.

"I find it amusing that you are so eager to oppose me—and to come after this," Morgan said. "Are you trying to get back to your pitiful life in the future?"

"I'm here to stop you from projecting your filth on the world."

"You? Did your uncle tell you that in our time, everyone involved in the Black Hammer security wanted to trust you and let you know about your genetic condition—for your own safety? But *your* family member thought you were too emotionally fragile to handle the information."

The words struck Will because he knew they might be true, at least as far as what his uncle must have thought about him then. He tried not to take his eyes off Morgan.

"Isn't it true, Chase?" Morgan called. "That you thought Will was too weak? Or was it that you thought he had a *predisposition* for terrorism and couldn't control his emotions?"

Will took a step back. He couldn't help glancing at his uncle, who was struggling to rise from his old and new injuries. Danny and Celeste were on their feet and coming forward.

Will waved a hand at them. "Stay back!" Then he glared at Morgan. "You don't know anything about me."

Morgan's lips twisted into a demonic smile. Then he lunged.

Will took several steps back. He wasn't strong enough or fast enough to fight the scepter's power, and he backed farther away with each swing.

Roland and Edmund were shouting for help, now forced onto the rooftop.

Morgan clearly enjoyed watching Will cower back with each stroke. He took a swing at Will's head and knocked his mace flying out of his hands.

Will fell onto his back and tried to shuffle farther away on the stone.

Morgan hoisted the scepter. "Goodbye, Donovan."

In the shadow of Will's body, the flash of his hand could hardly be seen. Morgan didn't realize what happened until the object hit him in the eye.

Morgan's hand flew to his face, and Will lunged up and struck the man's forearm. The penny fell and tinkled onto the stone as the scepter dropped from Morgan's hand.

Will caught the scepter.

As soon as his skin touched the hilt, a surge of energy channeled through him. His fatigue faded, and his muscles pulsed with renewed strength. His mind was clearer, and he felt more confident. Most of all, he felt like he was reuniting with a long-lost friend.

Will pointed the weapon at Morgan while blocking the path to his friends. Morgan looked stricken as he eyed the scepter. Even though his hands were empty, he looked like he still might lunge at Will. Then he cursed and swiftly retreated out of the same tower entrance.

Edmund and Roland were pinned up against the tower battlements, assailed on every side, about to be forced off the wall. Danny and Celeste were trying to get to them but were driven back by the men spilling onto the roof. Chase was on his feet but limping, about to face multiple attackers.

Dread for his friends grabbed his heart. Will pressed the white depression on the scepter's hilt, and the swirling flame flashed from the head of the scepter, catching the attention of several men as Will ran forward. Even with this newfound power, Will was still gravely concerned about his ability to fight these men. All of them had much more training and experience. His perspective of everyone else's movements slowed down. Not enough to keep them from killing him, but hopefully enough for him to compete.

Will swung as hard as he could into an oncoming sword. There was a dull boom and a brighter flash of light as the sword flew out of the man's hands. The attention of most of the soldiers turned to Will.

More men poured onto the top of the tower as Will fought to get closer to his friends. He struck a man in the chest, and the blow sent him flying into two other men.

"Witchcraft!" someone yelled, gaping at the mystic light.

Will deflected a poleaxe and knocked its owner careening out of the way. Barreling forward, he swung the scepter, blasting another man with the white orb.

He could hardly keep up with the oncoming array of sharp objects seeking to surround him.

A blow pounded into the chain mail on the back of his shoulder. He spun around, but the man had already stepped out of range, and Will met nothing but air.

He swung the scepter in a broad circle, clearing some more space, but he would always have blind spots, and the dauntless soldiers moved in like wolves. Will spun the scepter again, pounding away two oncoming poleaxes. Then he heard Danny shouting, "Edmund!"

The young noble had fallen to his knees, and Roland fought savagely to protect him. Chase, Danny, and Celeste couldn't get past the soldiers and were forced back as they tried to defend themselves.

The resentment Will had once borne against Edmund felt infinitely petty. Roland would also be down soon. They hadn't just become friends to Will—they were brothers.

Will let out an animal scream and swung the scepter in a fast circle, knocking away any man or weapon in reach, and tried to move to Edmund and Roland.

The shaft of a spear struck him in the face, and his head recoiled as he tasted blood. His swings went wild, no longer holding any form, shattering the spear that struck him.

Will felt his blood pounding up to his neck and skull. His fighting lost all orthodoxy as he assailed anyone in front of him. He charged forward, smashing, and bludgeoning, and screaming like a fiend.

He reached Edmund, now on the ground with a deep cut on the leg. The rest of the soldiers turned their attention to Will.

"Let me through!" a deep voice bellowed.

"Your Grace, please no! Don't approach the dark magic!" cried one of the men.

"Clear a path!" the king shouted even louder.

The soldiers stood aside, and King Edward III leveled his sword at Will. "Warlock! How dare you return to my castle!" Even in the starlight, Will could sense the intensity and determination in the warrior king's eyes.

41

———————

The king's men stood ready to attack, but Edward held his hand up for them to stay back.

"This isn't magic," Will said, "and I'm not a warlock. It's just something new that you haven't seen before—like gunpowder weapons." Words spoken by others when Will was in the accelerated state sounded much slower than normal. Will prolonged his rate of speech to match so they would understand him.

"You destroyed my supplies to make gunpowder weapons!" The king charged at Will with his sword raised. "Weapons that would help protect my people!"

Will kept the white flame ignited, keeping his reflexes sharp enough to avoid getting his head taken off. He dodged several strokes of Edward's blade while backing away.

"Your Grace! We do not wish to harm you," Will said.

"No? What of my men you've killed?" the king demanded.

"I've been trying to help you—trying to protect you from the Dreizack! They plan to kill you once you've paid for their gunpowder army!" Will shouted. The king was too good of a swordsman for Will to merely dodge the blade in an accelerated state, and he deflected the steel.

"You're mad! Just as Sir Madoc said you were," the king retorted.

"He's manipulating you like he does everyone else. He is no 'sir.' He's not a noble or knight. He doesn't believe in Arthurian values, a round table, Knights of the Garter, chivalry—it's all a farce to him. He's using you."

"Wait! My king, I can explain!" Edmund cried as he limped toward the king and knelt.

The king readied the sword to strike, and Will stood protectively next to Edmund.

"My humblest apologies, Your Grace." Edmund meekly averted his face as he knelt. "But he speaks the truth. The Dreizack intend to kill you and your children."

"You're English," the king said, still ready in an attack position. "You don't have their atrocious accent."

"Yes, my lord. Their leader, Madoc Morgan, told me himself that he intended to rule all of England. I would have come to tell you in person—"

"But you doubted I would believe you—not with so much promise in Madoc's offers. So, you attacked my caravan of expensive goods, trespassed in my castle, and killed my men!"

Edmund continued to bow his head. "And may have saved your life, England, and all of Christendom."

"Your defector friend said that you were going to try to hold me for ransom."

"If it were so, perhaps we could have assisted you without a soul being harmed. We believed it might be the most peaceful way we could make an exchange," Edmund replied. "We had no desire to fight or harm your men any more than was necessary to save your life and your realm, my king."

"Your friend said you didn't want money—you wanted

that." The king pointed at the scepter. "And his uncle pardoned, and for you to take the Dreizack as your prisoners."

"Yes, Your Grace," Edmund replied.

"Where are you from?" the king said. "You sound well-bred."

"My lord," Edmund said, still averting his gaze, "if my king desires it, I shall belong to all four corners of the realm. My body sectioned and sent to each."

"Why weren't you also going to ask for money? My ransom would have included lands, estates, titles, gold. It almost seems dull-witted not to also ask for these."

"To show our loyalty, Your Grace."

"What I should do is cut all of you to ribbons and leave your entrails to the ravens," Edward said, his sword still ready. "But my better judgment indicates that I should put each of you on trial to learn more. It would be wise of you to accept this opportunity to surrender."

"That is very generous—" Edmund started to say, but Will grabbed him by the shoulder and pulled him to his feet.

"I saw where my uncle was kept and the torture devices there. We will not be your prisoners."

The king gestured to Edmund. "He speaks freely. As long as you each cooperate, there would be no need for physical persuasion. Very few of our prisoners are put to torture. You would be treated well while the truth is ascertained."

Will took in the many soldiers behind the king, all eager to fight. "Your Grace, there is no need for more blood to be shed, but we will not surrender. We wish to part ways peacefully."

Edward pursed his mouth. He still stood as though he might lunge at Will—but then his features seemed to soften. "You must care a great deal for your uncle to risk your life in this attempt, and though I loathe you, I respect your courage. It reminds me of my friends when I was a youth. If they had not risked their lives by creeping into Nottingham Castle to free me from being a prisoner, I might not be king. I might not be alive. Surrender your weapons, and let us discover the truth."

"The truth is," Will said, "if it weren't for us entering tonight, Madoc Morgan might have kept you from a long life as king. I wouldn't be surprised if your friends killed guards in Nottingham Castle to save you. Please consider forgiving us. It's in everyone's best interest. I escaped this castle alone and unarmed. Now that I carry this weapon and have the help of my friends, many more of your men will die if you try to detain us."

The king's jaw was taut. He still looked ready to fight but was clearly calculating the situation. Will could tell the man before him possessed both the aggression and the restraint to be a great field commander.

"What proof is there that you won't continue to be a thorn in my side?" the king said.

"Your Grace," Will replied, "the proof is that we came to ask nothing of you that wasn't for your protection, that none of us are trying to attack you, and that I haven't and won't try to use this weapon against you."

"I will retain Madoc, though perhaps with fewer liberties, until he has taught us how to make his weapons," Edward said.

Will cringed inside, and Edmund responded, "We understand, Your Grace. There is nothing more we can do to warn you regarding that man, and we swear to never interfere with your affairs again."

King Edward glanced from the mystical light to the fallen bodies on the tower's roof. "I do not fear you, and I do not fear that." He gestured his sword at the scepter. Then he locked eyes with Will. "How am I to believe that you care so much for the fate of my kingdom?"

"I care a lot about your reign as the king of England," Will said. "Everyone knows you have great things ahead of you—with or without Madoc. England has long been at the heart of world affairs. If she were to fall, everyone's fate would be uncertain."

A dark cloud began to form, looming heavily over the castle. It slowly churned above them, obstructing the moon and stars. A tinge of green light rippled through it. The king looked from the cloud back to the white light from the scepter.

The king pointed his sword at Chase, who was standing several paces behind Will and Edmund. "I'm doing this out of the fondness I hold for my friends who rescued me from a castle prison. I will allow you to depart—with an oath to never again interfere with my affairs."

"Your Grace, I swear it," Will said. Edmund and the others behind also swore agreement.

The king's eyes flitted to the mysterious shadow of darkness twisting and intensifying overhead. "I command you to immediately take that object far from my castle. With the ransom most would have tried to take, you could have purchased a vast estate. It won't hurt me to spare you a few horses. My men here will allow you to depart. However, upon leaving my castle walls, your safety is in your own hands. Now go!"

Will wasn't sure what caused the cloud to form; he worried, as likely did the king, that it might be related to the use of the scepter. He extinguished the white light, and he and his friends quickly left the roof of the tower. A knot twisted in his gut. Where was Morgan?

42

———————

They wasted no time obtaining horses and riding out of the courtyard and through the first of many gates to get back to the city. A cursory bandage was placed on Edmund's leg, but the other wounds would have to wait.

The dark cloud remained above as they rode through the cobblestone section between two of the large walls. They galloped beneath the portcullis and onto the causeway going across the moat. The gates to the Lion Tower were also now up, and they rode through. They continued onto the narrow causeway to the last gatehouse at the end of the moat.

They heard the gate grinding behind them as it closed. Then the portcullis gate in front of them slammed down, biting off their escape.

"What's going on?" Celeste exclaimed.

"Shields up!" Roland shouted.

Archers appeared from the battlements on both towers and began firing arrows. They weren't bearing the emblems of the king's guard, but instead looked like the mercenaries Morgan had hired to protect the caravan.

There was no escape on the short, narrow causeway. Even if they jumped into the water, there was nowhere they could swim that archers couldn't hit them.

Roland turned his horse to help protect Edmund, and an arrow struck him in the shoulder.

"No!" Edmund shouted. The knight bared his teeth in pain, managing to move his horse alongside Edmund to shield both of them better.

The others also did their best to crowd the horses together and raise their shields in a protective circle. The steel-tipped arrows splintered away at the wooden shields.

Danny recoiled as an arrow went through his shield and grazed his shoulder.

Will noticed a man standing behind the gate in front of them with both elbows resting on the bars and a satisfied grin on his face—Morgan had them encaged, blocking their freedom.

Will held the scepter ignited with the white flame, hoping to have some advantage with sharper reflexes and to draw attention from the others. An arrow pierced through his shield, barely missing his face. He grimaced and hurled the scepter spinning overhead, the white flame still ignited, into the archer behind them. It struck the man, sending him reeling backward, and Will dug his heels into the horse to catch the scepter.

He wheeled the steed around. Morgan was gone, and the two archers on the forward gate had taken defensive positions behind the battlements.

Will charged his horse forward. Another arrow struck his shield. He dismounted at the base of the gate and beat at the metal crossbars, making a deafening sound until he made a hole large enough to slip through.

He couldn't see Morgan as he ran up the stairwell of the gatehouse. An archer swung a short sword at Will's face. Will pounded the weapon out of the way and struck the man, sending him off the tower and splashing into the moat. There was another splash as the second archer opted to jump rather than face the magical weapon.

Will surveyed the plaza beyond the moat going into the city, seeing only shadows. The dark cloud tinged with green light still loomed above them. He found the mechanism to raise the gate and frantically cranked it with all his strength. Then he returned to the others waiting for him on the causeway and mounted his horse.

Roland grimaced as he broke the shaft off of an arrow protruding from his left shoulder.

"Sir Roland, can I help you?" Celeste said.

"I'll be fine," he grunted.

"Let's move," Edmund said.

They directed their horses to the front gate, but then they stopped short.

The tight-swirling black cloud thickened and slowly descended. A startling flash of green-tinged light struck the plaza ahead.

"What was that?" Danny's eyes were wide.

"That wasn't natural—I haven't seen anything like it," Chase said.

"More dark magic?" Roland asked.

"I swear, it's not dark magic," Will said.

"My lord," Roland said, "can you fight?"

"It's my leg that is injured," Edmund replied.

They prodded the horses to the gate entrance and looked into the plaza. An ominous wall of black mist shrouded the city buildings from view. Within the great circle of darkness, the plaza's stone emanated an eerie, faint green light at the junctions between the cobbles.

Waiting for them in the plaza was a row of mounted horsemen, with Morgan, Wolf, and four mercenaries holding swords ready, daring them to advance.

Will looked around at his friends. Roland and Edmund were the only ones well-trained at fighting on horseback, and both were injured. Chase was also in bad shape. He saw the same fear and concern on the faces of the others.

"Will Donovan!" Morgan shouted. "You don't know the power you're up against. That scepter does not belong to you. I am sure by now your uncle has told you of its origin. There are beings who want it back, and they are not on your side. You know the power here lies with me and always has. They have supported me and not you. This is your chance to surrender peacefully, unless you want all of your friends to die."

"What is he speaking of?" Edmund demanded.

"He's gone mad," Chase said.

Will prodded his horse to take several steps toward the eerie spectacle.

"Will, come back!" his uncle shouted.

Will turned slowly to look at the others. "Let's face them—for Garrett and the men of Arundel."

"Keep close!" Roland commanded as he and the others aligned their horses next to Will in the plaza.

The knight let out a deep, guttural yell. "Charge!" He waved his sword and drove his horse forward. The others joined him in a thunder of hooves across the stones. Roland held his injured shield arm close, leveled his sword, and pointed it at the row of horsemen.

Edmund and Will were at his sides. The others followed in close formation.

Morgan waved his flame-bladed sword forward and shouted, "Attack!"

The horsemen crashed into each other. Wolf and one of the mercenaries were killed on first contact by Roland and

Edmund. Will sent a mercenary smashing to the ground, then he broke away from the fighting and went straight for Morgan. His heart raced, and he held tight to the scepter.

The commander leveled his sword at Will's head. Morgan's reach was longer, and Will was unsure if he could maneuver his horse well enough to strike first. Will's horse didn't share his accelerated state, and Will didn't think it would as long as the saddle was between them. He placed his hand on the horse's neck, and the steed quickened, nearly jolting him out of the saddle.

Morgan slashed at the horse, and Will pulled the mount to the side to protect it. The animal blustered, shaking its head, and Will felt its great muscles tremble. He removed his hand to allow the horse's perception to return to normal. The steed calmed, and Will guided it back at Morgan.

Will tried to knock the sword out of Morgan's hands, but the man twisted his blade and slashed downward. Will blocked it with the shaft of the scepter, then swung at Morgan, who dodged and tried to cut his arm. Will barely deflected it again. He tried to maneuver his horse around, but the man stayed just out of reach.

"Even with Black Hammer, you're too slow," Morgan said. "You've always been too slow, and you're no warrior—just a freakish alien mutt."

Will drew back his arm to hurl the scepter. Morgan smiled, anticipating it, almost welcoming it. The others were still in the thick of fighting. Morgan would end this before they could intervene.

Fast-approaching hooves hammered on the cobblestone behind Will. Will choked on his breath when he saw it was Danny. His friend was no match for Morgan.

Will tried to call out, to yell for him to stop, but Danny spoke first.

"Now, Will!" he shouted.

Will realized Danny was sacrificing himself so that Will could take a shot at Morgan—it was too late to stop him.

Morgan heaved his blade down at Danny. Will urged his horse forward. Danny took the blow to his shield and was knocked from his horse and onto the cobblestones.

Will was in striking distance. Morgan's face was desperate—he wouldn't have time to block the overhead blow. He stabbed his sword into Will's horse, and the beast jolted as it shrieked.

Will's aim was off-center, but he was able to redirect the edge of the scepter to just graze the side of Morgan's face. The bright flash of light slammed the man forward in his saddle.

Will's horse was falling toward Morgan's, and Will leaped from his saddle and tackled the man off the other side and onto the ground.

Morgan's body broke Will's fall onto the stone. Will recoiled off him, and the demon lay still as the green glow still emanated around them.

Will's chest was heaving with anger, and he bared his teeth. Positioning the man's neck with one hand, he placed the sharp point at the top of the scepter to slice it across.

The skin was warm against his palm, and he felt a faint heartbeat. The beard brushed against the top of Will's hand. Will exhaled and hesitated.

43

Will repositioned his hand on Morgan's neck, mustering the fortitude to do what must be done. He saw his handprint in blood on the man's offered neck. So much adrenaline pumped through him that he wasn't sure where the blood on his hands had come from. *Me? Morgan? Someone I've . . . killed?*

He felt sick and gritted his teeth. The people he had hurt up until now were actively attacking him or someone he cared about.

Whoever's blood this is—it's Morgan's fault. He deserves to die. This is simply a deed that has to be done. Like a butcher cleaning an animal.

Will cringed. *Butcher? Who am I?* He looked at the shape of his handprint on the person in front of him. Then he shook off the thoughts, inhaled, and pressed the point of the scepter firmly to the soft skin.

A voice broke his concentration. "Kill him, William!" Roland shouted. "You've earned it. Slit his throat!"

The command was jarring. *Earned it? This isn't who I am.*

This isn't how I was brought up. This might be how things are done here, but this isn't me. More than ever, he felt like he was in the wrong time. Not in this era, toying with the fate of the world.

"Do it, William!" Edmund shouted. "He would do it to any of us!"

He deserved it. He deserved much worse. *But where I'm from, sixteen-year-olds don't get to be judge, jury, and executioner.* But someone needed to cut the head off the snake. *Was he bluffing about knowing the beings who had previously possessed the scepter? Does he have information we need?*

He remembered Morgan telling him about the Dreizack in the future as a complex organization with layer after layer of security, secrecy, and networking. The organization wasn't a snake. It was a hydra. Cut its head off, and many more would grow to take its place. *We need to have real authorities force him to uproot the whole beast in our time.*

Will looked up as his friends gathered around.

"What are you waiting for?" Roland demanded.

"We should take him prisoner," Will said. "We need him in order to shut down his criminal organizations in our homeland."

Roland moved forward with his sword. "Or we can prevent *any future dealings* once and for all."

Chase spoke up. "There is a lot of value in taking him prisoner since we have the opportunity."

Roland raised his sword to strike.

"Wait!" Will said. "Don't you think he deserves worse than a quick death in his sleep?"

The knight lowered his sword and looked around for anyone else coming to attack. "Bind him. Quick!"

Danny pulled Will to his feet, and the looks of relief they exchanged spoke silent volumes to each other. Firmly, though briefly, they embraced.

All but Edmund dismounted to hastily tie every part of Morgan's body.

Then another flash of light appeared from the dark cloud, illuminating the steeple of All Hallows Church at the end of the plaza. The cloud continued to encompass the plaza, revealing only the steeple of the church and the figure who stood at its base, holding on to the spire with one hand. The individual wore a dark brown cloak, casting the face in shadows. Will's thoughts briefly went to Emma, and he hoped she fled the chapel as soon as she saw Geoffrey betray them.

The small group held their weapons ready, and the figure leaped through the air toward them, causing the ground to quake when it landed. Several of the horses bolted away.

"You go no farther," the figure said in a strong, low voice.

"Leave us be!" Roland said, leveling his sword.

The figure's stature, confidence, and ominous air about him made the group keep their distance. He pulled back his cloak, revealing a long, white-bladed sword with a large brown hilt. The blade bore similar craftsmanship to the scepter, with thin golden characters spelled out along the length of the white blade. He swung it in a wide arc, a trailing blaze of jade-colored fire flickering through the air.

The figure removed his hood, revealing striking white-blond hair, emerald-green eyes, and square, symmetrical features. His face was aged, but strong. "Your mortal battle amuses me, and I awaited its outcome. Now is the time to relinquish what you've stolen."

Will stood back, brandishing the white flame from the scepter. "Who are you?"

"I'm not here to answer questions from thieves."

"We do not have time for this sorcery! Let us make haste," Edmund said.

"Do not be foolish. You cannot travel faster than I, even upon your beasts."

"Is he from your land?" Roland demanded.

"No," Chase said.

"Need I kill you?" The figure lunged forward.

Will intercepted the blow. Even with the scepter illuminated, he was no faster than the being, and the attacks from their weapons carried equal strength.

The being was a much more skilled fighter, and his next blow sent Will stumbling back.

Edmund charged forward on his horse, swinging his blade downward.

The figure easily parried the strike, and his response shattered Edmund's shield, nearly knocking him out of the saddle.

In a broad swing, he hit Danny and Roland's swords, casting them out of their hands.

Roland drew his throwing axe and hurled it at the figure, who caught it with his free hand and prepared to throw it back.

"Wait!" shouted Will. "Someone from where you're from helped us get this scepter. Let's talk about this!"

The figure slid his fiery sword across the blade of the francisca, and both weapons emanated the fiery light. "I doubt your claim. How did you come by the Soul Scepter?"

"A map was given to me of where to obtain it, and I followed the map," Chase said.

"Liar! I'm the only one who knows where it was hidden!"

Chase glanced to Roland and Edmund then back to the figure. "This isn't our time—it was delivered to me. Far in the future."

The figure's lips curled back in anger and disbelief. "Only someone with the lifeblood of my friend could travel in time. Something I safeguard to share only with one worthy of taking up his legacy."

Chase hesitated. "My brother, Michael Donovan, said that a being he trusted gave him the map and three vials: one for him to take, one for me, and one for William there—my brother's son. Michael left the vial and the map to me after giving a vial to William."

Will ignited the red flame from the scepter. "See? We're telling the truth."

The figure's eyes widened, and he continued to hold the weapons, ready to strike. "Oh, how long it has been since I have seen your red beacon and the friend who crafted you."

"What are you bloody speaking of?" Edmund asked.

The figure ignored him, continuing to gaze at the red waves of light. "Do you fools not know how perilous it is to travel in time? My friend bore this power but rarely attempted it."

"We learned that the hard way," Will admitted.

"If what you say is true, then it is not my place to tell you how to use it, but it would be wise to decide where you belong and to stay there."

"That is wise council indeed," Chase said.

The figure continued, "The maker of the great Soul Scepter was the ruler of my worlds, long ago, but left in disillusion. He sympathized with this inferior sphere of clay you call Earth, and asked me to periodically watch over this planet after his death. My kind have stored your languages in our collective memory. Those who now rule the worlds I come from have a keen interest in your dwelling place. Interests that would not be to the liking of you humans. I suggest you find wisdom and exercise it. One day, your kind may be met with forces beyond your comprehension—forces that I may not be able to dissuade."

"What do you mean?" Danny asked. "What kind of forces?"

The figure looked at them intently. "Powers beyond the confines of your earthly experiences, things your minds could not understand, beings you are too weak to contend with. I will allow you to live—as the apparent heirs to our relic. Remember, as I said—find where you belong and stay there."

"What do the words on the scepter say?" Will asked.

The figure smiled. "*Stand, and fear not, for time is your ally. Be where you are meant to be.*"

He tossed the axe back to Roland, who let it clatter to the ground. The green light on its blade slowly dissipated. "There is great turmoil elsewhere, and others who need me. I will leave you to your own devices. William, you have been entrusted with great power. Do not think only of yourself as you wield it."

Will and Celeste each started to ask a question, but the figure had already swung his sword upward in a great arc of flame and leaped straight into the air, shooting up into the green-tinged cloud swirling above them.

The shroud of darkness slowly faded, as did the light from the cobblestones. The stars were again revealed in the sky.

"You will explain to us what happened," Edmund said. "But after we are far from here. The king had other guards in the city who chased Stephen. They may be inclined to ambush us."

Will said, "Sir Edmund. It's like gunpowder weapons—it's just something powerful and new beyond your understanding, and honestly beyond ours as well."

They hurried to gather and calm enough horses. Will insisted on riding with Morgan, and the seemingly lifeless body was draped across one of the mercenary's mounts. As they rode, Will kept an eye out for Emma and Stephen, hoping they were all right. There was no trace of the guards who'd pursued Stephen into the city.

The group rode close together, warily approaching each bend in the road, anticipating other possible attackers.

"Wait!" a female voice called out behind them. Turning, Will was elated to see Emma.

Celeste dismounted, and they embraced. "It's so good to see you!" Celeste said.

"Have you seen Stephen?" Chase asked.

"No, he led them deeper into the city, away from the river. I think he escaped, though."

"We must leave now," Edmund said.

Emma joined Celeste on her horse, and the group hastened on to London Bridge.

The road on the bridge between the three-story building lining both sides was mostly empty. They passed a man huddled sleeping in the street, as well as a tavern window revealing four men around a table, drinking from tankards.

Midway across the bridge, Chase shouted, "Halt! Wait!"

The others slowed their steeds, and Chase dismounted, waving for them to follow him inside an inn.

"We need to flee the city now!" Edmund insisted.

"We will. But there is something we must do inside. Bring Madoc."

Chase went directly to the innkeeper. "He's injured," he said, nodding to Morgan's body. "We'll take a balcony room. He needs fresh air."

The innkeeper saw their blood-splattered armor and weapons. He swallowed. "Of course."

Chase pushed through doors to an empty room, and the others followed close behind.

"We can't tarry here!" Roland said.

"We won't." Chase looked over the railing of the balcony to the water far below. "It will be easier for the two of you to sneak out of the city than for all of us to travel as a group."

"Separate?" Edmund said.

"We should stop taking chances. There are many ways you could sneak out. You'll understand soon," Chase said. "Will,

this distance below is enough space for us to transport without
—taking any stowaways."

"I don't see a way to climb down," Will said.

Chase smiled. "I'm not talking about climbing."

Will went pale. "I hate heights—and how do you know
where we might end up?"

"Touch the scepter to me before we hit the bottom. I feel
like we have to try." Chase paused. "We'll make sure we've thoroughly tied up Morgan."

Will took inventory for a moment. The Dreizack were no
more in this time. They hadn't manufactured any modern
weapons, and a third of the people they had interacted with
would die from the plague in a couple of years. The rest would
have their lives so shocked by the scourge that it might
outweigh influences by those from the future. But still, there
had been so many impacts. Who knew if it was remotely
possible to return?

"Are you ready to go back, Will?" Celeste asked, tenderly
touching his shoulder.

"I've been giving it a lot of thought. I want what is best for
the people here, and for everyone in the future." He glanced
out across the river to the sleeping city streets, the dark,
ominous cloud now gone. He reflected on how he'd thought he
might help save lives from the plague. But doing so just might
change the future enough that a new pathogen could evolve
that wouldn't have without his interference. Perhaps that
pathogen would be even deadlier in a world with limited
medical knowledge—maybe it could even lead to the extinc-
tion of the human species. He also remembered Garrett and
knew that staying here could hurt other individuals he cared
about. *Taking the risk to rewrite history shouldn't be my decision to
make.*

Will gave a firm nod. "I'm willing to try. It's kind of like tearing off a bandage—I just have to face up to my future life."

"Yes!" Danny said jubilantly.

"You're continuing to act very strange!" Edmund said.

"Sir Edmund," Will said, his heart feeling heavy, "I know you won't ever fully understand, but the time has come for us to part ways."

"No, I don't understand. We should all go back to Arundel. You'll all be welcome to stay as long as you like."

"Part of me would enjoy that," Will said. He swallowed as he looked at the people who had become like family. "I didn't appreciate you at first, but I've come to consider you a true friend. I don't think you'll ever know how big an influence you've made in preserving your country and the future of all other countries. Without the sacrifices of you and your men, none of us would be alive. I used to think you were noble only because of how you were born, but you've shown me that you're truly noble in character."

Edmund still looked perplexed, but then he smiled. "And I used to think you were named for William the Bastard." He gave Will a pat on the shoulder. "But you're William the Conqueror."

"Good one," Danny said.

"Sir Roland, thank you," Will said, remembering how diligently the man had mentored him. "For everything you taught me—and for leading us in battle."

Roland looked back seriously. "You don't need much leading now. But what are you speaking of? Where do you intend to depart to?"

"Home," Chase said.

"But William, you are her servant," Edmund said. "You're going to abandon her now?"

Guilt and hurt crossed Celeste's face, and she hugged

Edmund. "You'll never know how grateful I am. You saved more than just Arundel and my home. Thank you. I—I have to go with them."

"You're going to leave me?" Edmund said.

"Please trust me. It's for the better," Celeste said, clearly holding back emotion.

Edmund pressed his lips together, and his face filled with pain. "Your words grate at my heart—but you'll always have my blessing to come and go."

"But where are you wanting to go tonight?" Roland asked.

"Swimming," Chase said.

Roland glanced at the balcony. "No?"

"I'm afraid we must," Will said. His eyes met Emma's, and he knew he would miss her. He was glad he'd tried not to play with her heart. They hugged, and then Will said to Edmund, "Please promise me she will always be well provided for."

"Why wouldn't she be?" Edmund said.

"Will," Emma said, a little embarrassed.

"I don't want her or her future family to ever so much as worry about going hungry," Will said.

"Of course not. She saved our lives," Edmund said, somewhat confused.

Will and Emma exchanged smiles, and the others exchanged their goodbyes.

Those from the modern era locked arms around each other and Morgan. His head was drooped, and his eyes were rolled back in their sockets, but he was still breathing. They clung to each other and to Morgan as they edged to the end of the balcony.

"Wait!" Edmund said, grabbing the shoulders of both Will and Celeste. "If you insist on traveling by river, let us obtain a boat!"

"Just trust us," Will said. "We will never forget you."

"I won't let you do this to yourselves!" Edmund said.

Celeste spoke gently. "Edmund, remember the dragon, the guns, the light from Will's scepter?"

"Of course," he said, confused.

"Please trust us enough to let us do this."

He continued to hold on to both of them as he exhaled in frustration. "When are you going to return?"

Celeste couldn't hide the pain behind her words. "We can't—and please don't wait for us. We were never supposed to be here, but I'm very glad we were. You're going to be the best noble the world has ever seen."

Edmund's eyes were red, but after a moment, he slowly let go. "I'll not detain you, my lady."

"Ready, now!" Chase said, pulling on the others to help them over the rails.

They clung tighter to each other in fright as they were completely airborne, accelerating to the water far below, gaining more distance between themselves and the people above.

"Will! Now! Now!" Chase shouted.

The red glow emanated from the scepter, and Will touched it to Chase's forehead.

The world slowed down. In the corner of his eye, Will saw their friends staring down at them from high above. There was a great flash of light, and they were gone.

———

King Edward III and his son stood on the top of the White Tower overlooking the city. They saw the shroud of darkness that obscured the plaza, the dead bodies that remained, and the flash of red light from London Bridge.

"More of their sorcery," Prince Edward said.

The king nodded. "I did the right thing, sending them from my castle. The dark cloud over the plaza may have converged upon us, and we might be the ones lying dead."

"Do you think it's all from that—that fiery object he was fighting with?" the prince said.

"Perhaps. It may be a wand, or a wizard's staff. The priests will certainly have an opinion—although to them, everything is witchcraft. However, I'm certain there is some good in those people."

"Good?"

"When I look another warrior in the eyes, I see who he really is. The object may have had them bewitched, but I do not believe they were evil at heart," King Edward said.

"Shouldn't we do all we can to prevent others from becoming bewitched?"

"The clerics will continue their usual hunt for heresy, witches, and devil worship."

The king straightened and motioned back to the rooftop of the keep. "This was an embarrassment, and I'll have any of my men who speak of it placed on the rack. As to the fighting that commoners overheard, we'll blame it on the French, French sympathizers, and if necessary, witchcraft. That will give us even more impetus to continue our campaign. That blasted man jeering at the guards outside the moat used some French. I wish they would have caught him, but I'm sure there were other witnesses to his shouting."

"'Tis a shame we didn't learn the craft of making rifles," the prince said. "Do you still intend to try to develop their weapons?"

"We'll try. They gave us but little instruction, but we'll certainly try. That, and increase our focus on ranged weapons even more than before. Archers are less costly than knights anyway."

They were silent for a moment as they took in the night view of their lands.

"What of the execution the people expected tomorrow?" the prince asked. "Do we tell them the prisoner was pardoned?"

King Edward frowned. "No. My men have seen me show enough mercy, and I don't want the country thinking me to be soft. We have that daft whelp who betrayed his friends, lied to us about how they would sneak into my castle, and helped with the attack on my supply wagons and men. He'll do."

44

───────

Will found himself in a dream of the being who forged the scepter. He strode out of a palace with tall golden columns, sparkling crystals, and light dancing from the high ceiling. He held a position of importance and was leaving in a great hurry.

A woman called to him. She had a happy, familiar voice. He continued. There was too much at stake and no time.

She called again, and he stopped. Her dark brown hair framed her compassionate face and emerald eyes. She smiled and desperately beckoned for him to stay. Several of the being's male friends also stood at the steps and called for him to return. But there was no time. Other friends had betrayed him in the past and left him to die—and there were more important things to be done. The fate of their worlds depended on him, and he turned and continued to walk away. As he marched on, a weight sank into his chest. *Who am I doing this for?*

───────

Will lay on his back with his eyes squeezed closed, afraid of the reality he was about to face. He took a deep breath of the morning air. Will felt his heart quicken—it wasn't the dry mountain air of Idaho. He ran his fingers across the grass next to him, and his eyes shot open.

Sitting quickly upright, he continued moving his hands across the evenly cut grass.

Celeste sat several feet away, rubbing the side of her head. "Hey," she said.

Will was grateful to see her. He looked around for others and tried to orient himself. They were on a slight hill, surrounded by trees and shrouded in mist.

"This grass was cut by a lawnmower," he said.

Celeste checked that her sword was still at her side. "Yes, but I still don't want to get my hopes up until we know we're in the right time—and that it isn't a mutation of our own."

"Do you see anyone else?" Fear welled up in his voice. "Where's Morgan?"

Will sensed the scepter behind him and scooped it up without looking. He paused a moment, remembering what the figure on the bridge said to them. Were they where they belonged?

Will and Celeste stood, and Celeste drew her sword. They were encircled by fog.

"Danny? Chase?" Will called out.

There was no response except the caw of a raven.

They nodded to each other, then crept into the mist with weapons ready.

As soon as they emerged from the trees, they paused, taking in row after row of tombstones enshrouded in fog.

"What is this place?" Will said.

They continued, and hundreds of white, evenly spaced tombstones came into view.

"I think I know where we are," Will said in a hushed tone. "And I think Chase decided to trust the government. This must be close to where he felt he had the potential for what he wanted."

"Washington, DC," Celeste whispered. "Arlington National Cemetery. Maybe he was trying to get to the president."

They moved to an open stretch of lawn leading up a hill to a white building with columns and a large white rectangular tomb in front.

They stopped, and Will nodded. "I . . . I think I know what that is."

Celeste watched Will's face for a moment as he grappled with his emotions. Then she said, "My family visited here a couple of summers ago. It's the Tomb of the Unknown Soldier."

Will nodded, and it took a moment before he could speak. "Garrett—he won't have a tomb like that. None of them are going to."

Celeste glanced around, verifying that they were alone before putting her hand on his shoulder and lightly resting against his arm. "I understand it's a tomb for unidentified soldiers in multiple American wars, including against the Nazis. They're honored, and others whose bodies couldn't be brought home, are symbolically honored. There are also tombs and monuments to unknown people who paid the ultimate sacrifice all over the world, including back in England."

Will's shoulders relaxed. "Thanks—I needed to know that." He wondered if the scepter knew that arriving here would help him in the grieving process.

"I needed to remember it too." They were quiet for a moment before Celeste spoke again. "As terrible as the world can be, as long as there are people willing to sacrifice for what is right, there's still hope."

Will nodded. "Before Garrett—died, he asked if his sacrifice was for nothing. I wish he could have seen this far ahead. It makes me want to live in a way that shows I appreciate him and people like him." He let out a deep breath and turned to her. "Let's go find the others—and find things to live for. We had Morgan tied up pretty well."

As they quickly walked down the hill, Will remembered the being who was hurrying away from those he cared about in his dream.

"I'm really glad you're okay," Will said.

"I'm glad you're okay too," she said as they continued to walk.

"I'm also glad you're not engaged anymore."

She smiled. "Are you?"

As they reached the edge of the memorial and approached a paved street, Will felt Celeste's hand brush across his. The touch completely drew his attention, but he kept walking. Will realized she had switched the sword to her left hand, and he remembered the man from the dream. Her hand brushed his again, and he took it. Her fingers interlaced with his. He felt a rush of exhilaration, and for all of the hard decisions he'd had to make recently, he felt certain that he was doing at least something right.

———

Chase struggled to push himself up. He was barely awake though aware of dogs aggressively barking and running toward him.

He got to his knees in time to shield his face with his arms as a German Shepard bit into the loose sleeve of his tunic.

As he tried to pull away from the dog, he saw men in all-black combat gear, bearing assault rifles.

One of the men shouted something in German, and the dog released the fabric.

Chase moved his hand toward his sword in a daze, but one of the men shouted, "Keep your hands where I can see them! Don't even think about going for a weapon."

Chase raised his hands, and his eyes came into focus as he took in the men with "SECRET SERVICE" on their body armor —there was no mistaking the iconic white building behind them.

Chase swallowed and remembered that many of the police dogs in the United States were trained in German, partially so criminals couldn't understand the commands given to them.

"I need to speak with President Torres," Chase said.

"You can't just come in—" one of the officers started.

"Wait," interrupted another, "are you Dr. Donovan?"

"Yes. I need to—"

"We'll tell him you're here."

———

Danny's heart was pounding, as it often did in his recent dreams. He took several deep breaths as he woke. He hesitated before rising, and a smile slowly climbed his cheeks. He breathed in again, then stuck out his tongue, trying to more fully take in the aroma of stagnant car exhaust.

He was in a dimly lit alley, serenaded by busy stop-and-go traffic. His hand went to the hilt of his sword, but he saw that he was alone and moved to the street with apprehension.

Reassurance started to ease in as he stepped out onto the sidewalk and saw a city street arrayed with familiar-looking cars. He turned to see a black teenage boy wearing a football jersey walking toward him. He was eyeing Danny's disheveled clothing, chain mail, and sword.

"You're American?" A smile formed on Danny's tired face.

The teen gave Danny an odd look. "Yeah—nice costume," he said as he continued past.

Danny started down the sidewalk in wide-eyed awe. He didn't go far before slowly dropping to both knees and staring high above. Tears glistened in his eyes.

"There is a God," he said aloud as he looked up at the two golden arches of a McDonald's.

He ran inside and came to an abrupt halt at the long line in front of him. He took in the smells and the familiar items on the menu. A pang resonated in his empty stomach as he realized he didn't have any money.

He noticed a few people staring at him, and he brainstormed how he might get a meal.

Two brunettes about his age hesitantly approached him. It felt like ages since Danny had seen cute girls with modern hair and clothing. "You look like Danny Barrington—are you?"

"What? Yeah. How do you know who I am?"

Both girls broke into smiles. "Everyone's face who went missing during the attack in Idaho has been on the news all week!"

Others surrounded him, and several people were filming with their phones. "Where have you been?" someone asked. "Where's Dr. Donovan?"

A wide smile climbed Danny's face. "You know, I would love to tell you, but I could really use something to eat first."

Minutes later, on live TV, viewers could see Danny at a table strewn with food, the girls on each side.

"Can you please be more specific about where you've been?" a reporter asked.

"You know, the president might get pissed at me if I go into too many details. Let's just say it was the best of times, and it was the worst of times, and food-wise, it was the worst of times." He pushed a handful of fries dripping in ketchup into his mouth, then held the box of fries out to the reporter. He said through the food, "How can you not be eating this? Have some. I don't know how you can possibly restrain yourself."

"I'm okay, thank you. How long ago has it been since you saw Dr. Donovan and the others?"

"Seriously," Danny mumbled, "I don't know why you guys are so worried. I'm pretty sure they can handle themselves. I saw them not too long ago. I'm sure they're fine. The worst thing that can happen to you here is that you die of diabetes or heart disease, which let's be honest, is the American Dream anyway."

A few people laughed.

"What about the red speckles on your forehead?" the reporter asked. "That doesn't look like ketchup."

"Well, if you cut a dude's artery open when he's trying to kill you, the stuff has to spray somewhere," Danny shrugged.

"What?" one of the girls exclaimed.

"It's not like the guy's leaving you with a lot of options." He bristled and pointed to his chain mail. "Also, If I didn't have this little number on, I'd be dead. It's like I said, there isn't too much to worry about here—diabetes, heart disease, and too much email."

There was a commotion behind the reporter, and a man's voice said, "Turn off the cameras."

"Oh, c'mon," Danny said. "Don't be such an uptight bunch of suits. Relax and have some food. You know life is good when government reps don't need helmets."

The camera frame jostled, firm hands grabbed Danny, and the television scene cut out and transferred back to the network.

———

Will and Celeste eagerly borrowed phones to call their families from a bewildered couple walking their dog. Their disheveled appearance and strange clothing earned looks from passers-by. It wasn't long before a black SUV pulled up to the curb next to them, and four large men in suits and ties jumped out and approached them.

"Will Donovan and Celeste Barrington?" one of the men asked.

Will regarded them coolly. The scepter and his sword were secured at his belt. He scrutinized them, assuming they were from the government. One of the men had similar facial features as Tanner from paintball in the desert. Will felt somewhat amused as he assessed how soft their skin looked compared to the austere medieval men he had just been fighting. The idea of someone like Tanner ever bullying him again seemed outlandish. "Who are you?" he asked with a calm confidence.

Several of the men's faces registered faint surprise. Not that they seemed afraid of Will, but perhaps his strong yet relaxed tone and lean-as-a-rock posture weren't what they expected of a sixteen-year-old abductee.

One of the men said, "We're Secret Service. Your uncle said you would be dressed like this. He and the president want you to come with us to the White House."

"Really? Why the White House? Can we see some identification?" Celeste insisted.

"Sure." One of the agents reached for his badge. "It's for your safety. You have a whole terror organization after you. That, and we were told you helped Dr. Donovan save the president's life. President Torres would like to thank you personally."

———

Danny and Chase greeted them inside the White House and lamented that they hadn't seen Morgan. Government officials were scouring the city for him. The president was on Air Force One and rerouting back to DC, and their families were getting on the soonest flight out. They also learned that their teenage friends from the attack in the desert were all okay. Their videos of helicopters and the red sports car fanned public interest, but they hadn't seen what happened after they fled. Will tried not to worry about how much media attention might have gone to his family.

They received medical attention, hot showers, and clean clothes to wear. Chase needed more extensive treatment, and the group separated.

The White House staff had strict instructions to make them as comfortable as possible. Danny begged the staff for permission to stay in the Lincoln Bedroom, and they reluctantly obliged.

In the historic room, they gorged themselves on the finest of White House room service. The uncertainty of not knowing if they had really returned to their own futures still loomed over them, as did the fate of their friends in the past.

Celeste anxiously sat cross-legged at the head of the bed, looking up information on a tablet, while Will and Danny lay across the bed on their backs, holding their bulging abdomens.

"I'm glad we're in this room after what we worked to overcome," Danny said. "This is where President Lincoln signed the Emancipation Proclamation, declaring an end to slavery."

"That's been on my mind for a while, as well as wrongs the world still needs to end," Will said. He pulled out the 2006 penny displaying Lincoln's image. "Chase picked it up back on the White Tower after I threw it at Morgan's face. I used to think it was unlucky. It turns out, it wasn't—or maybe we just made our own luck. Either way, it wasn't something to be left back in time."

"Oh, my goodness." Danny placed his hand over his eyes. "I'm just bracing myself to find out what we screwed up."

Will shook his head and bit his lip. "Yeah. For now, I'm just grateful each of us is alive. In terms of history, I don't think anyone else has eaten as much in here in a single sitting."

"Ow," Danny said. "I can feel my pulse throbbing in my stomach."

"Are you guys ready to hear what I've found out so far?"

Will and Danny grew somber, and Will looked away. "It's so hard to think of everyone as—gone. We were just with them. But yeah, I'm ready."

"Okay," Celeste breathed, trying to keep her composure. "Not-so-great news. Edmund's father, Richard FitzAlan, was one of the wealthiest people in the world at the time, and shortly after we left, he had his marriage to Edmund's mother annulled by the Pope so he could marry another woman. This legally bastardized Edmund, who lost all rights to his inheritance."

"What?" Will exclaimed. "We couldn't have beaten the Dreizack without Edmund's help! Modern countries might not even exist without Edmund!"

"I hope it wasn't our fault that he lost his inheritance," Celeste said. "But he was away from home with us for so long, and so many of his men—his father's men, died. Maybe they found out he was fighting against the king's men too." She choked up for a moment. "Anyway, Edmund married at age twenty to Sibyl Montagu and had three daughters. He spent many years unsuccessfully fighting the ramifications of the annulment."

"Oh, man," Danny lamented. "A person was automatically disinherited if their parents divorced, or had their marriage annulled—but it probably had more to do with Edmund's father's love interests than anything else."

"Birth status was everything—it was everything to him," Will said. "It just isn't right. No one knows what he or the others did. It kind of makes you wonder how many others have sacrificed through the eons so that we can have our tranquil, indulgent lives."

A tear glistened in Celeste's eye. "Yeah, I bet he was really good to his daughters."

"I bet he was even better to his *wife.*" Danny grinned.

Celeste's face tensed, and her hand darted to grab a pillow. Will fully expected her to smack Danny with it, but she calmed and said, "I love you too, Danny. We made the right decision to come back." Her eyes lingered on Will's.

He gave her an encouraging smile. "Edmund also fulfilled his promise to his men to keep their homes and families safe. We can never be grateful enough for them." He worried about Emma but was sure Edmund still would have tried to be good to his word.

"You're right," Celeste said. "I also looked for information about the others. There were lots of knights, and lots of Rolands, but I haven't found anything about our Sir Roland yet, and so far, nothing about Emma. However, there is a ton of information about King Edward III and his son, the Black Prince."

"I hope it's unchanged," Danny said anxiously, bringing his fists to the sides of his head.

Celeste continued, "Well, they waged a long campaign through France, winning many battles despite being heavily outnumbered due to the increased range advantage they had from archers using the English longbow. They also used some cannon-like gunpowder weapons the year after we were there at the Battle of Crécy, and when laying siege to cities."

Danny exhaled in relief. "That's pretty much how I remember it. Any specifics about the gunpowder weapons that were made? I just remember them being pretty boring compared to what developed decades later."

"I haven't found a lot of specifics yet. It seems like they were just rudimentary cannons. But the king did finish building a gunpowder workshop in the Tower of London by the end of the year we were there, in 1345."

"Really?" Danny exclaimed.

"Is that new?" Will asked, his heart pounding.

"I don't have the date of everything that has ever happened memorized. I don't know. Technology was already developing in that direction anyway, and they would have to build the weapons somewhere."

"But Edward wouldn't have built it there, that year, if it wasn't for Morgan," Will said emphatically.

They were silent for a moment. Then Danny said, "What else could we have directly altered? What about the princes' skeletons found under the stairs we messed with? Did that still happen?"

Celeste's fingers raced across the tablet. "It still happened."

Danny got a far-off look on his face. "I wonder if, years down the road, they found loosened stones in the stairwell where Morgan hid the scepter, and thought it would be a good place to hide the bodies of the two princes."

Celeste shuddered. "I don't even want to think about that."

"What about the whole situation with the Hummer?" Will said. "From the moment that happened, I thought we could have permanently damaged history."

Celeste smiled. "Fortunately, it wasn't the only sighting of a demon, mythical beast, or dragon. I found countless records of dragon sightings in Britain during the Middle Ages. The accounts vary wildly in their descriptions, and I even found a record of the townspeople chasing a dragon to the river's edge, killing it, and pushing the body into the river—I don't know that we did anything more than help promote past superstitions and present fantasy-themed stories."

Danny pressed his hands to his head. "Yeah, especially with Will fighting like some kind of wizard. I'm going to forever blame witch hunts on you." He sighed. "What else could have —wait—do you think the history we grew up with wouldn't have happened if we didn't travel back in time?"

"That our present is because of our interferences?" Will said.

"I'll keep looking for things we can verify changed," Celeste said. "But if that's the case, then we were supposed to time travel, right?"

Will felt uneasy. "I don't know."

"Don't you wonder where each of us would go if the scepter touched us on red?" Danny asked. "What if we're supposed to time travel again?"

"Too soon, Danny. Too soon," Will said. "You heard the guy from another planet say how dangerous it was."

"And that the world is unprepared for them coming to take us over," Danny said.

"I don't know what we're supposed to do with that information," Will said.

"Should we tell the government?" Celeste asked. "I don't think they'd believe us."

"Even if they did, we don't know who we can trust." Will felt sick inside, remembering that Morgan used to work for the government.

45

Will, Danny, and Celeste waited on the steps facing the White House South Lawn, eagerly watching the black circular drive for their families to arrive. They wanted to meet them at the airport but had been asked not to leave for security reasons.

Two black government Suburbans pulled up, and before the first vehicle came to a complete stop, doors flew open. Two parents and three young kids rushed out and smothered Celeste and Danny in affection.

Will smiled as he walked toward the second vehicle. He knew its occupants would be a little slower. He felt a deep sense of love for the still-unseen people inside, and he was grateful they had only been worrying about him for a week instead of three months.

One door opened, and his grandpa slowly climbed out. The old cowboy gripped Will in a tight hug. "Good to see you again, tiger," he said as he thumped a coarse hand on Will's back. His grandma was close behind, wrapping him in her gentle embrace.

"I'm so happy to see you," Will said. Another door was open, but its occupant was still seated.

"Mom!" Will rushed forward and hugged her. He crouched to her level, and she brushed her hands across his face.

"Are you all right? You look different." She was smiling, tears on her cheeks and a familiar sense of concern in her eyes.

"I'm fine."

"Are you sure? You look—rugged, like your father coming home from a deployment or long operation."

Will smiled. "Yeah, I'm fine, I promise. I can't tell you enough how sorry I am that I made you worry."

"Oh, sweetie, that wasn't your fault." She held both of his arms as she looked into his face.

"Well . . . I did get into an . . . altercation that started it."

"The paintball? Oh, don't worry about that. I know what happened."

"How?"

"The other boys you were with came to our house to apologize."

"They came to our house?" Will said in disbelief.

"Not all of them, not the one who started the conflict. But after they heard about the attack outside the INL, they were really sorry. They said Tanner, I believe his name was, had shown violent and cruel behavior before, and now a lot of interventions have been made on his behalf. His family made sure he doesn't have access to firearms, including paintball guns, and he has started going to counseling."

Will let the information sink in. It was easy to hate Tanner, but the thought of him regularly going to counseling seemed to soften the way Will felt toward him. After what Will and everyone else had been going through, all of them would probably benefit from help talking through it. "I hope he gets the help he needs."

"Me too. It has been overwhelming how much community support we've received."

"Really? Our community?"

"Yeah, it's been really incredible—the kind messages and offers to help. We didn't ask for it, but some people set up online fundraising campaigns for us. It's almost silly how much so many people donated."

"No way. How much?"

"Enough that we're never going to be stressed about money again."

Will felt baffled that people would do that for *his* family.

They didn't speak for a moment, but of course, his mom was able to read his thoughts. "You and I have taken a lot of hate, but most people know we had nothing to do with the event that took your father's life, and they've never had anything against us. It only takes one person to make you miserable, and when that's happening, it's easy to forget that most people are good."

Will thought about how there had been so many moments in England when he felt ready to collectively write off modern society. Out of the corner of his eye, he saw the Barrington family hurrying over to greet him. No matter how depraved humanity might be, he promised himself not to forget that there were countless *good* people in the world too.

———

Chase was mostly absent for the next three days meeting with the president, while the others enjoyed downtime with their loved ones. President Torres arranged for a formal dinner and medal ceremony for Chase, Will, Celeste, and Danny. The attendance was to be limited to family and select governmental staff.

The night of the event, Will wore a suit and tie for the first time in his life—but he still felt naked. He had become so accustomed to always having a weapon at his side, or at least in close reach. Chase had agreed to have the scepter temporarily stored in a vault inside the White House, and without his patient coaxing, there might have been a fight between Will and the government officials. Will told himself he needed to move on, but he couldn't shake the sense that the scepter was calling to him.

He joined his friends in seats behind a presidential podium in the White House East Room, where he was seated between Danny and Chase. He took in the three large chandeliers and the gold curtains in the cream-colored ballroom. In the small audience on the other side of the podium, Will met the eyes of his mom, his grandparents, and the Barrington family—all smiling back at them.

The president came to the podium and, after some passionate words about what it meant for them to be there, said, "Dr. Chase Donovan's efforts to rescue me at the INL when we were under attack were nowhere within his job description. Most people would have just tried to save themselves, and maybe he should have. But without his courage and ingenuity, I wouldn't be standing here."

He continued, "In our escape, I would not have been able to get to safety without the brave intervention of his nephew, Will Donovan. I also understand that Celeste and Danny Barrington supported Will's efforts after providing medical assistance to others.

"Further details will not be released regarding the harrowing experience these four individuals faced at the hands of the Dreizack. We continue to ask everyone not to question them about what happened. We have become more aware of the Dreizack organization's threat to the safety of people around the world, and we will be relentless in our efforts to seek them out and stop them. These four individuals have shown great courage resisting this global enemy, and it is my humble honor to present them with these tokens of appreciation from a grateful nation."

The president paused for a moment. "Some people have discouraged me from affiliating with Chase and Will Donovan, let alone celebrating them, because they are immediate family members of Michael Donovan. Let me tell you this—Dr. Chase Donovan deserves our thanks on the merits of his scientific achievements alone. In addition to that, his bravery and the bravery of these three inspirational young people have helped our country more than I could begin to describe.

"I've recently been made aware of information indicating that perhaps in the hastiness to find someone to blame for the DC Tristalon Hotel Bombing, and in the desire to find closure, details were overlooked that suggest a real likelihood that Michael Donovan might have been framed. I am authorizing a special investigation to see if this is true. The people who died in the bombing and their families deserve to know exactly what happened. Closure and revenge should never be substitutes for truth and justice.

"But regardless of what happened—these two didn't do it, and they've been harassed for years for something they didn't do. What kind of people give back to a world that does that to them? I'll tell you who—people who have more moral character than you or I can begin to understand. They should never have needed anyone to say this, but those two, and their family, should be proud of who they are."

Will felt his eyes might start to water, and he tried to force them not to. He knew his mom and grandma would be tearing up, so he avoided looking at them. He raised his gaze upward into one of the large bright chandeliers and thought of the summer morning in the desert with Danny, before their worlds were turned upside down.

"Speaking of family," President Torres said, turning around to look directly at the four, "my wife, daughter, and son are equally grateful for what you did." He began to choke up. "This job only lasts a few years, and we are glad that, hopefully, we will have many more together."

President Torres individually called them up and placed medals around their necks. Danny smiled like a kid in a candy shop.

The four returned to their seats behind the president, and Torres continued speaking into the microphone. Will looked back at the glistening eyes of his mom, his grandma, and Mrs. Barrington. He smiled at himself for being right and because he loved them. Then he surveyed the rest of the small audience, wondering when the president would finally end his speech.

Will tried not to shift too much in the chair, remembering how King Edward III seemed restless while sitting on his throne. There was so much that could be done in life that he couldn't blame the king for not wanting to sit through a meeting. He thought about something Danny had said before they encountered the Dreizack—that the victors of wars determine the fate of history. He remembered his own realization that his individual fate was largely determined by overcoming the wars within himself. Will smiled. *That's a constant work in progress.*

Torres wrapped up the speech, and Will joined everyone else in the obligatory clapping. The president joined his wife and exited the room.

Will left the podium to embrace his mom and grandparents.

"I'm so proud of you," his mom said, beaming. "Your dad

would be so proud of you too. I went to many of his award ceremonies for valor."

Will took a seat next to her. "Thanks, Mom. I'm just relieved you aren't mad at me—for fighting."

"To save Chase and the president? Sometimes you have to stand up to people doing bad things. I'm sorry if I've been overprotective. You just mean the world to me."

As they continued to talk, a large, bald, black Secret Service agent approached them. "I'm Agent Hayes," he said, shaking each of their hands. "Thank you, and congratulations."

"This is the man who provided cover fire for the president and me to escape the INL," Chase said enthusiastically.

Agent Hayes smiled. "Yeah, we got our recognition earlier." Then his face became somber. "I lost a lot of friends that day, and since then, I've worked hard to figure out what led to their deaths. The president has temporarily given me a special assignment. If you're ready, he's requested that I escort Dr. Donovan and Will to meet with him."

Will's mom spoke up. "Chase told me a little about options you might have. He won't give me details, classified and all that. Words I've heard before. Will, I think you're able to make your own decisions. Just remember, you don't have to let them make you do anything. I didn't stand in the way of your father doing what he thought was right, and I won't get in your way either. And don't worry about us, we can afford to visit each other as often as we want. Home is wherever we're together."

Will felt perplexed. "Okay. Thank you. You're okay with me being involved in something *classified*?"

"I have been pretty protective." She smiled, then whispered in his ear, "Your dad wasn't the only one in our family who worked in espionage."

Will's eyes widened.

She leaned back, seeming to appreciate his surprised reaction. Then she said solemnly, "I'm certainly not encouraging you to do it, but don't use me as a scapegoat. You decide."

"Okay, thanks." Will only felt more confused. He turned to Agent Hayes. "What about Danny and Celeste?"

"It's just you for now."

"Is it?" Will met the eyes of his friends.

"Hey," Celeste smiled. "Don't forget about me when you're some kind of a big shot."

"The Princess of America? How could I?" Will said, a smile tugging at his mouth.

"But if they start interrogating you," Danny said, "completely forget about me. Don't bring me up at all—Celeste, yeah, probably fine, if you have to give them a name."

"Come on, let's go." Hayes urged Will and his uncle on.

———

Will took in the Oval Office with its rounded walls displaying grand paintings. He felt his pulse begin to race as he recalled narrowly escaping the king's chambers. He did his best to keep his voice calm and confident. "Mr. President, this is the nicest principal's office I've ever been summoned to, but I'm not sure if it's a good thing or a bad thing yet."

"Perhaps both," Torres said, with no humor in his tone. "Go ahead and have a seat."

"Thank you, Mr. President, but I'd rather stand. What's going on?" Will felt himself becoming more wary.

Chase and Agent Hayes sat together in chairs across from the Resolute Desk.

"Whatever you're more comfortable with. The thing is, we still haven't found Madoc Morgan," Torres said.

"I should have finished him when I had the chance!" Will fumed.

"Don't be hard on yourself. Now that we're beginning to understand the complex international financial power the Dreizack are deeply intertwined with, the idea of using Morgan as collateral to put an end to it wasn't a bad one—you can't beat yourself up. Not wanting to kill an unconscious man also says a lot about your character."

Will took a step back and looked at Chase. "How much does he know? Danny, Celeste, and I haven't told anyone anything."

"I trust him," Chase said, "and he knows. He has the final say on the project, and needed to know the—ramifications of what we've been dealing with."

"In your absence," Torres said, "our people have worked tirelessly to learn more about the Dreizack and the foreign artifact—this Soul Scepter. We better understand the type of future attacks we may see from the Dreizack. We better understand the genetics making you unique, and we've discovered some things about these beings who have been periodically visiting Earth."

President Torres stopped, maintaining eye contact with Will.

"That's really interesting. Please keep going," Will said.

"I'm afraid I can't," Torres said. "It's classified—and you're just a civilian, and a minor, and some would argue a threat to national security."

"But what about everything you said back there?" Will said, pointing behind himself.

"I meant all of it—and you can take the medal and walk away, or you can consider the opportunity of a lifetime."

"What opportunity?" Will asked cautiously.

"You have remarkable potential. We aren't exactly sure how we could use the scepter and your abilities, but I would like you to stay in the DC area. We have many training resources and can help you figure out what your abilities are."

This sounded too much like a speech from Bloody Morgan. "I don't think this sounds like it's for me."

"I understand this is a lot to take in," Torres said. "What's on your mind?"

"Well, do I even have a choice in this, or are you just going to kill me if I don't do it?"

Chase and Agent Hayes laughed. Torres held up a hand for them to stop. "Of course not."

"Will, I trust Alan Torres as a person," Chase said. "There are plenty of presidents I wouldn't trust, but I trust him. You don't have to do this. I just recommend hearing him out. He and I have discussed it at length, and I'll support whatever you decide."

Will nodded for his uncle to continue.

"Just because someone has power doesn't make them a bad person. In fact, that's where you have a lot of potential for good —whether you're interested in this, or you use your natural abilities to do other things."

"What else?" Will asked.

Torres had a calm and understanding look on his face. "Agent Hayes served in the Navy SEALS prior to the Secret Service and is willing to be your personal mentor in combat and spy training. I trust him more than just about anyone else I know. You'll be given access to a multitude of training and learning opportunities that any adventurous teenager would find exciting."

Hayes nodded. "So long as you don't screw around."

Will hesitated. "I never want to do any more killing."

"I would hope so," Torres said. "You would learn fighting techniques, but the point of the training would be for you to use the scepter to *save* lives."

"I'm never going to be anyone's puppet," Will insisted.

"I wouldn't want someone who could be a puppet to have

access to this much power. You'll always be in control of the choices you make. Also, bear in mind that there is no way you could ever touch the scepter unless we're on the same team."

Will's whole body tensed. "The scepter belongs to my family."

"It does," Torres agreed. "But in the interest of everyone's safety, I can't endorse a time-travel weapon going about unaccounted for and unprotected. You and the object have more capacity for changing the world than a hundred nuclear missiles. But you would be able to access the scepter as part of your training."

"What kind of training are we talking about?"

"Oh, driving fast cars, jumping out of helicopters, learning to use every weapon you can think of," Agent Hayes said. "We'd like for you to be well rounded."

Will tried not to smile. "So nothing too boring."

"Ha!" The agent grinned. "If you're worried about getting bored, I have a thousand and one cures for that."

"If I hypothetically were interested . . . would Danny and Celeste be able to join me in training?"

"We could look into that, but this really revolves around you," President Torres said.

Will thought about it for a moment and shook his head. He couldn't leave his family right now, even if his mom gave her blessing. As he turned to walk out, he paused, thinking of his family's safety. "There are threats against civilians?"

"Yes. We are talking mass casualty threats from the Dreizack and extraterrestrials. It will be a matter of when, not if, people will need your help. We can try to deal with this on our own, or you can be part of it," Torres said.

"They're really going to attack?"

The president nodded. "Unless we can stop them first, it's inevitable."

Will remembered Morgan's motives to crush the human spirit and his thirst for power. He thought of people he cared about and beings from another planet coming to destroy Earth. He wouldn't be quick to trust government officials, but he wanted to keep his loved ones and others safe.

He gave his uncle a somber look. "I know you, and I trust you. We've fought together, bled together." He looked at Agent Hayes and President Torres. "But I don't want all of you screwing things up."

Then Will smiled. "I'm *in*."

AUTHOR'S NOTE

I sincerely hope you enjoyed this book. I would love to hear about your reading experience. If you would like to contact me or receive a notification when the next *Soul Scepter* book is released, visit ericwestergard.com. If you liked the novel, please leave a review to help others discover it.

There were many compelling historical options to consider when selecting a time and place for the scepter to send Madoc Morgan. Interesting options in medieval England included two hundred years earlier in the time of Robin Hood, sixty years earlier with William Wallace, or a hundred years later in the War of the Roses. I felt 1345 was a good fit for Morgan's ambitions because of King Edward III's quest for expansion at the brink of the Hundred Years' War, the slow emergence of gunpowder weapons, and the impending shadow of the Black Plague.

Some people say they have felt the presence of ghosts as they've walked among tombstones. The closest I ever felt to that was after completing the first draft of this book and doing some further reading on the Tower of London.

A chill ran down my spine as I came across an obscure detail I hadn't seen before. In the year I chose for Morgan to convince the king to make gunpowder weapons in a secret location, I had him recommend that it be done in the Tower of London to be protected alongside the royal mint. I'm being completely honest—I didn't know that King Edward III decided to do precisely that in 1345 until after I had written it in the story. It was the biggest affirmation that despite possible historical shortcomings in my tale of time travel, at least I was getting one of the flavors right.

The geographic locations and buildings are all real. The Lion Tower is sadly rubble today, and I don't have any historical evidence that it had a sally port. However, many castles during that time did have sally port tunnels.

Multiple beta readers told me they wished I gave Edmund a happier historical ending for Celeste to read, but I didn't think it would be respectful to the actual person and the struggles he faced. He's nearly forgotten on the dusty pages of history, and it just didn't feel right to pretend away the little record of him that remains.

I do admit to taking some fictional license. The English language in 1345 was quite different than today's English. I knew readers would rather understand the medieval characters than have them be linguistically accurate, so I used what Hollywood portrays as medieval English.

I am exceedingly grateful to my editors, beta readers, family, and friends for their feedback and support. I would also like to thank the citizens of the United Kingdom for their work in preserving such a fascinating history and the compelling historical sites that I feel fortunate to have visited in my research.

A personal motive for me to include certain emotional themes in this book stems from the tragic and often ignored fact that someone commits suicide every 11 minutes in the United States alone. It's one of the leading causes of death for Americans ages 10–34. As a veteran, I view other veterans like family, and one of them takes their life approximately every 65 minutes. This is barely the tip of the iceberg for the number of people suffering from deep depression. One study concluded that there is an attempted suicide in the US every 31 seconds.

The occurrence of these constant global tragedies is a bigger problem than most of what we see in headlines—ignored partially because it's a painful topic.

How could I possibly help? Most individuals taking their lives probably weren't reading textbooks on techniques for overcoming suicidal ideations—but many people do turn to fictional entertainment when they want to escape.

I wanted to incorporate elements of characters digging deep to pull through desperate circumstances and sprinkle in nuggets of ways to find hope and resist self-harm. I didn't want to lean too heavily into the topic of depression because I felt it would detract from why many people seek out fiction in the first place—to temporarily avoid pain.

With this sensitive topic, I wanted to see how teenagers would perceive Will's inner turmoil. I was grateful to receive feedback from 42 teenage beta readers from 14 states. They answered many questions about the book and supported keeping in the scenes of resisting self-harm. Several told me they appreciated the theme because they have days when they don't feel like being alive. I spoke with them and made sure they were getting help and support.

I had a number of experiences growing up that challenged my resolve to keep pressing forward. There are strategies I've learned for making life passionate and fulfilling—but that's a whole other book—a memoir that I'm writing when I'm not working on the next *Soul Scepter*.

Rather than debating whether or not we have a problem, I think a more proactive approach is to see ourselves as striving for emotional wellness. Just like physical wellness, no one is perfect, everyone is different, and all of us have room for growth. Qualified professionals are available to help. Don't hesitate to dial **988** in the US for FREE emergency mental health services. As a friend to someone struggling, you could save a life.

For better *and* for worse, the victors of wars shape the world. The most important wars we fight as individuals are often personal ones. I wish you the best in being the champion in your own story.

-Eric